The Skull Cage Key

Michel Marriott

A Bolden Book

AGATE

CHICAGO

Printed in Canada.

Library of Congress Cataloging-in-Publication Data

Marriott, Michel.
   The skull cage key / Michel Marriott.
      p. cm.
   "A Bolden book."
   Summary: "Science-fiction thriller set in mid-twenty-first century Harlem"--Provided by publisher.
   ISBN-13: 978-1-932841-30-5 (pbk.)
   ISBN-10: 1-932841-30-X (pbk.)
   1. Twenty-first century--Fiction. 2. Harlem (New York, N.Y.)--Fiction. I. Title.
   PS3613.A7693S58 2008
   813'.6--dc22

                              2007042368

FICTION

6/08

10 9 8 7 6 5 4 3 2 1

Bolden Books is an imprint of Agate Publishing. Agate books are available in bulk at discount prices. Single copies are available prepaid direct from the publisher.

Agatepublishing.com

*This book is dedicated to my father,
Louis Bernard Marriott, Sr., whose life—
too short, too bright and too often misunderstood—
first stirred in me an insatiable hunger to wonder,
reach and write; to my maternal grandmother,
Georgia Bullock, whose death inspired the what-ifs
of someday being able to capture in a bottle the lightning
of a life well lived; and to my children, Khary, Tafara
and Olivia, whose lives daily renew in me the hope of a
future one day worth remembering.*

1

Wink

ARMY SWALLOWED HARD, AGAIN. The soft tissues of his palate and restless tongue were loud in his head as he squeezed the back of his throat, until his spit disappeared in a familiar ripple of peristaltic contractions, which eased past his heart until they, too, disappeared. Army blinked blankly in the darkened hotel suite, worked up more spit, and swallowed again. No use. He could not rid himself of the taste of her, any more than he could shake his addiction to satisfying her needs.

He smiled bitterly at the futility. It had only been a few minutes ago when he had helped himself to the flesh-warm leftovers of half-eaten Shanghai shrimp and curried noodles. Yet, still, there she was—the tangy, sea-salt aftertaste of sex commingling with the late-night snack he'd eaten without appetite.

He ground his face against the living room's soaring window wall. The knotted muscles of his upper back reflected the kaleidoscopic fireworks that flared silently in the room's darkness.

He wanted to hate her, but he could only manage to despise himself. Most of all, he despised his weakness for her, his need. It was as if he gleaned from her just enough pleasure—bursts of roiling yet all too fleeting satisfaction—to keep him perpetually chasing his tail as he chased hers. Each time, after, wallowing in depression and regret, he would convince himself that the next time would be different. That next time, she would give him more than she took from him. But it never happened.

Army's eyes focused, looking through his reflection to take in the scene thirty-five stories below. He could see the New Apollo Theater glowing like an anchor store in some old-fashioned, suburban shopping mall. Its marquee announced a special two-night engagement of Ames Browne, the James Brown impersonator the Downtown Lights found so fascinating. For blocks he could see poor Darks teeming along both sides of 125th Street, peddling home-cooked sweets, souvenir trinkets, and counterfeit DigiDots to hordes of tourists. Army welcomed the distraction.

He thought about the countless times he himself had walked the same Harlem Broadway, about how he once romanticized the notion that he was inhabiting the spaces where Hughes and Hurston, Garvey and Du Bois once inhaled a heady atmosphere rich with Negro possibilities. But that Harlem, Army reminded himself, had vanished long ago, like so many broken-faced monuments buried beneath deserts of forgetting. These days, few people, Dark or Light, seemed to care about the Harlem of his great-great grandfathers, the Harlem he eternally hoped to find.

Uptown Uplift had been its slogan shortly after the turn of the century. Developers and politicians at the time had called the area's economic resurgence the Harlem Re-Renaissance, Army's grandfather had once told him. Pride began to return to what was once known as the "capital of Black America." But that, the old man sneered, "was just before the white man sold us out one mo' 'gain."

Army surveyed the cheap glam-glitter of 125th Street as the first full hour of the Chinese New Year—the Year of the Dog—fell along its sparkling length. It sickened him to look too long, or too longingly, for what he couldn't see. Dread tightened another knot in his gut. The room seemed suddenly to become oppressively hot and itchy with sounds just loud enough to irritate. He shook his head violently as her music coalesced in his head.

Army had wished, like so many on the eve of a new year, to start a new life. During the first minutes of January First he vowed that he would finally make his break. But here he stood, he mused, bare-assed and broke, in a $20,000-a-night hotel suite in which he was woefully close to getting used to being used as that damn music rang and rattled in his ears.

He glared into the balmy February night as he rubbed his aching balls and struggled to throttle back his revving rage. The room flashed then settled into a low glow, triggering the fear-flee wiring that wheeled him around to locate the disturbance. He laughed under his breath when he found himself staring into the blubbery face of a gangster training an old shotgun on him.

The gangster appeared agitated. Army was surprised that—even without sound—he was drawn in, forcing him into a nearby loveseat to watch the gray-on-gray film character play on the living room's wall-sized viewpanel like an obscenely expensive nightlight. The man, dressed in a rumpled raincoat and wide-brimmed fedora, was shouting something into the receiver of an old rotary telephone. Army marveled at how large and crude the device looked. Then, in the corner of his eye, he noticed the hotel's palm-sized link pulsing from green to red before it purred for closer attention.

"You got that, Armstrong?" a voice rang from behind a cracked door of the suite's master bathroom, under which seeped the persistent strains of her cut-and-paste synth-jazz. "I said, are you going to pick up?" The tone was just sharp enough to tear a nasty edge. "My hands are all oily and I *really* don't want to have to get out."

Army nodded before he replied, before he leapt from the loveseat toward the link in a single athletic bound. An instant later, he surveyed the living room as he seemed to float across its creamy, carpeted expanse—beneath its ribbed cedar ceiling, over its carefully arranged postmodern modern furniture mixed with antique details and art objects fashioned from rare woods and vintage plastics. With gravity's insistence, Army finally fell hard just short of the link, his left heel rapping the curved corner of a coffee table. He landed with a double thud and a stabbing pain in his foot.

Army yelped as he snatched the communicator from the claw-footed end table.

"What!"

"Sir? Yes sir," a voice modulated for seamless deference recovered smoothly from Army's bark. Its source looked out from the link's flip-out, plasma-dot screen. Army found it surprisingly difficult not to stare at the expectant mug glowing in the link's Opti-Dot. It reminded him of the face of a circus pup just before it's tossed a doggy treat for some joyless trick it had been programmed to perform. "We only wish to confirm your order."

Army looked away from the link. "It's room service," he yelled in the bathroom's general direction.

He carried the link with him, a spidery bundle of spun carbon fiber and liquid optics, into the suite's enormous bedroom. He slapped the link against the wall, where it stuck like bad art before he threw himself onto the sunken room's queen-sized bed. The link automatically reoriented itself and began projecting its visuals on the room's ceiling.

Army stretched out on his back. The bed was still heaped with pillows and tossed blankets that smelled of Kattrel. He inhaled her deeply without wanting to.

"The salmon and caviar platter, fresh fruit bowl, another bottle of Moet '08—chilled—and our finest cannabis sampler," the room-service worker said. "Is it all perfectly correct?"

"Yeah, that sounds right," Army said, speaking at the slow march of overlapping images of the ordered food, drink, and smoke that appeared and dissolved on the pale-blue ceiling.

"Very good, sir. We'll be up in thirty minutes."

"Thirty minutes?"

"We apologize," the worker said. "We're running a bit behind. Chinese New Year and all."

"Ah, fine, okay. Just get it here as soon as you can." Army replied, reaching to shut off the link but catching a last glimpse of the man's face along the way. He looked irritated by Army's insistence. Good, Army thought. At least the poor son of a bitch is alive and not some fucking robot. Then he was gone and the link flipped back into its canary yellow standby status.

"So, when's the eats, drinks and, mmm, dry refreshments coming?" Kattrel called out. Army imagined her adjusting the buoyancy of the Jacuzzi, the tops of her long, lean thighs breaking the plain of the soothing waters to complete an ensemble topped with her lavishly wrapped head and hair.

"Fifteen minutes. They said about fifteen minutes." Army called, hoping to spare himself a tirade. He suddenly felt heavier with yet another burden.

"Yum. I'm planning to stay in this luscious tub as long as I can. Call me, Hon, the moment, the nano, everything arrives. Wait. When it comes, be a sweetie and pour me a flute and roll me a fat one. You know how I like it." Her voice was as light as a teenager's on prom night. "Bring everything in here. Okay? Yesss."

"Nothing would please me more, Katt," Army replied, wondering what he would do in fifteen minutes plus one nano-moment when there would be no chilled champagne, no eats, and no premium marijuana to present to Her Highness, bubbling away in her royal bath.

Retreating to the living room window, Army resumed his gaze on the celebrations below. His eyes shot to a crudely painted billboard for Ralph Ellison T-shirts and speak-and-sip coffee mugs. Army shook his head, rattling loose the memory of a recent incident in which he had noticed a few swollen copies of *Invisible Man* among shelves of junk books decorating the Jah Herb and Tea Garden Café on 138th near Abyssinian Baptist Church. He had seethed as he watched some slummers high on government-grown marijuana using a copy of Ellison's Old Century classic to level their table as they argued why no good literature comes out of Harlem anymore.

It was nearing the end of the first hour of Chinese New Year. The fireworks smudged the balmy, early February sky. The great paper dragon had danced from river-to-river along 125th Street, leaving in its wake cheering, praying-for-a-better-year crowds.

When Army was growing up, Chinese New Year was hardly noticed by people like him. It was something strange and exotic that happened in cities' Asian enclaves. But things, Army thought, often evolve in the most unpredictable ways.

Most think the holiday's mass adoption grew out of the Great Chinese emigration twenty-five years ago, when millions of Chinese men had come to Greater America to reclaim as wives the generations of their nation's discarded daughters who had been adopted and raised as Americans.

Army was more cynical. He was convinced that Greater Americans were obsessed with second chances. Mess up your January First resolutions? Don't worry. Next month everyone gets a national do-over. Chinese or not, who could resist it? The greeting card and champagne makers certainly couldn't, as they pitched in to make Chinese New Year more American than the Fourth of July.

Army picked through the layers of his familiar depression. Would he ever be able to celebrate anything with the abandonment of the tens of thousands of merrymakers in the streets below him? He searched himself for a reason to hope.

Here he was, twenty-eight years old and still a junior-grade text interpreter for Kattrel Avanti & Associates Talent Management Inc. Nothing to celebrate there, he told himself. From the minute Kattrel had hired him, Army recalled with mixed disgust and wonder (*How could I have been so stupid?*), she left little doubt that she had at least one juicy opening ready for him. Three years later, his primary duty was still filling that opening. And on this night—just like the first he'd spent in Kattrel's bed—he was spent, angry, and tormented with regret. All he could see ahead were luxuriously decorated downward spirals.

On an evening when so many people were able to convince themselves that they were happy enough, Army couldn't fake it. He shook his head, stopping only when his attention snagged on something in the churn below. He tried to imagine being part of that scene, and a smile passed over his face as he saw himself as a Viper, a screech-slanging street hustler. He envied the Vipers' freedom—no office, no mounting caseloads, no mounting Kattrel Avanti. He admired their strength, their independence.

Army blinked back into his skin just before he began dragging his index finger over the window until he traced a rectangle roughly the height and width of his face. He took a few steps back from it. Before he could fully inspect the unintended exactness of his handicraft on the dark, smooth surface, the outline of the shape began to pulsate in a melancholy shade of blue.

Never taking his eyes from the glowing rectangle, Army sharpened his voice and spoke in short, even tones.

"Magnify. Two hundred percent per tap. Magnify."

Army took a half step forward. He leaned toward the newly formed window within the dark window. He looked through it, first down and then out. He grunted admiringly as vivid details drew into sharp focus. The frenzied beadwork of colors that had been forming and reforming beneath the windows dissolved into individual bodies, heads, faces. He tapped the window again and again. Each time a chime rang out, barely audible over Kattrel's synth-junk that seemed to be coming from everywhere.

"Magnify," Army said, reshaping the window. He tapped the pane three times and looked more deeply into the crowds, only to occasionally double-tap to back away when he got too close. As he expected, he soon began spotting Vipers, their Spun-wound dreadlocks animated like dancing snakes. A few yards from a small group of Vipers, Army came across some pleasurists. They were working the shadows, hawking in expert whispers that he could lip-read to be "full-sensory experiences" with their Jellis. For, of course, the right price.

Then stepping out into the light, an especially striking pleasurist instantly stood out among the others. She looked about eighteen or nineteen, judging by the smooth, creaseless map of her face. Her figure certainly satisfied The Ratio—Army's mathematically precise characterization for women's proportions that inspired the slightest desire in him. Yes, he mused, this one measured up, as he ran his estimates of this pleasurist's height to weight, breast to buttocks, waist to hips, thighs to biceps. But there was definitely something more to her than mere shapes and contours. It was in her square-set shoulders, the way they rode high and back, complimenting the jut of her jaw. There was an appealing calculus of confidence and cunning in her attitude. As Army watched her, he became aware of a delicious weight filling his penis.

He followed her with his eyes. He tapped the pane, his gaze closing on the pleasurist in a way he'd never dared if he were among the people pressing around her, men and women, licking at her with eyes that seemed to sprout tongues.

Her name was Oooh, Army determined, after pushing the window to high magnification. The name dangled from a platinum-painted chain that dangled from her slender neck. Oooh, indeed, he thought as he zoomed in tight on her exposed, flat belly. A faint trail of hair snaked from her bejeweled navel to disappear beneath the low waistband of her snug skirt.

Oooh leaned against the stoop of a pre-Wars apartment building, the kind he knew she could never afford, no matter how hard she worked her Jelli. In the broken light of a steady procession of traffic, foot and vehicular, Oooh seemed to exist in her own space, under her own gravity. It was as if she was slightly outside the common kind of time that governed everyone and everything else. She appeared to relish being watched, being wanted.

Dressed in a loose-knit, mech-mesh, pleated skirt cut to emphasize her long, smoothly muscled legs, a gleaming breast band to match her silvery, lace-up boots and amber-colored night goggles. Everything she wore seemed to gleam, which played up the riveting contrast of her skin's velvety darkness.

Through the window, Army noticed that this pleasurist was not sporting the goggles for fashion. Judging by the spray of buttons running along the right side of her eyewear, she was wearing OptiTech5s. Street kids call them sunnyglasses, because they don't merely shield the wearer from the sun's glare and nasty ultraviolets—they also light up the night as if the sun was blazing bright.

If they weren't so costly, everyone forced to live and work in the dark would have them. But as it is, only the wealthy, cops, and criminals can afford them. And this woman, obviously good at what she does, was sporting some heavy-duty models, capable of who knows what with the right expansion packs.

Although Army couldn't hear a word Oooh was uttering, he found it surprisingly easy to understand what she must be saying. She was working: hot and cold, tease and torture. A lowered gaze here, a playful shove there, and then a pouty-lipped invitation. She was good, Army thought. She was—

"Armstrong! Where in the hell is my Mo'?" Kattrel screamed from the Jacuzzi. "Goddamn it. Are you going to let this hotel fuck up our lovely New Year? Armstrong. ARMSTRONG!"

Pulling himself away from the sight of Oooh, Army whirled on the balls of his feet, took a standing five-count for composure, then replied. "I'm sure everything will be here in a few minutes. Hey, it's Chinese New Year's. I'm sure we're not the only ones who want a few joints and a bottle of champagne tonight."

"If they are NOT here in two minutes," she said, "call them back and tell them—for what I'm paying for this room—if I don't get my Mo', I'm going to pop a cork off in somebody's ass."

"Don't worry," Army said, returning to the window and Oooh. "It will all be here—soon, soon… soon."

"It better," Kattrel said as the sound of the Jacuzzi bubbled louder. "Now I'm all tense. Why don't you come in here and rub something? I'll rub yours if you—"

"In a minute," Army deflected, before returning to his search for Oooh.

A few other pleasurists, veterans, he gauged, by their over-repaired ripeness, passed beneath his gaze. And then there she was, standing on the top step of the apartment building's crowded stoop. She just stood there looking up, up toward the thirty-fifth floor of the Robeson.

Startled, Army tapped the window until he felt as if he was standing a few feet away from her, her features partly obscured by three lazy tendrils of her dirty blond dreadlocks. In the next instance, she adjusted the angle of her face until, Army reluctantly came to think, she appeared to be staring directly up at him. Fear fingered the tender lining of Army's skull. He was sweating. Army tapped the window again and thought if he could only see her eyes, get close enough to see through her goggles' lenses, into her eyes…then he would know.

Could she possibly be able to see him in the suite so high and far away? Looking deep into Oooh's face, he saw her offer a coy smile. In the next moment, she snatched off her goggles. Her naked eyes were large, almond-shaped, the color of rusting pipes. Then she did something even more inexplicable, Army thought.

She winked.

Army didn't hear the soft rap at the door as he stood unclothed and dumbfounded before the window. Then the bell rang.

"The door. The goddamned door, Armstrong," Kattrel yelled out from her churning waters as the door's chimes sang out again. "Jesus Fuck! Get the goddamned door."

Army grabbed a silk robe the color of red wine and lunged for the door. Just as he reached, it he could hear a faint plea of someone needing help, something about a bad wheel on the serving cart. He didn't bother to see who it was before he began unlocking the door.

As he reached for the knob, it pulled his hand so hard that it slammed his body into the door with a force that stunned him. Before he could process what was happening his body went rigid, then numb. Rapid-fire jolts rifled through his limbs, causing his teeth to clench and his heart to palpitate wildly. Army's left cheek, torso and groin were held, flattened to the metal door as if he was little more than an insect splayed on the windshield of a speeding car. The room whirled and colors congealed into an unearthly sludge that dissolved into emptiness. Army desperately tried to scream. But he couldn't as the door hummed and trembled as if it were deriving some sort of satisfaction from his sweat-drenched body.

His throat wouldn't respond, not even to swallow.

Clawing to hold onto consciousness, Army could feel the door open. He could sense that he was crumpled to the floor, where people were stepping over him, scrambling past him and into the rooms. A moment later, he heard a scream.

Kattrel.

Her name was the last thing Army clung to as complete nothingness swallowed him whole. The last thing he heard was her bad music blaring in his ears.

2

Death Dreaming

IS THIS DEATH?

It certainly felt like hell, Army thought. He seemed strangely formless, yet, in no way free. Army had to remind himself that he had once inhabited his very own sack of flesh and fluids. Gone were the demarcations where he existed and the rest of the world didn't. His physical self seemed as if it were part of a fractured memory, as if the pieces of his life had been pasted into some amorphous Romare Bearden collage tiled with shards of other peoples' lives, too. And, to his surprise, there were bubbles of calm in his low boil of sightless, soundless panic.

Nevertheless, he felt like dying, like surrendering. But he couldn't be certain that he was not already dead. Confusion churned up briefly and then passed. Kattrel. Helplessness. Numbness.

He felt himself tumbling without any perceivable motion. This was his damnation come due, he confirmed. He had lived a life—petty, unremarkable—that convinced him that he had earned this gentle torment. He had not been a particularly bad man. He had never murdered or flagrantly cheated. But, God knows, he thought, he had not lived an especially giving life. He had squandered his gifts of intellect and patience, as well as his lottery scholarship to University. And his affectionate nature had been sucked dry by an employer—a woman almost his mother's age— he permitted to exploit him. Army thought of Kattrel. No more anger. Then he found himself thinking of his mother. His sister. He missed them badly.

Without warning, he convulsed with fear. He was dead, buried, and forgotten. Infinity bared its teeth. Then the fear released him as quickly as it had seized him. He could see his mother wiping the sweat from her forehead, thick-limbed and substantial, with comforting girth and wisdom. She was in her kitchen, which was warm and fragrant with good foods baking, frying, and simmering.

What day was it? What time?

"Mama. Are any of these people still here in Harlem?"

Army was a child again, visiting the Schomburg Memorotorium, where sepia-toned photographs of a living Harlem hung on dingy walls from braided wire. Each picture possessed an urgent energy that animated every frozen expression, every streaking streetcar, every stride-bound figure, capturing in the spell of a camera, transfiguring the mere lately into legacy.

Army inhaled the age that had settled in the long undisturbed dust along the tops of the pictures' frames. He tasted time, bitter and gritty, on his tongue. He was remembering that his mother had taken him to the Schomburg, and that her answer to his child-innocent question shocked without the intention.

"Maybe in the graveyard, baby."

"They're all gone? Everybody in these pictures? Even the children playing in the streets and the babies in their mommies' arms?" he asked.

"Yes, Lord… 'fraid them, too. These pictures were taken way back in the 1920s. Those people are in Harlem heaven, sweetie. 'Cept for the scoundrels."

Harlem heaven. Maybe that was where he was going, Army wondered. Had he been a scoundrel? He was certain that his stepfather was.

It had been many months since he'd sworn to his stepfather that he would never return to the apartment. Ever since, most of his communications with his mother had been by way of handwritten letters and the occasional viewpanel chat. None of this constituted genuine visiting, according to his mother. ZaNia was profoundly old-fashioned that way. A visit must pass her hug-and-kiss test.

Army was born holding on to his mother. His stepfather, Jae-J., often reminded him, in that tone of his that struck the ear like an indictment, that when he was lifted out of ZaNia's overworked womb, he reached down and grabbed hold of her abdominal zipper. "And you're still holding on to her," Jae-J. reminded Army the last time they stood eye-to-eye, the night everything changed.

The conflagration had started with an innocent remark, Army recalled. Then, suddenly, it was as though he was there. Army tried to convince himself that he was simply dreaming—death dreaming. He was back in the old apartment, 200 Claremont Avenue. It was that night two years ago. Jae-J. was drunk again. Army had been a man for years now but felt like a frightened little boy, a boy who had always been deathly afraid of his father.

Then the memory passed. Maybe, he mused, he was in some sort of coma. The thought calmed him for a while, until he realized that comas were a thing of the past, familiar only from old movies. When a coma occurred, it was usually medically induced as a prelude to body-part harvesting and research. Time seemed to be passing, but he had no idea if it was going by in seconds or in weeks.

He began to find it harder and harder to access his memories, to gather the finer details of his mother's face, voice, gestures, the smell of her hair when he bent down to kiss her cheek. Suddenly, only his freshest memory appeared easily retrievable. The attack. His murder. There was a swirl of images of Kattrel, their lusty recreations at high-priced resorts, her handiwork of humiliations, her surprising acts of kindness when it suited her.

A new image then looped into crystalline recall: the pleasurist, the one who winked at him from the Harlem streets. Oooh. Even when he wanted to stop thinking about her, he couldn't. The scene played out over and over, for hours. Or was it days?

He could see Oooh staring up at him, his fear fusing disaster and desire. He wanted her. He wanted her, but not to simply enter her like a foreign body. Army wanted genuine intimacy. Why he felt he could find such a thing with a stranger—let alone a stranger who makes a living selling her pleasures—he did not know. He just knew.

Army found himself repeatedly drawing and redrawing how they might actually meet, what he might say, what she might reply. He occupied himself for what seemed a long time, finger-painting possibilities in his mind.

Excuse me. Ah, it's Oooh. Isn't it?

That's what my clients call me. Don't feel you have to, 'kay?

What do you prefer?

Well, "bitch" makes my skin crawl.

What is it about me that makes you think I would ever call you, or any woman, such a thing?

I don't know. Something in your way tells me that you have a murderous hatred inside you, just barely inside you.

Fuck you, bitch!

See?

No-no. I'm teasing.

That's not funny. Asshole.

I said I was just teasing, really. Come on. Let me buy you some tea and let's talk awhile.

I got a better idea, muscles. Let me introduce you to my Jelli and let's do some business.

You make me laugh. You want to have some laughs?

If that's what you want to call it, yeah. Let my Jelli tickle your funny bone.

Army was engrossed in his fantasy, molding and remolding it. He liked the personality he gave the pleasurist: smart, sassy, seductive. He realized that she was probably just another cheap hustle, a Jelli whore. But he preferred the Oooh of his imagination. And he definitely preferred his fantasy version of himself—confident, charming. Choosing it was the prerogative of a dreamer, he assured himself. If time had no meaning, he thought, nor could anything else.

Inexplicably, he could hear himself calling from deep in his thoughts. He had not been ready to die.

Momma.

3

S.C.U.L.E.

"MA?" IMANI ASKED, HER VOICE FRAYING WITH FRUSTRATION. "Have you seen my S.C.U.L.E.? I've got a test in two— TWO HOURS!"

"*No*, child."

Her answer was as firm as the snap ZaNia delivered to the young chicken's neck. The scent of hot blood mingled with the scoured cleanliness of the kitchen as the bird's body shook in feathery flops. Imani's mother twisted and pulled at the chicken's head, yanking the squawking knot of eyes, beak, and tiny brain until it popped off into her hand as naturally as a cork might from a bottle.

"Did you look in your room? With all that plunder in there, it's no surprise you lost your S.C.U.L.E. Again. What color did you make it this week?"

Imani didn't answer. Instead, she bugged her large, dark eyes but was careful to keep her narrow back to her mother so ZaNia couldn't see the irritation hardening her adolescent features. But Imani's involuntarily pronounced exhalation betrayed her.

"Don't be getting mad at me, girl." ZaNia shouted over her shoulder as her ginger-brown hands tussled with a tuff of feathers that clung to the dead bird's back. She shook her head, crossed herself, and mumbled to Allah to give her strength to survive her daughter's teenage years. She grinned at her own dramatics as she listened to Imani stomping off to her room.

ZaNia Justus mindlessly wiped away some errant feathers that had settled on the sweaty places on her chin and high forehead. Her thoughts settled on the glow of anticipation radiating deep from her matronly bosom.

Her only son was visiting for Chinese New Year dinner. ZaNia's excitement over cooking for the family, the whole family, brightened her eyes and flared her nostrils as she busied herself like a much younger woman around her cramped kitchen.

But her excitement was dampened by a creeping concern. It was early afternoon and she had still not heard from Army. He had promised to contact her around noon and tell her what he planned to bring for dessert. ZaNia found herself staring off, day-dreaming without a plot, place, or characters. She began to hum as she collected herself and returned to her work.

The dinner had to be as satisfying as it was important. Her son deserved the best she could muster, ZaNia thought. No radiated, gene-jacked groceries were going to find their way onto her dinner table this evening. Nothing re-constituted. Nothing re-sequenced. ZaNia was not unlike most mothers through the ages. She wanted to prepare a home-cooked meal to nourish the body, but perhaps more importantly she wanted to satisfy her own appetite to demonstrate her love for her boy.

She prayed that he would see all the fixings as an overture toward a greater family peace. She knew she still had her hands full with getting her husband, Jae-J., in line.

ZaNia had been thinking about Army and Jae-J. for weeks, long before the notion of a reconciliation dinner came to her. Perhaps it was her psychic pelvis acting up again. Jae-J., when he is feeling particularly spry, calls her hips his magic wishbones. But ZaNia had never thought for a moment that her husband's nickname for her thick, brown hips had anything to do with the accuracy of their clairvoyance.

"Um, um, um," ZaNia muttered under her breath as she checked the fire under her great-grandmother's stout, black pot. The chicken, she knew, would soon be cooking in a stew of garden-grown peppers, green onions, baby potatoes, and windowsill herbs. She already had the corn pudding baking in the oven and its sweet, caramelized aroma scented her every breath. ZaNia knew she should check the viewpanel for her old friend April-Mae's cornbread recipe. *That would have to wait*, she mumbled to herself. Imani had promised to toss the fresh salad and pick some flowers from the roof for a centerpiece. ZaNia planned to start the brown rice and put the mincemeat pies in the oven just as Army arrived.

For the moment ZaNia was content to lean her broad buttocks against the kitchen sink and study the empty table. She could see the family, all of her family, seated noisily around its dark, pressed-wood rectangle, chatting busily, laughing, reaching for seconds of her famous herb chicken and rice, merrily passing the pan-fried cornbread and complimenting her cooking and hard work.

The hours cannot pass fast enough, she thought, mildly amused to hear herself again humming a very old song from her childhood. It was from Jamaica, like her mother's people.

> Don't worry about a thing.
> 'Cause every little thing going to be all right.
> Say me don't worry about a thing
> 'Cause every little thing going to be all right.

The lyrics, even when heard in her head, gave her a conditioned comfort that stemmed back to when her mother first sang them to calm a little girl frightened by fiery nightmares after the first attacks on the city. Almost fifty years later, the song still comforted her; it made her feel wonderfully close to those she could only hold in her memories.

For a few minutes she didn't hear the blasts of data streams playing over her kitchen viewpanel, which flashed with multiple portals pouring news, weather forecasts, and Imani's music, along with various family notes and schedules. For a few minutes she didn't think about Imani thrashing about in her room looking for her S.C.U.L.E. She didn't think too much, either, about all the work that was still to be done before Army would ring the buzzer and return home, if only for a few glorious hours. She didn't even wonder why he had not called her.

From the elbow of the apartment's cramped L-shaped kitchen, ZaNia looked out into the living room. It was a typical mid-20th century space long ago repurposed for mid-21st century demands. It had made a perfectly adequate home in which to raise her family. Now only Imani, Jae-J. and her father, G-Daddy, shared its rooms overlooking West Harlem.

"Ma. Ma!" Imani called from her bedroom.

"Yesss," ZaNia answered absently.

"I've been calling and calling," she said as her voice grew louder and closer.

"Well, what do you want, Baby Sister?" ZaNia asked, as she summoned her concentration.

"Mommy," Imani said, pitching her words into her mother's expressionless face. She only glanced at her daughter between glares at her steaming pots. "Ma, G-Daddy says he knows where my S.C.U.L.E. is. But he won't tell. And I'm running out of—"

"Daddy's up?" she asked, turning to look into her daughter's eyes for the answer.

Imani stomped her feet. "Are you listening to me, Mom? Mommy? He won't give me my S.C.U.L.E.," Imani said. "And I think he's been drinking again." Imani's voice was overloud, competing with the pulsing rhythms of one of her favorite DigiDots firmly pressed onto the ridge of skull behind her right ear. Its hyper-volume had transformed the fifteen-year-old's head into a flesh-and-bone resonator.

"Yeah?" ZaNia's voice turned almost as sharp as the long knife she was wielding to chop celery stalks. "I think you are forgetting who you are talking to, girlie."

Imani's gaze fell to the floor. "I just…"

"You just nothing," Imani's mother said, scratching one of her two tightly wound mounds of silvery braids glistening with oil and perspiration. She turned heavy-footed on her flat-heeled sandals to look Imani directly in her drawn face.

"You tell G-Daddy to come here this minute and talk to me. And when you're talking to your elders, girl, you better watch your tone. And did I ask you if G-Daddy'd been drinking? Mind your business. You understand me?"

Imani, her eyes still tracing the cracks in the kitchen tile floor, said nothing.

"You hear me? You will not disrespect any adult in this house. You hear me, girl?"

"Yes." Imani's head was still bowed.

"Now go fetch your grandfather," ZaNia ordered. "And will you please turn your head down. I can feel that nonsense you're listening to all the way over here. It's rattling the last of my natural teeth."

Without a word, Imani did what she was told.

"And honey," ZaNia sweetly called to her retreating daughter. "Look behind your grandfather's books. I've got a feeling that's where he hid your S.C.U.L.E. this time."

Imani grinned as she trotted off to G-Daddy's tiny, makeshift room, yelling his name.

4

Happy New Year

IT HAD BEEN A GOOD COUPLE OF NIGHTS, SO GOOD THAT OONA DIDN'T FEEL the slightest capitalists' remorse as she closed her sweet-suite a couple of hours early on a holiday week. Six of her steadies came on schedule. A seventh client, apologizing profusely for being twelve minutes late, insisted on a double session for triple pay.

Each gave her a generous tip. In between, she made a respectable haul of Harlem street trade—faces, bodies, and moans she had not known. Judging by the sugary smiles on their lips when she softly kissed her guests goodbye, Oona knew she was likely to experience them again.

She knew the axiom of The Trade as if she had written it herself: Every Johnny and Janey was not a job, but an investment.

But what about that job with the glasses? That was nothing more than a quick buck, she thought. And no matter how much she thought about it, Oona couldn't figure out why Rattle, of all people, would pay her so much for doing so little. She surprised herself with how much she enjoyed holding that Dark's attention on her while she kept an enhanced eye trained on him. It was the easiest cash she'd made in a long time. Four full bricks of old money.

There're lots of possibilities with paper money, she mused, most of them barely legal but all of them dizzying lucrative and, better yet, anonymous. Keeping a spy-eye on the Darkie must have been mighty important to someone. Oona's imagination galloped away in a cloud of inference and fantasy.

A jealous wife? Perhaps. His spurned boyfriend? Could be. Oh, maybe both of them doing each other in nearby shadows, itching for confirmation that—"yeah-yeah..."—their big, black sperm whale was—"ahhh... harder.

HARDER… y-y-y-yessss…"—in the room, and—"right-right there"—all sexed up—"oh, Jesus, yes!"—wrapped up in somebody else's arms and attentions on Chinese New Year.

A broken skull for a broken heart? Huh, maybe. But Oona knew that her conjectures were more entertaining than likely. Rattle had supplied the OptiTechs and just enough information for her to do what he wanted. And when it was over, Rattle, her only family, retrieved the glasses, delivered the cash, and disappeared before she could count her wrinkled presidents. Her silence was implicit. *One good thing about family*, she thought, *he could trust her and she him.*

Rattle made it clear that she was only to transmit a signal to him if the Dark left the hotel window before 1 A.M. It got touchy near the end. But that wink nailed him. Oona congratulated her resourcefulness. So the big Dark stayed put. But for what purpose?

Oona sucked her teeth as worry shivered up the 'S' curve of her lower back. The questions faded in a flash of realization that her luck couldn't hold. It never had for long. Her lapse in letting herself feel a few moments of joy for the good nights and the windfall stirred her with trepidation. Something, something terrible, was destined to happen to her, she thought. Experience had taught her not to doubt the clockwork recurrence of personal disaster for people like her, the so easily disposable and forgotten. She knew that her string of good fortune would, sooner than later, rope her into calamity.

That detective had been bothering her again. Sniffing around like a dog confusing her for ready tail.

Oona shook her head as she sat before her tiny night table. The rim of its large rectangular mirror-monitor glowed brighter the closer she pushed her weary face to its luminous, bluish surface. She stared deep into her reflection, which strangely refused to stare back. She found it hard, especially after a busy night, to look Oooh straight in the eye.

She reached for a dermal rejuvenator. She ran the egg-shaped device over her face. Layers of make-up peeled and powdered over the table's shiny, narrow surface. The rejuvey's fine vibration sputtered, then restarted, but not before nipping Oona's left cheek.

"Shit!" Oona jerked the device away and pulled up multiple views on her mirror-monitor of the star-shaped wound burning an inch below her half-closed eye. "Shit. Shit. Shit," she whispered, as she rolled a HurtOff over the spot.

Oona couldn't get that detective out of her head. "Sick old fuck," she spat. The rest of her facial appliqués fell away as she discarded them in a feathery heap on her night table. She reexamined her damaged cheek. It was red and raw. Sometimes it was much more painful to be Oona than her professional persona. She re-powered the rejuvenator long enough to pass it twice over her lower belly. The trail of fine, dark hair there curled and fell to the floor like a dead caterpillar.

That damned detective, she thought as she stood up, wiggled out of her work clothes, and stepped into her shower. She had been taking two-minute showers all week, saving her allotment for a full twenty-minute blast for the end of her workweek. As soon as her weight was squarely on the center of the shower stall's floor, the water warmly blasted her body with millions of microscopic fingers, jabbing, stinging, soothing.

She stepped on a button tile and a honey-scented shampoo-bath gel mixed into the shower's spray as the center of the shower's floor began to slowly rotate, turning her body in the steamy stall like she were some exotic art object being readied for re-sale.

She was starting to feel like herself as she watched her spray-on gloves melt and the last of Oooh wash away and whirlpool into the drain. Then she thought she heard chimes. A few seconds later the sound of someone banging, banging hard, at her door spiked her sense of anger.

"Who the hell?" she growled. But she knew before she stepped out of the shower and grabbed her robe. *No one but that goddamned detective would pound on my door like that, and this late at night.* She glanced at her mirror-monitor as he stomped, damp and cold, toward the door. "Time?" she shouted at it. "3:19 A.M.," it replied and displayed in oversized, green numerals.

"So, you gonna let me come in or are you going to stand there and play with yourself?" a man's raspy voice barked before dissembling into moist snorts and grunts of self-inflicted amusement.

Oona stared into the sentry screen. Her fear was confirmed. She was thankful that her sentry screen was one-way only. *If he could see her face,* she thought, *he'd arrest me for looking like I wanted to strangle him with his own large intestines.*

"Yes, Detective," she said with an airless tone. "What can I do for you?"

Oona regretted the words before the last syllables left her lips. She was tired and getting careless.

"Oh, let me in and we can talk about what you can do for me," the detective replied, looking to take advantage of any opening the young pleasurist offered him.

"I'm closed for the night."

"My badge says you're always open for me."

Oona tried hard to see a few moves ahead in this dicey game of chicken and chicken hawk she was being forced to play. She realized that she knew very little about the detective, except that he was some Department once-was with a grudge. But she had been a pleasurist long enough to know who to butter to keep her license secure, and keep the worst of the bad news from her door. And being a Dark, she might have to grant an occasional freebie to ensure her clients weren't hassled by overzealous security.

"Rattle." She spoke her cousin's name as if it were a curse. She blamed him for the detective banging, for now, at her door. Always playing the big man, Rattle had invited her to lunch at the Hotel Theresa. That was months ago, before she finally decided to relocate her operation to Harlem. Before she realized it, this detective—the hotel's "head dick" of security, she recalled him describing himself—was seated uncomfortably close to her at their table.

"Rattle never was much of a judge of character," Oona whispered with a scowl.

But Rattle wasn't there. She realized that she would have to negotiate this potentially nasty bit of business herself. She hadn't figured out how the detective figured in her world. Oona knew his badge gave him no official authority over her. But he probably had friends, maybe old Department pals who could be bad for earnings. This time, she reasoned, she might have to give a little. The thought tumbled her empty stomach.

"Hey, sugar tart. I just want to dance a little with your Jelli," the detective's voice crooned. "That's all. Dance a little."

"Shit, he's all toxed up, too," Oona said to herself as she stared at the detective's image.

Her doors shook as the detective resumed his pounding.

"Listen," Oona said over her sentrycom. "I'll let you in, but just for a while. Give me a minute to get my Jelli ready, and then you come in, and then you go. Understand?"

"In and out," the detective whispered drunkenly. "That's the way I like it. In and out." Another snotty laugh.

Oona's outer door unlocked. The detective stumbled in and waited for the pleasurist's inner door to unlock and open. When it did he staggered in, slinging his weight from side to side like a retarded orangutan. He practically walked over Oona.

"Where is she? Where's that hot Darkie piece of ass?" the detective, visibly confused, asked. "The one they call Oooh?"

"I'm Oooh," Oona answered wearily. "Oooh is my working name, Detective Reynolds. I'm not working now."

"Yeah, yeah," the detective mumbled as he lumbered further into the sweet-suite, suddenly indifferent to the woman standing in front of him.

"Cams up?"

"No," Oona replied. "No cameras. I told you. I'm closed."

Without a word, the detective began shedding his rumpled clothes, all the while rubbing his crotch so vigorously she thought he was either trying to start or extinguish a blaze between his legs.

"Slow down, cowboy," Oona protested. "What the hell do I get out of this?"

"Damn, you don't look like much up close."

"Charming. Why don't you take your sweet nothings to some other girl's bedroom?"

"Because I'm here, bitch," he snapped. "It's New Year's and I want to see your Jelli. Hurry up. And let me tell you something. If you gonna work here in my Harlem, you're gonna want me as a friend. Understand? Take that fucking robe off and let me see your a-coochie-ments."

Oona swallowed hard and said nothing as her robe fell open before she let it slide to the floor.

"Show me your Jelli, gal."

"Come over here to the bed," Oona resigned, leading the detective, who tiny-stepped forward with his trousers tangled around his ankles.

"Is this what you want?"

"Can I touch it?" he asked with boyish wonder.

"That's what it's made for, Detective," Oona purred, going into auto-Oooh by habit. She softened for an instant when she noticed the gnawed-off stub of a finger on the detective's right hand. She lowered her voice.

"Let me help you get out of these clothes so you can—"

"Just the pants!"

Oona cringed as she guided the detective's bloated, half-clothed body, clumsy with age and slippery with sour-smelling sweat, to mount her Jelli.

"Damn, your Jelli's soooooo sweet," he said between hoggish snorts.

"Yeah, sweet," she said, as she helped him find a rhythm that would empty his balls and get him out of her bed, out of her home, as soon as possible.

"Arrhhh, fuck. Your slot machine was made for me," he yelled as his eyes rolled back white and sightless. "Hmm, this Jelli is sooooo goddamned goood!"

"Come on, big daddy. Come on," Oooh whispered in the detective's hairy ear hole. "Make Mommy happy. Mommy's calling. You coming?"

The detective closed his eyes and bit the color from his lower lip. He thrashed about trout-like, his face reddening, and the gelatinous fat that collared his neck jiggled violently.

"Hap-Hap—Happy—FUCKING—New Year!" the detective hollered. Then he grunted, and his body stiffened as if he had been shot in the head at close range.

"Yeah, Detective," Oona hissed, as she stared at her ceiling. "Happy fucking New Year."

"Now that we're friends," the detective said, staring at the lifeless Jelli, "call me Reagan—like the President."

5

Brain Drain

ROMARO DIDN'T KNOW WHAT TO MAKE OF THE CLUMSY COMMOTION in the back of the security office. He was on his dinner break and really didn't want to be bothered with anything more pressing than finishing his pressed meats sandwich. But against his better judgment he opened his big mouth to intervene.

"Can't you see a man's trying to eat in peace?" Romaro said, waving his floppy sandwich overhead as if no other words were necessary. "Is there a problem back there, ladyboys?"

Two men, half Romaro's age and dressed in ill-fitting ValuMartCity security jumpsuits, looked at each other for a moment before answering. They knew the big man who had long ago made himself at home in their security shack. But neither knew Romaro well. He was Department, after all, and both were surprised that such a high-ranking cop would occasionally hole up in a department-store security office to eat his dinner. One of the guards remembered something about him saying the food in the employee cafeteria reminded him of when he used to accompany his father to work. Something about how his father worked in a department store. But somehow that explanation, the guards felt, did not fully explain why the Department captain showed up in their security shack once or twice a week.

Romaro was an intimidating man in both manner and stature. He made the guards nervous and self-conscious. But that did not stop the taller guard from engaging the captain whenever he could. The young guard still harbored fantasies of some day joining the Department. He wanted to show initiative.

"Sorry for the noise, Captain," he said. "It looks like the visuals in the third-floor West-L restroom are acting…well…kinda crazy."

"It's all wrong," the other guard volunteered. "It's fucked!"

"Do you want to take a peek, sir?" asked the taller guard, looking over his shoulder to deliver his invitation with eye contact.

Romaro exhaled with disgust as he rose to his feet with a middle-aged grunt. His big, square head nearly bumped the room's low ceiling, from which hung aging viewpanels watching every corner of the old Herald Square mall. "This better not take more than a minute," Romaro said as he dropped his sandwich on a table cluttered with security logs and daily feed routes now splattered with mayo Flav.

Romaro stepped over to the men and parted them with his outsized shoulders and thick, overlong arms that moved with a rigidity suggesting they were bolted on. The captain had always carried a top-heavy build, but over the years his legs and hips had thinned, giving him the disproportionate profile of a giant, walking lobster. His perpetually ruddy complexion only accentuated the resemblance.

"Here," the taller guard said, pointing to a beat-up viewpanel angled down to reveal two rows of four cubed views of a third-floor restroom. Each view periodically flipped like children's blocks to reveal ever more detailed views.

"So what's the problem other, than you two getting your gooeys watching people take a shit?" Romaro asked, turning from the screen to get a glimpse of his sandwich sitting in the near distance. He could smell it, hear it calling him. "Don't make me lose my goddamned appetite. I bought a freeze cup of choc pudding for dessert."

The shorter guard shook his head a long time, before the taller one blurted out his concerns. He explained to Romaro that the security's Augmented Auto-plotting Intelligence was zeroing in on statistically suspicious occurrences. It had locked in on the restroom for a reason, he insisted, even if three trained human beings with their organic intelligence couldn't see what that reason was.

"The AAI is looking at something," the guards said in a unison that unnerved Romaro.

Romaro leaned in and narrowed his eyes as he studied the VP's key screen.

It was an overhead view of a rather typical department-store bathroom, large by today's standards, probably built more than fifty years ago when toilets still used perfectly good drinking water to shit in. Original black-and-white tiled floor, Romaro noted, while trying not to calculate its worth on the Underground Eco. All the ceramic sinks had long been replaced with metal ones, which themselves had recently been replaced with low-grade plastic ones. Standard glass mirrors had given way years ago to reflective wallpaper.

Romaro shrugged and took a deep breath. Nothing looked out of the ordinary, he thought. It was the day after Chinese New Year, so the store was crowded with bargain hunters of all kinds. The view flipped back to detail: an overhead of the bathroom's six stalls. Romaro didn't really want to watch two elderly women and two teenage boys defecate; there still was his chocolate pudding to consider.

He glanced at the young guards. He had to admire, if ever so briefly, their intense concentration on the doings in the bathroom stalls—four occupied and two vacant. Time passed like a kidney stone, Romaro thought, as he and the guards watched people enter, shit, and exit the stalls. Everybody has to shit, he mused, the high and low, the Dark and Light, the young and old. Apparently, he observed, this didn't mean that they were all equally compelled to wash their hands.

Romaro and the guards watched a dozen shoppers come and go when he realized that he had done exactly what he had hoped he wouldn't. He'd lost his appetite. And he was pissed.

"Funny," the shorter guard said under his breath.

"What the fuck's funny," Romaro replied, barely moving his lips. The back of his neck was getting tired from looking up at the viewpanel.

He took a loud, long breath before he turned to the taller guard. "Don't tell me that you see something funny, too."

"No sir."

The shorter guard scratched his clean-shaven chin.

"Isn't it strange that no one used the two center stalls?" he asked. "In the last thirty-five minutes lots of people used all the other ones, but not those two. Whyathink?"

He rubbed his finger over the image of the two empty bathroom stalls as he waited for a response.

"Maybe somebody peed on the seat, or they stink," the taller guard said dismissively. "I don't know."

"Damn," Romaro whispered. "I'll be damned. You're right. All this time and not a single bitch-of-a-whore took a squat in those stalls. Not a one."

"Then why you think, Captain?" the taller guard asked, trying to get back in the game.

"Because somebody's fucking with us," Romaro roared. "That's fucking why."

Romaro got to his feet so quickly that he toppled his chair. It struck the aluminum-tiled floor and bounced with a great clap and clank. The guards jumped. Romaro kicked the chair out of his way as he walked to an adjacent viewpanel, tapping his link that clung to his right ear.

"Najima... Yeah. It's me."

The guards looked on, their faces illuminated in the silvery light of the overhead viewpanels. They listened as their hearts raced to catch up with their speculations. Something big was happening. They knew it. A Department captain wouldn't get involved in some routine shoplifting incident.

"I'm not coming straight back from my break. I'm still here, yeah, at ValuMartCity, in the security shack. I need you to tie into the shack's security streams. The boys here will give you prime access. Something wrong is going down in one of the public bathrooms. Yeah... No joke.

"I'm heading in there to take a look 'round for myself. Tell me what you see as soon as you tap in."

Romaro looked at the taller guard and nodded. The guard fumbled with a control panel until he fixed on Romaro's link frequency as the captain flashed the code by holding up his fingers as he spoke.

"You," Romaro barked at the taller guard, "stay here and monitor the situation and stay linked to my surveillance officer; she'll link you to us.

"You," Romaro said, pointing to the shorter guard, "come with me."

With a bang of the door, Romaro and the guard were gone. The remaining guard fumed that he was not chosen and then decided he would do his best to impress Romaro's surveillance officer.

6

Saved You A Plate

ZANIA LAY ON HER RIGHT SIDE, HER THIN PILLOW SCRUNCHED INTO A three-cornered ball between her right cheek and shoulder. ZaNia always slept on her side so Jae-J. could sleep on his stomach, which he preferred. Their twin-sized bed was simply too small to accommodate Jae-J. and ZaNia sleeping on their backs, which she preferred. And their bedroom was far too small to accommodate a bed any larger. It was, ZaNia convinced herself, a small sacrifice. She would sleep standing on her swollen feet for this man. There were those times when they lay on each other, times when the inadequacies of the bed, the room, the world, ceased to matter.

But on this night she could find no peace, not on her side or even in the arms of her husband. It was the second night she had not heard from her son. She had made a dozen VIDsit requests to his office and his home, and three more to his WaveWeave service. Nothing.

Just before going to bed, she had broached the subject of turning to professionals for help.

"It's too soon for that," Jae-J. cautioned. "Anyway, they don't take you seriously until a person is missing for at least a week. Plus, a young Dark male? They're likely to take our action deposit and just pocket it. Do nothing but put us on some list to be watched more closely. And what we going to do then? Call the police? File a complaint?"

He laughed without humor and glared at her forehead, as if he could see straight through its bone and count the wrinkles of a brain gone sadly defective.

"Yeah, why don't we just call the police, Nia?" Jae-J. asked, not expecting an answer. He turned his back to ZaNia, signaling that the conversation was over.

ZaNia opened her mouth to shoot back an explosive shell of a reply, but stopped. The woolly blanket hadn't completely covered her husband's back, exposing his tattered T-shirt that in turn exposed his bare shoulders, back, upper arms, and neck. He looked especially vulnerable lying there, inches from her touch, with his badly scarred skin in plain view, she thought. Her eyes slowly followed the bumpy, patterned wound that covered much of his back the way gravel sets into a dusty, country road.

She tried to imagine what that skin felt like before he forbade her to kiss or touch it, before the bio-bomb exploded on that clear autumn afternoon so many years ago. Five hundred died before they could be air-rushed to treatment. Two thousand more, including Jae-J.'s mother, father, and teenage sister, would be dead in less than a week after the bomb's bio-agents infected them with a hyper-aggressive strain of V-HIC.

Jae-J. survived, but not without scars known and unknowable. ZaNia ran her fingers a breath above her husband's wounds. As she did, her irritation dissipated. She knew him. She knew that he, too, was worrying. Just in his own way. Moments later, Jae-J. mumbled goodnight and kissed the air, turning over one last time to face her just as he drifted back into the deep end of sleep. Nothing deprived Jae-J. of sleep, and she envied him for that.

ZaNia realized that Jae-J. was right, at least about how a detective would perceive Army's absence. It was a holiday week. Lots of people lost themselves in the celebrations, not showing up at loading docks and stockrooms, offices and workstations and marital beds when they were expected.

But this was Armstrong Justus Black. ZaNia knew how much it would take to prevent her son from keeping his promise to her. Could he be sick? Hospitalized?

Worse?

She dismissed the questions as quickly as they passed into her racing mind. Army was a good boy. And if he had been arrested, even mistakenly, he or someone would have contacted her by now. *So, what could have happened?* she asked herself, as her desperation deepened.

ZaNia lay in bed for two more hours watching Jae-J.'s shadow-shrouded features, which after that long began to annoy her with their dreamy calm.

She'd considered getting up an hour ago, but she'd heard G-Daddy going to the bathroom down the hall. The last thing she wanted to do in the middle of the night was hear her father complain about his weak bladder, or reminisce about flush toilets.

For the last thirty minutes she had heard little more than rare silence. She convinced herself that a cup of cool tap water would help her sleep. She could still get in a few hours of sleep before she would have to rise to make the family breakfast and start her day. She eased out of the covers and slid her feet to the bare floor. She wrapped herself in her robe and stepped into the hallway, stopping just long enough to snugly close the door behind her.

Everyone must have been asleep, even the apartment itself.

ZaNia padded through the living room and into the kitchen. She looked toward the sink and saw her HARLEM HAPPENS mug sitting mouth-down on a mat next to it. But she was drawn to look toward the viewpanel on the other side of the kitchen. She glanced at its motionless, deep blue screen; it was apparently in sleep mode as well. But when she approached the screen, it stirred.

"GOOD-"

"Shhh. Quiet,"

"-morning…"

"Good morning," ZaNia whispered, quickly adjusting the VP's volumel to 'low-low.'

"Any messages, any VIDsits today?"

"Yes," the VP replied. "You have eleven messages and four VIDsit invitations as of 11:49:21 P.M. yesterday, February, 2041."

"Any high priority? Any from Armstrong?"

"None priority. None from Armstrong," the VP said, its horizontal expanse filling with beckoning windows and gateways and pulsating lists, color-coded directories cross indexing to live and filed clips of breaking world, national, and local news. And weather.

Disappointed, ZaNia said nothing for a few moments. "Thank you, now go back to sleep mode—NO! Wait. Wait…"

ZaNia walked to the kitchen's doorway and peeked as far as she could see into the darkness of the living room and hallway that led to her family's bedrooms. Satisfied with what she didn't see or hear, she turned to the VP, this time carefully pulling up a chair to sit directly in front of its newly energized viewpanel.

"Stand by for a VIDsit," ZaNia whispered.

"Of course. To whom?"

"To my son, at his HOME ONLY. Tag it 'highest priority'."

"Understood," the VP said, blinking and then sweeping its offerings to its borders and opening a large, black, outlined window in its center. The top third of the window played a loop of Army's face, a silent, full-motion clip he had recorded for VIDistors. The avatar made him appear to be listening even when he wasn't available to make the VIDsit or decided he wasn't up for one.

ZaNia cleared her voice and tightened the knot of her hair that had grown fuzzy and loose.

"Ready... begin."

ZaNia saw her face reflecting back to her on a lower corner window, just beneath the image of her son's virtual rapt attention. She cleared her voice again and started to speak.

"It's way past midnight here, but everybody is so worried sick about you that I don't think anyone is getting any rest. I know I'm not. I'm a worrier, just like my mother was. I can't close my eyes, Army, not until I know where you are, how you are."

ZaNia could feel herself choking up with emotion. She placed her hand lightly on her chest and closed her eyes before she began to speak again.

"I made all your favorites: stewed chicken, cornbread and corn pudding... everything you like. But I don't know how long I can keep it from spoiling, honey. You knew I would save you a plate. And G-Daddy promised that he wouldn't touch the rum until you come home. 'Not a drop,' he said."

"You have ten seconds," the VP softly interrupted.

"Well, Army, my VIDsit is almost up. If you are getting any of this, please call your momma. Okay? We're worried sick. Sick. It's been two days. Call. Call us."

The VIDsit screen went dark. She lowered her head and shook with tiny waves of despair. ZaNia was determined not to cry. She clenched her fists. When she lifted her head, she was startled by the sight of Imani standing in the darkened kitchen doorway. It was something in the angle of Imani's more-child's-than-woman's face, the way her fingers held too tightly to the edge of the doorway, that loosened ZaNia's grip on her own emotions. Tears ran down her cheeks faster than she could swipe them away. Imani started to cry too, her throat resonating with a hiccupping, wet whine.

Imani ran over and coiled herself like a housecat in ZaNia's ample lap. ZaNia held her daughter, more lanky legs and arms than anything else, in the modulating glow of the viewpanel. She cradled her daughter's head and fixed her glassy eyes on the torrent of information that rained across the VP.

Floods of information. Information. Information, she thought, but not a drop of knowledge about her Army. As she consoled Imani, ZaNia could feel her eyes begin to clear, but not the dread gathering in the place deep inside her, the empty place where her overworked womb once had been.

7

Getting a Head

ROMARO STEPPED FROM THE DEPARTMENT STORE'S CREAKY CABLE elevator looking as if he wasn't interested in anything more than buying a new all-season blazer. The security guard trailing two steps back tried to ape the captain's practiced nonchalance—though his cranberry-colored security guard coveralls made that attempt more futile than he realized.

"Hey kid, tell me your name again." Romaro asked as the two of them walked along an aisle overhung by thickets of men's clothing racks. Only a few shoppers looked up. It was almost closing time.

"It's, ah, Kofe. Sir."

Romaro stopped so abruptly that Kofe stepped on the backs of Romaro's heels.

"What kind of name is that for a Light?

"My maternal grandmother was a Dark, and Kofe was her grandfather's name, an African name. West African, I think," Kofe said, without apology.

"Oh," Romaro said as the two men began to walk again toward the bathroom in the West L section of the department store. A few more shoppers turned to see the men pass them. No one looked alarmed. Romaro looked more like a store manager than a Department captain, Kofe thought.

Romaro tapped his link.

"Najima, are you seeing what I'm seeing?"

"Yes. I have full access," she replied. "And I've got an eye on the bathroom stalls too. No change. Your little buddy in security cleared and locked down the bathroom. He was surprisingly subtle for a store cop. No commotion."

33

"Good," Romaro said as he pressed closer to the bathroom. "Good."

Romaro signaled Kofe to take up a position next to the door. Romaro pressed himself against the wall on the opposite of the door. Kofe studied the door. He had seen it and dozens of others just like it thousands of times. It was an ordinary, lightweight metal door that now bore a hastily handwritten sign that screamed OUT OF ORDER.

Romaro reached under his black suit jacket with his right hand and slowly brought out a standard issue Department penetrator. The oversized handgun's smooth, black composite skin gave off a grim gleam in the store's overbright light. Kofe read Romaro's eyes and removed his shock baton from his waist holder.

"You stay here," Romaro said as he inched closer to the door. "Make sure no one comes in and make damn sure if anyone other than me comes out of there, drop 'em like your drawers on prom night. Understand me?"

Kofe wanted to tell Romaro that he understood, but his heart was in his mouth. He made do with nodding, as he held his shock baton high in attack position.

"Real good, kid," Romaro said, as he inched the bathroom door open. "Najima? Any change inside?"

"Negative. No change."

Standing, Romaro crept into the bathroom with his weapon drawn. He swept the L-shaped room with his eyes. He could see nothing out of the ordinary. He heard only the hum of air exchangers and the deodorizers firing every few seconds. The room smelled of artificial pine. Romaro realized that he had never smelled the real thing; he associated the scent with shithouses, not forests.

Romaro stepped slowly to the row of sinks to his left and craned to see the stalls located just beyond the bend of the L. His link vibrated in his ear.

"Yeah," Romaro whispered. "Got something?"

"Think so, Captain," Najima replied, her voice low, her words slowly falling on his ears. "Been analyzing the security feed on the stalls. The perspective is off, just a hair. And the resolution... I don't know."

"You don't know what?"

"I think someone, maybe two or three people, are in there, hiding in the stall." Najima's words went flat and heavy. "I think they're using some kind of obscura. Sophisticated stuff."

"Shit," Romaro said, checking his weapon with a glance. "I need to know if there's one or more in there. How many? A number."

"I'm giving you the best I've got," Najima said. "My best guess is that it's probably one; likely just one. But we're not talking some crackle head with the runs, Cap. Want me to call in backup?"

"Naw. I think me and the kid can handle this," he whispered almost loud enough to be a warning. "Probably some fancy shoplifter scared shitless 'cause he knows he's cornered."

But Romaro couldn't even convince himself of the lie. He knew that cornered prey was the most dangerous, and that whoever was clever enough to tech-conceal himself so completely in a department store bathroom was cunning enough to make *him* the prey. Romaro realized that he would have to be extremely careful. He was fighting back second thoughts about posting the kid outside the door as he got down onto his hands and knees. He was trying to see if he could peek under any of the stall doors. But all of them extended to the floor, and a rush of vulnerability made him scramble back to his feet.

Romaro was sweating. His penetrator felt slippery in his hand. He cursed to himself as he hoped the stalls' interior partitions wouldn't extend to the floor. From inside one, he could look along the floor and might see feet, or some other suggestion of what he was up against in the neighboring stalls.

Romaro inched toward the stalls, stepping slowly, silently—toe-heel, toe-heel—over the room's smooth, tile floor. When he reached the first stall, he smiled to himself. He loved being the hunter. He reached the stall's door and eased it open only enough for him to slip into it, placing first one foot and then the other a top the stall's toilet.

His link throbbed. He had no choice but to ignore it; he was too close now to give away any advantage. He braced himself against the stall's wall and slowly lowered his head and shoulders until the top of his head touched the floor. Just as he turned his head enough to get a look under the partition he saw another set of eyes staring back at him from three stalls away.

Startled, Romaro lost his grip on the wall and crumbled to the urine-stained floor with a crash. He instinctively tried to catch his fall with the same hand that gripped his weapon. The penetrator fell and bounced loudly under the toilet behind him. He saw himself a turtle on its back in the sun. He felt a migraine approach from the back of his left ear like distant thunder.

Before Romaro could get to his feet, there was a second crash. Romaro knew it was the door of the last stall. The whole set of stall walls shook with the force of the escape, as Romaro's heart felt like a bound fist trying to escape his chest. He heard feet—two feet. Someone was running hard and crashing through the bathroom door.

Screaming curses, Romaro retrieved his weapon and scrambled out of the stall, his right knee aching and swelling. Seconds later, he pushed through the bathroom door. He could see Kofe chasing someone running at least fifty feet ahead of him. He took a deep breath and pushed himself to join the chase, huffing through the pain in his banged up knee.

Romaro tapped his link.

"Where?" he asked, sucking for air.

"Target is moving fast for the east staircase. I have security holding all elevators and escalators. We are evacuating the building."

"What? What are we dealing with?"

"Hard to say, Captain," Najima replied. "The store's security systems are badly out of date. And I suspect that the target is using some kind of vidi scrambler. We're just getting a dark blob. No face. Nothing. Can't tell you if it's a man or woman, Light or Dark. Just that it's moving fast and on the stairway to the second floor.

"Shit," Najima yelled. "That kid, the discount cop, chasing him, he's down. On the east staircase, half way down."

"Fuck," Romaro yelled as he made it to the top of the stairs. He could see Kofe sprawled face down on the raw concrete stairs. He stepped quickly to the kid, grabbed him hard by his shoulder and pulled him over. As he did, he was first confronted by the sickening sound of a man being emptied out. His eyes then registered the blood that gushed down the stairs, leaving behind Kofe's intestines, spleen, liver, and stomach. He could smell the kid's last meal. Beef stew. Or was that the smell of the wound? Romaro couldn't be sure.

The kid had been opened up. Romaro had seen it before, many times before. A homemade hot laser device, a gut buster, had burned through the abdominal wall in a single, close-quarters stroke. The guy didn't have a chance.

"Where now?" Romaro asked Najima.

"First floor. The target disappeared for a minute, but is moving again. Without a face, without a decent ID, we could lose this one in the crowd."

Romaro limped down the stair and went into a slow trot when he reached the mall's main floor. He could see a couple of hundred shoppers trying to squeeze out the three double-door mall exits as rent-a-cops did little more than direct the pedestrian traffic. Romaro's headache was throbbing in counterpoint to his swollen knee.

"Captain," Najima said uncharacteristically excited. "I think we just copped a break. I can't make out the assailant, but I just noticed that an overcoat disappeared on the first floor when the target paused by a rack of winter coats."

"What in Buddha's balls," Romaro hissed as he stopped and scanned the crowd of shoppers moving toward the mall exits. "We've got his murdering ass. Describe the coats left on the rack."

Romaro nodded as he walked slowly toward the exits, searching for anyone wearing a knee-length, gray woolen trench coat with wide lapels, epaulettes, and buckled belt. It was a chilly night. And most shoppers were in their coats. And gray was a popular because its popularity made it an inconspicuous color in a time when most people knew that being conspicuous could get you killed.

The throbbing in Romaro's head and knee hardly registered anymore as he was once again caught up in the hunt. This was his kill. He realized that store security was required to call in city police for a homicide. But it would take at least ten to fifteen minutes before they got there, and longer to deploy. That was more than enough time, he thought, to fire off an explosive charge into the head of Kofe's killer and rack up a clean Department kill for himself.

Romaro flipped his coat jacket lapel to reveal a Department glow badge. He held his right arm straight down, the nose of his penetrator looking as if it was about to blast the mall's gaudy, threadbare carpet. Two store security guards spotted Romaro and were about to herd him to the exit when they stopped in their tracks, one noticing the badge, the other the frightening weapon in his huge hand.

Romaro, growing frustrated, tapped his link hard.

"Najima!"

"Nothing. The target must be hiding again. Keep a close watch out. The assailant has to, sooner or later, make a run for it. The target has to come your way."

"I'm going to try to flush this bastard out."

"Remember, Captain, he's armed and—at least at close range—very dangerous," Najima cautioned.

Romaro said nothing, but headed for racks crammed with coats, new and used. Before he completed his second step, something big crossed his path, knocking him back. Romaro fell hard on his back, but this time never lost grip of his weapon. He heard screams and an explosion of broken glass as he got back to his feet. Without thinking, he ran toward the noise and an overpowering smell of popcorn and cashews. He saw a tall, broad-shouldered Dark wearing goggle-glasses, a jade-green stocking hat and a long, loose-fitting gray coat. The man was running like an athlete, with a large shopping bag rolled up and tucked under his arm like an American football.

Romaro was running again, his weapon leading the way like a lethal hood ornament. Just ahead, no more than ten yards away, Romaro could see the man had paused, as if confused about the certainty of his escape. Romaro aimed and fired. The penetrator's charge exploded into the forehead of a haberdashery mannequin. Hunks of the exploding head and its electronics sprayed Romaro's target as the man fell, face first, into the mannequin display, which launched into a clamorous chatter.

Dropping to his good knee, Romaro struggled to steady his breath and aim and fire again. But the man in the wool coat had gotten to his feet with remarkable speed and bolted with his red ValuMartCity shopping bag now swinging from his hand by its plastic handles. The man barely shortened his stride as he banged his way through the panicked crowd that parted and then closed behind him.

"Najima? Do you still have that fucker?"

"No, he's gone. Nothing on store or street vids. He's disappeared, ghosted on us," she said. "I've got lot of city cops, though. They're speeding up Seventh Avenue."

"Captain, this is Barnes—you know, the other guard, from the security shack."

"Yeah, go ahead," Romaro said as he watched the first of the police burst into the mall.

"I'm in the third-floor, West-L restroom. I'm standing in what was stall four and five. "

"Huh? Four and five?" Romaro growled. "Just tell me what the fuck you see."

"You've got to see this, Captain," the security guard said into Romaro's link. The seasoned detective registered revulsion and shock dripping from the younger man's words. "Whoever killed Kofe," the guard said after taking a couple of deep breaths, "warmed up on some poor soul in the bathroom."

Romaro was in the dark, and he didn't like it. He listened as he snatched his glow badge off of his jacket and held it prominently over his head as a gaggle of city police officers stormed in his direction.

He heard banging over his link and then the guard speaking to Najima.

The security guard was kicking a small projector off the lower edge of the stall's wall.

"Can you see this?" he said to the ceiling directly above him.

"Yeah," Romaro heard Najima say, as anger flickered into her voice. "All too well."

Romaro broke into a slow trot and then, despite a growling pain in his head and knee, picked up his pace as he made his way back to the store's bathroom. "Tell me what you see," Romaro screamed as he huffed and puffed and trotted.

Romaro stormed into the bathroom just in time to see the guard, Barnes, standing over the body of a man slumped over on a dry toilet. Judging by the man's neatly pressed woolen trousers, silk and tweed vest, and cotton, pinstriped shirt, the man was likely a person of some means. An antique uPod watch was still fastened to the man's pale wrist. His wingtip loafers held a brilliant shine.

"Why isn't there any blood? There should be lots of blood," the guard asked Romaro, who was still trying to catch his breath as he took a few steps closer to the body, which appeared undisturbed except for its missing head.

"Lock this whole, damn thing down, Najima," Romaro ordered his surveillance specialist before throwing his beefy arm around the guard's shoulder and walking him out of the stall.

"Look, Barnes," Romaro said with uncommon tenderness. "It is Barnes, right?"

The guard nodded yes as he allowed Romaro to lead him away from the murder scene. "Everything you've seen is going to be part of a special Department investigation. In a few minutes, this whole place is going to be swarmed with city cops. Tell them nothing. Refer questions or anyone asking questions to me."

Barnes nodded that he understood.

"My specialist will provide you with all the contact info you'll need," Romaro continued. "This is important, and I won't forget how you performed here tonight and how you're gonna perform on this thing in the future. You got me? Yes, I'm sure you do."

Romaro and Barnes could hear people approaching the bathroom's door.

"No worries," Najima assured Romaro. "It's locked down and one of our evidence units is en route."

"Remember," Romaro reminded Barnes. "Not a word."

"Not. A. Word," Barnes replied and then looked back at the stall where the body sat. "Where do you think the head's at?" His eyes were wide with terror.

Romaro shook his bulldog's head at the question.

"Where? Where do you think it's at?" he said brightly. "Our fucking bargain hunter got away with it in that bag at a cut rate."

Romaro laughed alone.

"Now no more talk," Romaro said abruptly. "Our people will be here soon. They'll take you to Department C3, ask you some questions, then take you home. Cooperate. Hear?

"I'll owe you one, kid."

8

In-Site

REAGAN REYNOLDS CARESSED THE FELT OF HIS RAIN-SLICK PORKPIE, which he'd perched on the bar stool to the left of his. Chinese New Year had passed better than most in recent memory. He found some comfort in that. Almost four days had passed and he could still smell the Jelli's musty sex oils on his fingers. But even that little extra was not enough to boost his mood.

It was getting late. Reagan's graveyard shift as the house detective at a Harlem hotel would begin in a couple of hours. He hated the job, but after his almost 20-year-long career as a Department detective had ended so badly, and with his pension held up in endless executive reviews, he'd had to take what he could. Temporary hardened into permanent before he realized it. But being a house dick in Harlem had not been without its perks, Reagan thought, as he lustfully recalled his early-morning adventure in the Harlem sweet-suite.

He glanced at the time and reminded himself that as long as he was reachable, the hotel management wouldn't pressure him too much if he was a few minutes late. He usually drifted through the hotel's back door shortly after midnight. He liked to grab a fried egg sandwich from the kitchen and gobble it down as he strolled up to the lobby. Once there, he'd uproot some hapless bellboy from his favorite chair and take up his station by the potted fern. Or he would roam. It depended on his mood.

Besides intervening in some lovers' spat, or chasing off some Vipers, pleasurists, and other assorted unsavories that ventured too close to the hotel entrance, Reagan had little to do. That was the part of the job he despised the most. He understood that management was more interested in the appearance of security rather than the expensive real thing. Some nights, Reagan felt like little more than a scarecrow, a scary old face peering out of an empty suit installed to spook off neighborhood Darks. But… there were the Jellies…

"Another coffee?" the bartender asked.

Reagan looked up from his empty cup and into the bartender's pale, unremarkable features.

"Why not? Yeah. And put a nigger more of something extra in this one."

"Excuse me. Did you say put a nig—"

"You heard me?" Reagan's voice boomed. "I said a jigger. Why would I want a tiny Darky in my coffee? It's black enough." Reagan's pale green eyes smiled.

The bartender realized the old cop was kidding, but that didn't upgrade the humor above annoying. He took a cleansing breath, then spilled a splash of Scotch into Reagan's coffee. The bartender hoped the liquor would keep this ill-tempered regular civil, at least. He had seen him lose it before. Lucky he hadn't killed anyone that time, he thought.

Almost every night, the bartender reflected, Detective Reynolds sat at this bar, and by osmosis the bartender had come to know more about him than he cared to know. He knew, for starters, that Reagan was named for a long-dead president, and that he was a year or two from his sixtieth birthday. He lived nearby and he drank too much. And he talked obsessively about how the Department had screwed him into an early retirement, and how his dying mother and meddlesome baby sister were driving him crazy.

He also knew that Reagan could talk endlessly and bitterly about the Darks—how they had ruined his career, how they had ruined the country. His sister had married a rich African who, he said, treated her like something he might fling from his nose.

"More Scotch?"

"Huh?" Reagan said, too lost in his many resentments to have noticed the inquisitive expression the bartender was training on him.

"I said, do you want another shot in your coffee, Detective?"

"Yeah, more Scotch," he replied, taking note of the respectful tone the bartender struck when he called him Detective. He appreciated that. Good listener. Good man, Reagan thought as he glanced again at the tavern's only clock, a large, suspended glass cylinder filled with animated gases forming and reforming the time when it wasn't forming whiskey brand names and house specials. The clock read 10:17:31 P.M.

As Reagan loudly sipped his drink, he gazed around the tavern, Freddie's, which was wedged in a row of SRO tenements and rundown shops on a stubby Bronx stretch of Fernando Ferrer Avenue. Its mostly unadorned shotgun space was practically empty except for a youngish couple huddled at a back table. A shabbily dressed woman sat alone, facing the wall and nursing a beer. A few men stood at the end of the long bar, chatting in a blue vaporous haze with the bartender, who looked as if he wished closing time had come an hour ago. The tavern's wraparound viewpanel was playing fragments of two Japanese baseball games and the Earth Cup quarterfinals between Israel and New Palestine. No one was watching.

Through the tavern's bullet-resistant windows, Reagan could see the infinitely more interesting drama of Ferrer Avenue, a tumbledown side street that attracted a mix of low-grade hustlers and their hustled. The street was crowded, as it was always crowded, with people too overworn and impoverished to escape to anywhere better. Then again, some were so fried by hard times that they probably didn't realize how fucked they were, Reagan mused. The other night, he'd watched a half-naked Dark, dressed in filthy sheets he had thrown over his shoulder, strut past as if he were a Roman emperor.

It's strange, Reagan thought, how the hopeless are hardened by life while at the same time softened up for fate's final blow. He lingered on the slow procession of pedestrians, thinking how so many of them looked like crabs that had misplaced their shells. Everyone seemed to be dressed in variations of the same loose-fitting government grays and greens, tunics, trousers, and jackets.

Metro Health and Sanitation workers regularly sniffed Ferrer and its tributaries to bag bodies that were too tired or too V-HIC-ridden to take another foot-dragging step. Death and deterioration were such a part of streets like Ferrer that few—whether among the powerful or the powerless—believed it could be any other way.

"Fuck 'em," Reagan said, almost loud enough for someone to hear. "Especially the monkey men and all the other assorted Dark mutants thrashing up the world."

He looked to his left, then slowly turned to his right. Only his hat sat next to him at the bar.

"Didn't you think the 21st century was going to be better than this?" Reagan mumbled.

"What?" the bartender asked, turning a look of annoyance in the detective's direction.

Yelling now, Reagan repeated himself: "I SAID didn't YOU think the 21st CENTURY was going to be BETTER than THIS?"

"I say give it sixty years," hollered back one of the two Light men who had been talking to the bartender.

"In sixty years, the century will be done, over," Reagan hollered back to the man, who was dressed in a Health Services jumpsuit and heavy, knee-high boots.

"Yeah, I know," the man said, pleased with his stab at sarcasm.

Reagan groused, then gulped the rest of his coffee. He shoved the empty cup and saucer toward the bartender with a rattle. He stood up, snatched shut his oversized raincoat, and grabbed his hat with the three good fingers of his right hand. In a fat man's huff, he left the tavern without paying or saying a word.

A few steps outside, Reagan found himself breathing hard. As he stood collecting himself, he spotted a knot of uniformed figures two blocks away near the bright lights of the Grand Concourse. At least a dozen officers and two Department vehicles were in the street, which was barricaded with yellow laser wire. Reagan quickened his step and headed for what he prayed was trouble. His long raincoat blew open as he waddled at an uneven pace, running, walking, running, up the swollen slope of the narrow, cracked street. A light rain painted his white shirt gray where it stretched the tightest over his overhanging stomach.

Reagan Reynolds, panting from his wide-set mouth, didn't notice the spitting rain as he waded into the crackle of what he hoped was a fresh crime scene.

Spit trembled as he reached deep to catch his breath. He and Zulu had just scaled five flights of rickety stairs, and neither man thought he was capable of another step. But the sight of their door gave them a second wind. Besides, the MethPops they'd downed like jelly beans minutes earlier were kicking in, making their heads, legs, and feet feel as light as children's laughter.

"C'mom, Zulu," Spit said through clinched teeth, a frightful many of them chipped or missing. "Bring your tired black ass up here. A few more steps to go.

"You want them frezzpacs to overheat?" Spit shouted over the building's ceaseless chorus of voices, screams, coughs, baby cries, thuds, thumps, blaring audios, and poor plumbing. Then he laughed like a man who just realized that *he* was the joke.

Zulu nodded and began to drag their load into the single-room apartment.

"Might be too late," Zulu said as he sniffed around the room, walking like a zombie toward the apartment's only window. It was more like a ship cabin's portal and opened out from the bottom. Spit gagged as the men's watering eyes met briefly in disbelief. Then, each covered his mouth and nose as Zulu popped open the window, under which stood an old-fashioned Styrofoam cooler.

"Put 'em all in the there," Spit instructed Zulu, who struggled to get the frezzpacs out of the cloth sack in which they hauled them.

Both men, frail from consuming more drugs than food, stood over their handiwork and peered down into the cooler.

"This is the shit," Spit said pointing into the cooler.

"Well, it smells the part," Zulu replied, not taking his eyes off their booty.

"What's in there is going to take us high over happyland," Spit told Zulu, whose heavy-lidded eyes were beginning to succumb to a MethPop crash. "Ahh, man... we're going to the penthouse. The fucking penthouse without ever leaving this shithole. That's the motherfucking beauty of it."

Zulu sighed. "Is it going to make us happy?" he asked, waving his nose in the haze of incense he lit by dragging its tip across the floor. "I mean real happy. Happy for real?"

Spit closed the cooler and sat on it, poised to lecture.

"Look man, happiness is just a trick of chemistry, a spark in your brain that tickles you this way or that way." Spit paused, wiping the foam of saliva that gathered in the corners of his mouth whenever he got excited.

He continued. "Are you happy when old lady Chin gives you a hand job?"

"Yeah," Zulu replied lazily. "If I can close my eyes and don't have to look at her."

"Okay," Spit said, looking pleased. "Are you happy when you think about that nut you bust on her?"

"Yeah," Zulu said, smiling.

"Okay, okay, but you didn't bust that nut when you're just thinking about it. Did you? The happy you feel is some shit in your brain that tricks you, chemicals, bullshit that makes you think your tired ass is happy."

Zulu looked at the cooler and blinked.

"Now stay with me," Spit said, growing excited again. "What's in that box will trick your brain to make you feel happier than you have ever dreamed about feeling. I watched JoË Dots use this stash here to shoot up a whole room full of motherfuckers, rich motherfuckers, who were shooting their loads in their pants they were so happy because of what's in this box here."

Zulu looked up at Spit, disappointment drawn all over his sagging face.

"But I don't want to shoot my load in my pants."

Spit hopped off of the cooler and put his arm around his lifelong friend. He looked into Zulu's widely spaced eyes, which were the same shade of caramel-brown as his skin.

"On this one, buddy, I guess you just have to trust me. Okay?"

Zulu nodded and then nodded off to sleep.

"Mag-fucking-nificent," Spit said under his breath.

Awake, but still groggy, Zulu dropped to his elbows and crocodiled to the corner of the room where Spit was working by candlelight. He could see night at the window. Even in the room's uncertain light he could make out the shiny outlines of two injectors laid out on a piece of shocking white cloth. Their needles were long, thin, and impossibly sharp. Each needle glowed with a red so bright they looked hot to the touch. At the end of the injector's body was an ergonomically molded plunger the color of dead bone.

Each injector bore precise markings along its length to measure whatever substance they were about to dispatch. Spit couldn't stop thinking of the hatch marks as notches, each denoting every time these instruments had been used to prick the seam that held a user's body and soul together.

"How did you get to know so much about injectors, Spit?"

"I just picked it up around the way," he replied, a thick joint dangling from his lips.

The sleep had reset Zulu's senses. He lowered his voice and turned serious. "Show me how these things work."

He watched Spit deftly handle the injectors, checking and rechecking their mechanisms and membranes. He tapped the injectors with his index finger and carefully observed each injector hum to life. He explained that each injector held the proper amount of a new kind of trans-neuronic enabler, a special kind of memory enhancer that a lot of young, rich Lights were getting into. Spit said that JoË Dots himself told him that the enhancer is made out of the stuff in the brains of people they kill for it. "That's why they call this magic shit 'Hedz,' " Spit told Zulu with an airy reverence.

"He showed me how to draw it out of the lobes of their brains, to measure it, and then shoot it," Spit said between draws, holds and coughs of marijuana. "He gave me this one," Spit said, motioning to the open cooler, "for all the help I've been giving him with disposing of the empties."

"Is this a empty?" Zulu asked, raising up from the floor enough to look into cooler.

"Naw," Spit said. "If we can keep it chilled enough, we can shoot Hedz off of this one for a while, a long while. Boss man told me to think of it like a steak bone with lots of steak still on it."

Both men giggled like monstrously mischievous children. Serious again, Zulu asked one more question: "Will it hurt?"

Spit shook his head.

"These injectors' got something on them so the needles dull your nose as they drill in," he said. "You think those milk-fed Light boys would stick needles up their noses if that shit hurt?"

Spit laughed alone. Then he turned somber.

"Watch!"

Never breaking eye contact with Zulu, Spit guided the injector up his right nostril, filling it with the needle's red glow as it penetrated his nasal passage, then the base of his skull. Spit's eyes watered. A teardrop ran quickly down his left cheek, slowing when it reached the stubble that framed his weak chin. He grinned, then grimaced.

The sun had just flattened and fell into the Jersey horizon when a young sergeant first noticed the fat man waddling into Freddy's Tavern. It had been a mild diversion from the boredom that crept in after the first hour of crowd control. Despite its reputation as a canyon of crime and premature death, the Crimson Hills section of the South Bronx offered little resistance as the Department secured a square block of decaying tenements and SROs.

The following hours of the sergeant's sentry had been mostly uneventful. People, he reminded himself, tended to either respect or fear police, and were absolutely terrified of the Department. *Who in his right head wants to be on the wrong side of a Department line?* the sergeant thought, as he turned to see a squad of Spook Operations officers a few yards away, checking their weapons and equipment.

Only twice did he hear the WHOOP of an alarm and the telltale pop and crackle of laser wire on flesh. Only once was the contact severe enough for him to catch a whiff of something like frying dog. The smell told him that someone—he prayed not a child—had ventured too close to the yellow beams and had paid with an ugly burn. Someone had tossed a brick in an officer's direction, shattering it on a wall a fair distance from the assembly point. The incident seemed too inconsequential to mount a response. Time passed slowly.

But now the fat man was back, and he was running toward the operations scene. The helmet visor's zoom-sight revealed that he was a pre-elderly Light, job-dressed in a white button-down with a knotted necktie, raincoat, and hat. Just in a hurry to get home to the wife? Maybe he missed his transport, the sergeant reasoned as he turned his reconnaissance southward and continued to scan the streets for anything remotely menacing. Just as the sergeant's visor locked on a half-dozen Dark figures congealing into something worrisome, his helmet screeched like a frightened finch. When he turned his head toward the direction of the proximity alarm, he saw nothing at all.

He flushed with fear as he fumbled for his firearm.

"Hey, boy. Take it easy," Reagan yelled with a mix of amusement and annoyance. He hadn't meant to sneak so close to the inexperienced officer that his body's bulk blocked the sergeant's visor-vision. "I'm one of the white hats—good guys—you know…"

The sergeant eased his hand off his weapon as he regained his composure.

"Step back…Step back NOW!" he barked in a boyish voice reaching for more. "Who the hell are you and what business do you have here?"

Reagan laughed at the sergeant before he spoke. "I'm retired Department, son. Scan my U.I.D. You'll see what you need to see."

The sergeant's visor checked Reagan's universal identity card still in his jacket and discovered that the fat man was telling the truth. He also learned that Reagan Reynolds worked overnight security at the Hotel Theresa in Harlem. But he found no reason or authorization for the man to be on site, and he told him so.

"Look," Reagan said, standing perilously close to the laser wire, "I was in the area, just up the street, and saw the lights, the heavy vehicles. Just wanted to know what's going on and if I could help out."

"I don't think—"

"Who's in charge?" Reagan asked, speaking through a dismissive, you're-bothering-me-boy yawn. Then, with surprising speed, he reached over the laser wire and grabbed the sergeant by the shoulder. "I asked you nice—who's the head cheddar?"

Before the sergeant could respond, they both heard a booming voice coming from the opened hatch of a command vehicle idling in the middle of the street.

"Is there a *problem* here, Sergeant?" rumbled a voice thick with bees and honey. Captain Jon Romaro climbed down from the vehicle, obviously perturbed with all the noise on his perimeter.

"No, Captain. No problem," the sergeant replied with appropriate snap. "I've got this civi here who... "

Reagan leaned forward, the laser wire burning his raincoat, and focused on the man who was stepping out of the darkness.

"Captain?" Reagan asked as if asking himself.

"Reagan." Romaro replied with a raised eyebrow.

The men hugged like lumbering bears, Reagan actually lifting Romaro off his black-booted feet twice.

"Sergeant, give this man an all-access," the captain ordered. "This tough old son-of-a-whore used to be my partner."

"Yes, sir," he answered and nervously tried to attach a green access tag to Reagan's singed raincoat as the detective and the captain walked to the command vehicle.

"It's real good to see you, Rome," Reagan said, matching Romaro's rooster-strut step for step. "I heard on the vine that you were transferred to Washington."

"It was a training thing. Office politics, career stuff, you know. Nothing long term," he replied.

Reagan stopped and spun slowly around to take in the in-site, a small hive of Department work—work he felt the Department brass had stolen from him. He envied Romaro, but tried hard not to show it.

"So what's all this shit about?" Reagan asked.

"A tough, tough case, Ray," Romaro said before starting his climb into the command vehicle. "Can't you smell it? High-level shit. The kind of hard-assed shit you used to eat for breakfast."

Reagan struggled to follow the captain into the vehicle, ascending a short steel ladder before stiffly folding his body into the vehicle's darkened interior. The windowless compartment, barely large enough for four people, was so crammed with winking and blinking consoles and viewpanels that it seemed better suited for a pair of rocket wings than three sets of knobby, TorqueTek tires.

He could see a surveillance specialist wired to a bank of monitors and control decks. She sat in a bubble in a section of the vehicle that was slightly higher and forward. Her dark blue uniform and angular build made her look as if she was just another piece of hardware. Everything was bathed in a misty green light. "Captain," the surveillance spec said softly but firmly, "the second set of voyeuristics are in place and are reporting. We've got solid data streams."

"Good," Romaro said, swinging around in his command seat in the sunken rear of the vehicle to study two side-by-side screens now drenched with data.

"Damn," Reagan said under his breath. "Is this an operations scene or another mission to Mars?"

"We strongly believe that what's happening in that apartment building up the block on Ferrer is part of this case I was telling you about," Romaro said, glancing from his screens to Reagan's openly impressed mug. He roughly cleared his throat before he spoke.

"Look, I was just in a meeting this morning at C3 and pushing hard for a bigger budget to pick up a few more street contacts."

"You mean snitch ants?" Reagan asked as he scanned the equipment-crammed command vehicle. "With all this shit you still need some loser assholes on the street?"

Romaro shook his head hard and then laughed.

"Still the hard-ass skeptic," Romaro shot back. "No... NO. I'm talking about smart, well-placed civis who know the fucking difference between steaming bullshit and steaming borscht. Someone like you, old partner, old pal."

"Well, I never liked borscht. Both are bullshit to me," Reagan replied with a chuckle. "But I do know bullshit, and I gotta tell you, old partner, old pal, I smell it on your breath. After all these—"

"Ah," Romaro hollered. "You believe in coincidence?"

Reagan shook his head.

"Me neither," Romaro snapped. "I've got the job. I've got the budget. And now I've got the man. If you haven't impregnated any small animals lately, I don't think getting you clearance would be too hard. I can bring you in, Ray. Bring you in."

Reagan looked around. He felt himself mentally fingering something he hadn't had in his reach for a very long time: a genuine opportunity.

"Can't give you details, not until I get official clearance, but I promise you that we'd be working together again," Romaro promised. "I'd bring you in as a, eh, eh... consultant."

Reagan was dizzy with what he was hearing. Department? Consultant? Then he began worrying about all the very real dirt he'd done over the years, and wondered what the Department would do if it found out about it. Instead of a job, he might get a prison cell.

The surveillance specialist broke in. "Captain, Sets 1 and 2 are confirming that we have human remains in the apartment."

"Yes. I told you we'd find it here, Najima," Romaro responded. "Is that a visual confirmation?"

"No, not yet," Najima reported. "We're getting some old WiFi-microwave feedback, but I'm confirming with very strong scent indications. The voyueristics are also picking up heavy traces of human excrement; might just be the apartment's sanitation or another marker for body parts. Wait. I'm getting some pretty heavy masking odors, too. Something artificial. Fruity. I'd say incense—cherry, maybe strawberry."

"Sounds like foul play," Romaro cracked, but no one laughed.

"Shit," Reagan whispered in disbelief. "We got buggies that can smell now?"

"Smell, taste, and feel around, too," Romaro told Reagan. "These little remotes can crawl up the sides of buildings, up elevator shafts, without making a peep. Unless you get real close to them, most people think they're just puny, New York City cockroaches. They can spy a hundred times better than the ones we used when we worked these streets. But we still need human assets on the ground, Ray."

Without missing a beat, Romaro asked Reagan, "What can you tell me about this building, 2911 Ferrer?"

Reagan shrugged. "It's your basic shithole SRO. Full of slum scum," he replied. "Some prickheads, heavy users, a few petty criminals, a few more pensioners maybe, some pups too. Mostly Darkies. Mostly deficients."

"Anybody in there who can shoot back?"

"Probably," Reagan said.

"You know anybody on the fifth floor?" Romaro asked as he looked off into space, as if he were hearing voices.

"Nah. I might know some of them by face, but no names, not in that pile of bricks."

Romaro turned his attention to a communications panel and began preparing his officers for a stealth assault. He introduced Reagan to Najima. She was a slender woman who Reagan did not find unattractive—if she'd lose that unchanging, no-nonsense scowl.

She explained to Reagan that intelligence gave them "high confidence" that there were two men in the northwest corner room that measured fifteen by eight feet, with a six by six feet setback that contained a shower, toilet, and sink. No closets. No overhead compartments.

As she spoke, multiple views of the building's façade and floor plans flashed across viewpanels in front of her. Najima said the target room had a single window that was much too small for entry or escape. The room was practically identical to scores of others single-room apartments in the building. Only a standard steel door and a hardware store lock stood between the room and the gathering waves of Spook-Ops.

Najima yelled out over increasingly noisy squawks of communications between the command vehicle, the squads assembling inside the building, and Central Control Complex downtown: "We're getting full sight and sound from the room now."

"Put it up," Romaro yelled back.

Reagan listened and watched as fuzzy multiple views of two men in a dingy room lit up the command vehicle's main screens. Romaro ordered Najima to clean it up.

Reagan wiggled out of his raincoat. Not only was the command vehicle cramped, but with the three of them huddled together, it was getting warm, too. He was damp with sweat. He regretted turning down Romaro's offer of bottled water. He loosened his tie and folded his coat into a tight square and sat on it. His butt was growing increasingly numb from sitting on the unforgiving metals and composite plastics that formed the inner confines of this "piggy bank"—the nickname street kids had given these oversized Department vehicles. He felt around in the blue dimness for his hat and realized that he must have lost it during his tussle with the sergeant. Hell, he thought. He loved that hat.

"Yes, yes, yeah," Romaro said pounding a fist into his open palm. "That's it. Good fucking job."

The scenes' colors found their register. Everything came into sharp focus. Reagan was staring into the back of a man's head. Another angle revealed a second man, a Light, thinner than the first and with a face like a penguin's. He was sitting on his haunches in front of a hand towel that bore two injectors. Reagan recognized them right away.

"This is what we're looking for, people," Romaro screamed.

The second man, a stout Dark with an undersized head and round face, appeared to be listening to the Light.

"Is this a empty?"

"Naw. If we can keep it chilled enough, we can shoot Hedz off of this one for a while, a long while. Boss man told me to think of it like a steak bone with lots of steak still on it." Laughter.

"Will it hurt?"

"These injectors' got something on them so the needles dull your nose as they drill in. You think those milk-fed Light boys would stick needles up their noses if that shit hurt?" A laugh. *"Watch!"*

Romaro spoke to a team leader: "Get me critical mass on the fifth floor. Now!"

Reagan, Romaro and Najima watched the Light man drive the injector's scarlet needle into his nose and then scream, dropping it and falling back. The man was clearly in great pain, flapping his arms and legs against the floor as his nose dripped blood and what appeared to be brain matter.

The Dark man grabbed the Light one, screaming his name.

"Spit?" Romaro asked Reagan. "Is that a name that means anything to you?"

Reagan, overwhelmed with what he was seeing, and with watching it from inside a Department vehicle with his old partner, only shook his head.

Romaro stared at him for a moment and then tapped his link: "Take 'em down. Go, go, go. Go!"

The main surveillance stream was filled with the Dark screaming and crying as he cradled Spit, wrapped in a blanket soaked with blood, brains, and vomit. "Don't be dead," he pleaded into the man's lifeless eyes, opened wide. "We're going to the pennhouse… Remember? The pennhouse…"

At that moment Reagan heard the apartment's door shatter on its hinges. SpookOps officers charged into the room with the butts of their assault rifles locked into their hips.

"We're in," Reagan overheard the team leader report on Romaro's link.

"We can see," he replied. "Secure the scene and targets. I'll be right up."

Grabbing a handrail and pulling himself into a crouch, Romaro made his way to the vehicle's hatch. He held out his hand to Reagan. "Come on, this is where I can use your Sherlocking. For now, just work it like a regular street crime. You understand?"

Reagan nodded that he understood and assumed he was already on the job.

Zulu's apartment, 5-E, was now Evidence Site QXR-11-2846-J. Scores of Spook Operations and patrol officers, as well as Department medical and forensics staff and technicians were involved, each busily engaged in their specific tasks. An evidence lab buzzed in the hallway while patrol officers set up ceiling-to-floor laser wire barricades on every floor.

All of this was lost on Zulu, who began to rock faster as more strangers pressed into the room. He felt someone pry at his fingers as he felt a twinge of pain, like an insect bite, radiating from a spot on the back of his neck. A breath later, his arms fell slack. Spit tumbled into Zulu's lap, hung there for a moment, and then rolled to the floor like a hideous rag doll.

A gushing noise brought Zulu partially back to his senses. Horror pounded in his chest at what he saw. Forensic technicians were hosing down evidence with a silver liquid that instantly hardened into a rock-like gray mass on contact. He watched as the techs sprayed everything in the room and then stood over Spit, his body strapped into a gurney.

Zulu screamed and screamed and screamed as the form spread and swelled over Zulu's feet, legs, and chest.

"Captain, this one is in really bad shape," said a technician. "The medics say his vitals are almost non-existent. Whaddaya think? Suspect, or evidence?"

Romaro walked over. Reagan trailed. The captain motioned for the chief medic to join them at the gurney.

"Well?" Romaro said, bouncing his glare from the medic to Reagan. "Frankly, he doesn't look like he'll survive the trip downtown. Let's concentrate on the other one."

Reagan looked at the other man, who was whimpering in a pool of his own piss.

"Hand me a can of gloves," he ordered a passing technician. Reagan rolled back the shirt sleeve and used the can to spray, in smooth even passes, a translucent, rubber glove onto his right hand. He then ran his gloved hand over Zulu's chalky face, smearing and then wiping away the blood and vomit that had covered it.

Romaro watched intently.

"I think I've seen this man before," Reagan ventured, studying Zulu's face. "I didn't recognize him on the feeds. But up close… I'm not sure. I think I've seen him hanging around with some local assholes, Vipers, at Haines Point."

"That's not a crime," Romaro said into Reagan's ear.

"I know it ain't much," Reagan said. "But it's all I got on short notice."

"So, do we foam him, Captain?" the technician asked.

Romaro looked at Reagan and Reagan shrugged. Romaro turned to the tech and nodded.

The tech happily resumed his work, covering Spit's shoulders, neck, and head. Zulu screamed and screamed, but the screams were heard only in his head.

"Hold it!" Reagan shouted, using his gloved hand to wipe the spray from Spit's nose and mouth. "I think this bastard will tell us more alive than dead."

Romaro shrugged this time. "It's your call, buddy. That's why you're here."

Two medics prepared to remove a heavily sedated Zulu on a gurney.

"Hold up," Romaro shouted. "You've got to play him his rights."

A worn-out recording of an officious woman's voice began playing from a patch on a passing officer's uniform.

"Under the provisions of section 215-RU4-USA of the Gonzales Guidelines, you are under arrest. Anything you withhold may be held against you in a court or tribunal of our choice. Due to the nature of your charges, you are hereby deemed a threat to national security. Therefore, your rights to counsel, outside communications, and visitation are waived for a period of incarceration not to exceed ninety days."

"Do you understand?" the officer asked Zulu.

He blinked twice before whispering that he did. The medics hustled him off to await transport for processing downtown.

"Captain," Romaro and Reagan both turned toward the voice. "I think we've found something you were looking for."

Romaro and Reagan walked toward the forensics chief. He was a lanky Dark with girlish shoulders who spoke with mechanical precision. The chief pulled back the flap of an evidence tent he had constructed around the cooler. To his eyes, Reagan thought the box looked like a typical cheap picnic cooler. But Romaro and the forensics chief were scanning it with handheld instruments and studying the readings closely. Reagan knew they weren't expecting to find beer and sandwiches inside.

A crowd of officers, medics, and technicians gathered around as Romaro knelt before the cooler. He grabbed its lid and lifted it slowly with a crackle. The tent filled with noxious odors so thick that Reagan could feel the weight of them filling his lungs. Romaro waved off the crowding of faces to look inside.

"Frezzpacs," he shouted over his shoulder as he reached in with both hands. He ignored a medic's offer of spray gloves.

"I have something." He pulled out one hand and found it covered with hair the color of spoiled corn silk. It hung from Romaro's fingers in long, wet, matted clumps.

"Damn, it's cold in there," Romaro said as he plunged his hands deeper into the case. "Okay, I think I got one. It's fucking cold. I think… Get. Ready. Reagan."

A technician handed Reagan a large, clear evidence pouch. He held it up and at the ready. "Okay. I'm ready."

A large, hairy mass rose out of the cooler. A short toss landed it in the evidence pouch, with what Reagan thought was surprising weight. Drying his hands, Romaro grabbed the pouch back and quickly began running his eyes and fingers over it.

"Hello again, Mr. Eric Todd Harrington, Jr.," Captain Romaro said, speaking directly into the marbled blue-white flesh webbed with veins and bloody eruptions where there had once been a face. Everyone crowded around knew the name, but most only knew Harrington himself from celebrity vids. They knew he was the only child to inherit the fortunes that flowed from his father's company, Wind Spin Energy Unlimited. And in his considerably free time, young Harrington had taken up filmmaking, with considerable success.

But, Romaro explained to Reagan, he had actually met Harrington, in a manner of speaking, several days earlier in a restroom stall in the ValuMartCity Mall.

"Why would a man like this be in a bargain mall?" Reagan asked Romaro as the two stared into evidence bag.

"Apparently," Romaro said as he ran a finger along the large, perfect slot cut into Harrington's skull, "he was there to lose his head." He turned and stalked out of the tent.

Reagan pushed through the flap in an effort to catch up to Romaro who, he thought, was no less driven than when they had been partners, too long ago now to count the years. But Reagan was not the same man he had been, not the same man at all, he thought, as his resentments crawled under his skin. Romaro had everything: career, authority, respect. Reagan seethed as he considered his life, post-Department: shame, seedy hustles, suicidal boredom.

"Fuck," Reagan said, just within earshot of Romaro.

"What?" Romaro asked. "Left something back there? Your nerve?"

Romaro laughed a little too loudly, Reagan thought.

"No," he said flatly, looking at the hallway's floor then the ceiling. "I forgot to call in to my job. I meant to, then got so… y'know."

"Yeah, I know. Don't worry," Romaro said as he started to talk again. "I had my people contact your hotel. It's taken care of. One way or the other, you'll be with me—at least until we sort this mess out a little better."

"I've been cleared?" Reagan asked incredulously. He felt his tired old heart leap in his chest like a sportfish on the hook.

"Cleared enough," Romaro said, laughing again. "Let one of my people take you home. Get some sleep. I'll contact you in," Romaro looked at his old analog watch, "…six hours. It'll be like old times. Or else like two old-timers trying to get the hard-on to actually solve a case together."

Reagan found himself laughing. "Just try to keep up. I'll be waiting for your call."

Both men laughed as they left the tenement, walking with a kind of purpose Reagan hadn't felt in years.

9

Talky Heads

TWO MEN, EXTRAORDINARILY ORDINARY, WALKED BRISKLY ALONG A minimally lit corridor. Its smooth, tubular walls were devoid of windows, doors, bulletin boards, iconography, or adornments of any kind. The general dimness emphasized the yellowish light that glowed like a distant sunrise a dozen yards ahead of them.

When they reached the end of the tunnel, slender shafts of blue light played over them. Each man was dressed in a freshly fabricated lab coat. Seconds later, heavy glass doors parted with a *whis-s-s-h*. The men, their manner silent and formal, entered a cavernous chamber where they joined dozens of other men and women, all identically dressed in ankle-length, spotlessly white lab coats. Once lost in the crowd, the men let their body language speak fluent casual.

The others seemed to be governed by a well-ingrained routine as they moved purposefully, but unhurriedly, along walls of polished steel drawers. Oppressively powerful lamps and clusters of precision-tooled instruments hung from pods high overhead that were, in turn, attached to still longer cables suspended from the chamber's cathedral-like ceiling.

"Good morning," a woman's voice boomed through the chamber. The speaker's face appeared, large and opaque, from inside a great transparent shaft that rose fifty feet above the chamber's floor. Her expression, timeworn and solemn, heightened the import of her responsibility as Deputy Department Commissioner.

"We have only a few announcements this morning," the commissioner said, as quiet chamber music played soothingly beneath her words. "Our work here remains especially sensitive and vital. Please document all autopsies closely and carefully. And make certain that you have firm confirmations all the way up the investigative chain of command.

"Work closely with your supervisors and remember, this is a secure operation. Follow all security protocols to the letter. Questions?"

The chamber's workforce gathered around the conference tube as the image of the deputy commissioner dissolved into a receding mist. They began buzzing about it as if it were some kind of high-tech totem, reading, chatting and pointing their electronic clip pads at it as the pads drew all pertinent data for the day's work.

The two identical men—forensics specialists—dutifully checked their clip pads, nodded, and headed off to T Section, Fourth Wall, Drawer A.

"Looks like routine fluid replacement."

"Yeah," the other worker said. "Nice way to start the day. E-Z."

The walk turned out to be longer than the specialists anticipated. It had been weeks since either one of them had been in the back corner of the Department's special operations morgue. Once they arrived at T-4-A, one of the men reached for the drawer's circular hatch. He mashed his thumb on its biometric keypad and waited for the corresponding muffled clang. The hatch's wheel began to glow green.

The forensics specialists slipped on their breathers as the area's filtration scrubbers overhead activated with a rumbling hum. Both men yanked on the wheel lock until the drawer opened with a hiss and the slab tank began to inch into view.

The clip pad shattered before the assistant realized that he had dropped it. Neither spoke as they stared, paralyzed by their shared disbelief, at the thrashing figure submerged in the dark-green suspension medium.

"He's conscious!" one shouted.

"I can see that," the other shouted back. "Check the monitors. We've got to stabilize him."

"That's crazy," the first one said as his fingers danced over the suspension cylinder's controls. "Get a doctor over here. Get a doctor!"

The drawer wheel was pulsing blue and red as a general alarm rang out. The morgue's machine-like order collapsed in a swarm of white coats flying like wasps to T-4-A to save what life was left in suspect Armstrong Black.

"We should arrive in about thirty minutes, sir."

Reagan hardly noticed the driver's update.

Comfortably alone in the rear passenger compartment of a Department car, Reagan had swiftly grown reaccustomed to the invisible hands of acceleration and deceleration pushing and pulling at him. The seating curled around him as if it cared. He seldom looked out of the car's deeply tinted windows as the silvery sedan surged through openings in Manhattan's early morning traffic.

Reagan wasn't the least bit weary, even though he had hardly been able to get more than a few hours of sleep. He was almost giddy to get started on his second day on the case as a consulting detective. He shook his balding head in wonderment at his improving fortunes, wondering what he had done to deserve his good turn. He couldn't thank God or Karma. Reagan was a devout nonbeliever and proud of it. But here he was, reviewing case history on the backseat viewpanel of a private car heading to Justice Square. "Jesus," he said, without irony.

Romaro's people were good. The case files had been meticulously prepared, spilling across the screen in multimode references: text, graphs, maps, photos, vids, and analysis with audio HELP tabs liberally affixed throughout. Romaro was not exaggerating when he called the case a nasty number, Reagan mused, as he studied a time/space symmetric of high-value murders. All were beheadings, like the one in the mall, and most had occurred in the last three months. Harlem, by far, was the epicenter of the slaughter. But why hadn't he heard a thing about any of it?

These victims were among Greater New York's most privileged—rich, young, educated, and from some the best connected families. Then Reagan realized that he had answered his own question: These were not the kind of people who usually turned up in the daily personal crime postings, those endless lists of rapes, robberies, beatings, and murders. These were the beautiful people, even if somebody out there was separating their beautiful heads from their beautiful bodies. This was clearly more than simple murder, Reagan told himself.

His first thought was that this was the work of terrorists. But who? What groups? There was no indication—not even a hint—of anyone taking credit for the killings. Plus, the Terrorist Wars had been over for years. He couldn't even imagine anyone insane enough to try to reignite those horrors. No, Reagan thought, agreeing with Romaro, these were not assassinations but some different sort of targeted scheme at play. But what? Why?

Six murders—four men and two women—since mid-November, and an official blackout of the whole thing. Romaro told him that the Department's position was that premature word of the murders could panic a public still jittery with war memories, from the days when severed heads were strewn about the streets like spoiled cabbages.

"Shit," Reagan said to himself as he tapped up morgue images of the dead, watching each face in life dissolve into its grisly death mask, their heads hollowed out for no reason he could understand. He didn't buy for a minute what the MethPopper had said about getting high on a dead man's brains. Besides, he had already read the pharmacology report on the injectors' contents. Rancid brain tissue and ginger ale. No wonder that Popper nearly blew his lights out with that shot.

But there had been a consistent method to the mutilations, Reagan observed.

All the heads had been bloodlessly severed from the bodies. The cut, through muscle, tendons, and bone, was almost faultlessly clean. There seemed to be little sign of struggle on the bodies. The female victims showed some light bruising on their arms. None indicated a chemical means to subdue them, Reagan noted.

"Why and how and who?" Reagan asked himself as the car glided into Lower Manhattan. The car seat cushions sensed that Reagan wanted to recline, so the seat eased back thirty degrees and coaxed Reagan's broad back to accept a more relaxed position. The names and faces of the dead played across the viewpanel until Reagan asked them to stop, hold, magnify.

He closed his eyes to search for his own conjectures. "What the fuck am I looking at here?" Reagan repeated softly to himself as he flash-forwarded through the victim profiles in his head. "What are you headless fucks trying to tell me?"

"I hope I'm not disturbing you, Detective."

The Department driver's face intruded into a particularly gruesome autopsy vidi playing on the VP. Reagan hated when people VIDsited without invitation. But he knew if he were in the driver's place, he would have done exactly the same thing.

"Sorry to interrupt, but I think Captain Romaro is trying to get your attention. We're pulling in to Department HQ and he's standing over there at the lower lobby entrance. Is your link up?"

"What? What?"

"Your link, Detective. Are you wearing it?"

Reagan pressed a control pad and cleared the tint from his left rear window. He peered out and saw Romaro frantically pointing to his ear. He fumbled to get his link out of his coat pocket. He was not accustomed to wearing a link, and hadn't felt it scratching for attention in his coat's pocket.

Reagan pulled the spindly, translucent tubing from his coat pocket and held its base near his face as it reached for his left ear like a toy spider. His touch had awakened the device.

"Where have you been?" Romaro shouted into Reagan's ear. "I've been trying to reach you for half an hour. There's been a change of plan."

"Sorry," Reagan said, talking to Romaro as he snatched open the car door and shoved his way into the backseat. "My link was in my pocket and—"

"It's supposed to be in your goddamned ear," he snarled. "If we're going to work together, you and me, you've got to keep it together. You got me? You're not at some broken-down hotel—unless that's where you'd rather be."

A wave of humiliation, then anger, crested inside Reagan. He had seen Romaro upset before, but they had always swapped ire as equals. Reagan wanted to holler some punchy retort in Romaro's reddened face. But he realized that, one, if he did he would probably be right back at the Theresa; and two, if he tried to speak at all, his voice would likely betray him. Instead, he nodded as he adjusted the link into his ear. He didn't say a word as the car sped off, the two of them stewing in the backseat, heading fast for Midtown Manhattan.

He wondered why Romaro hadn't contacted the driver sooner if whatever he had to say was so goddamned important. He looked out of the sedan's window as the car emerged from the Department's underground exit ramp.

"Bitch ass," Reagan whispered under his breath.

Reagan felt terribly self-conscious as he walked into the forest of fake fir trees that greeted shoppers entering ValuMartCity's main floor atrium. Reagan seldom shopped, and when he did, it wasn't in places like malls. Even this one, with its reputation for low, low prices—which were never quite low, low enough for his tastes. Everyone he saw, even the Darks, was dressed in better and newer clothes than his. And he was wearing his best suit to impress Romaro.

"Over here." Romaro motioned for Reagan to join him at the foot of a spiral escalator that was depositing a slight, boyish-looking man dressed in a store security jumpsuit. Suddenly, Reagan felt superior to someone as he puffed out his chest and strolled to Romaro's side.

"Say hello to Barnes," Romaro said, referring to the man who offered his hand. Reagan shook it hard then dropped it as if it were covered with a V-HIC rash.

"This is the one I told you about," Romaro continued. "His partner is the one who died in the line a few days ago. Brave boy."

"Kofe," Barnes meekly injected.

"Ugh, yes," Romaro said. "His name, Reagan, was Kofe. Brave, brave boy. Shame. Well, show me why you called me this morning."

Barnes nodded and showed the men to a nearby elevator. It was nearly empty when they entered it, but before the doors closed, a pack of shoppers pressed inside. A four-year-old girl crammed in next to Reagan, her feet standing on his. Reagan smiled uncomfortably at a woman he figured was the girl's mother, perhaps grandmother.

She didn't return the smile.

"Sorry about this," Barnes said as the elevator door opened and they stepped off. An owlish looking man walked up to them with a self-important stride. "The store manager wanted to show you this himself." The manager introduced himself and promptly reinstalled the men in the elevator, then escorted them to the store's first-floor rear exit.

Despite some tidying-up of the scene, Romaro knew exactly where he was. Reagan scanned the area, noticing about ten yards ahead that shoppers were being redirected away from a large display. It sat at the edge of the store's busy patterned carpet, which gave way to a wide, badly scuffed, tile floor. The area was lined with hooded stands of confections like candied apples, varieties of nuts, popcorns, and hot dogs. But the display, fenced off with blinking caution cones, did not seem as if it belonged near the festive-colored food court. Romaro arched his eyebrows when he fully took in what was before him: a haberdashery display table.

Reagan heard the store manager explain that the display had been one of the most advanced of its time, a major leap forward in shopping technology. But as the decades passed, habits and tastes changed, and the costs of the display's maintenance and operation became higher than the profits it once brought to the store. A few years ago a maintenance worker found it, repaired it, and brought it out of storage to amuse shoppers' children. It had been a big draw ever since.

Reagan, who had never seen anything like it, circled the display with amazement.

"Wait until I turn it on," the manager told him with pride as the manager punched buttons on a remote controller that was more than twice the size of his hand.

The banquet table-sized display began shuddering, clattering, and clucking to mechanical life. Reagan took a half step back as Romaro pressed closer to examine the noisy electro-mechanical machinery—especially the badly functioning robotic head he had nearly blown off its steel and plastic neck.

"Okay, where's the eyewitness you said you've got?" Romaro asked Barnes, who stood several feet away from the rattling display of seven robotic heads mounted to the table in a zigzagging line. Four were clearly designed to appear male and the remaining three female. In the center of the tabletop was a set of long, slender arms topped with synthetic hands that looked, if they had been real, as if they would have belonged to a dancer.

The heads, except the damaged one, wore a variety of hats. The hands and arms were draped with what Reagan thought were the most beautiful scarves he had ever seen. He had to remind himself that he hated scarves.

Romaro stared skeptically. The robotic heads were now blinking their crudely made eyes and opening and closing their equally crude mouths.

"Yeah, cute antique, but the eyewitness?" Romaro asked a second time, with much less patience than the first request.

"Wait," Barnes insisted. "Wait just a few more seconds."

As if on cue, the robotic head that resembled a grade-school boy began twisting wildly in its pedestal base while it loudly squawked: "He was a stinky man. He was a stinky man. He was a stinky man. He was a stinky man. He was a stinky man. He was a stinky man. He was a stinky man. He was a stinky man."

"Can you turn that thing off?" Romaro shouted over the screaming robotic head

The manager explained that he couldn't, not without shutting down the entire display by executing a second hard reset. A second reset so soon, he believed, would wipe its short-term memory. Barnes jumped in to say that he had cautioned the store manager not to reset it at all, not without allowing Romaro to take a look at it first. The display, he confessed, was the eyewitness.

"I know it's not really by-the-book, Captain," Barnes told Romaro, who looked as if he was about to tear Barnes' head off with his bare hands. "But c'mon. Listen-listen. These heads saw something, smelled something, felt something too, I bet."

Reagan started to see what the security guard was trying to say.

"Look, Rome, these things—and, yeah, I know how it sounds—are kind of like witnesses. You said the security systems here couldn't pick up a thing other than globs on a screen."

"That's right," Barnes butted in. "Whatever that bastard was using to scramble our vids, it probably wouldn't work on the heads."

"The optics in their eyes," the manager added, "are very old tech, rudimentary really, but more than adequate to do what they were designed to do: expertly sell hats and scarves."

Romaro asked why some technoids couldn't just plug the display into a retriever get the data out. But Barnes said the system was too old to interface with a retriever. The only way was to interrogate the heads.

Romaro looked stricken. He cleared his throat, and bent down over the screaming robot head. The other heads settled and looked blankly ahead while the robotic hands caressed a silk, aquamarine scarf that had been laid over its forearm.

"Do they have names?" Romaro asked, feeling stupid.

"Yes," the manager said, gesturing toward the screaming head, "the little head's name is Woodrow."

Barnes folded his arms at his chest and watched intently. Reagan could not take his eyes off the robots. Their appearance unnerved him, but early 21st century technology intrigued him. What a sight it must have been in the 2020s, when second-wave artificial intelligence became cheap and plentiful enough to harness to less-than-critical operations. A thinking, talking, charming department-store display table. Wow, Reagan thought. And now it's little more than a creaky A.I. toy. Reagan began to wonder what the world would make of him in another twenty years.

Pacing in front of Woodrow, Romaro began tentatively.

"Now, Woodrow…" He punched the air then turned to face Reagan. "I can't do this. It ain't even alive. It's a goddamned store mannequin."

"C'mon," Reagan said, stepping forward. "Pretend it's more. We've dealt with witnesses that had less sense. Let me take a shot, huh?"

Romaro stepped back, and Reagan took his place in front of Woodrow. Reagan turned to Barnes and barked an order: "Get me a chair."

Reagan never took his eyes off the squawking head as Barnes eased a chair under his wide ass.

"Woodrow? May I call you Woody?" Reagan began, speaking firmly to the head that was only inches from his face.

"He was a stinky man. He was a stinky man. He was a stinky man," the head screamed nonstop. Its primitive machinery lent it a bug-eyed expression that reminded Reagan more of a ventriloquists' dummy than a robot.

"Now, Woody," Reagan whispered gently. "Let's talk. Okay? Just talk."

"He was a stinky man. He was a stinky man."

Reagan reared back and slapped the robot in its hardened rubber and plastic face.

Woodrow blinked his doll-like brown eyes and then went silent. A moment later it turned, as all the other heads turned, to look directly at Reagan. The robotic hands balled into a fist.

"Better," Reagan soothed. "And I'm really sorry I had to do that, Woody. I really am."

"Well, you ought to be," said a head that looked as if it could have belonged to an old-time English gentleman, complete with a finely trimmed mustache and a proper black bowler perched on its head. "That awful man last night crashed into him and bumped him into an alarm loop."

"Yeah, yeah," Reagan said, fidgeting in his chair with anticipation. "The man, the stinky man, from last night. Tell me more about him. Whatever you can recall."

"Rude," injected a woman's head that looked as if it had been modeled to appear as if she were the Englishman's young wife.

"Yes, yes, yes, rude," a choir of the remaining working heads rose in a cackle of aging joints.

Reagan nodded his agreement. Romaro, standing next to a beaming Barnes, only shook his head in more disbelief than he thought he could stand in a day.

"Why do you say that the man, the man last night, was rude?" Reagan continued, with a sensitivity that caught Romaro off guard.

"No manners," the woman-head said, preening in a flat-brimmed straw hat with a midnight velvet ribbon tied in a bow beneath its slender, vacuum-molded neck.

"He hurt me," Woodrow said. "Stinky man."

"Could you smell him?" Reagan ventured.

Woodrow turned away from Reagan and then snapped back to face him.

"Uh-uh," it said. "But he looked and felt like he would stink."

"How'd he look and feel?"

Woodrow opened his hand-painted mouth a full beat before its words tumbled out. "He was dirty, dirty. His hat was made from sack cloth. Dirty, thick sack cloth. His clothes, cheap synthetics, were wet with sweat."

"What about his face, Woodrow?" Reagan asked, his heart thumping in his chest. "Did you see his face?"

"I saw it," said a dark-skinned female head that wore a halo of amber tiny curls. "He wore a heinous turtleneck shirt that was pulled up to his nose."

"And those sunglasses?" the Englishwoman added. "Perfectly dreadful."

"But when he slammed into Woodrow," the Englishman said, "his glasses fell to his nose, and his face become fully visible for 1.6 seconds. Frightful man. A Negro. I'm certain of that. A Negro. Yes."

"You mean an Afro-citizen," the Dark head firmly corrected.

Reagan stood up and stepped back. "Please, all of you, please. Give me details. Everything. Anything. Height, weight, complexion, eye color, hair color, texture, length, visible scars, facial hair…"

"Yes, of course," the Englishwoman said in voice that sounded like tiny bells ringing. "But first, could you answer a question for us?"

"I'll try," Reagan replied, sitting on the edge of his folding, metal chair.

"Who destroyed the head of Woodrow's family, Old Man Bloomfield?"

Romaro stepped forward to confess. "It was a terrible accident, and I promise each and every one of you that I will have Mr. Bloomfield returned to working order as soon as humanly possible."

The heads all snapped to face Romaro, and then snapped back to face Reagan. The Englishman bowed his head and closed his eyes before jerking his face into what struck Reagan as something half way between a sneer and a smile.

"Then, that, sir," the Englishman's head said dryly, "will have to do."

The other heads began to cheer. The pairs of hands applauded with great clicks and clacks.

10

Typed

"**G**OOD JOB. I MEAN IT, RAY. DAMN GOOD JOB BACK THERE," ROMARO said, speaking to the top of Reagan's head as the two climbed into the rear seat of the waiting Department sedan.

Reagan nodded his thanks as the car's engines whined and a heavy hand of acceleration shoved the men hard against the back seat cushions as they sped east. Reagan pulled his bulk back to the edge of his seat with a huff to study the rear viewpanel, which danced with criminal threat profiles.

"Once I got them to stop jabbering about fucking hats, they were some of the best eyewitnesses I'd ever seen," Reagan said with more self-satisfaction than he wanted to reveal. "Fact is that no human could have been so dead on with so many observations as those talking heads."

"Yeah, details and corroboration in one package," Romaro added as he joined Reagan's search for possible matches. "But you know none of it will hold up in court."

The driver swung the car sharply into FDR Drive and nosed the vehicle toward downtown.

"Doesn't matter, if we get our man," Reagan said as he more closely examined two particular profiles on the screen. "And I think we've found him, Rome."

Romaro tapped his link to standby as he lowered his face to the screen.

"Gordon Gaines McCoy," Romaro read aloud.

"Rattle," Reagan said with disgust heavy on his tongue.

"You know this piece of chicken shit?" Romaro asked.

"N-no—nah," Reagan stammered. "I mean, I've seen him around the hotel a few times. Low-level drug dealer. A Viper."

"Then we've got 'em, buddy," Romaro said, slapping his old partner on his back. "And you've got a job. I'm authorizing an immediate upgrade in your Department status on this case. My street connections have gotten rusty. But you're out there still ass-deep in it." He grinned at Reagan, lifting his eyebrows. "I need what you've got on this one. You know Harlem—the new Harlem, and the old one we used to work. What do you think about that?"

"I think I'm the luckiest bitch of a bitch in the world," Reagan said, permitting himself a smile. "But does this mean I have to work weekends?"

Romaro slapped Reagan on his back again. This time Reagan could feel the whack sting beneath his cheap dress shirt.

"Welcome aboard, Detective-Temp!"

Reagan liked the sound of Department consultant better, but decided not to complain. He could feel his foot firmly in the door. Maybe this could really work, he told himself, as he tried to ignore Romaro's knack for clumsy condescension.

The Department sedan slowed just before plunging down a spiraling ramp. Natural light was replaced with a flash of hydrogen halo lamps. Reagan realized that he was descending into the subterranean Central Control Complex—C3, a great inverted pyramid impaling the granite floor of Manhattan with 50 stories of top-secret research labs, libraries, study lofts, conference rooms, and offices. Romaro leaned back and closed his eyes as the sedan descended.

Only the pyramid's great, broad base was visible above ground. Its ten stories of post-apocalyptic architecture offered the Department's public face. Reagan, like practically everyone else in New York Metro, was familiar with this view of C3 from VP stories and announcements. These offices were always bright and airy for visitors and news conferences. The artwork of precocious children shared wall space with portraits of smiling officials and "Citizen Officers of the Month." Neighborhood watch groups regularly met in its community rooms, and tourists toured its black-mirrored corridors and sipped free mint tea.

Of course, Reagan knew, the most popular and photographed part of the complex was its roof: Justice Square. Its ten acres of poured, polished black granite was the nation's chief memorial park dedicated to Greater Americans lost in the Terrorist Wars. As the sedan pulled up to Red Port 6F, he wondered if the many faces and names in his case files might someday join the thousands of others sprayed and spoken into the sky by the square's Twin Fountains of Remembrance. But he and Romaro were going somewhere else—down.

Romaro escorted Reagan to Deck Two, two levels beneath a reinforced firewall built from layers of blast-resistant cells. It separated what the Department's calculations determined were clearly acceptable losses from what it believed were not. The reverse numbering of C3's floors—the higher the number, the lower the floor—deepened the sense of its otherness. Until he could orient himself, Reagan's strategy was to stay close to Romaro.

Just inside, two security desk officers met Reagan in their sentry station, an anteroom that reeked of overheated electronics and metal cleansers. The officers scanned Reagan's newly issued Department U.I.D. card as Romaro looked on. Reagan was directed to press his palm against a security pad and recite his entry key code as he walked through a portal that scanned his body to the bone.

Once Reagan emerged on the other side, one of the security officers, a Dark, wordlessly began pressing an access badge onto Reagan's chest. Reagan winced in surprise when he felt a tiny prick beneath the badge and the officer's continued pressure.

"Hey!"

"Procedure, Detective-Temp," the officer replied dully to Reagan's protest.

"You're fucking stabbing me with this stupid-ass pass," Reagan shouted at the officer, who avoided eye contact.

Before Reagan could slap the officer's hand away, Romaro grabbed his arm and laughed.

"Hold it, tough guy," Romaro said as he slowly wagged a finger. "It's just a pin prick."

"I'm always the pricker," Reagan growled. "Never the pricked."

Romaro shook his head.

The security officer stepped back without expression and slowly returned to his desk, rejoining the other security officer staring unblinkingly at his console.

"He's typed," the second officer said flatly while maintaining eye contact with his console.

Romaro motioned with his eyes for Reagan to follow him out of the sentry room and into a darkened, curving hallway that quickly led into an expansive gray-on-silver corridor, a bit brighter and louder, with uniformly bland dressed men and women rushing about. Reagan was struck by how directed everyone looked: no casual conversations, no horseplay, no play of any kind. Reagan was also struck, startled even, by all the targeted acoustics: warning klaxons, beep prompts, roster announcements that passed in and out of his earshot, like walking beneath audio spotlights, moving in and out of sound trained directly at him.

"A lot has changed from the days when we were on the street," Romaro said as the two men walked toward a modest bank of elevators, his voice steady and loud over the intermittent noise of C3's routine. "Take, for one, this place. It's nothing like old Centre Street. I've been all over the world, Ray, seen the best of the best in Berlin, Tokyo, Singapore… and there is no place, no operation, that remotely approaches what we have here at C3."

Romaro paused next to a set of shiny, blue-steel doors.

"Expect the best here and here the best is expected," Romaro said as his eyes glistened with something Reagan hadn't seen on any job he'd worked since leaving the Department. Reagan glanced again at Romaro to be sure. Yep, he confirmed, the old hardass's eyes were definitely shining with pride.

Romaro caught Reagan's gaze and threw it back in a glare.

Reagan saw his opening. "Why'd you let that nigger stab me like I was some goddamned prize bull?"

Romaro laughed then coughed in the hollow of his fist to suppress a chuckle.

"You should have seen your face. 'Always the pricker…' "

"I'm glad you find it so fucking ha-ha. That nigger—"

"It's a new kind of smart badge," Romaro interrupted. "We just got them about eight months ago. The badge sticks you so it can sample your DNA and a few other unique markers. Your badge is now typed to you and only you. Anyone else tries to wear or use it and all hell breaks loose."

"So, it's going to nip me every time I put it on?" Reagan asked stroking the badge as if to soothe it.

"Hell no. Only does that the first time," Romaro explained as he pressed his thumbprint harder than he needed to into the elevator's control pad.

"Security badges that bite like rats and a headquarters where up is down and down is up—shit *has* changed since I was Department."

"Yeah," Romaro replied, looking both ways before speaking again, this time in hushed tones. "Another thing has changed, Ray. Watch yourself with that 'nigger' talk. That kind of thing is really frowned on down here now. It's—how can I put it?—unprofessional. You were one of the best I'd ever seen on the streets. We need the old Ray—but with some slight adjustments. Are you going to behave yourself?"

Reagan frowned, then nodded as if he understood. But all he understood was that Romaro was not the same man that he had worked the vicious streets with, apparently too many years ago. Reagan wanted to laugh in Romaro's face. *Niggers are niggers, no matter what Romaro wants me to call them. And deep down, Romaro probably knows it too.*

The elevator doors opened with a somber chime and Romaro and Reagan stepped into the empty space without a word between them. The elevator sounded a double chime as the doors closed in a rubbery kiss.

"Destination, gentlemen?" the elevator asked with officious inflection.

"Tier 36, central conference room," Romaro replied.

Reagan gripped one of the elevator's handrails and chewed at the inside of his cheek. He couldn't explain it, but ever since leaving the sentry station he had been feeling like a kid entering a carnival ride. He knew it would be a mistake to let Romaro see how giddy he was feeling, so he struggled to maintain the scowl of the hard-bitten detective by chewing his cheek even harder.

The elevator slowly began to move and then, without warning, plunged in a whistling descent. For a moment Reagan believed that his body stood at the edge of weightlessness. He found Romaro's reflection in the polished elevator doors and noticed that the lower half of his deeply lined face was drawing back, like tiny stage curtains, to form something feral, something that struck Reagan as a genuine expression of pleasure.

Reagan tightened his jaw and braced his resolve not to scream, not to scream what his heart would if it could it sing to its own up-tempo beat. He settled for a whispered *whoooppppppeeeeeeeeee.*

11

Tough Tit

THE "TOE TAG BOUTIQUE," AS REAGAN LIKED TO CALL THE MORGUE, never bothered him. He was at peace with the dead; it was the living who raised his suspicions. So he strolled into the Special Operations Morgue like a season ticket-holder heading for his box at the opera. Few heads turned as he and Romaro made their way to the far side of a vast chamber that reminded Reagan of a gigantic wine cellar, something he'd expect to find beneath some European estate, or better yet, a castle.

Romaro slowed and pointed to a midnight-blue structure, a tent. Reagan could see that it was affixed to the wall and looked large enough to house a meeting. But why were they meeting in a tent?

"… you should have the full autopsy index up on your clip pads…"

Reagan could hear a breathy, weak voice speaking from inside the structure as he and Romaro drew close enough to pull back its flap door. Romaro stuck his head inside for a moment before urging Reagan to join him.

"Ah, Captain Romaro," wheezed the bald, stooped man who had been speaking. "And your associate. Yes. It's good for you both to finally join us."

Romaro clenched his jaws. Reagan scanned the tent and was surprised that it appeared even larger once inside. Besides the skinny old man doing the talking, there were four other men and a woman standing around a long, gunmetal-blue plastic table. Where the tent was attached to it, the morgue's wall was dominated by two, large circular doors. Reagan assumed that the drawers held slabs and the slabs held bodies.

The old man returned his attention to his clip pad and to the others standing motionlessly around the table.

"I want you to pay particular attention to the upper nasal cavities," the man said, his voice little more than a mumble. Reagan glanced at a clip pad one of the others had shoved into his hands when he entered. He learned from the pad that the old man was Detective Commander Michal Kobec. His sunken eyes and jutting jaw line had struck Reagan as vaguely familiar. And the voice. Then he remembered. For years, Kobec had been the face of the Department's forensics-training vidis. Reagan had studied them during his earlier days at the Department.

All the vidis began the same way: Kobec standing in a long, spotless, white cloth lab coat before an uncovered corpse and intoning with academic correctness, "Remember, forensics is not a precise science, but an artful application of precision and science."

Kobec was old then, Reagan thought. To get this fossil out of retirement said more than enough for Reagan about how big this case really was. Reagan felt his clip pad vibrate. When he looked down at it, he saw that Romaro had texted him a note: *The Department's forensics chief emeritus. Michal Kobec. Pay attention. He's running the multi-agency task force on this one.*

Reagan looked up from the pad just in time to catch Kobec staring his way.

"The subject in life was Seth Seasons, a male Light and a petty criminal known to his associates as Spit," Kobec croaked. "He expired yesterday evening at 10:47 from massive neurological complications that resulted from a self-administered injection—through the olfactory epithelium in the left upper nasal cavity—of an illicit substance that appears to be a rather haphazard amalgam of decaying brain matter, ginger ale, and a number of crude hallucinogens and opiates that had been present in the subject prior to the injection."

"Haphazard? Easy on the 'hap' and heavy on the 'hazard,' it seems to me."

Reagan turned toward the voice at his left to see, just inches from his own, a set of features so distorted with genuine glee that they seemed to form a grinning fist. Reagan's eyes darted to his pad's staff index and noted that Mr. Glee was actually Lieutenant Charlie Gaghan, described as an accomplished, much-decorated officer. Reagan awkwardly acknowledged the man's puny pun.

But he had other things on his mind, and his stomach. He strained to suppress a shudder as cold fear rumbled in his head and belly. The Methpopper he had urged Romaro to save was now dead. It wasn't that he cared about this drugged-out lowlife. But he had staked what meager influence he was trying to rebuild with Romaro on the value of keeping the man alive. Why hadn't someone told him sooner that the shithead had died? Reagan wondered. Just his luck, just as he was beginning to—

"Tough-tit break," Romaro whispered in Reagan's right ear, as if he were speaking directly to Reagan's doubts.

Reagan could feel that his shirt clinging wetly to his back. He could hear Kobec still speaking, but paid no attention to his words until he heard the ancient pathologist issue a single word.

"Purpose?" Kobec placed his skeletal hands on the table in front of him and leaned forward. "Yes, purpose," he said being careful to emphasize the question by making eye contact with each of the detectives arrayed around the table.

"Can any of you tell me why one human being would inject the brains of another human being?" Kobec asked, stiffly scanning the room for an answer.

"To get smarter? Religious ritual? Aphrodisiac? Sleep aid? To get high?" the tent thundered as the detective tossed their guesses into the air.

"You, Detective Reynolds," Kobec turned, training a finger on Reagan. "…'to get high?' Yes. A means of achieving a sort of intoxication we have not yet discovered. This is a highly plausible possibility."

The forensics chief instructed the detectives to look at their clip pads. Reagan and Romaro immediately recognized the head spinning slowly on the pad in multiple perspectives. It was the same head they had retrieved two days ago in Reagan's Bronx neighborhood.

The data tracking across the clip pad confirmed that the head belonged to Eric Harrington, a thirty-one-year-old filmmaker who lived alone in his home studio on Park Avenue South. It noted that his wealth was inherited, but his success was apparently his own. Harrington's film credits scrolled down the pad as if they had no end. Reagan recognized some of the later ones, screamers popular in Harlem theaters. But he had never heard of Eric Todd Harrington, Jr. before his head turned up in a picnic cooler in a grungy Bronx tenement.

"You may further examine Mr. Harrington's biographical data in your pads on your own time," Kobec said, interrupting Reagan's musing about how such a man may have lived his life. His U.I.D. showed extensive travel outside Greater America, with many extended stays in difficult-to-enter locales like St. Tropez. Reagan's mind wandered. He realized that he didn't know a single thing about St. Tropez, except that it was the sort of place the very wealthy would go—or at least, very wealthy people talked about it in the movies.

He tapped the city name with his index finger to reference it. The pad immediately flashed with global locators, 3-D photographs, and live aerial feeds of beaches and hillside villas. There were text and audio descriptions of the place. Reagan satisfied himself with reading the locator and was surprised that it was a gulf city in France. His first instinct was to imagine it an island somewhere off South America or India. Reagan was doubly surprised to read that it was named for a saint who, legend had it, was beheaded for refusing to give up his faith; his body was thrown into a boat that eventually came to shore at this tiny, old town of the mega-rich and famous.

"Do you think that such a man as Harrington would willingly come into contact with a Spit Seasons?" Kobec asked. Reagan looked up to see the forensics expect staring at him. Reagan was relieved to realize that the question was only rhetorical.

When Reagan's eyes returned to the clip pad he noticed that Romaro has sent him another message: *Keep your head in the fucking game!*

Reagan nodded without looking up. Kobec scratchily began to describe the condition of the head, the image of which on his clip pad graphically split in half and opened like a book.

"Most intriguing," Kobec said while directing the detectives to examine close-ups of the head's badly damaged brain, "is the work done around the specimen's hippocampus and amygdala. As you can see they have been removed with remarkable care. And yet, in other areas, there are wounds that represent nothing short of butchery."

Lieutenant Gaghan leaned into Reagan and spoke wetly into his ear again. "This definitely wasn't a New Jersey."

"A New Jersey?" Reagan asked against his better judgment.

"Yeah, no Hack 'n' Sack."

Reagan could not only hear Gaghan's satisfied laughter, but could feel it as the man leaned into him, his love handles jiggling under his dark, regulation Department suit, white shirt, and dark tie.

"So, sir, what do you think we're looking at here?" Gaghan suddenly asked Kobec, speaking up more loudly for the whole room to hear. The question obviously threw off the old man's timing.

"Well, we certainly have a pattern, don't we, Lieutenant? Six beheadings, all bloodless and expertly executed. Each victim young and wealthy. And with few exceptions, most of the murders occurring in Harlem. And now we have the late Mr. Seasons found with one of the victims' brain tissue injected into his own brain—with fatal results."

Kobec tapped his lipless mouth as he looked at the detectives arrayed before him.

"I am grateful that in this respect, I am like an interpreter for the dead," Kobec said, drumming his bony fingers against his concave chest. "Mr. Seasons clearly has more to tell us. But in the meantime, we might do well to listen to the living. Not my first choice, but then that's me."

Kobec laughed softly into his hand, prompting the attending detectives to join in on his thinly veiled joke.

"Watch your pads," Kobec ordered.

Reagan was startled to see how much the man he'd helped to apprehend less than 24 hours earlier had deteriorated. Zulu Skinner's round, dark-brown face fell slack, its jowls drooping like a cartoon hound's. His skin had grown ashen, strangely complimenting the man's lifeless, unblinking eyes, Reagan thought.

"This is, if you recall, the man Detectives Romaro and Reynolds brought in yesterday. Skinner was Seasons' roommate, and apparently old friend and partner."

Reagan felt as though he could sense Romaro perceptibly stiffening. He must have been pleased with Kobec's recognition of his work, but Reagan realized that he would be miffed that Reagan was mentioned as well. And even worse, Reagan had gotten equal billing.

The pads showed Zulu sobbing. An off-camera interrogator spoke first. "Would you like an absorbent?"

Zulu nodded wildly and reached outside the frame, his hand returning with a glistening, white wipe he repeatedly ran over his eyes and oozing nose.

"Feel better?" the interrogator asked calmly.

Zulu nodded, this time more calmly.

"Now again," the interrogator's voice sharpened, "tell me precisely why you and your friend had a human head on ice in your apartment."

"I told you that I had nothing to do with that," Zulu screamed. "Why don't you tell me how Spit's doing…he looked bad…bad! Is he alive?"

The interrogator: "I've told you. You tell me something and I tell you something. Let's stop wasting each other's time. Huh? We're talking murder here, maybe terroristics too, and—"

"Terror?" Zulu cried. "No terror. I swear on my momma's soul, no terror shit. No! Spit said we were just going to get high, real high."

"Shooting somebody's brains up your nose?"

"Well… I… I don't know," Zulu said.

"The brains, the brains, Mr. Skinner," the interrogator pressed harder. "We knew he was injecting someone else's brain tissue into his brain. But why brains? There're easier ways to get high. Right?"

"Are you gonna to let me see him? Let me see him!"

"Yes, yes, of course I am. I promise… but first tell me about these injections."

Zulu shook and began to weep again. He wiped his nose with the back of his detention jumpsuit's sleeve. Reagan looked around the tent and saw everyone staring unblinkingly into the interrogation vidi.

"You promised to let me see Spit! You promised!"

"Right, yes, I promised."

"Okay. Okay. The only thing Spit told me about this brain stuff—he called it Hedz—is that it gives people a special kind of high. He wouldn't say too much because he wanted me to find out for myself."

"Did you?" the interrogator asked.

"Never got a chance. As soon as Spit shot it, you people came busting in. Never got a chance. You know what?" Zulu asked as he looked down and shook his head. "I don't think Spit did either. That's all I know. All I know. *You promised.*"

"Not yet, buddy… One last thing," the interrogator continued. "Who did Spit work for?"

"I don't know," Zulu said, growing more agitated. "Lots of people."

The interrogator's voice grew louder and more demanding. "Did he ever mention someone named Rattle? A Viper who calls himself Rattle? What about somebody called JoË Dots?"

Zulu was cradling his head in his hands and rocking. "I don't know no Rattle, no Dots, either. Can I-I-I talk to Spit?" Zulu pleaded.

The interrogator's voice sounded dark and flat.

"You can talk to him, Mr. Skinner, but I don't think you two are going to have much of a conversation."

Zulu shook his head from side to side so violently that his flabby jowls made him look like a deranged clown.

"I am sorry to inform you—"

Zulu shrieked and began heaving.

"Dead. Your friend is dead. Died a couple of hours ago."

Zulu grasped his shoulders and rocked more violently, crying and screaming.

"Are you sure that you can't tell me anything about this Viper, Rattle, and Mr. Dots?" the interrogator asked, shouting over Zulu's one-man din. "They are the ones who killed your friend, and they would have killed you too if you had taken that injection."

"Dead? Spit? You're lying, trying to trick me," Zulu hollered.

The vidi halted on Zulu's twisted face before the detectives' clip pad cleared.

Kobec smiled or winced, Reagan couldn't be certain.

"Thanks to Detective Reynolds, we have a bit more to share."

Romaro chewed his lips. Reagan puffed up with pride, although he had no idea what Kobec was talking about.

The clip pads flashed again with a full-pad vidi. It was Spit, clearly near death and struggling to speak. The vidi lasted for only thirty seconds.

"Dots, JoË Dots." Spit's voice was raw, his words weak and brittle as they fell unevenly dribbled from a mouth so distorted it appeared anal. "Told me the head was good. Good." The vidi showed the man's eyes rolling back into his head and blood and brain tissue oozing from his nose.

He fought to speak again. This time, his voice firmed and grew remarkably strong.

"Tell Zulu that I can see the penthouse. Tell him I'm getting off the elevator and it was a fast, much too fast, ride."

The vidi went black.

Romaro turned and gave Reagan a congratulatory raised eyebrow, but Reagan could tell it was an empty gesture.

"Did he say anything else?" a detective called out.

"Nothing," Kobec replied as he stepped slowly to stand in a spot between the two morgue drawer doors. Slowly, he turned his full attention to Drawer B, verified its identity on its reader, and then began unlocking its door. With a *spissh* it began to open, gradually spilling into view a woman's bare, white feet, then her legs, hips, torso, shoulders, neck. But no head.

Reagan looked over the body, mostly bluish, and cold and stiff on the slab. In life, he thought, she must have been some kind of organ grinder. Even in death, even with the heavy jagged scars of a thorough autopsy and some odd, purplish blotches here and there, he could see that she had been athletic, well maintained, firm yet giving in all his favorite places. Her pubic mound was expertly trimmed and he thought he noticed a glint of gold just between her slightly parted thighs.

"This is, or rather, was," Kobec said softly, "Kattrel Christine Avanti, a 44-year-old Light who was the wealthy operator of a global executive employment agency. The whereabouts of her head are still unknown to us. But this is what she looked like before its unfortunate theft."

A holographic projector glowed overhead as it cast a ghostly, three-dimensional image of Kattrel's head, hair, and face as she might have looked asleep in her bed. Reagan felt a tinge of shame pass over him as he stared at the body and felt stirrings of sexual arousal. Then the projector shut off.

"Apparently," Kobec said, "we have a seventh victim. Pertinent data will be linked to your pads momentarily."

He walked to the head of the slab and pointed. "Notice her neck. Same M.O. And —despite her age—her profile and lifestyle are very similar to those of the other victims. We have done extensive work on this subject."

"With the exception of the removal of her head, of course, little trauma was inflicted on this body. By the way, whoever did this was clever enough to neutralize her embedded medical alerts. As far as her vitals' monitoring stations are concerned, Miss Avanti is still in the pink and not definitively dead in our morgue."

"Exactly how was she killed—beyond the obvious?" Gaghan asked, straight-faced and with no hint of nonsense.

"We've determined that she was startled while in her bath in an Elite suite at the Robeson Arms Hotel in Harlem. Yes, another homicide in Harlem. She suffered some sort of paralyzing shock," Kobec said, reaching for a laser pointer to underscore his points. "There are light bruises on her arms and back, indicating that she was handled by at least two individuals. And death occurred some moments after the head was harvested."

"Harvested?" Reagan asked, surprised as much as anyone else that he, a mere Detective-temp, would have the nerve to interrupt Kobec.

"I choose my words carefully, Detective," Kobec replied. "I believe we might be dealing with a group of 21st century headhunters. These heads are clearly being snatched for a purpose, one that transcends any sadistic cravings or political statements. There is a higher purpose at play. Perhaps it is precisely what Mr. Seasons and Mr. Skinner told us—a new kind of intoxicant that can only be produced with elements of the human brain."

The silent tent was filling slowly with the sickly sweet smell of a flash-frozen human body.

"If this is what we are dealing with, Detectives, human brains as the raw resource for some new street thrill... " Kobec turned from the detectives and looked as if he was about to return Kattrel's body to cold storage, but did not. Reagan's gaze lingered on the body's still-rounded breasts and erect, caramel-colored nipples. "... if this is what is driving these homicides, then brace yourselves. We will soon have more headless corpses than we will have drawers to store them."

Gaghan turned to Reagan and feigned fear. "We're going to have to get a bigger morgue."

12

CONfession

REAGAN WAS EAGER TO GET BACK ON THE STREETS. HE FELT claustrophobic after spending so many hours so deep beneath the ground, breathing an atmosphere that had long ago lost any resemblance to fresh air. Even the prep-packed sandwiches and bottled water served in the canteen and lounge had an overly artificial taste, Reagan thought, as he stared at the lounge's simulated windows.

"Amazing, right?" Romaro said as he dropped into a leathery recliner next to a hardback chair Reagan had dragged beside one of the windows.

"Yeah," Reagan said absently, his eyes on people walking casually, backlit by the approach of a late-winter sunset. "Is this some kind of canned vidi we're looking at?"

"Hell no," Romaro said, before tearing into a pressed meats sandwich dripping with mayo Flav. "That's the view from topside. Let's see. We're looking west, just south of City Hall Park."

"So," Reagan asked, "this is what we'd see if we were up there on the streets?"

"Yeah, guess so," Romaro replied, sipping on a box of soy choc milk.

"Are we ever going to get the hell out of here?" Reagan asked quietly, looking around to make sure no one was around him to hear his blasphemies. He lowered his voice and talked to Romaro's sandwich as it collapsed into his old partner's mouth. "I like meetings as much as the next guy, but I think we need to get back on the streets. We're not going to crack shit down here in this fucking hole, 'cept another box of that choc milk you love so much."

Romaro spoke with his eyes until he swallowed the last of his sandwich. Reagan didn't need to hear the words. But Romaro supplied them, nonetheless.

"Listen, Reagan," he said as he sat deep in the recliner. "Don't let a few kudos make your fat head swell. I'm still running this case. How do they say it in Washington? Yeah. You serve at my pleasure."

Reagan felt the old rage rising again, and for a moment he forgot what Romaro had plucked him from, all the humiliation and obscurity of his life post-Department. He inhaled the fighting words smoldering on his lips, then he turned to look back at the piped-in picturesque. With his back to Romaro, he tried his best to choke down the resentment and anger he felt.

A beat later he spun back to face Romaro.

"I'm not some first-year cadet," Reagan said, barely concealing the heat forging his words. "I know the deal. I don't need you or any-fucking-body else humming nursery rhymes up my ass. Okay? All right?"

Romaro stood up now, his back as straight as a Spartan's arrow. Reagan stood too, and stuck his nose inches from Romaro's fuming face.

"Do what you got to do," Romaro said in a rumble from deep in his gut.

Reagan leaned forward, bringing his nose so close to Romaro's that they almost touched, close enough to kiss, close enough to kill.

"I'm saying, look, this case is bigger than your dick; even bigger than mine," Reagan said, cutting the slightest of smiles. He lowered his voice into a stage whisper. "The question is, are we gonna fuck up in breaking this Hedz shit wide open because we're gonna be too fucking busy trying to break each other?"

Reagan took a big step back and threw up his hands.

"Remember?" he said, smiling coolly. "I'm one of the good guys."

Romaro flashed his own grin.

"I say let's stop fucking around, cowboy," he said, standing down from his own red alert. "Kobec's office is on my link. He wants us back in the tent in ten minutes."

"You gonna to drink the rest of that choc?" Reagan asked, reaching for Romaro's milk box.

"Nah," he said as he held out the half-drank soy milk. "Take it. Knock yourself out."

* * * * * *

Reagan and Romaro joined the file of detectives making their way through the morgue. When they reentered the tent, they found Kobec in hushed conversation with three men, all dressed in dark blue suits and dark shirts and patterned ties. Romaro whispered to Reagan a single word: "Washington."

Kobec reconvened the meeting and introduced the mysterious men as his senior advisors on the case. He said nothing about Washington or any federal oversight. But Romaro texted Reagan his take—that Washington might try to bigfoot the Department with a separate investigation, one that could assign the New York operation only a support role on its own case.

Kobec cleared his throat and took his place, standing again in the narrow space between the two morgue drawers. Without a word, the old man reopened the drawer containing the recently declared seventh victim. Reagan watched the "senior advisors" stare at Kattrel Avanti's headless corpse.

"During the break, I received a number of questions from some of you," Kobec began, his voice more airy than it had been before the break. "Questions regarding physical evidence found on or in this body. We have an abundance of such evidence. I advise you to consult your clip pads.

"To begin with, we have traces of semen deposited over multiple occasions within a three-hour period of time in practically all of her major orifices. At this time, we will not go over the number of unlawful sexual contacts this represents.

"We also found bits of skin under her nails, as well as foreign pubic hair in several areas—some expected, and others not so."

Several detectives, including Romaro and Gaghan, stepped forward to pass their clip pads over the body to record additional images and evidence.

"Now," Kobec said as he tottered a few feet to Drawer A, never breaking eye contact with Reagan, "we have another piece to ponder."

Kobec began opening the drawer. Its slab began to roll out, revealing first the large feet and then muscular legs of a Dark man.

"I caution you that this is going to be a bit unorthodox," Kobec said as the full length of the man became visible. The smell, sour and biting, prompted several detectives to cover their noses and mouths. Reagan looked at Romaro, who was drawing close to the slab, bringing his face inches from the man's fully intact head. Romaro looked back at Reagan without expression.

"Yes," Kobec said over the rising murmur of comments. The mysterious other men said nothing and registered nothing on their faces. "This man is alive. He has been held here in suspension for the last seven days. It is his semen, pubic hair, and skin that we found on the Avanti body."

Fuck me. A goddamned nigger, Reagan thought. "I should have known a bunch of niggers would be part of all this headhunting shit," he hissed, just loud enough for Romaro and a detective standing next to him to hear.

Romaro shot Reagan a look that Reagan ignored as he studied the man on the slab. His body was covered in a thick, greenish gel that glowed spasmodically with flashes of red and blue. Thick tubing—tubing that throbbed and twitched, as if it was somehow feeding or feeding upon the figure's flesh—was roped around its neck. A wide metallic belt pulsing with digital readouts and control pads was drawn tight across its chest as smaller, silvery tubes snaked from a large cup that appeared to be sucking at its groin.

Gaghan flashed a mischievous grin. Everyone who caught a glimpse of it knew what he was thinking.

"Meet Mr. Armstrong Black," Kobec said, stepping toward a thicket of buzzing detectives. "He was an employee of Ms. Avanti's and, evidently, her lover. He is also, at the very least, an eyewitness. At the most, the murderer left behind an accomplice. Difficult to say at this point. He was found unconscious and injured at the murder scene.

"I trust you may help bring clarification to points I can only offer as educated guesses," Kobec said to the detectives as his fingers moved like a concert pianist's over control pads attached to Army's slightly rising and falling abdomen.

At that moment one of the blue-suited men stepped forward. He talked as if his authority was evident. No one questioned it.

"Washington has a great deal of interest in this case," he said in a cooler tone—one bordering on hypothermic. "We agree with your superiors. But we must add that we believe these murders may well represent a national security threat."

The man took a few soundless steps toward Army on the slab, whose breathing was growing noticeably more regular.

"On my instructions, this man was moved here and kept in a semi-conscious state. It is our hope that these... special lodgings... may ultimately make him more cooperative and more, let's say... receptive to your questions. Be creative."

Kobec cleared his throat with some trouble. He said he wanted Romaro, Gaghan, and Reagan, who fought, but failed, to conceal his exhilaration for having been chosen, to lead the questioning. "Give him a moment or two, gentlemen," Kobec said as he tapped a final sequence into a control pad.

Army's eyes and mouth opened in a silent scream.

"Mr. Black... Mr. Black..." he heard a voice say. "How do you feel?"

Army looked up blankly, blinking his almost sightless eyes—he could detect light, but couldn't see anything clearly beyond vague shapes. Someone behind him was periodically spraying something that felt like warm, faintly salty water into his mouth.

"Can you hear me?" the same voice continued, in a friendly tone. Gradually, Army could make out what looked like a large face, close to his own. He must be on his back.

"Am I... am I...?" he whispered, "Am I in hell?"

"No," the voice said gently. "If you were in hell, then that would make me the devil. I assure you that I'm no devil." Gradually the face—large, beefy—became more clear.

"You are very much alive," Army heard a second voice say, "but your boss, Miss Avanti, wasn't so lucky."

"Kattrel?"

"Kattrel," the second voice said. It was coming from another face on the same side of him, beside the first. Another man's face—also heavy, not young. Army's head pounded but was slowly clearing.

"Kattrel is dead. But you know that. Don't you?"

Army heard the stranger tell him that Kattrel was dead, but the statement lacked weight. He was still getting used to the idea that he wasn't dead as well. His body, clammy and unresponsive, felt distant and disconnected. Yet, he was beginning to feel the cold, hard slab beneath him. Army's thoughts were a nauseating jumble. Every sight and sound nearly unbearable. Yet fragments of memory were knitting themselves into some coherence.

"Kattrel. You remember Kattrel Avanti?" the first face said, now slowly circling Army, who began to track it with his eyes.

"Tell us what happened the night she died," the second face said, lowering his voice.

"Yes. Tell us what happened in the early morning of Chinese New Year at the hotel," Romaro said. "There was champagne, romance..."

Army felt his memories growing firmer. He began to grasp that he was in some kind of institution. But not a hospital. These faces hovering—definitely not doctors. Too many questions. Then it dawned on him that he was naked and covered with something slimy. And tied down, somehow, to the slab he was lying on. Cops. These guys looked like cops.

"Why did you kill her?" a third voice screamed from behind him. "We got your sorry black ass on enough sex crimes alone to bury you under the prison."

"No. We know you were attacked," the first voice countered. "Tell us who attacked you."

"Why did you kill that woman, a pretty Light woman, you perverted son of a bitch?" the third voice hollered. His face—younger than the other two men's—was right over Army's now, damp with sweat.

Why, he thought, was he strapped down? Why were these cops screaming accusations at him? Fuck you, he thought, aiming his deadliest glare at the baby-faced Light man whose voice was the loudest.

"Just tell us what you remember," the second cop cooed.

For a moment, Army considered complying. He thought of his mother and how, if she were here, she would be pleading with him to cooperate. *You have nothing to hide, honey*, she'd counsel.

"What did you do with her fucking head?" the young cop screamed, as he grasped Army and roughly twisted his head to the left. Army could see a crowd of darkly suited men staring at him. Then he could see some of them taking unsteady steps to their left, some to the right.

The next thing Army realized was that he was uncontrollably thrashing about on the slab. One of the policemen had moved a woman's headless body less than a foot from him. Someone was forcing his eyes open to look at the pale, ruined flesh. At first, the fright of naked death lying so close to him was enough to unhinge him. But before Army could calm himself, a razor-sharp realization ripped through his soul.

It was Kattrel lying next to him.

"What did you do with her fucking head, you murderous motherfucker?" the screaming policeman was shouting in his face again.

"Look! Look at what you did to your Kattrel, you black beast!"

"Fucking nigger," the second cop joined in, caressing the words. "Fucking murdering nigger."

"I didn't kill her," Army whimpered. "I didn't kill anyone!"

Army kept his eyes on those of the second cop, the one who'd just called him a nigger. "I'm telling you the truth," Army insisted. He began to sob. "It's the truth. I was knocked out. Out cold. I came to here. Just now." He closed his eyes and cried like a lost child.

"It sounds like a con to me," Gaghan said, standing behind the sobbing Army's head and smiling at Romaro and Reagan. "Sounds like a goddamned CON-fession to me."

Kobec feebly raised one of his hands. The tent fell silent.

"A fair job, gentlemen," he said, as he patted Army's head as if it were a family pet. "A promising beginning. We will take it from here. Thank you."

The trio of Federal men formed a small circle around Kobec and dropped their heads into whispers.

"I guess this means we're dismissed," Reagan said to Gaghan.

"Yeah," Gaghan replied as he trailed Reagan and Romaro out of the tent. "By the Three Wise Men from D.C."

13

Greater Hands

OUCH. OUCH. OUCH!!

It was his feet. Army registered the pain, but somehow abstractly, as if he were in a dream. Then he realized that he had been in a dream—but the pain burning through the soles of his feet was real. He awoke on his back with a start, more enraged than afraid.

"What? What?!" he shouted clearly enough in his head, but the words leapt from his swollen lips as an animal's bark, fury without focus. His body didn't feel as though it was entirely his own; it was vaguely the way it had felt back in the morgue, existing between uneven intervals of wrenching consciousness. Army shuddered. Then the pain returned, but this time it was preceded with a sickeningly loud WHACK!

His feet were flames involuntarily scrambling to find the cool ground. His head felt as if was packed with wet sand.

"Don't make me have to bang you again, boy."

Army opened his eyes to see a face the color and smell of raw meat. Police. But not like the police in the morgue. As the man jerked Army up into a sitting position, it became clear to Army that he was outdoors, and that the policeman was dressed in the dark blue uniform of a City Hall patrol officer.

"You want me to kick your monkey ass back into the cage, jailhole?"

Army shook his head no without thinking. Yes. He was in City Hall Park on a mild winter day. He must have fallen asleep on one of its benches. The officer was shoving him toward the park's gated exits. Army could see Broadway, its gingerbread of early 20th-century towers and older-still churches casting evening shadows on afternoon streets. But all the street-level shops and office lobbies were barricaded. And people—day-workers, service staff, shoppers and many others who seemed strangely out of place—were being roughly herded by squads of police. In the distance he could hear a stew of amplified voices—speeches, directions, chants and songs.

Army felt the impact of a shock baton striking him flush across his left shoulder blade, sending him forward and down to his knees in dizzying pain.

"This here is for decent people," Army heard the officer scream over the rising roar of people massing in angry circuits along Broadway. "Get your Darkness out there with the rest of your filthy tribe. Go. Go on now!"

Another crack across the back as Army got to his feet and stumbled into a crowd of chanting Darks, hundreds of them stomping and rhythmically thrusting their fists into the air. Some beat drums and blew cheap whistles. He inhaled the crowd. It had, he thought, an honest odor of sweat, musk, and overheated indignation. Army found his sore feet taking up the rhythm as he stomped and marched along with them, although he had no idea what they were marching about.

His mind began to clear. The Department processing agent had warned him that he might suffer some short-term memory loss for the next few days. The agent had also told him that he might have some trouble staying awake for the next eight hours. Guess he wasn't lying, Army thought. He realized that he didn't remember going to sleep and had no idea how long he'd been asleep.

He jerked his arm up to check the time. His gut clenched when he found only his bare right wrist. The platinum antique wristwatch Kattrel had given him during their Christmas "business trip" to Singapore last year was gone. He remembered slipping it on when he was being released by the Department. He remembered the processing agent making some kind of snide remark about how he must have really earned it when he read its inscription.

Stolen. The watch must have been stolen when he fell asleep, Army surmised. His rage flared anew when he thought the policeman might have taken it. Did he have any money? Army wondered as he stood flat-footed and jostled by the exuberant crowds surging for blocks along Lower Broadway.

Army reached for his pockets, then realized that he didn't have any. He was wearing a Department-issued suit of disposable slacks and a Velcrofastened jacket, and hardened paper sandals on his swollen feet. No wonder the cop knew he had just been released from detention, he thought. Yes. The folder the processing agent gave him: it held a temporary U.I.D., travel pass, a meal card, and a link call credit.

"Fuck," Army cried, but even he couldn't hear his desperation in the din of the churning crowds. He must have dropped the folder somewhere.

If Kattrel could only see me now, Army thought. How hard she would laugh at him, falling over him with her warm, soft weight, accepting him and dismissing him all at the same time. Coming to his rescue, she would howl laughing with a mouth that so naturally drew into a perfect O.

But Kattrel was dead, and he was still a "person of interest" to the Department in connection to her murder. He tried not to remember the way he last saw her: cold meat on a slab. Headless. Army was numb, wishing he could awake yet again and assign every moment of the last week to the most terrifying nightmare he had ever had. His world was collapsing, and all he wanted to do was to call his mother.

A protester whose bony body was painted lemon yellow stormed up to Army's face, screaming, "Live Free! Piss Free!"

Army felt himself tumbling backward in a reflexive recoiling from the nearly naked man's nose-to-nose snarl. But Army quickly regained his footing when he discovered that there was only enough room in the crowd for him to fall against, not down. He watched the protester repeat his face-screaming as the man wiggled through any momentary gaps among the demonstrators. Before Yellow melted away, Army could see the words—NO TO SWEETBREEZE—crudely painted across his back.

"So, this is what this is about," he said under his breath as he pushed against the riptide of determined humanity. He twisted his neck and confirmed what he had only gotten a glimpse of a moment earlier. Aged clock faces jutting from buildings near Duane Street showed 2:10. "I got to get to Harlem," he said over and over again. "Got to get home."

ZaNia was the first to notice the VP alert.

Imani was much closer to the ominous blinking of the viewpanel's status bars. But she had been too occupied with another corner of the kitchen's VP, gossiping with S.C.U.L.E. pals in San Juan and Sao Paulo, to see the alert pulsing with a distressing urgency.

"Ma," Imani complained. "This old VP is locked up again."

But ZaNia had already bumped past Imani and was frantically fingering the VP, abruptly ending Imani's VIDsitations, snatching the panel's audio back from personal, and tapping up vidi links to coverage of clashes between protesters and security forces near City Hall.

"What! What are you doing?" Imani whined.

"Quiet," ZaNia shot back. "Get your granddaddy. Get him!"

Imani's back straightened and her spine tingled from the base of her skull to the tip of her tailbone. Like fire and smoke, fear and terror filled her. The kitchen's commotion closed around her in a noose of noisy disorder. Army must be there, ZaNia told herself. "Jesus no!" she whispered as she managed to get six feeds of the riotous City Hall scenes playing on the viewscreen. "I know he's there. I can feel it in my hips."

ZaNia's stubby fingers danced over the VP as if its surface was griddle-hot. Her right hand deftly demanded the main viewing window to resize into a sweeping panorama of Broadway from Vesey Street north to Walker Street. Her left hand called up recent images of her son—his face (frontal and profile), his full figure (clothed and unclothed).

"Need further assistance?" the VP asked, its synthvoice low and an upgrade short of sounding earnest.

"I do," ZaNia answered, yelling over the colliding voices and footfalls of Imani and G-Daddy entering the kitchen.

"What you got, baby girl?" G-Daddy shouted, loudly pulling up a kitchen chair to sit behind his daughter, whose face was glued to the big screen.

"Give me a minute, Dad," she replied, and then drew closer to the viewpanel.

"Initiate a full visual recognition search for subject, Armstrong Black, in thirteen-block area along Broadway from Vesey to Walker."

ZaNia whipped herself around, nearly striking her daughter, who had wedged herself between her mother and grandfather. "Look, baby," ZaNia said, her breath growing short in her chest. "Get your father on his link. Get him!"

"What?" G-Daddy asked.

"Allah be merciful," ZaNia cried to no one in particular. "Jae-J. might be down there in that mess, too. He told me that he had to pick up an order at the Hardware/Software Collective. It's on Worth, around Church and Broadway."

"Relax, girl," G-Daddy said as he began rubbing ZaNia's shoulders like he used to when she was a frightened child.

"VP assist," she shouted at the viewpanel. "Expand your VRS to include Jae Jerrod Justus in the identical Broadway corridor. Visuals are uploading. Blend search vectors to include any hits on subjects' U.I.D.s newly entered in public security and medical databases. Recheck status on thirty-second cycles."

"Understood and searching," the VP replied.

"You know your shit, girl," G-Daddy said proudly, as he settled his tall, thin frame back into the straight-backed, wooden chair. "If anybody can find them you can. Always was good with that tech shit."

Imani stared at her grandfather while he spoke, wondering why he always said the same things over and over, like age just didn't make him old, but weirdly defective. She could tell that her mother had already tuned him out and questioned why G-Daddy had been summoned at all. Imani could smell rum on his breath. *Old drunk*, she thought, but dared not say.

It was 4:35 and Imani was trying to make sense of what was blazing across the viewpanel as she tried and retried to reach her father on the link. But she was repeatedly blocked with the same embedded apology about communications in the VIDsit area being "temporarily suspended for security priorities."

"Still nothing, Ma," Imani shouted over the VP audio feeds. She could feel her mother's heart sink along with hers.

"That one. Pull in that one," G-Daddy shouted as he stabbed his finger into the left corner of the viewpanel. "That's DEF and the Smiley girl."

Imani rolled her eyes, thinking, *Not at a time like this*. She knew that her grandfather had the hots for Kenya Smiley, the street anchor for Darks Entertainment Feed. In a flick of her wrist, ZaNia pulled the feed to center screen and popped up its audio.

"… demanding an end to what the leadership is calling a demeaning and humiliating affront to poor people with the introduction of the controversial SweetBreeze4U2 deodorizing agent into the public drinking water. What began here in front of City Hall this afternoon—about three hours ago—as a peaceful demonstration has turned tragic.

"That's correct, Douglass, medical workers told me ten minutes ago that there are at least ten dead and thirty-three others wounded, some of them critically."

"I'm sorry, Kenya, can you be certain about that? No. No word has been released about deaths. We are awaiting that momentarily from Central Authority."

"Nee-Nee," G-Daddy shouted into the back of his daughter's head. "Ask her if she has any identities of the dead and injured. Ask her!"

ZaNia knew she should. It was an obvious question, one that must be flooding into the newscaster's viewer response Weave wires. But she couldn't bring herself to finger in the question and power drive it through the feed. She desperately wanted to hear that neither of her men was among the dead, even among the badly injured. But she didn't want to hear it so publicly, and with no more solemnity than a soccer score.

ZaNia's fingers curled into fists and laid paralyzed in her lap.

"Let's just watch and listen awhile," she said softly. "Okay?"

G-Daddy got out of his chair and bent down to give his daughter a frail but loving hug.

"Yeah," he whispered. "Let's watch a while."

"But keep trying to get your father," ZaNia ordered Imani.

Six feeds were pouring scenes of carnage and confusion onto the viewpanel, each from different viewpoints and varying perspectives. The story was strikingly the same. Demonstrators were being beaten and rounded up as security squads stormed through the crowded streets swinging their shock batons, cracking bones and shattering resolve.

Imani flinched when she saw a young woman fall under the wheels of a police transport that was slowly plowing into City Hall Park from its eastern entrance. G-Daddy was on his feet shouting and waving his fist into the air. "Bastards! *Bastards!*" he screamed hoarsely.

ZaNia was overwhelmed by the full-screen tableau of the riot violence. She could see thousands of bodies straining at security barricades, withering in the crush of chaos. Any one of them, she kept thinking, could be Army, could be Jae-J.

As she searched for her son in the preceding days, ZaNia had directed the viewpanel to gather, aggregate, and display any area crime, injury, and arrest report that held a mid-to-high mathematical probability of involving anyone who fit Army's profile. For nearly a week she had waded through lengthy daily logs of those who met their end naturally, accidentally, by neglect, or by their own final act of will. She combed health records of the sick and hurt. She had been overwhelmed by the seemingly endless litany of death and injury inflicted by local barbarity; she was stunned by both its creative cruelty and mundane regularity. Torture, mutilation, rape, pedophilia, cannibalism, shooting, beating, stabbing, strangulation, electrocution—and nearly every such act ended with murder. Fortunately, ZaNia thought, Army had not been among the victims. He was there, somewhere in the teeming crowds in Lower Manhattan. She knew it.

"Nee, get that one, that one," G-Daddy hollered, snapping ZaNia out of her terror trance.

"What? Which one, Daddy?"

"That one, there, the white man, left corner."

"We don't know how this could have happened," the white-haired correspondent said, disbelief visible in his cool blue eyes. "The lobby of the historic Woolworth Building, that's the 128-year-old tower, the tallest in the world when it was completed, is engulfed in fire."

ZaNia dropped the feed back into the matrix of six others, then accessed six more, than six more until the viewpanel was bursting with feeds, all reporting on the Woolworth Building fire in multi-views, text tickers, blurb bubbles, and background balloons.

"Did anyone catch anything about deaths and injuries?" ZaNia asked as she wrestled with the VP for more information.

"Just property damage, Mom," Imani shouted back over the VP's disharmonious chorus.

"Typical," G-Daddy cried as he paced like a man a third his age. "Fuckers don't care about people. Not black people. Put it back on that Smiley gal."

G-Daddy caught Imani rolling her eyes at his suggestion.

"I trust that girl," he said defensively. "Yo, I knew her grandfather. He was a good brother. Good brother."

ZaNia complied. The VP reoriented, allocating most of its screen to the DEF coverage and relegating the others to a moving mosaic frame.

"Yo-yo-yo, girl. Turn her up," G-Daddy demanded. "She say something about body count?"

"…Again, I caution viewers that what we're getting is unofficial," Kenya Smiley reported, trying to hold her ground as protesters crashed about her. She was screaming, her curly, dark hair blowing into her unblinking eyes. "Yes, we are getting some preliminary reports now, we're hearing from reliable sources that the body count will be high this evening. We have reports of at least twenty-eight deaths and dozens of injuries, many, I'm sad to say, severe."

"Jesus," Imani moaned.

ZaNia said nothing, but reached for her father's shaking hands.

"At this point we have no way to determine whether the dead and injured include protesters, passersby, and law enforcement officers. We are getting some information that at least two persons were badly burned in the Woolworth fire, a fire, we are now being told by fire officials, is under control.

"We are bringing up two eyewitnesses to tell us, from their perspective, what caused the peaceful protest to explode," the reporter said as she pressed a woman dressed in a torn and bloody tunic to face her camera.

"They just started beating us, beating us for no reason," the woman, a Light with missing front teeth, spit into the camera. "No reason. No reason," she cried again.

"I must ask you to stop this," Kenya Smiley could be heard saying off camera. "We are conducting an interview. I... I must—"

The feed went black and then resumed.

"We are being told by City Hall police that we have to move for our safety; we are being forced to move..."

A VP alert flashed across the screen.

ZaNia muted the feeds and potted up the VP audio.

"Standby," the viewpanel said flatly.

ZaNia squeezed her father's hand hard. Imani looked as if she was praying.

"Standby..." the VP repeated. "Whereabouts report: Armstrong Black. Released from Department detention: today, February 14, at 9:58 AM. Charges: pending. Condition upon release: good. Current whereabouts: searching."

ZaNia screamed. "I knew it. I knew it."

"Where's Department detention?" Imani asked, unsure if her mother was pleased or terrified by the VP report.

G-Daddy piped up. "It's downtown, near where the old police department headquarters was for years. Big place, mostly underground."

"And it's near City Hall," ZaNia said weakly, as her voice regained its strength. Graphic and aerial maps of Lower Manhattan dominated the VP. "He's down there. He's down there some place. And he and Jae-J. are alive and well. I can feel it in my hips."

* * * * *

Army awoke in the hand of a giant Buddha. He didn't know how he had gotten there, but realized that time had raced ahead without him. The late winter sky was a darkening purplish blue, the color of a bad bruise. And the city was oddly quiet. He peered over the slightly raised forefinger and knew immediately that he had somehow made it to Chinatown.

He was facing south and could clearly see against the night sky the brightly lit tops of the New Municipal Building and the majestic gothic glint of the Woolworth Building. He could also smell the sour bite of stale smoke on damp air. Below, he found more trash and debris than vehicles on streets he had once worked as a freelance text interpreter, helping the less-than-literate interpret their insurance forms, tax documents, and other important materials. Mott and Mulberry, Lafayette and Centre.

Army crawled on his belly to the edge of the Buddha's thumb and discovered two things: His ribs were sore, and pockets of police and city safety squads remained in the area. He could see some of their floodlights glaring in the distance. Occasionally he heard the whoop of a siren.

Blinding light!

Army groaned and squeezed his eyes shut as he slid back into the giant statue's upturned palm. He clenched his face in his own inadequate palms, leaving his ears open to the assault of a rumbling baritone voice that resonated in his bones and forced his eyes to see again. A great face, the color of new bark, looked down on Army as it spoke with the certitude of God.

He recognized the face—its searching brown eyes topped with graying brows that angled into an apex like the raised roadbed of an opened drawbridge. In a flash of synaptic sparks, Army placed the voice, too. Both belonged to the Reverend Dr. C. Donnell Cosi. The sight and sound of the controversial activist-minister were being streamed over municipal news monitors affixed to the upper floors of Buddha Bob Koon's Sporting and Outdoor Wear Megastore, which is where Army realized he'd ended up—in the heart of Chinatown.

Army realized that Chinatown screens were glowing to life all over the area. *The riot must have triggered a power outage*, Army speculated, as he settled back into the palm and watched the enormous monitor across the street. Its great screenshine illuminated him like an electric sun.

"…unmitigated tragedy. It began as a peaceful assembly, a rightful protest. We are not violent people, just violently opposed to injustice. And Order 24/7-365.2, my brothers and sisters, is N-just. It is our democratic right… Did you hear me? It is our demo-cratic right to give voice to our full and complete opposition to the city's insistence to pump SweetBreeze4U2 into the public drinking water. You know as well as I do that a people, any people hoping for a future they want to live in, could not stand by and permit such a pollution, such a violation.

"We only pray…"

G-Daddy was on his dirty stocking feet, pacing stiffly as Rev. Cosi's voice, a smoky rasp flickering with embers of compassion and indignation, rattled the dented speakers of an aging radio.

"Turn it up, yo!" G-Daddy shouted at Imani, who was tending to the antique boom box on the kitchen floor near the viewpanel. "That's Cosi's station. And Rev's telling it like it ain't gonna be told nowhere else. Damn skippy, yo!"

"We all only pray that the city administrators will see the error of their misguided ways," Cosi said, in an obviously prerecorded message reaching out over Greater New York from his tiny radio station.

"Jesus knows," Cosi continued, as his voice began to decompose into a storm of static, "they know not what they do."

Army crossed his palms behind his head and smiled as the monitor went black. He jerked his head around to see all the screens glowing over Chinatown blink black, one after the other, like falling dominoes.

The Man must have pulled the plug on the old troublemaker, Army thought as he considered the reverend's last words: "They know not what they do."

ZaNia pulled her chair closer to her father's prized radio. Could it be capable of delivering more truth in its old coin bag of transistors, resistors, capacitors, and dry cell batteries than the Weave and all of its otherworldly ingenuity? She dismissed the notion and turned back to the viewpanel, half-listening to both it and to G-Daddy's ranting radio.

"Our government had demonstrated its willingness to transmogrify our righteous rage into a murderous, state-sponsored rage. Yes, I said it. The truth is as plain as the black of my face. Plain and simple…"

G-Daddy was prancing around his radio screaming, "Preach, preach, tell it, goddamnit. Sheee-it!"

Imani shook her head and stared at her grandfather with watery, wondering eyes. Like all old people, G-Daddy was a time machine of sorts. To Imani, he was as alien as the Martian fungus the Japanese astronauts had brought back to earth to farm. It seemed to her that G-Daddy refused to travel any further forward in time than the late 1990s, back when he was still a young man—when Darks called themselves "black," when music and movies played on shiny saucers, and when people, like he would still say, stood for something so they wouldn't fall for anything.

Imani watched the old man stoop low, from his belly, and turn the radio up as loud as it could go.

"Let your eyes see what carnage has been unleashed upon simple truth," Rev. Cosi continued. "We had prayed—prayed real hard!—that the city would listen to our pleas for reason. Now we pray that no more innocent lives will be lost today. As for tomorrow…"

It was getting late. Army could feel it in the chill that slipped into his bones as plain old cold; he could see it in how the daylight had melted into the darkening, starless sky overhead. He wished he hadn't lost the pack the detention agent had given him when he was discharged. The travel pass would have gotten him Uptown. The link credit would have let him reach his mother—let her know that he was all right, where he was. He could imagine Jae-J. jumping on a train to retrieve him like a runaway child. He could have tolerated that humiliation if it meant getting back home, he thought. If he had at least the folder's aspirin drops they would have helped him sleep. Without any of its meager contents, all he could do in his thin paper clothing was embrace himself and try to rock himself to sleep in the Buddha's giant palm.

But instead of drifting into the release of unconsciousness, Army's mind began to sizzle with snatches of memory.

He was a capital murder suspect. He knew this because he remembered the detention out-processing agent spitting the words in his face from him behind a laser screen in a dark, cramped, subterranean room. He recalled a rat-like man with grayish skin and lots of tiny pointed teeth. Or was this recollection just another trick from his mangled memory?

"Armstrong Black."

"Yes," Army had struggled to speak clearly through the still-swollen glands in his throat.

"You're a T-3 case. Active investigation. Close perimeter release," the agent had told him. His memories were gelling, and Army could see the man more clearly now in his mind's eye.

The agent told him that his release status marked him as a possible low-grade "threat to the nation." This required that his Universal Identification Card be seized and replaced with a FU-Blu ID card, which severely restricted his movements in public places.

Until further notice, Army was now banned from higher security-rated areas like the city's gated communities, high-rise residences, premiere retail centers, and star-rated restaurants. Nor could he enter airports, hoverports, MagnaRail train stations, or even use taxi and car services. He could not enter skyways, city plazas, and most parks. Most places of higher education and all private recreation zones were now off-limits. His FU-Blu status also meant that he could not leave the island of Manhattan without notifying and receiving approval from a Department T-3 case manager. After 9:00 PM, his new security rating would prevent him from going anywhere but his or his mother's apartment, which he had designated as his secondary residence—even though he had not set foot there for almost two years.

"Can I go to the corner deli for a sandwich?"

"Depends," the out-processing agent said with easy nonchalance. "If you want that sandwich after 9:00 PM, then you're shitty-shit-shit out of luck."

"What if I have it delivered?"

"Nope again. FU-Blu holders can't order deliveries."

The agent informed Army, in a single-breath spiel that he obviously repeated to offenders on a frequent basis, that "any and all violations, no matter how slight, would subject the FU-Blu status-holder to immediate re-arrest, further security degrades, and vigorous prosecution that could lead to conviction, fines, and/or imprisonment."

Army remembered that the agent ordered him to memorize the rules just before he pushed Army away from his counter with his eyes. "Remember, your status is on your card. Lose it and the Department will have it embedded in your scalp, the same way vagrants and the mentally deficient wear their U.I.D.s."

More memories... The agent breaking his façade and laughing out loud after their exchange. Realizing the man's tiny teeth were not the result of unfortunate heredity, but a self-inflicted product of bad taste. It was a silly style, even for an uneducated Light, he thought, feeling superior to the agent, who himself had derived obvious satisfaction from feeling superior to an educated Dark likely to be dead or slammed back into detention before the month was out.

But as the Koon store news monitor glowed back to life—this time playing a 3-D animation of a waving American flag against a backdrop of interstellar space—Army welcomed its warm glow. His thoughts bumped lightly against one another as he turned on his side, lay his head on a pillow of praying hands, and pieced together much of the jigsaw of the day: his release, how he had fallen asleep in City Hall Park only to awaken stripped of everything of any value—no watch, no aspirin, no U.I.D., no complimentary travel pass, no temporary link credit. No meal card—his stomach took that opportunity to grumble emphatically. He thought about the riot and how lucky he had been to survive its crush of passions and poisons. He shook his head, but it failed to shake loose the remaining question.

For the life of him, Army thought with a tingling astonishment, he could not remember how he had gotten into the open hand of a giant Buddha.

14

Contact

IMANI HAD FALLEN ASLEEP AT THE KITCHEN TABLE. SHE AWOKE TO FIND her chin wedged in the drool-gooey crook of her left forearm. Her impulse was to bolt up from her nest of flesh and crossbones to see who was catching her so unguarded.

At least the kitchen was dark.

Looking to her right, she realized that she could count G-Daddy out. Good. He would never let her forget how she had collapsed like a baby in the midst of a family crisis. Might as well have slept sucking my big toe, she thought.

Imani's embarrassment eased as she watched G-Daddy sleep, knocked out in a kitchen chair. His spindly legs and arms splayed, his boxy head bobbing with each heave of stale breath. And oh, goody-goody, is that snoring? Yeah. The old rap dude, with his dark glasses hanging ridiculously off his nose, was snoring, she said to herself.

"You up, child?"

Imani swung her head around. Her mother was exactly where she had left her, sitting in front of the viewpanel before Imani decided to take a "little nap." The VP's audio was muted, and its images and text seemed quieter too. The riot was clearly long over. It was 2:33 in the morning.

"Sleep well, baby?"

Was she for real or just reminding me that I had fallen asleep on duty? Imani studied her mother's face for any sign of news, good or bad.

"How 'bout you, Momma?"

Imani stalled and looked hard at her mother. She looked okay. She had oiled her braids and, yes, she had washed her face. Maybe brushed her teeth too. She was still wearing the same shapeless dress from the day before, though.

"I didn't sleep much. Sipped this jar of fresh tea most the night. Good for the nerves. But still not a word about your father..."

"I was just gonna ask 'bout Daddy."

"I know, sweetheart." ZaNia spoke in Imani's direction but not directly to her. She adjusted her girth in the hard wooden kitchen chair positioned a few feet in front of the VP. She rubbed her eyes. "I know."

Imani felt the sting. Of course Imani cared. She loved her father, she screamed in her head. She was also grateful that sleep had given more than her body some rest; her mind had been spinning out of her head with what-ifs.

"How long has G-Daddy been sleep?

"He dropped off about an hour after you did. About midnight, I guess. And hasn't gotten up once, not even for the toilet."

A slender silence stood between them, then swayed before snapping. Imani cleared her throat. ZaNia spoke to the viewpanel, ordering it to restore its audio and broaden its search of police and medical data banks for Jae-J. Imani decided to go to the bathroom, pee, and wash up. Maybe catch up on some S.C.U.L.E. work. She knew she could never go to bed, not with her mother in full martyr regalia.

"You want to get a little nap, Ma? I'll watch the VP."

Imani was not sure where the words came from or why she had uttered them.

ZaNia stared hard at her daughter. She weighed the words and what she saw in them as a childish challenge. She suppressed an urge to hurl her hurt at Imani, to have what her Mississippi grandmother used to call an N-fit.

"No. That's all right," ZaNia replied, surprised by the thickness of the honey in her tone

"Fine," Imani said, thankful that her mother had apparently taken no offense at the suggestion that she was merely human.

G-Daddy began coughing in his sleep, deep rheumy sounds.

Then, like a voice calling from almost too far away, ZaNia's link rang.

Imani heard its electronic beckoning coming from somewhere behind the basket of holographic fruit that had for years been the kitchen table's forever-ripe centerpiece.

"I got! I got it!" Imani said, sock skating back to the table from the kitchen's doorway. G-Daddy stirred but did not wake.

At Imani's touch, the retracted bundle of tele-electronic tubing and liquid optics sprang to programmed life, reaching for the teenager's ear.

"Mommy. It's Daddy! Dad-DEE!" Imani hollered, this time yanking G-Daddy from his sleep. "He says he's fine, being held in a church."

With surprising agility, ZaNia reached Imani and snatched the link from her daughter's ear.

"Jae-J., Jae-J.," she whispered into the link as it attached to her ear. "You were there, there in the riot. And you're not hurt?"

ZaNia collapsed into her wooden chair, sobbing as her father and daughter rubbed away at her burden.

"Cutie. Heeeey cutie."

Army wanted to dismiss the woman's voice. He had been sleeping lightly for much of the evening, catching snatches of voices that occasionally drifting up from the awakening streets below. But this voice seemed to be taking shape around him.

Maybe it was coming from the alley behind Koon's. Maybe it was the kooky acoustics of Chinatown playing tricks on his ears. His empty stomach and his full bladder were of more pressing concern than locating a disembodied flirtation.

"Hey sweet thang! You up there?"

Damn, Army thought. He wormed about on his belly and worked himself to a rounded ridge of fiberglass that formed the meatiest part of the Buddha's left hand. He peered over its slick, shiny surface, letting his eyes follow down along the gaudy, pleated folds of the Buddha's molded red robes.

"So you *are* up there, devil," said a woman with a heart-shaped face and, Army was quick to notice, a heart-shaped bottom to match. She looked to be about his age. Certainly no older than her early thirties. She wasn't dressed like someone he should fear—no uniform, nothing that suggested anything more than a loose woman in tight clothing. Intrigued, Army pushed his head out over the edge of the Buddha's middle finger.

"How'd you get way up there, heartbreaker?" the woman asked, giving him a little show and tail as she walked in small, languid circles. "My name is Starr, and this is my corner of the universe."

"Your corner?"

"Yeah, baby, Chinkies need loving, too. And some Darkie hiding in a Buddha is bad for business, even this early in the morning."

Army cocked his head like a dog unsure whether to growl or run. He decided to reappraise her. She reeked with an overtly commercialized sexuality and was so ballsy that Army began worrying that she just might have a pair; worse, a pair bigger than his own.

"Well, you coming down, you handsome sonofa—"

"Armstrong! My name is Armstrong."

"Nice name, Daddy—uh, I mean, Armstrong."

"Starr? That the name your momma gave you?" Army asked as he took a closer measure of her figure, compensating for the distortion of seeing all her parts from so high above.

"Starr? Yeah, my old lady took one look at me when she pushed me out and said, 'Shit, this skinny little bitch looks like a star.'"

"So you're a pleasurist?"

"So you're a dumb-ass? I just told you I was here to sell some lovin' to the Chinks here in Chinkytown," Starr said with a casual air. "Yeah, me and my Jelli deliver the kind of pleasure worth paying for. You should see my Jelli go. Nice…very nice… I keep it in very nice condition."

"What's its name?"

"Plasma."

"Plasma?" Army chuckled as he let himself roll over to rest against the Buddha's little finger. "Plasma, like the stuff stars are made of?"

"Ah, so you're not a dumb-ass after all, huh? I like the name because it's hot. Didn't know stars were made out of the shit."

Starr rolled her eyes and readjusted a mound of vanilla-scented ringlets uncoiling in the river air.

"You leaving or what?" she asked Army abruptly. "These streets gonna be full of clients soon, begging for a ride on my Plasma. You've gotta go, lover boy."

A single car appeared out of the smoky night, its approaching headlamps backlighting Starr so intensely that she, for a few moments, was reduced to nothing more than a curvy cutout. The car passed slowly, its single passenger eyeing her closely. Starr flashed a figure with her fingers, only to watch the car speed away and disappear.

"Cheap fuck!" Starr screamed at the car.

Army was straddling the Buddha's left wrist.

"Did you know people died down here today?" Army asked, trying hard to bend his voice into a more serious shape. "Wonder where all this smoke came from, why they've been washing the streets for hours?"

Starr looked over her bare right shoulder just long enough to say she had heard something about the trouble. "A little smoke ain't going to stop people from tending to their pleasures. Besides, like my momma used to tell me, there's opportunity in chaos."

Army looked down on Starr, his face filled with unconcealed disgust. He hated her type, the business-as-usual predators who baited the weak with promises of exactly whatever it was that they didn't have, and what they were unlikely to ever have. And the promise of no-consequence sexual pleasure was, especially now, the most alluring and ensnaring promise of all.

Army had never actually met a pleasurist. Not knowingly, he thought. He had never had trouble finding erotic adventure. The notion of sex without consequences always intrigued him as a kind of performance art. But paying for it? No way. Especially with a pleasurist and a Jelli's insult to authentic fucking. "Nah, no way," Army said, just loud enough for Starr to hear.

"No way, what?" she snapped, now visibly losing her patience. "You ain't coming down?"

Army felt his anger surge. Surprisingly, he thought, it wasn't so much directed at Starr, but at himself. She reminded him of Oooh, the hot pleasurist he'd seen from the Robeson's window the night of Chinese New Year. Shit—she had been watching him the night Kattrel was murdered! He realized that she could actually exonerate him. She might have even seen the actual murderers that night with her goddamned super glasses.

He had to find Oooh; he had to speak with her, persuade her to help. But that was crazy, he told himself. All he knew about her was that she worked in Harlem.

"Hey! I ain't playing," Starr was screaming now. "You better come down or I'll get somebody to yank your dusty butt down. I know you hear me. Hey!"

Army poked his head out and looked down on her. "Listen," he replied gently. "I can't come down unless I can get somebody to take me home. I'm a FU-Blu. Just got released."

Starr looked up and wore the closest thing to sympathy Army had seen on her all night. "What 'cha do?"

"Nothing."

"Then, Negro, you's in trouble," Starr said with a chuckle rattling in the back of her throat. "A big buck like you can get 50 to life for doin' nothin'. Where's home?"

"Harlem. My family's from Harlem, from before it got so fancy you gotta sell your kidney or your ass to live there."

"How'd you get a place in Harlem?" she asked like she really wanted to know.

"It's my mother's place—she and her husband," Army said. "He's the building's super. Been the super just about all my life."

The gray lie stuck in Army's throat like a fish bone, poking more than choking. It wasn't that anything he had said about his family and Harlem was untrue—except for the part about the old apartment being his home. He lived miles away, in New Rochelle. It was where gaggles of young bootstrappers like him with good educations and almost decent jobs lived in a safe, vacuum-sealed, suburban stupor. It was where they daydreamed of the day they could call any overpriced corner of Manhattan home. New Rochelle was where Kattrel helped him get a good deal on a short-term cooperative after he confessed to her that he'd end up killing his stepfather if he lived another day under *that man's* roof.

Army half-wondered if he had not told the Pleasurist, of all people, a truth he had long been reluctant to accept: His apartment had never been a home. He had to admit that it began as little more than a declaration and never amounted to much more than a sparsely furnished statement. He spent more time in hotel rooms, working or fucking, or, all too often, both.

Army was thankful that the pleasurist was walking away. She wouldn't see him shaking his head like a deranged MethPopper. Army was beginning to question his grip on truth—knowing it, telling it, living it. So much of his life had been a lie, a fact that he did his best to lie away. Then he heard his mother speaking in his head. There were no words, just the shiny way she made him feel when she stopped the world from spinning just long enough to tell him what he needed to hop back on. She was telling him that her little piece of Harlem would always be his home. She was calling him back.

* * * * *

Starr glanced over her shoulder and half smiled, half frowned at Army. He could see that she was digging into a hip purse. When she turned a few moments later to face him, she was holding a silvery card with large blue and red letters that Army recognized right away as a MoGoTel card.

"Here, take this and call somebody to come get you," Starr said with one hand on her hip and the other holding the card over her curly head. "Come and get it and call your momma."

"Yeah, hold on. Don't go anywhere." His heart pumped faster as he slipped around the Buddha's open palm.

Army straddled its wrist and began to work his way down to the gently curving right arm, down to the figure's generous, wide-set lap. Army discovered as he climbed down that his body was more stiff and raddled than he had realized. Twice he almost fell, but even the fear of falling could not shake his faith that he was going home.

Starr watched Army as he dropped the last couple of feet to the vacant sidewalk. She took three steps toward him, the whole time holding out the MoGoTel card as if it possessed some powerful juju.

"Take this and get the hell outta here," she said, her eyes hard but her smile soft.

With each step closer, Starr appeared to age a year in Army's eyes. Her latte-brown makeup was thick and cracking at the corners of her eyes and mouth. And when he took the card from her, he noticed something that seemed overly workaday, rough and scarred, about her hands.

Army retreated with the card to the alley behind Koon's. He called out a last thanks to the pleasurist as he stepped deeper into darkness. He looked around to make sure he was alone. He kneeled before a discarded plastic crate and began to activate the card. He swept the plastic crate's top clean with the edge of his hand and used his dirty fingernails to release two rubbery feet from the card's backing. He carefully stood the MoGoTel card up until it looked like a tiny billboard.

All Army could think about was his mother. He anticipated the sound of her relief as he pinched a corner of the card until it pulsed green and spit a pink thread of light that struck the crate's rough-cast surface, projecting there a lightware keyboard and miniature viewpanel.

Army dropped to his knees and began typing in his mother's access address until the card voicelessly responded. It confirmed his mother's address and then informed him that he had three minutes of communications with unlimited range and full visual-audio capacity.

"This is a great card you gave me," Army shouted excitedly toward the spot on the street where he had left Starr. He didn't even notice that there was no response from the pleasurist. All his attention was on putting through his VIDsit to his momma.

"BeThereBeeThereBeeeeeThere," he chanted under his breath as the virtual viewpanel brightened and indicated that the VIDsit was in progress.

15

Rikki's Mourning

RIKKI ROSE BEFORE MAC\SHEEHAN COULD REMOTELY ROUSE HER from lavender-scented sheets, and the warmth from her body seeped into a bed that never forgot her delicate contours. She stiffly wandered toward her living room, enjoying the springy thickness of peasant-woven rugs arranged on mahogany floors like lily pads beneath her bare feet.

She lingered at the double French doors, pausing just long enough to exorcise the pangs of misgiving that stirred her empty stomach.

Her brother was coming. She had sent for him.

Rikki knew how much Reagan detested traveling. But she had been forced to force the issue, she told herself, trying hard to rationalize her rare insistence. They had to talk. They had to come to some agreement.

Rikki had done her best to make his trip from New York agreeable. She knew he would never admit that he feared flying; nonetheless, she secured elite-class accommodations on a MagnaRail Cruiser. How could he refuse a scenic seat on *The Philadelphia Glider*? The train was her favorite mode of inter-urban transportation, and the *Glider* was her favorite train. It should be good for his mood, she assured herself.

Yet Rikki knew all too well that she and her older brother were entirely different people, with entirely different attitudes about life. He did not share her soft touch for teasing out life's delights—or even recognizing them, for that matter. Where he was plodding, she was a wind dancer. She smiled. He growled.

Rikki glanced at a viewwall. It read: Condition CRITICAL. She didn't bother getting close enough to read the fine print scrolling along its upper and lower edges. She knew too well what was being reported.

The same all week, she thought. She took a deep breath and tried again to coax the anxiety in her belly to uncoil. She shook her head slowly for relief before walking into her country kitchen.

"'Morning, Mac," Rikki called in a voice not yet fully awakened. "Chai with a touch of steamed goat's milk."

"Yes, indeed, I know just how you like it, Miss Rikki," answered Mac\Sheehan, whose bodiless presence followed her from room to room. "Anything else?"

"Hmm." Rikki thought as stood before the kitchen's spotless beverage dispenser. It trickled steaming chai tea into an oversized ceramic teacup crafted to look like cupped hands. She inhaled its misty richness as Afrika Tumba's "Sweet Morning Suite, Symphony No. 3 in F Minor" swelled into the kitchen and surrounding rooms. "Yes. Please give me a travel update on my brother."

Mac\Sheehan responded in a voice carefully calibrated to please. "The train on which Detective Reynolds is a passenger is 42.7 miles north of 30th Street Station Complex. It is on schedule for a 10:21 AM arrival. Anything else? Morning Weave briefs?"

"No. No, thank you," Rikki said, between sips of tea. Still in her sleeping satins, she shuffled out onto her home's open-air terrace. Its Arabian tile floor warmed automatically under her feet as she stepped into the infant day. A breeze blew tentatively at her hair, which fell loose against the nape of her neck as she looked eastward over Fairmont Park and Preserve.

Center City Philadelphia loomed in the near distance as a forest of soaring towers. Somewhere deep in that thicket of gleaming glass, metals and polymers sat the LifeTek Healing Center. And in that, Rikki knew all too well, lay her mother, the withered rind of the woman who gave her life.

Rikki strained to imagine Rose-Pearl Reynolds in her hospital bed; she tried to imagine her mother not struggling for each tomorrow, for each new breath.

With all of her wealth, her connections, and her influence, there was nothing more she could do for her mother, other than bear witness to her last act. She lifted a tear from the corner of her eye with her little finger. *Already crying, and the day's just started,* she thought.

Rikki drank her tea. She reminded herself to embrace her suffering;

she wanted to see how close she could draw it to her. But almost reflexively she found herself considering the much vaster suffering, the misery of the poor and forgotten, of the misused and discarded. They were there, too, in Rikki's Philadelphia, and she couldn't forget them any more than she could forget the suffering of her mother.

She dropped her head and closed her eyes.

"I hope I am not disturbing your meditation, Miss Rikki." Mac\ Sheehan's voice spoke barely louder than Tumba's kalimba sonata, playing for the second time. "It is 10:26 AM."

Rikki's pulse quickened. Reagan's train must have arrived in the station.

"Detective Reynolds is en route to the Schuylkill Expressway. His limousine should arrive in no more than twenty minutes. Do you want him delayed?"

"No," Rikki said, as she jumped up from a terrace chair she didn't remember sitting in. Her agility surprised her. She stooped to pick up her teacup and walked briskly through terrace doors, which parted at her approach. She loosened the cord at her waist and stepped out of her nightclothes, kicking them to a corner of the terrace before stepping naked into her living room.

"Thank you, Mac," Rikki said as she practically skipped toward her bathroom. "Start my shower—and order beer, lots of beer. I think my brother is drinking instant. I don't know the brand."

"Very good, Miss Rikki. Mac will improvise," the familiar voice replied.

Reagan stepped into Lift Two of the Towers Majestic North, catching a full frontal glimpse of himself in a flawlessly mirrored wall as he did. He liked what he saw. His new ultrasonic shaver had finally rid him of the bluish shadow that had semi-permanently darkened his jowls for years. Weeks of full-night sleeping had unpacked the bags beneath his eyes. His thinning hair glistened with a restoration hue that reminded him of the days when his chest still entered a room before his belly.

Reagan especially admired himself in his new suit. It was a camel-colored, one-button number hand-made in Chinatown to expertly fit his unfashionable bulk. Back on the Department payroll. He was doing well, and he wanted the world to know it at a glance. *Looking damn good.* He adjusted his new porkpie on his head.

"Floor, sir?"

"Penthouse," Reagan told the elevator as it gathered its ornamental gate before lifting off like something late for a countdown. Reagan watched the floors race by on a viewpanel that displayed news briefs, weather forecasts, stock quotes, and aphorisms of the day: "Beauty in things exist in the mind which contemplates them."—*David Hume (1711—1776)*

"Now, ain't that some shit?" Reagan said over the notes of music so vague that it annoyed him. "I think this goddamned elevator is trying to fuck with me."

"Floor, sir?"

"I already told you PENTHOUSE! The fucking PENTHOUSE," Reagan huffed, watching his face redden.

He kicked at the elevator's gates until it rang out in alarms.

"Beer?"

"Rikki, that's the third time in—what?—thirty minutes you asked me if I wanted a fucking beer. What's it with the beer? Mr. OogaBoogaMan importing beer now, too?

"Nothing, Ray," Rikki said meekly as she drew trembling circles on the glazed-glass top of her terrace table. "Sorry. You just seem a little tense to me. And I thought, uh, a cold, glass of beer might relax you."

"It'll take more than a beer."

The elevator had deposited Reagan in Rikki's living room almost an hour ago. The ritual of reconnection consumed the first ten minutes: obligatory hugs (fifteen seconds); compulsory compliments: hair, weight, (two minutes, 23 seconds); compulsory compliments: home, interior design (three minutes, 11 seconds); comparative train travel talk (three minutes, 14 seconds); comparative weather: New York/Philadelphia (42 seconds).

But the next twenty minutes had been anything but mundane mutterings. Reagan's manner had lightened when Rikki asked, almost as an afterthought, about his work. He sat down and sank deep into the living room's cashmere sofa and crossed his legs at the knee. Rikki noticed his spit-shined calfskin loafers. She found herself realizing that her brother was not simply uncharacteristically well groomed, but he had, seemingly overnight, developed style.

"…it's damn tough to believe, Sis. I know. I know. But what I'm telling you is true. All true. Too true."

"Yes, yes. I'm sure it is all true," she faked, strategically opening her eyes and nodding in agreement. "But take me through it again—slowly, this time."

"Okay. But try to keep up this time," he began. "I probably shouldn't be talking about any of this shit. But I know I can trust you. Right?"

Rikki, curled up in a matching cashmere recliner, wildly nodded yes.

"Promise that you're not going to say a word of any of this to anybody— not even with Mr. Dark-ness. Okay? We straight on this?"

Rikki agreed, while habitually suppressing her urge to react to Reagan's equally habitual insistence on insulting her husband. Reagan had never forgiven Rikki for marrying a Dark. And the fact that her husband was also an African, and a wealthy, well-respected businessman, was more than her brother's politics, prejudices, and insecurities could tolerate.

Reagan could not even bring himself to call his sister Rikki, the name her husband had bestowed on her on their wedding day in Lagos. It was a name she felt better suited her sensibilities than Richie, an unvarnished stand-in for Richard, the name of her maternal grandfather's hero, Richard Nixon.

"I told you that I'm back with the Department for a while, that I'm working this special case," Reagan said as he looked over Rikki's head and out on the approaching noontime sky. "Sitting up here in your crystal tower, you think nothing could be wrong with the world. But believe me when I say that the world is a terrible place, full of terrible people who want to do nothing but terrible things.

"I've seen a lot of terrible things… But there's something, something voodoo-hoodoo, some techno-mind-sucking shit going on. And it's been going on for a while…"

Rikki reached for Reagan's cupped hands, but he pulled away.

"Listen, Sis… Somebody's going around chopping off people's heads and selling what's inside their skulls to people."

"Their brains?"

"Yes—well, no. Well, we're not exactly sure yet," Reagan said, biting his lips. "We think they are selling the victim's *feelings*. Maybe more."

Rikki looked at her brother's stricken expression. Then she let her head drop. "I'm listening," she said speaking to the shine on his shoes.

"What about your, uh—"

"Mac?" Rikki asked, raising an eyebrow. She opened a small drawer on an accent table next to her chair. "Mac."

"Yes."

"Some privacy please," Rikki commanded, while using the control pad to set the parameters for Mac\Sheehan to return to full attentiveness.

Turning back to Reagan, Rikki patted his knee. "Relax. You can speak freely here. See?

"Mac!" she called.

There was only the faraway-sounding polyphonic harmonies of a Batwa pygmy song, a new favorite Rikki had discovered last year while vacationing with her husband in the rainforests of Cameroon.

"Go on, Ray," Rikki gently pressed. "Tell me more about your work."

"Well, I'm damn glad to be on it," he started, avoiding Rikki's questioning eyes. "This is important work. Even got some feds looking over our shoulders. They think it might be terroristic."

"No," Rikki gasped.

"Well, I don't. But, but I ain't never run across anything before that's this, this… Well, this fucked up. I can't figure it out. At first I thought it was some kind of cheap hallucination, a trick, maybe some mass hysteria bullshit."

Rikki whispered that she understood. She didn't.

"Then I started pressing people, talking to garbage heads—Vipers, trippers, slummers, and some Freds and Gingers—you know?—rich party boys and girls. They all say the same thing: There's a new underground high, a new kind of shit-scary narcotic out there. It's been so underground that even the lowlifes can't get their hands on it."

Rikki shook her head. "What does this have to do with people getting their heads cut off?"

Reagan straightened his legs and began nervously rubbing the full length of his thighs.

"Are you listening?" he cried. "Don't you hear what I'm telling you?"

He stood up and cast his words down on top of Rikki's head.

"Their *brains* are the drugs!" he hissed. "Rich people's brains. People like you that go around smiling and whistling all the damn time. Happy fucking people. All right? *Happy people*! It's like they're snatching their good feelings, pieces of their happiest times.

"They call it Hedz," Reagan continued in a voice that seemed suddenly tired. "And I hadn't heard a fucking thing about until almost two weeks ago. Nothing. Right under my nose and nothing."

Rikki slowly rose and walked to her kitchen. Without a word, she returned with an enormous glass stein brimming full of beer.

"Instant?" Reagan asked with disappointment.

"I thought you said you were cutting back, watching your weight," Rikki offered.

He eyed the pitcher and spoke again, this time more haltingly. "They're telling us that this Hedz is real hard to get, that you got to know the right people. Golden circles and shit like that. And you have to pay for it in pounds of good, old-fashioned, untraceable cash.

"Some old-timers say it reminds them of how cocaine first hit Harlem way back in the old century, not long before it was cooked into piss-cheap crack. That was way before it got purified into crackle and controlled by the government.

"But this," Reagan said into his clammy, closed palms, "could be a million times worse than crack."

"Is it actually that bad?" Rikki asked, wishing she could have sounded less Pollyannaish.

Reagan shot her a you-gotta-be-kiddin' look before replying in a quiet voice.

"How about we got a Department morgue full of headless bodies? And more every week?"

Rikki's face recoiled in fear.

"It gets worse," Reagan said. "An informant told us that there's already a bunch of Hedz addicts who can't get enough of this shit, too seen-it-all-done-it-all to bother with nightclubs, fine restaurants, even sex. They'd rather sit on their asses and shoot somebody else's good times up their noses."

Rikki looked puzzled. "How can a substance hold somebody's memories?"

Reagan shook his head. "I can't say anymore. Shit—I've already said too much. Do you have any goddamned beer in this house that's worth drinking, or at least worth pissing?"

"Never mind the beer. Talk to me, Ray," Rikki pleaded. "You're carrying too much to deal with all this alone."

Reagan got up and stalked over to a glass table near the entrance to Rikki's terrace. He reached for the stein of instant beer, which Rikki had set next to a silver platter of finger sandwiches. He reared back and gulped down a huge swallow of the beer, then helped himself to two of the finger sandwiches. The next moment he pulled himself within a few inches of Rikki's startled face. Rather than rant, he whispered.

"I better get the hell out of here," Reagan hissed. "You already know too damn much. I don't want you too scared to visit Mother. I don't want you too afraid that somebody's going to lop your head off when you ain't looking and get high on your multiple orgasms over the Amazon rainforest."

"It was the rainforest in Cameroon," Rikki corrected, softly. "And I did enjoy myself."

"Be careful," Reagan said, urgently. "I don't know about Philadelphia—yet—but in Harlem, there are a whole bunch of folks who would kill for a chance to steal your head and sell what's inside like cotton candy at the circus."

Rikki shook and tried to look brave.

"I have an old bottle of Jamaican run," Rikki said meekly. "Do you want a real drink?"

Reagan smiled weakly before reaching for Rikki's hand.

"Yeah. I could use it," Reagan said, surprised that he suddenly wanted something stronger. Discussing the case with a real person—not a clinician, not a Department supervisor, not another detective—*had* been therapeutic, he admitted to himself. This was his sister, after all. Even the instant beer really wasn't that bad, he thought. But his eyes brightened when he saw his sister enter the living room with a stout bottle of Appleton Estate 21-year-old Jamaican rum.

"I want to talk about Mother," Rikki began, completely crushing the moment Reagan was allowing himself to enjoy. "She's dying, Ray."

"She's *dying?*" Reagan sniped. "She's been dying for years, Sis. She's had a good life. Did you think preventive PPS injections were going to keep the V-HIC in check forever? C'mon. We all knew that one day her immune system would fall apart, just like ours will some day. All the fucking medications, transfusions, transplanting, rebuilding..." He paused to run his hand over his surviving hair.

"Pretty soon there ain't going to be nothing left of the original but her name. She's old, damn it. Let go."

Rikki only shook her head no.

"You know, I went to a Department funeral a few days ago," Reagan continued, looking away as if to collect his thoughts. "An old minister spoke. He was so fucking tired and old that I was taking bets that it just might be a double send-off. But there was one thing he said that stuck with me. He said we all got an appointment with death; and that's one appointment we all are going to keep—no matter what.

"Mom's just trying to keep her appointment," he said. "You've got to understand that. She was always fucking punctual, anyway."

Rikki listened quietly before she spoke.

"I do understand. I know she's old, Reagan," she said. "Her eighty-fourth birthday was last month, and not even a VIDsit from you."

"Ahhh, you're trying to change the subject," Reagan said firmly. "And you know, like I know, that in her state she couldn't tell whether it was me or Spanky the Talking Asshole wishing her a birthday."

Rikki's stomach clenched and anxiety spiked. She could feel the skin of her face superheat with frustration.

"I don't want to argue," Rikki said in a single breath of exasperation. "I just want us to agree on a solution. I am her sole legal guardian. I know I don't need your permission."

"Permission? Permission for what?"

"I want to bring Mother here to live with me."

"You mean die with you," Reagan sniped again. "No. Not that again. Why? Ain't Rosy Pearl getting enough attention at that medical center you're paying top credit? I thought it was the best of the goddamned best."

"It's not the care," Rikki replied. "I'm enough of a realist to know Mother will never recover. I simply want her here with me. Maybe she'll rally, get strong enough for long enough to tell me something, to share a secret, to tell me everything is all right. I don't know."

"That's the point," Reagan replied, his voice obstinate. "You *don't*. I'm so sick of this. Do what you want. You're gonna anyway. Right?" Reagan said, pushing his wide-mouthed glass, half-emptied, with the stub of his missing finger. "Do what you want. But what about your husband?"

"He's fine with whatever decision we make."

Reagan wobbled to his feet.

"Of course anything *we* decide is okay with him," Reagan boomed. "That sorry-assed, Nigger-gerian is never the hell here.

"Why do you put up with it?" Reagan kicked the leg of the chair that Rikki was sitting in so hard that Rikki felt the force bang into the bottom of her ass. "I know he tells you that he's away on business, but I know what kind of business he's tending to."

Rikki stood and turned toward the terrace. "Why do you have to be so vulgar? So angry all the time? You've always been that way."

"Because I'm an angry vulgarian. That's why. But your husband is the one fucking some African whore he's probably calling his wife, while you sit here alone carrying on conversations with talking walls," Reagan yelled, loud enough to wake Mac. "You've got to know that she's giving him children, lots of shiny black babies that you're too old and used up to answer with babies of your own."

Rikki leapt at her brother. "You have a lot of nerve passing judgment about us and prying into our lives. Are *you* still sleeping with sex puppets and those women who pull their strings?"

Reagan glared at his sister.

"What would Mother think if she knew that you are so messed up in the head that you can't bear human intimacy? That you *pay* to grunt your seed into the bowels of a *machine*? A machine, Reagan? A ma-chine?"

Reagan bit his tongue. He felt foolish and ashamed standing before his sister's assault. Clear sky, clear sky. His anger manager had told him to see himself as a cloudless sky.

"You have the audacity to assail my husband, to denigrate our lives, which *work*, at their worst, far better than yours, at its best," Rikki pressed, knowing she was recklessly close to crossing a line she would regret.

Then she crossed it.

"Tell me, Ray, when you're humping your machine in the dark, do you pretend it's that poor dead girl who wrecked your career?"

Reagan slapped his sister hard across her face and grabbed her wrists so tightly that his knuckles looked like rows of white pebbles. The Y-shaped vein at his temple swelled from lowercase to capital.

"Stop it," Rikki yelled, trying to twist free. "Let go. Let go!"

"Sit down and shut the fuck up!" Reagan yelled. His shirt had pulled out of his pants and his jacket, damp with sweat and spilt liquor, was falling from his shoulders.

Suddenly another voice interrupted, coming from everywhere around them. It wasn't as loud as Reagan's shouts, but somehow, it was more penetrating. "Ms. Rikki, are you in distress? Are you in need of emergency assistance?" It was Mac\Sheehan. Rikki replied that she was unharmed and that it could override its emergency protocol and return to normal status.

"Acknowledged," Mac\Sheehan said. The two siblings fell silent.

Reagan glared at Rikki. "Tell your fucking machine to call me a car," he said finally before tossing back the rest of his rum. "I never should have come."

"Yes, I think it's time for you to go," Rikki said to Reagan's back as he stomped toward her apartment's front door. "Don't worry. I'll tell Mother you love her."

"Tell the old woman what you want," Reagan said, stopping at the opening door. "But I'm telling you for your own good: Let her go."

Rikki ran up to her brother from behind. She thought about pounding her fists into his fat back. Of hurling one of her Zimbabwean stone sculptures at his piggish head. Instead, she handed him his coat and hat. Reagan turned, grabbed his hat and coat, and spun back around just as fast.

"Mac. Front door," Rikki called, doing her best to control an urge to kick her brother's ample backside.

"Thanks, little sis, for a lovely afternoon," Reagan said over his shoulder as he yanked the outer door that led to the elevator. He tried his best to slam the steel door behind him.

Mac\Sheehan intervened. The big door stopped inches short of closing, and then eased shut with the gentlest of clicks.

16

Baghdaddy's

REAGAN FELT LIKE A CHAMELEON WITH A SKIN CONDITION. No matter how much he tried to blend into the crowd pressing him toward the nightclub's entrance, he appeared to be exactly what he was: a middle-aged cop who had no business among these young, stylish and perversely rich partiers, other than official business. This was Generation Alpha-Omega, the ones who had convinced themselves that they owned everything that mattered, he thought.

Reagan's face contorted in a twitchy play between amusement and resentment as Freds and Gingers jostled him. To most of them, he was a dismissible oddity: a swollen, hard-edged personage, probably one with some authority. The clubbers were desperate to get inside. It was Saturday night. Even if it meant an hour's wait beneath the artificially oxygenated coolness of the club's block-long awning, an artful slice of architecture that took its full length to spell B-A-G-H-D-A-D-D-Y-'-S, that would be fine with most of them, Reagan groused. All to celebrate a meaningless occasion that clashed with the décor.

For the last several years, the nightclub had been a favorite among good-timers driven by an insatiable hunger to consume all things Harlem. This night the banquet was being set yet again in this Middle Eastern-styled behemoth of brick and fantasy done up in pointed arches and onion domes at 116th and Farrakhan Avenue. Reagan knew the place. Its predecessor had been on his beat when he and Romaro had free rein over most of Harlem during their days as Department street officers. Occasionally, he slipped in through the back to do a favor for a favor. But he had never liked the place.

"Excuse me," asked a clear-skinned bloom of a man. He stepped up to Reagan with a genuflection that struck the detective as mocking. A girl on the boy's arm was tugging at him to step back into the crowd. Yet the boy persisted.

"Yes, excuse me," he said, a bit too brassy. "Aren't you the fellow who plays Piss Puss the Clown at children's parties?"

Reagan could see himself wearing the boy's ass on his right foot like a house slipper. But he needed to enter the club without incident, so he smiled and tried to laugh off the insult.

"No," he replied. "I'm not a clown."

"Then why are you dressed like one?" the boy shot back as the girl began apologizing for her boyfriend, who was lost in his own laughter.

"That's okay," Reagan assured the girl. "I get that a lot. It's the face. It relaxes people, makes 'em laugh, I guess." He puffed out his cheeks and rolled his pupils back into his head until they looked like boiled pigeon eggs. Mortified, the girl shoved her boyfriend until they dissolved into the crowd.

I should get a medal for that, Reagan thought as he looked skyward. Without meaning to, he began studying the club's ornately ugly façade. It was hard to believe that an actual mosque once stood on the very spot, and that a famous Dark, Malcolm X, used to work there.

That, Reagan reminded himself, was a very, very long time ago, back when his grandfather was a badass cop busting black asses every time he got a chance. A sharp elbow into Reagan's shoulder blade startled him, sending him stumbling back into the present. The clubbers were lurching with anticipation. Some cheered as they got their first clear glimpse at Baghdaddy's massive brass and leather-laced doors.

Reagan's heavy face couldn't muster up any of the joyful expressions that played over the faces that surrounded him. Even his most faint smile sagged at the edges. It had been a long time since he was in the company of so many people who seemed, literally, to have been born yesterday. Fluffy, stupid, disrespectful sheep, was all he could think as he looked over the crowd of mostly Lights, some Darks, and a sprinkling of others he couldn't clearly determine what they were. As always, he mentally dispensed with any annoying ambiguities by applying his granddaddy's adage: *When in doubt, they're niggers.*

Lights or Darks, these were not his people. What did they know of the world? Reagan wondered as he eyed them, all made up, all dressed up, hoping to get all joyed up on an Uptown Saturday Night. What did they know about the world beyond their nightclubs, their bottomless appetites, their treats and retreats, conceding nothing except eventually getting old and dying, just like everybody else?

What could any of them know of his world, a place of long shadows where he goes to bed with headless corpses and awakens shaking and sick with more questions than answers? Reagan tried to swallow his bitterness, but it stuck in his throat as he watched these people laugh, laugh, laugh.

Bread and circuses, bread and circuses, Reagan thought, as he drank in the club's overdressed appearance. He remembered learning in school that the Roman Empire regularly resorted to pacifying unrest with gaudy distractions. How was Baghdaddy's any different—or for that matter, the whole of Harlem any different? Reagan asked himself. Then it dawned on him. It wasn't the masses who were being showered in deflecting amusement. It was the young wealthy—the only group that could mount a creditable challenge to the old order of things, if it wasn't so busy partying.

No wonder they laughed, Reagan thought. They probably know that when they stop laughing, they'll find themselves grimly installed at the same levers of power their elders are chained to. As if to underscore his thinking, a young blond woman standing inches from his ear erupted into uncontrollable laughter.

Reagan turned, in hopes of staring her into silence. But her delicate features stunned him—not their allure, but in their power to recall a recent memory he had been desperately trying to suppress. The blond was a dead ringer for the serenely dead face of a head Romaro's team had found stuffed in a discarded baby carriage beneath the 125th Street trestle.

Both were pale Lights, the dead one due to a lack of blood and the one in front of Reagan by way of heavy make-up. Either way, they looked like twins, or at least sisters. Reagan felt his chest tighten. He was still trying to forget. His musings were interrupted when the blond turned to him, jabbing a finger so vigorously in his face that a nail scratched his right nostril.

"What the fuck are you looking at, you creepy fat fuck?" she screamed in his face. He could smell the unmistakable aroma of good whiskey and cheap MethPops on her breath.

"Huh?"

"Huh? Huh? I'm *talking* to you, shittrash!"

Reagan was ashamed that he flinched at the verbal battery. *Shittrash?* He said nothing. He wished he could summon projectile vomit and launch it at this screeching siren. Was this a test? He wondered. Two assholes in twenty minutes.

Reagan turned his back to the woman, dropped his shoulder, and plowed his escape through the parting crowd. From behind he could hear the girl and some of her friends. They were, of course, laughing at him.

Their naiveté unnerved him. Their gumption annoyed him. But most of all, their class, which afforded them boulevard-wide margins of error, infuriated him. They had their whole lives ahead of them to debase, abuse, ignore, or exploit anyone they deemed beneath them. It was their lives' work.

Reagan broke the brim of his new fedora until its shadow obscured everything except his thin-lipped mouth and full double chin. He hitched up the waistband of his slacks from where they settled just under the ample swell of his lower belly. He felt a surge from behind as feet began to shuffle along the strip of burgundy carpet leading to the club's entrance. He took another look at the crowd and cursed under his breath.

Reagan passed through without incident. The elite-class club membership the Department had secured for him was apparently in order.

"Good evening, Mr. Reynolds," a reed-thin, olive-skinned man said, stepping forward and bowing slightly before Reagan. "Thank you for selecting Baghdaddy's."

Reagan slowed for a moment only to snort at the charade. Reflexively, he fell in behind a trio of women that seemed to float in a cloud of exotic fragrances and crudely cultivated glamour. Nevertheless, he found himself hypnotized by the supple sway of their hips, each accentuated by the low ride of tightly wrapped skirts on flawless bare skin. When their belly chains occasionally caught the flicker of artificial torchlight, Reagan discovered how easy it was to forget that he was still in Harlem, still in the mid-twenty-first century, still trailing leads in a case that was beginning to terrify him.

The women drifted on, stopping only a few yards later to part a sheer curtain the color of passion fruit and then disappearing with only the swish of silk against silk. Seconds later Reagan followed, stepping through the curtains and into an avalanche of beats, bass, and brass. Reagan felt the music pounding in his chest, in his belly, in his head, long before his ears could make sonic sense of the Persian rocket roll.

His eyes quickly adjusted to the low light. Stretching before him was the familiar billowing heart of Baghdaddy's. From the beginning it was intended to be an adult playground, fashioned to look and feel as if it were some potentate's tent. All the dress up was never to his taste. But the ever-present smell of marijuana was, as it hung low in the club's moist, warm air. Reagan took a deep breath and held it, hoping for a passive high.

Hmm, he thought. *Harlem does have its perks.*

Once seated, Reagan noticed that his membership card indicated that he should double-tap it along his table's edge. When he did, Reagan watched the rectangular tabletop glow into a private viewpanel. Menus for drink, food, and dry refreshments slid into view; there were gambling games and other amusements, too. A window opened to inquire if he would like to run a tab; another, which stated club rules and legalese disclaimers, Reagan closed immediately.

Beats the hell out of the back door, he thought as he browsed the menu.

He sought out Baghdaddy's IC-UC system. From the tabletop VP, he could pull images and sound from the four common areas of the multileveled nightclub. For a premium fee, he could see almost every corner of the upstairs Harlem Harem. And with permission, he could open conversations with anyone who wanted to play.

Since he was on the Department's dime, he thought, he could make unrestricted use of the system as an investigative tool—or at least that could be his cover story. He decided that he better throw in some gratuitous voyeurism—the baser the better—to help make his story more convincing.

Why not start with the nude greeters? Or the caged slave dancers? Or the three juicies he'd followed through the lobby?

Reagan ordered a strong drink, licked his lips, and fingered the IC-UC into a frenzied game of seek and spy. He glanced at his watch. He'd have about ninety minutes before he'd have to meet his informant in the Harem upstairs. For a moment, Reagan's head felt as if it was spinning. With so much wrong going on in the club, he wondered how he'd find the right wrong. But as soon as he noticed Cutter peering at him from behind a curtained wall, he knew he was in a good place for bad things.

Reagan stirred his bourbon and peeked in on a pleasurist plying her trade in an fourth-floor sweet-suite. "Ahhhh…" he sighed after a stinging gulp of the drink, which was cooled by sugared cocaine ice. *Work that Jelli! Work it. Work it good.*

* * * * *

"Dots."

"Whachawantwidmeee?

A small-boned man no larger than a runt schoolboy peered from behind a thick drape. His scar of a mouth hardly moved when he spoke. His icy glare had long grown used to doing most of his talking. The glare was why he was called Cutter. The fact that he ran practically every aspect of Harlem's vast underground economy lent him a stature that far exceeded any muscle and mass that nature may have slighted him. And it didn't hurt that his club, which he started as little more than a front, had grown over the years to be one of the most popular in Harlem.

"Whacha-luknnNat?

Cutter's stare went laser, directing JoË Dots' unfocused gaze to a large mound of man sitting alone at a table near the circular bar.

"Isn't that your inside guy at the Theresa? The dirty dick?"

"Whohe?" Dots asked, as he strained to see through the club's designer darkness.

"Yes. That man," Cutter said, slightly raising his voice.

"No-B," Dots replied, barely moving his big man's head fastened to a bigger man's body. "HeInaTopDollarSquat. NoBheee."

Cutter studied his table's viewpanel under his child-like fingers, which were adorned with Blackish rings. "Looky here. It says that our guest there was formerly with the Department. Oh, shame. A dishonorable discharge fifteen years ago.

"And, oh, you might find this interesting, Dots. It says he is a member of the security staff at the Hotel Theresa. Humor me and look again, Dots."

JoË Dots drew back the plum-colored drapery that obscured the table and turned his shovel-shaped face until he could draw a clear bead on the man who had captured his boss's interest. For longer than Cutter wanted to wait, JoË Dots said nothing. Then with a "Humph!" he fell back into his chair. "YeahMeeeknowum," he said, mush-mouthing bursts of screech-slang. "Howdhegitamemship?"

Cutter spoke softly and clearly. "Invite him over."

JoË Dots nodded, agitating his nest of roiling dreadlocks before he put his beer down with a bang. He peered at Reagan, realizing that he was staring at a dead man who didn't yet realize that his life was over.

Before he stepped away from Cutter's table, JoË Dots dropped his slang and mischievously added, "That's a mighty big, handsome head on his shoulders."

"I bet it's as empty as it is big, too," Cutter said as his lips came as close as they had all evening to a smile. He looked as if he was about to actually laugh, but coughed hard instead.

"More rind than fruit," Cutter said as Dots started toward Reagan's table. "Not worth the effort."

As Dots rose, Cutter grabbed the big man by the sleeve of his Italian-cut suit and pulled him back to the table. "Changed my mind. Watch him. I don't want to see him anywhere near tonight's party. Use as many bodies as you need. Keep him the hell away from the 'Scape. Understand me?"

"No'Scape4ho-dickeee," JoË Dots assured Cutter. "DoneDealeee."

"Good," Cutter continued. "He can stay, for now. But why not scare the shit out of him? Don't beat it out of him this time."

"Pural," Dots rumbled, then smiled. "InI."

Taj rubbed and kneaded a stranger's flesh as his mind retreated to a distant place in his head, some place far from the permanent midnight of a Baghdaddy sweet-suite.

"That feels good, boy," the client moaned as she grabbed a satin pillow and buried her face in it. "Mmmm... just... like... that."

Taj obeyed, trying to ignore the ache in his bony shoulders and the greedy demands of a pampered body that flexed and beckoned his hands to rub harder, deeper.

Taj opened his eyes long enough for the sweet-suite's purple darkness to saturate his vision.

Beneath him was a scrawny, pasty-skinned woman who, like Taj, was only recently out of her teens.

But somehow, in a Möbius twist of fate, he thought, she was privileged and he was poor. As a consequence, she could afford to be the mistress, while he was always the slave. For the last twenty minutes she'd lain on her belly insisting that he massage her back, her thighs. Now she was loosening the towel that covered her ass.

"Boy," she said, with no affection, "I paid for the full treatment. How's your Jelli?"

He cleared his throat. "I have two, mistress. A male and female."

The client turned and slowly sat up, readjusting the towel across her breasts.

"Let me see the Dildojian."

Taj stood and handed the client a fluted glass of plum wine. "Give us a moment," Taj said softly, before sliding back a painted screen that stretched three quarters around a bedroom nook. Less than a minute passed before the client heard music, faint but as intoxicating as the crackle she inhaled from an amulet she wore on a gold thread.

Taj called to her, "My mistress, your desires are our desire."

The woman pulled back the screen and stood in the space. The suite appeared much larger than it could possibly be, a deception deepened by strategic candlelight and designed illusion. The nook was not much larger than the perfectly square platform bed that dominated it. In the bed, beneath gauze-thin blankets, lay Taj, thin and taut and rubbing the bare chest of what appeared to be another client, a large man who, suggested by the tenting of the blanket covering his crouch, held a large promise for the evening.

"Please come. Come in," Taj whispered, still rubbing the chest of the broad-shouldered figure lying next to him. "Join us," Taj begged, speaking more in breaths than voice. "Please."

The woman smiled broadly. She dropped her towel and walked, woozy with anticipation, to the bed. Taj pulled back the blanket so the client could get a better look.

"What-what… what is your Jelli's name?"

"AnJoi," Taj replied, adjusting his own loincloth to ensure that his genitals remain tucked away and fully in compliance with regulations. "I think he likes you."

The client studied the Dildojian's enormous erection. She licked her lips as Taj rubbed oil along its heated, pulsing length. "Yes, look at that. He wants to love you," he said, as if reciting lines from a school play.

Taj ran his hand along the Dildojian's thick neck, his touch prompting it to slowly part its bulging thighs to reveal testicles the size of limes. Taj squeezed a triangular control just beneath its left armpit. It began to gently snake its hips.

The client roughly rubbed her vagina with one hand while stroking Taj's boyish cheek with her other. Without a sound, she slid her hand to Taj's shoulder, then used him to lower herself onto her knees. Very gradually, she adjusted herself over the Jelli—grunting like a feeding sow—and onto the Dildojian's handmade penis, which was hard with electrically activated transpolymers.

Taj sat on the Jelli's chest to face the client, who he embraced with something that might pass for tenderness in the dark. She rested her head on his shoulder as she whimpered, sobbed, shuddered, merging her rhythms with the Dildojian's. Taj rubbed his oiled hands over the client's lower back, her narrow hips, the tops of her thighs, her breasts, while, from time to time, expertly reaching behind him, finding and manipulating discreet controls on the sex machine.

Sensing the moment, Taj initiated an orgasmic sequence that hastened the Dildojian's hips to more furiously meet the client's, stroke for stroke.

Taj closed his eyes, but could not shut out his anxiety. In less than an hour, a detective was going to enter his sweet-suite, and he was not going to be interested in taking a ride on or in a Jelli. The detective was going to want information, dangerous information. The Department left him little choice but to cooperate. If he didn't help, he could lose his job, and perhaps his license.

The client was bucking and screaming above a hunk of neuro-sensors, micro-motors, molded musclewear, and synthskin.

"Ahhhhhhhh... I'm-I'm-I'm!"

"Yes, I know. Come to me. Yesssss." Taj wetly whispered in the client's ear. "Let go of it. Let go. Yes, like that. Oohh..."

Taj kissed his client softly on her cheek, still hot and wet. As he did he spoke in a low, airy voice. "Oh, how we love to love you."

He shot a glance over the client's shoulder to see the time glowing in the lower corner of the bed nook mirror. The detective would be at his door before he could shower the client off him, before he could catch his breath. Taj knew that he had to convince the detective that he was doing his best to be helpful without helping much at all.

The detective was Department, and that scared him. Harder to fool, he thought. He clenched his jaw as he slipped into his virgin silk robe. He had been stupid. He knew he should have never told another pleasurist what he thought he saw after last week's 'Scape. *Could have been fake. It could have belonged to a Jelli*, Taj said to himself, rehearsing the lie.

Then his expression of worry faded into a look of confidence. He watched his client stumble naked toward the suite's shower stall, a woman who was convinced she had just had a good fucking, even an illusion of romance. He was, after all, a pleasurist—a professional conjurer of delicious lies.

17

Collision

HER HEART. IT WAS HER HEART.

ZaNia pressed her fingers into the bumpy ridges of her breastbone and rubbed. The narrow valley of sweat-dampened skin stretched tight over the bony place, one of those places like the spine, the shoulder blades, the kneecaps, the forehead, where the skeleton insists on staying close to the surface. It was a reminder of the framework just beneath the flesh, of a utility of divine design that, like the spines of a snowflake, made her structure remarkably individual. The bony places also reminded her of the longest night to come—when all the bones would emerge, when all that would be left would be the bones.

ZaNia pressed her open palm to her heart and tried to soothe its palpitations.

"Momma. Momma, you all right?"

Imani had seen her mother drift away before. She noticed how ZaNia could disappear into herself in the days just after Army had disappeared. When it was Jae-J.'s turn to vanish, the spells of disconnection became more frequent, sometimes leaving ZaNia almost catatonic before she'd return to herself.

Imani had hoped that now that her mother had her men back, now that the family was whole and under one roof, her roof, she would get better. Not worse. It had been three days, and now they were supposed to be celebrating their reunion. Imani couldn't understand why her mother seemed so listless.

"Nee? What is it?" Jae J. asked, turning away from G-Daddy, leaving him drooling with yet another what's-wrong-with-America argument on his lips.

Only an hour earlier the Justus living room had crackled with dinner chatter. The old dining room table had been set up where the couch usually sat. Food had filled the table, all neatly arranged on the special-occasion tablecloth ZaNia's mother had made when she was a girl. The living room still smelled of stewed chicken and rabbit, steamed carrots and beets, peas and grits and coldwater cornbread. It was the kind of meal not likely to be had again for a long, long time. Plenty of fresh honey bread and chilled dandelion wine was left on the table, inviting the men to nibble and sip as they talked.

ZaNia looked around the living room. She turned her head slowly from side to side. Her eyes glistened with feelings so sweet that she couldn't imagine there were words ripe enough to convey.

"Momma," Army whispered, approaching to kneel at her side. "Tell me what's wrong."

All eyes were on ZaNia.

She began shaking her head again, this time with a closed-mouth smile from which she hummed without melody.

"I'm just happy," ZaNia said, her voice firmer with each word. "I'm just so happy that we are all here, alive and safe. I feel like I'm going to burst. My heart can hardly stand it."

Army squeezed ZaNia's hands and looked into her eyes. He was gripped by how much older his mother's eyes seemed. For a moment he embraced, then dispatched, then embraced again the question: Had the pride that drove him from home cost his mother more than he was prepared to accept?

"I'm fine," ZaNia said, looking up at her son and then at Jae-J. and her father and daughter. "I might of overdone it some with all the cooking. But I'm fine. Go. Go back to your talking. Go ahead Jae. Daddy."

"You sure, baby girl?" G-Daddy asked, rearing up from his seat more in a gesture of concern than any intention of actually leaving his chair.

Jae-J. said nothing but stared at his wife as if she were molded in damp brown sugar.

"Imani," ZaNia said, just short of a shout. "Could you get me a glass of cold water, child?"

Imani hurried to the kitchen. "You want it in your big cup, Mommy?"

"That'll be fine, baby. Just make sure it's got plenty of ice."

Jae-J. cleared his throat and nodded to Army, who nodded back. They looked to G-Daddy, who was motioning that ZaNia needed her rest.

As if on cue, ZaNia piped up. "Don't mind me. I'm going to wash up and go to bed. I've got a lot of sleeping to catch up on."

G-Daddy, Jae-J., and Army each kissed ZaNia goodnight before she stood and shuffled toward her bedroom.

"Tell me again why tearing up the goddamned city and rioting like they did made more than horsefly's sense to do," Jae-J. said as he reared back his chair. "If they don't want SweetBreeze in their water, there are other ways to get it stopped."

G-Daddy smiled to himself as he poured himself another generous glass of dandelion wine. "Like calling their Council member? First thing is that nobody pays attention to 'em. Who even votes anymore?"

"So a riot is the answer?" Jae-J. pressed.

"It was an insurrection," G-Daddy countered.

Army spoke up. "Whatever it was, it was scary as hell. There were times I thought I'd never get out of there alive."

"Lucky you did, boy," G-Daddy said. "The po-lice like to shoot and beat down big negroes like you. Seen 'em do it in L.A. in '92. 'Can't we all just get along?' Hell no!"

"Bullshit," Jae-J. cried. "You can't have a society without order and what happened at City Hall was no fancy insurrection. It was a riot!"

G-Daddy grinned and arched his wiry old eyebrows at Army, who was trying hard not to get drawn into a fight between his grandfather and stepfather.

"There's a *hell* of lot of difference between a riot and an insurrection," G-Daddy said, stopping to roll a joint. "A riot, yo, is a bunch of hoodlums and idiots burning and looting with no purpose. You know what I'm saying? Tulsa and Rosewood and Cincinnati… now those were some riots. But you, yo, don't know nothing about none of that."

"And your argument is?" Jae-J. asked.

"Listen, Jae, you know those people stormed City Hall for a reason, yo, and it didn't have nothing to do with breaking windows and getting an ass beating. They don't want to drink that poison your government's gonna put in the water supply. That SweetBreeze4U2."

Army picked up the thread. "That is some crazy stuff. But I read that it does make a decent defecation deodorant—"

"And piss deodorant, too," Jae-J. injected.

"But it ain't nothing like what the rich, white folks use to make sure their shit don't stink," G-Daddy said.

"That's for damn sure," Jae-J. shouted. "Ever smelled a rich man's toilet? I used to clean 'em. Smells like a fucking rose garden."

"I don't care what they smell like, son," G-Daddy said before lighting his joint. "Yo, that's besides the point. The point is that this SweetBreeze shit is bad, bad news. Besides giving you the shits, yo, I heard on the radio that it turns your fart gas green."

"Green?" Army asked, laughing. "C'mon, G-Daddy. Green? I don't believe that. How?"

"No," Jae-J. added, trying hard not to laugh himself. "I heard something about that too. Like when some bastard cuts one in the subway, wouldn't do him a bit of good to blame the stink on somebody's dirty diaper. Everybody could see for themselves 'cause there'd be a big-ass green cloud coming out of his asshole."

Jae-J. almost fell off his chair laughing. Army and G-Daddy found themselves laughing just as hard. "Now wouldn't that be some shit?" G-Daddy added, between spasms of his herky-jerky laughter.

Jae-J. stopped laughing and looked at his father-in-law and stepson as if their chuckles were suddenly irritating him. "They don't have to drink it. Right. Nobody's forcing them to drink the water."

"What?" Army asked as he noticed a wild look burning in his stepfather's reddening eyes.

"Hold up, yo. We talkin' po people, mostly black and brown like you and me and Army, Jae. Know what I'm saying?" G-Daddy snapped. "Shit, ain't never been no picnic for us in this country. But when government started spending trillions on the T-wars and hardly nothing on education, jobs, housing... damn, black and brown people—"

"They ain't no more black and brown or white or yellow or red people any more, man," Jae J. screamed. He banged the dining room table, rattling empty dishes. "We're just Greater Americans. Some lighter and some darker. That's all."

G-Daddy rolled his eyes.

Army shook his head and felt like a child in the company of men—men who'd had too much drink and smoke.

"Oh, so there's only Lights and Darks because your government says it's so?" G-Daddy roared back. "What my man Reverend C. say? Race still matters, yo."

"The Dark people ain't never going to get anywhere if they keep holding on to all of this black-white bullshit," Jae-J. insisted. "And puh-leeeze don't start talking about slavery and how your reparation check bounced. I don't want to hear it!"

G-Daddy closed his eyes and shook his head. Army bit his tongue. Jae-J. had always been an angry drunk, and he was getting drunker, and angrier, by the minute. Good thing Imani had gone to bed, too. Army's stomach knotted just like it used to when he was a boy, when he had to endure his stepfather's drunken rants.

"Army, what's that energy fabric, the computer-designed stuff used to pull curtains and shit like that?"

"Spun?" he said.

"Yeah, yeah. Spun," G-Daddy said. "Jae, you see all these black people, them Vipers, that wear their hair like a nest of nasty snakes?"

"Yeah. So?" Jae-J. replied.

"Then you seen them at night, when they let their snakes dance."

Jae-J. looked exasperated as he let his forearm slide deep into the table, loudly plowing plates of half-eaten food into a heap.

"What's your fucking point, old man?"

Army wondered, too.

"My point is that our people, yo, are gifted with genius. That when the American Navy left all their metal barrels back in the islands a hundred years ago, back in World War II, what did our Caribbean brothers do?"

Army had to admit to himself that he had no idea what his grandfather was talking about. And he worried that Jae-J. was going to explode with frustration.

"Well, yo, they took them garbage cans turned them into steel drums, pans, and made music—*beautiful* fucking music. Damn skippy, Skippy."

Army smiled.

"And these Vipers, yo, that figured out how to braid this Spun into their dreadlocks, twist them up, and turn them loose," G-Daddy continued. "It's all the same tradition when they make their dreads dance and shake. You know what I mean? Just think where that kind of making something-out-of-nothing smarts could take our people if the Man wasn't always standing on our necks," G-Daddy said, sitting back in his chair with satisfaction lifting the corners of his mouth into a grin. "Black genius! Just think about that."

Jae-J. dismissed this argument with a lazy sweep of his hand. "Waste of time. The ugly motherfuckers should get a job—and a haircut."

"C'mon, man," G-Daddy pleaded. "Niggas gotta represent, gotta stand up for each other."

"I ain't no *niiiiiigger*," Jae-J. screamed, slurring his words. "And you're talking shit, old fool."

G-Daddy laughed, then leaned into the table and pointed at Jae-J.

"So you ain't a nigga? I guess that's why they locked up your son, froze him like a pork chop, then tossed him in the street like last week's leftovers.

"I guess that's why your daughter ain't got no school to go to. She gets her lessons remote control, on some Etchy-Sketchy bullshit that some slick-tongued politicians had the nerve to call a S.C.U.L.E. What that stand for, Army?"

Startled, Army spoke up: "Student-Controlled Universally Linked Educator."

G-Daddy leaned toward Jae-J. "You ain't a nigga? Then, yo, tell me what you thought you was when they were cracking nappy heads all around, when they herded you into that church basement and told you you couldn't leave until they were damn good and ready to let you leave? You's a nigga, just like me and everybody in this house, Mr. Justus," G-Daddy whispered before he fell back into his chair. He licked his dry lips as if tasting victory.

Jae-J. gazed through half-closed eyelids at a roach that crawled slowly across the windowless wall. He started to speak, but didn't.

Army cleared his throat. "I think G-Daddy has a point," he said tentatively. "You know how the police like to ride young Darks, loading their U.I.D. cards with silly charges. By the time they're old enough to look for decent work, their security ratings are so low they can't leave their neighborhoods to take a job. No one will hire them. So what do they do? Most of them stay in the neighborhood and get in trouble, get caught, and get their U.I.D.s even more restricted."

Jae-J. whirled around in his chair to stare into his stepson's open face.

"What... what do you know, boy?" Jae-J. asked, moving only his lips. "You won your high-falutin' education in a lottery, and the only work you do on that fancy job of yours is lick your boss's ass. Oh, right. Can't do that no more 'cause you cut her fuckin' head off."

"What?" Army said in a voice so frail that it shamed him.

"Hey, hey, hey, hey," G-Daddy yelled.

"You heard me," Jae-J. said, glaring at Army through one open eye. "What was wrong? You didn't like the way she fucked you?"

"Hey, man," G-Daddy said, throwing up his arms as if to call time out. "What's your problem? You know your boy ain't no murderer!"

"He *ain't* my boy," Jae-J. hollered and pounded the table with his fists. "And *you* are my problem. All you fucking people in my fucking house is my problem. You understand me, G?"

Army felt his mouth go dry as he watched G-Daddy retreat inside himself.

No one spoke for a few seconds. Army's heart beat so hard he crossed his arms over his chest to ensure it wouldn't leap out. Memories spewed like vomit, bitter and stinking. In the brief, uneasy silence, he found himself freezing time and digging up memories he had tried for two years to bury.

It was that night again. His mother's birthday.

Jae-J. had been away scoring spare parts for the apartment building's failing boiler. ZaNia and her best friend, April-Mae June, had cooked all day, and the apartment smelled like a hungry man's heaven.

Army always loved his mother's birthdays, even more than his own. And as long as Jae-J. was away, he knew the day's celebration would be certain to be wonderful. That late September afternoon, he sat on his bed watching his mother and April-Mae dance in the living room to Bob Marley music playing loudly on the Quadbox. He marveled at how expressive his mother's movements were, despite her long, hard life as a Maternal and the many surgeries and procedures near-permanent pregnancy necessitated.

ZaNia always refused to tell him how many children had passed through her rented womb. Only a few, she once told him, shared any of her genetic material. For the most part, they were other people's children, people unable or unwilling, to carry and deliver their own offspring. They were mostly people wealthy enough to pay a Maternal Order for this very expensive service.

But everything changed, she was fond of telling Army, when she was impregnated with him. She felt it in her hips that he was more than another job. She knew he was special and he was more hers than the client's. In a few months, the client ordered that the fetus be aborted because it turned out to be male, after she'd specifically ordered a daughter.

ZaNia quit the Order rather than abort this last fetus. Army knew the story so well. ZaNia had the baby, had him. The actual day of his birth was inconsequential, Army came to think. His true beginning, he realized at an early age, began with the birth of his mother.

For months he had been searching for just the right expression for his adoration of his mother. Less than a week before ZaNia's birthday, he was sure he had found the perfect present in the back of a Harlem tourist shop. It was a double fist-sized heart made of rare glass. It was filled with a red fluid that absorbed light throughout the day and gave it back at night as a warm, amber glow.

He had wrapped the heart the night before and hid it in the back of the closet he shared with G-Daddy. Army had planned to give her the heart after dinner, after the birthday cake and happy birthday songs. Army remembered how he was filled with sparkling anticipation.

Then Jae-J. came home, stumbling drunkenly through the door. By the time he reached his late teens, Army came to discern an explanation for the pattern Jae-J. established with nearly all of the family's festive occasions. During times of giving, he forbade anyone from giving him anything, and he got drunk when anyone expected him to give them anything.

But this day, Army remembered, had been magic—until Jae-J. came home and ruined everything, chasing off April-Mae with his brutishness so fast she forgot to take her slice of homemade birthday cake with her. Army wanted to retreat to his bedroom, like he usually did when his stepfather came home drunk. But this time he had decided to stay at his mother's side.

He could feel the hurt building up inside her even as she tried to smile her way through her torment.

"You know every birthday is another birthday closer to your last one," Jae-J. told ZaNia as she busied herself to get his dinner on the table. "It's the worms that should be celebrating birthdays.

"Happy feeding time to you," Jae-J. sang loudly and badly off key.

Army didn't realize it at the time, but he was standing in front of Jae-J., shaking his head as he looked down on him. Army was seated at the table where the birthday cake and Army's unopened gift sat.

"What you looking at, boy?" Jae-J. roared at Army.

Army bit his lip before his answered. "Nothing."

"What you say?"

"I said I ain't looking at nothing," Army said, a challenging edge in his voice. "Nothing at all."

ZaNia called from the kitchen doorway. "Come here, Army. I need you in here."

"Yeah, damn near thirty years old and still running to your mammy's apron strings," Jae-J. hissed. " Help her get my dinner on the table. Been working all day. I'm hungry."

With his last word, Jae-J. wobbled to his feet and used both arms to sweep everything from the table to the floor in a sickening crash.

Army and ZaNia came running into the living room, their eyes and hearts unwilling to accept what they were seeing. The birthday cake sat in a pink and white heap on the floor, its icing splattered over the birthday cards and festive paper plates and cups. And just beyond the pile of cake, Army saw his neatly wrapped present to his mother. Half of the crumpled box was soaked through with a bloody fluid. It took weeks to wash the glowing stain from the old floor.

Army turned to see Jae-J. holding his knife and fork in his hands as if nothing had happened. He looked back to see his mother stooped over, picking her birthday cards out of the mess.

"You know, you are an asshole," Army screamed at his stepfather. "You're an asshole, you drunken son-of-a-bitch!"

"You lost your goddamned mind, boy?" Jae-J. screamed back, the cutlery still in his hands. "I ain't going to be disrespected, not in my own house."

"You give respect, you get respect," Army said, taking a step closer to Jae-J. But ZaNia grabbed him by his T-shirt before he could take another.

"Look here," Jae-J. shouted. "I don't care who's your momma. You take another step closer to me and I'll open up your belly with this fucking knife here."

Jae-J. held up the serrated steak knife to emphasize his threat. "Ain't nobody too big to taste their own blood, and I ain't too small to make you taste it."

Army tried to take another step toward his stepfather and realized that his mother was still holding his T-shirt. He turned to see her teary face grimacing in anguish.

"Don't," she whispered up at him. "Please don't. Please."

* * * * *

Army opened his eyes to see G-Daddy stretched out on the living room couch, his ridiculously large headphones cupping his ears. But his memories kept washing back to that night, which ended with Jae-J. passed out on the table, his outstretched right arm resting in an upturned bowl of cold mashed potatoes.

Remembering Jae-J. that way reminded Army that Jae-J.'s worst punishment was, simply, being Jae-J. Then his musings ended in a crash that shook the apartment's ceiling and flickered the living room's lights.

Army and Jae-J. were the first to reach the electro-bolted door to the roof. G-Daddy, trailing more than a flight of stairs behind, could hear them pounding their bodies against its dented, steel stubbornness before it gave.

"G-Daddy! G-Daddy!" It was Army, and the shrillness of his voice straightened G-Daddy's back with fright. "Stay where you are. Don't come up to the roof."

Jae-J., sobered by the dash into the night air, joined in. "Listen to him and stay down there! You hear me?"

"Go back and make sure Momma and Imani stay in the apartment," Army called again. G-Daddy, looking up the flight of stairs, could see his grandson silhouetted in the doorway. He couldn't make out his features but he could read his defiant stance. "Go back and make sure, make sure they don't come up here. I'll explain later."

"Cool, cool. I'm going, but somebody, yo, better tell me what the fuck is going on," G-Daddy said as his voice receded and then disappeared.

The rooftop was bumpy and uneven under Army's and Jae-J.'s feet, difficult to walk on in the dark. But Jae-J. was reluctant to activate the roof lighting until they knew what they were dealing with. He didn't want the attention it would draw, and then the need to explain to the building's maintenance board why he'd flipped on the big lights in the middle of the night. Instead, he grabbed a flexiflash he kept on a rack behind the door.

Whatever had fallen or broken loose had landed somewhere near ZaNia's animal pens on the southern edge of the roof, Jae-J. thought, as he slowly followed his ears to a great commotion of clucking and scratching coming from that direction. Army was crouching, inching closer toward the same sounds of frightened, confused chickens and rabbits.

A thin beam of bluish light went out ahead of the men, feeling about here and there like the tip of a blind man's cane. As the men stepped forward, the light began picking up clumps of feathers, some of them held together by globs of blood; one mass of feathers still held fast to a hunk of freshly torn flesh.

"Over there," Army said, pointing to his left.

Jae-J. aimed the light where his stepson motioned, slowly swinging its fading length until it stopped on a section of ribbed muscle spilling purple and green entrails. Two slender bones rose out of the mass at an angle and ended in snapped stumps.

"What's that?" Army asked.

"It's some kind of fur... rabbit, I think."

"Damn," was all Army could say.

The sounds of the chickens were almost deafening as the men walked less cautiously toward the pens, stepping over dead animals along the way. Jae-J. handed the flexiflash to Army, who watched him pull away broken and bent pens. He could see something large, something that did not belong on the roof, lodged beneath a pile of upturned cages.

"A little closer," Jae-J. whispered. "Hold the light higher. Steady... steady."

Army obeyed, adding nervously, "Momma's going to be upset when she finds out so many of her good stewing animals been wasted like this."

Jae-J. puffed and snorted as he yanked away cages to get at the object. Both of them could see it clearly now. It was a box, taller than wide and shaped like some sort of capsule. It was black, expertly engineered, and about the size of an old-fashioned hatbox.

"What the hell is it?" Jae-J. asked as he reached out to further examine its military-green, metal skin.

"I don't know," Army replied. "Looks like some kind of medical canister, maybe."

"It's kind of heavy," Jae-J. reported as he began to yank it clear of the pile of ruined cages.

Army joined him, running his hands carefully over its surface, feeling for buttons or hidden latches.

"There're no markings on it," Army said calmly. "I doubt it's hazardous."

"Where do you think it came from?" Jae-J. asked, looking up at the starless sky and then quickly surveying neighboring rooftops.

"Well, damn sure nobody tossed it all the way up here," Army said as he tilted the canister back and felt beneath it. Something clicked, and a silvery centerline appeared on the canister. "But any kid with a toy hoverplane could have remoted up here from another rooftop."

"Fuck! What's that smell?" Jae-J. asked, turning his head away from the stench pouring from the vertical crack in the canister.

"Smells like bad meat," Army said as he fingered the now icy crack, urging it to open wider.

"Don't. Don't open it, Army!"

Too late. As Army tried to pull his freezing fingers out they triggered some sort of release that sprung the canister wide open, spilling its contents onto the roof with a hollow thud. Both men dropped to their hands and knees to search in the dark.

"Where's the light!? Get me the light," Jae-J. whispered loudly. "I think I feel something down by my feet."

Army pulled the snaking light loose and aimed it down at his stepfather's feet.

"What?" Jae-J. asked, afraid to show that fear was beginning to paralyze him.

"What?" Army asked, then commanded: "Look!"

Army moved the smelly clump around with the head of the flexi.

"It's a fucking head," Jae-J. screamed from the back of his throat. "A goddamned, fucking head."

Army spoke quietly. "Kattrel. It's Kattrel's head."

"What the fuck, Army?" Jae-J. whispered. "Why in the hell is your boss's head up here on my roof? Talk!"

"I don't know. I don't know," he said as he nervously rubbed his hands over his scalp. "What—you don't think I stashed it up here! Look at the cages, Jae-J. Somebody dropped it here. You heard the crash just like I did."

"Who is going to believe that bullshit?" Jae-J. asked. "Dropped from where? Fell off Santa's sleigh?"

Army drew his face nose-to-nose with his stepfather's. "Let's start with what you believe. Okay?"

Jae-J. glared back. "It ain't going to mean shit what I believe when the police swarm this place."

Army turned away. "You're right. Whoever dropped Kattrel's head here wants me found with it."

Army turned off the light and sat on a broken crate. He blew his breath into his cupped hands, then looked over to his stepfather, who was pulling up an empty cage to heave himself onto. A long moment passed.

"Somebody wants to make me Kattrel's killer. No telling what they'll do next. I gotta go." Army said. "Jae-J. I'm sorry, I'm so sorry. I don't think it's going to be safe here—for you, Momma, everybody."

Jae-J. reached out in the darkness and grabbed his stepson by the shoulder. "Don't you worry about us. I got this. But you? Start runnin'—*now*. We'll be okay."

Army looked out over Harlem. It was an unusually quite night. He could hear a few sirens in the distance, someone's japjams playing loudly from a distant window.

"Tell Momma that I love her, and I will contact her as soon as I can," Army said softly. "Tell her not to worry too much. You know it isn't good for her heart."

"Wait," Jae-J. said.

Army watched him walk a few yards and then melt into the darkness. Moments later, Jae-J. returned, carrying a dusty old lockbox under his arm.

"Take this," Jae-J. said as he lifted bricks of old-century currency out of the opened box. "Here's about $30,000 in paper," Jae-J. said, stacking the money in Army's overflowing palms. "I know it isn't much, but this stuff ain't like credits. It's hard to trace. Paper gold on the streets. I keep some on hand for black-market parts this old building couldn't live without."

Overwhelmed, Army found it difficult to speak. So he didn't. He shook his head and hugged Jae-J. tight, slapping his back all the while.

"I better go now." Army whispered in his ear before kissing him on the cheek. "Go." Army repeated the word, saying it as much to himself as to his stepfather: "Go."

The slam of the roof's rumpled metal door shook loose the panic that Army had been struggling to keep locked away in some useless part of him. His fears were clawing their way out of his head, and with them, wretched eruptions of confusion and desperation. So much had happened so fast.

If he stole a car, perhaps he could make it back to his apartment undetected, he began to tell himself. But then what? He was still a person of interest. His New Rochelle apartment was probably already crawling with local cops. Plus, he was no car thief. His only chance was Harlem. But he would need a weapon. No, he needed a change of clothes. No. He needed to get a hold of himself. Breathe. No. Think. Think!

Army realized, standing dumbly in the night still gripping the bricks of money Jae-J. had given him, that his first priority was to get away from this building. Draw all attention he could away from his family. He had put them all in danger. The bare-assed fact of this made him want to die. For a moment, longer than he had ever imagined possible, Army considered throwing himself off the roof, beating his demons—inner and outer—by plunging into an eternal, dreamless sleep.

He shook his head and slowly began pushing his panic back, squeezing and folding it into ever smaller recesses of himself. In its absence, Army felt suddenly clear-eyed and clear-headed. He dropped to his knees and began stacking the money into more manageable bundles.

Then a spill of yellowish light washed over him from behind and quickly pooled around him. The roof door was open, again. Army tried to readjust his eyes as he turned into the doorway's glare. Before he could demand who was there, he saw ZaNia step into the darkness that mopped up the light as she closed the old door behind her.

"No, Momma," Army said weakly.

ZaNia shook her head as she slowly closed the distance between her and her son, still on his knees amid the ruined animal pens. She didn't say a word; nor did Army, who could feel himself trembling with sorrow and shame.

When ZaNia reached him, Army reached out and encircled his mother's hips with his muscled arms and held her the way she had when he'd been a frightened little boy. Even over the Harlem night noise, Army could hear her, hear his mother humming the melody. In his mind's ear he could hear the refrain: "Everything's gonna be alright."

He began to cry as he felt her cradle his face and kiss him on the top of his head.

"Momma," he said hoarsely as she began to step away from him, "I've got to go."

"I know," ZaNia said in a voice heavy with sadness. "I know you do. Just come back to us when you can. Stay safe, Army. Promise me that." Army nodded as he got to his feet. Mother and son hugged in a way that only two who were once one could. Then, when Army permitted himself to open his teary eyes, she was gone.

He took a deep breath and returned to his knees and the money he'd need to escape.

18

Hat Trick

ABUMP OF AIR FLATTENED BENEATH THE SPOON-SHAPED UNDER-carriage of the hoverplane as it gently banked northeast into midnight. For thirty minutes it had been following the inky undulations of the Hudson River fifteen thousand feet below.

Carmaya drifted near the surface of a nap. She smiled and squeezed Philip's hand. He turned for a moment from the seatback viewpanel on which he half-watched an old movie and a vidi he had shot hours earlier, half a planet away. Grudgingly, he took occasional notice of a stock ticker gliding along the VP's lower edge. The Saturday-morning markets in Tokyo, Singapore, and Johannesburg were down. He looked away.

"How are you feeling, Carma?"

Without opening her eyes Carmaya wrinkled her new pixie nose and sang her reply.

"Marrrr-vel-ous-ly... happy... hon."

"Me too."

He softly rubbed Carmaya's hand and felt overcome with love for her. A silly thought tugged at him: Why had he hesitated so long before accepting her marriage proposal? He was a different man then, a less trusting one.

A vidi of Carmaya cracking coconuts on the beach filled the upper left quadrant of the viewpanel. His eyes smiled at the recent frolic. The sight of her again in that cotton sundress stoked memories of their last afternoon on the island.

The trip had lived up to their considerable expectations, Philip thought. Despite their work-hard-play-harder lives, he was certain that they required a thorough getaway. Philip had been able to clear his calendar at the commodities cluster for three full weeks. He hadn't even carried a link while they were away. It was their fifth anniversary, and for months he and Carmaya had been conspiring to escape New York, escape the ceaseless, frenetic pulse that enslaved a certain class of people that seemed to outsiders to possess exactly what the world craved: the freedom to be free.

The hoverplane dipped its starboard wing and sliced downward through dissolving wisps of cloud cover. Harlem materialized, rising up like a pincushion of church spires and minarets, offices and hotel towers—and lights, so many lights, Philip thought, as he tried to remember the flame dance of torches that lit the open sands surrounding the private bungalow they'd left behind on the Indian Ocean.

"Philip and Carmaya... I hope I'm not disturbing you two, but in a few minutes we will be touching down at D.N.D."

Carmaya opened her eyes and nodded to the viewpanel a couple of feet in front of her window seat.

"Very good, Skipper," Philip said, holding eye contact with the hoverplane's captain on the VP. He lifted himself a few inches in his deeply cushioned seat and looked over the craft. Its sleek cabin balanced an elegant efficiency with a luxurious array of pampering conveniences.

Philip was pleased with himself for wrangling one of the executive hovers in the company's fleet so he and his wife could make the J.F.K.-to-David N. Dinkins hover hop in solitary peace. Besides the captain, there was a steward onboard who was tidying up the aft lounge and adjoining galley.

A company limousine was waiting at the port to whisk them to the Hotel Theresa. Philip had reserved a week in the honeymoon suite to ease the transition from the island to Manhattan island. They were scheduled to check out on Chinese New Year's Day.

"What are you looking at, love?"

Carmaya was eyeing the five white-bright ovals that marked the landing decks suspended over the Harlem side of the Hudson. "We're almost home, Phil." Her voice was raspy with sleep and disappointment.

Philip stuck out his thin bottom lip and arched his sandy brows. Speaking in his most impish voice, he panted "So, where are we going for summer vacation?"

"Hmm." Carmaya playfully replied as she tapped her forehead. "Somewhere nice."

"You can bet your life on it."

They hugged and laughed as the hoverplane shuddered and then eased to a landing. The captain's door slid open and a smiling, silver-haired pilot made small talk as he directed them to a canopied, portable escalator that self-assembled as the hatch swung open.

"Thank you again and bye-bye now," the captain repeated as he waved gleefully until the escalator retracted and the hatch slammed and sealed.

On the ground, a short, barrel-chested man trotted up to the couple and shouted something over the din of the hovercraft throttling up to return to its New Jersey hanger.

Philip frowned. "Where's Darrell?"

"Couldn't make it. Sick. I new driver. First day on job."

"So what's your name?"

The driver turned away from Philip to scream orders at porters struggling to cram Philip and Carmaya's luggage into the idling limousine's trunk. The black, six-wheeled suprastretch glittered eight yards away. The driver ran ahead and was now vigorously gesturing for the couple to join him in the limousine. Its rear gull doors were opening with the hydraulic grace of a mechanical bird about to take flight.

Carmaya was wearing only a raw silk pants suit and complained to Philip that she was cold in the river breezes. They clutched each other at the waist and ran clumsily to the wing-like doors. Philip suppressed a curse. He didn't want to upset Carmaya. But in his head he was shouting, *WELCOME BACK TO NEW YORK FUCKING CITY.*

The driver was already waiting behind the wheel with one leg inside the car and one leg out, an unshined shoe tapping his impatience on the tarmac.

"Hurry, hurry," the driver said without apology. "Got to rattle and roll."

"You could help us," Philip yelled, a little too loudly, over the rumble of hoverplanes, shuttle trams and taxis. Carmaya held tightly to her husband's arm when they reached the limousine. He couldn't stop thinking, *What's this guy's problem?*

The instant the couple reached the suprastretch, the driver sprang from the car without a word. He practically snatched Philip's and Carmaya's small carry-on bags from them. Before the couple could protest, the driver tossed the bags in the trunk, leaped back into the car, slammed his door, and closed the trunk from a dash switch. They climbed into the backseat, fuming.

"Driver!" Philip tapped at the translucent partition that separated the passenger section from the driver's. A viewpanel flickered into poor focus in the partition. It was the driver, a mud-colored man with shaggy reddish hair and lips, Philip thought, that seemed ill-designed to ever completely close. Philip thought the driver looked about thirty, his own age, but he reminded himself that with these people it was hard to be certain. The chauffeur's cap shaded much of the rest of his face, which was further obscured by the limousine's badly functioning VP. The rapidly overlapping small slights and confusion were unnerving Philip almost as much as the pained expression Carmaya wore as she stared silently out the limousine's deeply tinted window. The car's engine growled and the car lurched.

"You going to the Theresa in Harlem? Yes?"

"Yes, we have people expecting us there," Philip white-lied while he tried to place the odd man's even odder accent.

Carmaya shot Philip a look and then reached for his hand. He was ashamed that it was cold. "I should have worn some gloves out there."

Carmaya shook her head. Philip knew she didn't buy the line. He was getting scared, and his fear grew as it became harder to conceal.

"What did you say your name was again?" Philip asked the faulty VP.

The driver said nothing as he steered the limousine out of the hoverport parking lot.

"I said, WHAT IS YOUR NAME?"

"Excuse," the driver said. "I sometimes get turned around 'round here. I want concentrate. What you say?"

"YOUR NAME?"

"Oh, it is Tito."

"Like the Old Century leader, the head of Yugoslavia?" Philip asked, struck that this man's family could have been versed enough with old European history to even know such a name.

"Naw. Don't know that guy. It was grandfather's name and he got it because his father worked for a fella with same name. I think he singer... YES... sang with his brothers. Very rich."

"I see," Philip said, trying hard to relax as the limousine inched through traffic toward the 125th Street exit sign.

Carmaya screamed. "You idiot! You missed the exit!"

"What?!" Philip twisted around just in time to watch the 125th Street exit recede into the night.

"Look what you made me do!" the driver protested. "All this talking, talking, talking."

"Hey," Philip cautioned. "Calm down and just loop back. Okay?"

"Philip, let's get out and call a taxi," Carmaya pleaded. "Philip, listen to me!"

"It'll be fine, Carma," he said, trying to reassure her as well as himself.

"I loop around," the driver said. "Relax."

The limousine powered onto Riverside Drive and merged into speeding southbound traffic. Carmaya and Philip watched from the spacious passenger compartment. Then suddenly everything inside went black—the VP, the sparkle of courtesy lights sprinkled along the ceiling and edges of the floor. The car vibrated and began to slow.

A small sliding door in the driver's partition opened with a snap.

"Sorry. Car trouble. Bad fuel cell. Really sorry."

"Car trouble?" Philip asked incredulously.

"Philip, let's call a taxi," Carmaya renewed her plea, but this time with a weaker voice.

"Not to worry," the driver said. "I can pull over there and get help."

As the limousine slowed, it swerved to take an exit that wound down to a small, abandoned parking lot below the highway and near the high grass at the river's edge. Philip had no intention of waiting there with his wife until help arrived. He reached for the limousine's link to call a cab, but was horrified to discover that it was dead, like all the other power-driven systems in the car.

"Carma, let me use your link to call the cab."

She looked panic-stricken. "It's in my bag. And my bag is in the goddamned trunk," she cried as she dug her perfectly manicured nails into her husband's bare forearm. "And—and my taserspray… It's in there too."

"Quiet. He'll hear you," Philip whispered.

"You don't think this is some kind of robbery? A kidnapping?"

"No. I just think this guy is incompetent. Think about it. There are lots of easier ways to rob a couple returning from abroad. Stay calm."

A flash of white light burst across the limousine's rear window. Philip jerked to look for its source.

"See, it's a wrecker coming to help," Philip said brightly.

The limousine came to a stop on a surface that suggested concrete and gravel, judging by the crunch the tires made when the engine died. Philip tried to listen to the driver when the wrecker pulled next to the limousine.

"Relax. Going to be okay now," the driver said, pushing his ill-shaped lips through the hatch in the partition. The driver killed the limousine's lights, and the wrecker's driver did the same.

The darkness unsettled Philip and Carmaya, who could hear their driver release the car's hood, then open his door and walk to the front of the limousine. Only muffled talk. Carmaya tried the windows and found that without electricity, they would not budge. Philip yanked at the door releases and confirmed the same was true for them.

"We just have to wait here until they repair the problem," Philip said. But his worried expression discounted any consolation his words may have conveyed. Carmaya stared straight ahead and sat on her hands to keep them from trembling so hard. Philip's eyes swept the passenger compartment for anything that could be used for a weapon—in case he was wrong.

"Listen," Philip said.

"Yes, I hear it."

The sound of men and the familiar buzz and bang of tools were ringing out from the front of the limousine, as well as from beneath it. The car started and the driver shouted over the revving engine that they would soon be on their way. A second later, the VP and lights flickered on.

Philip slapped his knees in relief. "See, look. Even the link works," he said pointing the reactivated communicator toward his wife.

Carmaya worked up a lopsided half-smile.

"Please call a taxi now, right now," she said in a tiny voice.

At that instant Philip and Carmaya heard the crunch of several pairs of feet approaching both sides of the passenger compartment. The doors unlocked simultaneously and flew open. The driver peered inside on Carmaya's side and two beefy, dark-skinned men leaned inside next to Philip. For a moment he thought he vaguely recognized the two men. All of them were holding tools, but none of the tools appeared greasy and automotive, but rather shiny, almost surgical.

"Phil-ip?" Carmaya cried softly. Her eyes were wet and open wide.

The driver spoke first. "You can thank me later, but at this moment we are in a bit of a hurry. Plus we want to give you both something nice." Philip was struck that the driver's bumbling manner had vanished, along with his nondescript accent.

The driver grabbed Carmaya, roughly pushing her down to her knees and to the car's floor, clamping a smoldering hand over her nose and mouth as her body crumbled into submission.

In a split second, the wrecker's two crewmen turned to Philip, one man wrestling him to the floor while the other held two hands over his nose and mouth. As the limousine's doors quickly closed, Philip struggled in what were now extremely close quarters. He watched helplessly, between the fingers of one of his captors, as the driver ripped his wife's jacket and blouse away from her neck. He could feel hands clawing at his own shirt collar, popping his shirt's buttons.

"Hold them still," a voice from behind him shouted.

Philip felt something cold and curved being pressed hard against the back of his neck. He smelled antiseptics.

His body tensed so hard that he bit his tongue. Three sharp jolts and his muscles loosened; he could feel his own urine running hot against his pant leg. He could not move. His sight was failing. Everything was growing blurry and dark.

Philip strained to see Carmaya. He couldn't find her, although he knew she had to be only inches away. He could hear men moving quickly in the cramped compartment. He could hear the clinking of metal instruments, the beeps of electronics. He could smell more antiseptics. Then he heard the driver speak.

"Get me a hat box for the man. Give him another jolt for good measure."

Closer now.

"Like I was saying, Phil," the driver said speaking so close that his nose occasionally bumped Philip's. "You can thank me later. Right now I'm about to give you and your lovely wife something really nice. A gift… A timeless gift that's always in season, always in fashion." He laughed. "I'm about to give you—drum roll, maestro. I'm about to give you both im-mor-tal-ity. But cha-gotta die first."

Philip never heard the last word. His consciousness burst like a soap bubble. But somewhere between a clock's tic and toc, Philip's mind eked out a final thought: *Fucking bastards.*

He remembered where he'd first seen the wrecker's crew.

19

GottaRun

TOO BULKY, ARMY SHOUTED IN HIS ACHING HEAD. STILL TOO BULKY.
He could feel his back damp with sweat in the cold night as he wrestled with the uncooperative horsehide duster G-Daddy insisted that he take. *Funny old man*, Army allowed himself, thankful to be thinking of anything except the journey he knew laid before him.

Got to calm down. "Think. Be smart," he whispered to himself on the tarry roof of his stepfather's building. He realized that he had to find a fuller measure of courage than he had ever possessed before if he wasn't going to be captured or killed before sunrise.

He took a deep breath and began to quell the trembling in his long, slender fingers. Clawing clumsily at the bricks of paper money Jae-J. had given him was not going to help. *Think.* He had to find a way to pack away the bundles of paper money into the full-length coat without drawing attention to himself. *Think. Think.*

Army was glad Jae-J. had already raced back to the apartment. He didn't need a security cam to see his stepfather ordering the family to take only its essentials, escaping into Harlem back alleys, getting as far away from Claremont Avenue as they could before dawn brought its glare of scrutiny upon them. Army wished he could go with them: Be a kid again, let Jae-J. make all the crucial decisions, let his mother wrap her big, soft arms around him and soothe away his terrors.

He flicked another gaze over his shoulder. Yes. He was alone and shoving the last stack of hundreds into his pants pocket when his stomach knotted and he doubled over with dry heaves.

Blood!

Was that blood running down his face? His face and neck were suddenly hot, wet. Sticky.

Had some Department sniper already heat-sighted him and silently squeezed off a micro-explosive shell in his face? He had seen something recently on the Weave about how Spook-Ops snipers were using new munitions—tiny, smart shells that soft-pierce some sorry soul's cranium, confirm the culprit's identity, and when satisfied, detonate with deadly finality.

Army felt nauseous, short of breath, and unsteady even on his knees. He clasped his face in his hands. The ache in his head pounded harder. It felt like the very seams that held his mind together were bursting apart. *Don't let it end like this.*

Then Army tore his hands away from his face. There was, to his surprise, no blood. In the faltering light of the dying flexiflash curled up at his feet, Army saw only tears, sweat, and mucus shimmering on his upturned palms. He began to sob.

Armstrong… Armstrong, you bitch-ass little nigger, he heard his grandfather's voice saying in his head. He climbed to his feet and, still whimpering, struggled into his coat. He whispered as if he were trying to remember long-forgotten lyrics to a favorite song. "Focus. Focus." He crushed the flexiflash under his boot and stepped to the stairway door. "Focus over fear. Focus over fear. Focus."

As Army descended, his plan began to solidify. He knew that, just like his family, he first had to get out of Harlem. Whoever had planted Kattrel's head on the roof certainly must have alerted authorities to its whereabouts, and there were certain to be accusing fingers pointed straight at him.

Army realized he couldn't afford to simply take the money and run. He'd have to run smart; he'd have to know who he was really running from—for damn sure, he thought, not only the police.

Oooh.

More than ever, he thought, he had to find that pleasurist from Chinese New Year. He was convinced she was the key.

He pounded his weight into the apartment building's back service door. It opened with a hallow CHA-JUNK! He slipped through, stumbling into Harlem's black embrace.

"A little more time. Okay?"

For the last half hour, Army had been seated in the rear of the Black Star

Coffee Shop and Cafe. It was little more than a dingy crack in the wall. Its coffee was thick, strong, and cheap. Whenever he went there, looking for Harlem ghosts, the place always smelled to him like old urine and cheap air fresheners, but it was an odor that he found reassuringly human.

Hotel workers, pleasurists, and Vipers frequented this place, which was always loud with muffled conversations. It was close to some of Harlem's biggest hotels and the cafe's management seemed to welcome their kind even more than their business. Tourists steered clear. A little too authentic, perhaps, Army mused.

He entertained himself with the cafe's two-panel picturegraph menu, dotted with neat, tiny rows of pictures of food and drink. Very little of it carried any type. There was a smattering of English, some Spanish and an occasional Chinese character sprinkled around icons of steamy noodle dishes. A stick-on icon of a small coffee cup and icons of two slices of toast with a picture of a pat of butter noted $10 Credit $6 A.U.C. (American Union Currency). He knew that he could dine here all week on an old, U.S. $100 bill—without questions or second looks. He regularly popped glances over the edge of his upturned menu to the cafe's wrap-around, front window.

But even with such a vantage point, Army found his attention wandering, fixating on the most inane details. The jittery ceiling light over his head seemed to be flashing in code. There was definitely a pattern, Army was convinced, until the light sputtered and went dim and as dumb as he felt.

Army looked up to stare into the face of a waitress who only vaguely looked in his direction. Even when he ordered, the waitress looked blankly ahead, as if his words were of no more value to her than the sound of spilled silverware. She pointed at the menu and then the reader, obscured in a cluster of sweeteners, creamers, and spice sticks. Army inserted the menu into the reader and listened to his order confirmation as it beamed itself to the woman's waitress pad. With that she shook her head dismissively and ambled off.

He was grateful that the waitress engaged in none of the social gestures that minute by minute confirm human identity. She'd hardly acknowledged he was even there. *Fine*, Army thought. After all, he reminded himself, he was trying to recast himself as a shadow. And who passes pleasantries with a shadow? Army knew all too well that as he sat in the Black Star, his name and face was likely being added to the millions of others who would be making the morning's Hunt List.

Surely his FU-Blu card had already called, and he had not pinged it back to assure his keepers that he was precisely where he was supposed to be. Soon, very soon, Army realized, the Department would be coming for him. Nonetheless, he found himself settling into the kind of ease that prizefighters conjure just before they step into the ring to hurl fury at one another.

Army scanned a full half-block cross-section of 125th Street. It was an angled sweep of grand hotels, modest storefronts, and stoops darkly aglow in street lamps beneath a low-hanging sliver of moon. Army smiled when his gaze returned a third time in as many seconds to a brownstone's colonnaded entrance—its cascading, steep-set steps, where he first saw Oooh.

How quickly so much of his life had been harshly reshuffled: no job, no home, no woman, and soon, if he was not more careful than he had ever been, no life.

He studied the street swarmed with pump bikes, scoots, and cell-cycles. It was busy, too, with tourists and traders and bottom-feeders eager to lap up whatever sap of crime and commerce dripped their way. He closed his eyes and rubbed his temples with the knuckles of his thumbs. His headache was subsiding yet his head still felt heavy and foreign. Before he could draw open his eyelids, he heard a cha-cha-chink and felt a slight tremor of his tabletop. He smelled the coffee before he saw it. The squareish backside of the waitress receded toward another patron.

Where is she? Army asked as he slurped the coffee before swallowing the gulp whole and hot. Two pleasurists were sitting on the wide, concrete banisters of the stoop where Army had hoped to find Oooh. The steps were crowded with prospectives and hangers-on who gathered to gawk and, if the pleasurists were feeling generous, get a grope—free of charge.

Where was Oooh?

The bigger question, Army mulled as watched the pleasurists, was, what would he say to her if he found her?

More than an hour had passed and Army was growing desperate. He couldn't stomach another cup of Ethiopian Rift blend or eat another stale square of crumb cake—crumb by crumb. At least the sudden rain had suddenly stopped, leaving the night shiny and wet as if it were waiting for something lusty and illicit.

Just as Army was preparing to take his chances outside, he couldn't move. His heart twitched and sweat beaded on the bridge of his nose. He had to remind himself to breathe. *It was only a glimpse.* Then another. *There it was again*, he told himself.

At first he saw only an arm, long and brown and well muscled, jabbing through the shadows that shrouded the brownstone's entrance. It was enough for Army to know that he had found her. A few moments later he saw Oooh follow that arm into the face of another pleasurist, a much larger woman who seemed to be all thighs, hips, and buttocks.

Army turned up his coat collar as he stood and briskly headed for the door, pausing only long enough to press a $100 bill into the waitress's outstretched hand.

"I might be back and I'll need this table," he told her, as if the money had paid his check and purchased her obedience. The waitress tucked the tightly rolled currency behind her ear and smiled faintly. But Army didn't notice.

Outside, Army was beginning to feel comfortably invisible and, for a moment, invincible. He was convincing himself that he was blending well enough into the petty pedestrians. The night would hide him, he assured himself.

That had been Oooh—Army knew it as he quickened his step and weaved around the slower moving. Finally, he thought to the exclusion of everything else, finding Oooh would mean finding answers, and maybe finding a way out of his deepening nightmare.

A shock of red. A police car—pulsing red and blue glow—was gliding toward him. Army froze and pleaded with fate that the local patrollers were not scanning for U.I.D.s. He didn't have one. The car slowed a few yards away from him and roared off when the stoop pleasurists stood up and mooned the officers, who flickered their car's lights in gratitude.

Army kept his head down and his hands shoved deep into his duster's oversized pockets. He was feeling exposed. From his location across the street from the stoop, he could hear a group of Chinese men playing spades. Someone was smoking what smelled like homegrown marijuana. A girl who looked too young to be out after youth curfew sat alone on the stoop's bottom step, nursing a listless infant on a bud of a breast.

"Som goo-ward smoke-key, boi."

"Pardon me?" Army asked as he bared his teeth to a stocky man who was doubling his pace as he approached.

"I say I got damn kill-yar smoke-weed. It nat-true-ral. Earth-growed. Git-ja God-high."

The Viper stepped close enough into Army's face for a few of the man's Spun-wound dancing dreadlocks to brush across Army's forehead. Instinctively, Army stepped back, but not far enough that he wasn't overwhelmed by the peppery smell of the man's breath and body.

The Viper grinned as he upped the amperage of his intimidation, stepping forward into Army's face and firmly thumping Army's breastbone with his index finger to accent every other word of his sales pitch. Army only thought about the money, a small fortune on the streets, crammed not-deep enough into his pockets.

"Dis gooood stuff (thump!), bredda-mon."

"Nah, not interested, my brother Dark."

"Awright, I give it to ya chee-ape, (thump!). Cheap, cheap, real (thump! thump!) cheeeap, Dark."

"No," Army said, his voice growing rough enough to throw off some sparks of its own. "Not interested. Naw."

Army stared into the Viper's eyes, ink-black dots set in whites the color of piss-stained snow. He thought about running back to the café. *If he takes my money, he takes my life.*

Army took a side step, but stopped when the Viper sidestepped into his path and grabbed Army's shoulder with startling strength. Without thinking, he broke free of the Viper's grip. The men glared at each other. Then the Viper laughed, hard. His nest of hyperanimated dreadlocks swayed and uncoiled to the grunting laughter.

"How much you got, brother? I'll make a dee-eel, huh?"

Army could feel the Viper leaning his greater weight against him, pushing him toward the dark space between the street's brownstones. *Could he feel the money?* The Viper laughed again and slapped Army's shoulder, as if inviting him in on the phantom joke. At that instant, Army felt something hot swim the length of his left arm just before it began to go numb. His vision blurred and he stumbled back into one of the brownstone's wall.

Moments later, Army could feel himself being dragged, taken deeper into the black, narrow gap between the buildings. He could hardly swallow as fear grew in his chest like a cancerous lump.

"Rattle, Rattle, you know I saw him first."

Army twisted robotically toward the voice. Materializing out of the darkness, it was her. It was Oooh. Her dark skin seemed to glow in contrast to a tight silk T-shirt the color of sunset. With another step, he could see that she was wearing black spray-pants that, despite the Chinese scarf she had tied into a skirt, emphasized the nudity just a coat of fabrasized paint away.

Oooh. He uttered her name without the benefit of his voice.

Her eyes were shaded by antique wire-frame shades, but the rest of her face was bare, smooth, and alluring. The Viper stuttered some obscenities before releasing Army, who struggled to stand on his own.

"Oooh, my darling cuz," the Viper said, turning stiffly around to meet her voice. "Just tryin' to makes a little transaction with da fella here. Plus, you don't know what I know 'bout him. I got big business wid 'em."

"You know this is my spot," Oooh said with eyes unblinking, mouth unsmiling. "Any action—trans or otherwise—gets done by me. We plural on that, cuz? C'mon. Look at him. You're lucky I came along. I think I saved you from an ugly stomp-down."

"Why ya talk to me like dat, Oooh?" Rattle asked with a grin. "Just buz. That all. Dooing buz-nest is all. And fight? Got a dose of TumbleDown in 'em. Was thinkin' 'bout selling 'em."

Army was surprised that he could lift his arm enough to rub his left shoulder. He looked from Oooh to the Viper and then back to Oooh. He felt like the Viper was talking about someone else.

Rattle smiled like a choirboy, then cleared his throat. "Mesorry. HeYouends."

Oooh motioned to Army to walk toward her. He took a few stumbling steps as he could see pleasurists, clients, and other passersby go about their business in the other end of the gap. Oooh walked past Army and kissed Rattle softly on his forehead. They held hands for a moment before Oooh's mood darkened.

"You want to make some real money, cousin?" she asked Rattle in a voice that was flat and urgent. "Come by my door in a few hours. I think I want to take you up on your transport offer. Think I need to take a break."

Rattle shook his head hard, aggravating his dreads to dance ever more vigorously in approval, before backing out of the gap and giving a two-fingered salute.

"I be by tomorrow night," Rattle called out. "Gotta big job2do in the morning."

"Tomorrow night, then," Oooh called back before walking toward Army and offering him her hand.

"You all right?"

He nodded like a lost child found.

"You realize I know who you are?" Army asked, trying to keep his jitters from leaching into his voice.

Oooh flipped up her lemon-colored lenses and winked. "And I remember you too, loverboy. Happy New Year."

Army's eyes widened before they nearly closed.

"Come on. Follow me," she said, like a woman who was accustomed to men coming when she told them to. "We have a lot to do. We gotta get the hell out of here. Gotta run."

20

First Last Days

"**M**ISS RIKKI?"

"Yes, Mac."

It hasn't been difficult to notice lately that you haven't been feeling, well... like yourself. I mean, I know your concern with Mother's health has been heavy on your mind, and as for your brother's visit last week—that certainly didn't help. And I see that you did not cast a vote on any of the daily referendums this week, not even the environmental ones I know you support."

Rikki stirred sleepily in her bed before slowly pulling herself up to her elbows. Her bed folded itself beneath her back in an offer of support.

"No, no, I didn't, Mac," she replied as her face settled into a subtle divide between confusion and loss. More than a minute passed before Rikki moved an inch or uttered a word. Mac\Sheehan was perfectly patient in her stillness.

Rikki took a long, deep breath, held it, and then exhaled quickly.

"I have been feeling, mmm, especially blue, lately," Rikki said in a voice that was beginning to find itself.

"Blue? Melancholy. Low spirits. Depressed," Mac\Sheehan responded, in a tone just flat enough to draw attention to the artificiality of its intelligence.

"A little bit of all of those, I guess. You know as well as I do that Mother is being brought here today." Rikki roughly cleared her throat before blinking back a tear. "I have no illusions about what that means. I know she's coming home to die.

"Today," she said slipping into a rasp, "marks the first of her last days."

"Yes, that may be true, Miss Rikki," Mac\Sheehan said trying its best to match Rikki's mood and modulation. "And then again, isn't that true for all organics, from the first moment of your lives? A 14th century English proverb says, 'Death is a shadow that always follows the body.' And almost a thousand years earlier, Buddha observed: 'To watch the birth and death of beings is like looking at the movements of a dance. A lifetime is a flash of lightning in the sky. Rushing by, like a torrent down a steep mountain.'

"I find such imagery greatly comforting," Mac\Sheehan said, without a hint of self-awareness.

Rikki's complexion looked gray in her bedroom's filtered light. Mac\Sheehan's visual acuity noted tears welling in her eyes. In a nano-moment spent crunching compassion calculations, it decided it was best to say nothing.

Without warning, Rikki snatched her blankets from her body with a loud snap and sat up. Her face brightened. She clapped her hands and grinned bravely. "All right, Mac, let's get going. What's our inspirational quote for today?"

"Miss Rikki?" Mac asked tentatively. "I was wondering if we could depart from our usual morning regimen."

"And do what?" Rikki asked as she swiveled in bed to bring her feet gently down onto a carpet that fingered her toes like enlivened spring grass.

"I composed something."

"You composed something? For me?" Rikki's voice lightened with curiosity and delight. "Yes, of course. Please. By all means. Let me hear it."

Rikki fell back into her bed, which silently readjusted again for her comfort. She closed her eyes, folded her palms across her breasts. "Okay, Mac. Begin."

"My pleasure," the system said with a likable tone that almost sounded anxious, even nervous. "I call it a compassion poem."

It lowered its voice to a crisp, warm whisper.

"The day awoke troubled and gray. Its air, moist and chilled from the night, was restless and fretful as it fingered treetops and chased its tailwinds in great, invisible circles; it rudely tossed loose leaves and rattled the windows of the sleeping. There was fatigue in the lengthening rod of light lifting, yet again, the ancient weight of the dark heavens from an evening's imposition on its favored, round-faced child. Nevertheless, the horizon glowed with insistence, and the new day obeyed the ordained order of things, a delicate, spiraling pattern made of billions, upon billions, of yesterdays. The sun rose. The sky brightened. Dawn stretched, then smiled her pearly, watercolor welcome. And life went, as it always does, relentlessly onward."

Rikki only shook her head, nodding in silent affirmation with the sentiments carried on the words of her P.H.A. Once again, she felt enlivened, strangely restored, she thought, by of all things, a machine embedded in her home.

The sound of the morning intruded through a bedroom window that Mac\Sheehan had cracked to offer her a rare morning breeze. Rikki leaned forward, stopping to rest her forehead against her uplifted knees. She listened to her own deep, steady breathing and to birdsong rising from the park far below, where tree leaves sang a wordless chorus with every passing breeze. A new day had just been born; Mac\Sheehan understood that and now, she thought, she was beginning to as well.

"Thank you, Mac," Rikki said. "I mean it. Thank you so, so much."

"You are most welcome, Miss Rikki."

"Now, let me ask you a favor," she said slowly, as if she was uncertain if she should give voice to a sudden notion. "Mac?"

"Yes."

"I need you to do some detective work."

21

Offender Bender

NAJIMA SAT SUSPENDED IN THE SURVEILLANCE BUBBLE. HER EYES darted over Times Square's wrap-around silicon-vapor screens, shimmering with ever-shifting digital mosaics. Her link tied her into the bubble's Bio-Cybernetic Assisted Intelligence, which chewed low probabilities to spit out vastly higher ones that indicated where targets were going—some even before they knew where they were going. But this target had been especially elusive. It was cunning and perhaps, Najima thought, incalculably bold.

"I'm getting soft-alert coordinates to begin locking down the 200 block of West 43rd Street between... wait... wait. Okay. I got it—between Broadway and Eighth Avenue."

"That's right under our noses," Romaro hollered over his link. "Shit, it's just around the corner. That's where the old Times building is. Bunch of automated government offices and clinics. And a hell of a lot of foot traffic, standarounds. It's going to make it damn difficult to isolate and track a target."

Najima glanced at Romaro's face, drawn and lined with frustration, staring at her from an insert in her upper center screen. She knew that look, knew it all too well in the scowls of men like him—men of smothering responsibilities, men like her father had been. Life taught Najima not to overreact, not to stumble in the wake of such unrealistic expectations.

She paid little mind to her captain's complaints. She summoned her calm and studied the data patter on the screens that encircled her and tried to listen only to the sounds that were fed to her rather than those that simply leaked into her auditory range. But she couldn't. There was the whirl of the vehicle's vent jets sucking air that always smelled to her like sweat and motor oil; the hums and moans of the vehicle's mechanicals correcting, adjusting, assisting; and the muffled noises from outside: rumbling cars, bikes, and transports. People rustled like dry leaves before a storm, curious, but keeping their distance from the command vehicle that rode as much on intimidation as it did on its six TorqueTek tires.

Najima's seat lifted a few inches and swung her swiftly in a leftward turn toward a far corner of her main screen. Then she rode her seat as it whirled her 180 degrees to face two rear screens, one tracking heat and scent signatures and another scanning Times Square for fine movement markers.

"Huh uh…" is all she said as she fingered controls that returned her to the main screen, as the rear screens slid forward to align themselves behind layers of silicon-gas screens repositioning in front of her. At Najima's word each screen became opaque, overlaying all their tracking information into a complex but clearly coherent picture before her eyes.

"You got that fix yet?" Romaro barked from his command pod nestled deep in the rear of the command vehicle, several feet below Najima's surveillance bubble. "Been sitting here in this stuffy CV on this goddamned traffic island for—what?—45 minutes? And still haven't found this fucking head snatcher.

"How hard can it be?" he asked rhetorically. "It's the same sumbitch I shot at in the mall. I know it!"

"Hold…on," Najima whispered. "I think I've got it. Target sighted and… and… *confirmed,*" she shouted.

"Where?"

"It's moving east, at moderate speed, along the northern side of West 43rd Street. Not quite mid-block," Najima said, sharpening her imaging of the target, which appeared on screen as a throbbing red blob spilling numbers as it moved in and out of dozens of smaller, silvery blobs. Najima pressed her equipment to give her more—more clarity, more detail, more certainty.

"Captain, I'm patching my images into your monitor," Najima said. "That's him. Definitely male, reading male-mass hot spots."

Romaro could begin to make out a tall Dark wearing a long, dark overcoat, brown scarf, and black flop cap. Judging by the size of the large bulge on the man's back, Romaro figured some sort of backpack was concealed under the coat.

"But can't get much on his face yet," Najima said. "But based on what I have so far, I would say that his face is not inconsistent with the description Detective Reagan got from the hat-display mannequins. Even the coat seems to match."

"Is he armed?" Romaro asked sharply.

"Can't tell. His hands are stuffed in his pockets," Najima replied flatly. "And the voyeuristics aren't much help in this crowd. I'm not reading any lethal-force components, but I would advise max caution."

Romaro checked his staffing grid. He had Gaghan at mid-block on the east side of Broadway moving south and Reagan holding at Eighth Avenue looking westward. He ordered both men to seal 43rd Street. Their Opti-Dots lit up with target coordinates and surveillance beamed from Najima. Each flashed ALPHA RED in their eyes.

"I want this stain mopped up so we can call it a day," Romaro told all his detectives. "I want to be home in time for Sunday dinner with the family."

Najima was troubled. This Viper had already made fools of some of the Department's best—including her. The target had been tracked from 118th Street over a network of security sensors, sky peeps, and embedded cameras from street to subway to gypsy cab to a spot just inside the northeastern edge of Central Park. Routine stuff. Then the target simply disappeared. And now, for almost an hour, the Viper had eluded every means and device the Department had, including dozens of detectives on the ground. Most troubling, Najima thought, she couldn't explain how this target managed it.

"Captain."

"Yeah," Romaro growled.

"I've got Bobbie Starr's crew reporting in from Central Park South. Do you want me to patch you in?"

"Not unless Lieutenant Starr wants to tell me that she and her people are rocketing their asses to Times Square."

"Do you want me to reposition them?"

"YEAH," Romaro roared. "Get them to split up and back up Gaghan and Reagan. NOW!"

Romaro fumed. "How did Starr's boys lose this fucker in the first place?" he muttered, just loud enough for Najima to hear. Then he asked himself the same question.

The target had been cornered in Central Park hours ago. Sniffers had confirmed that he was carrying human remains. Romaro was still disgusted that no one could figure out a plausible explanation for how the Avanti woman's head ended up on the roof of a Harlem tenement. Neither he nor Reagan bought that the Black Popsicle, Armstrong, hid it there. It was clearly dropped there, he thought. Planted. But why?

"Shitty," he grunted. "Just shitty work. Some heads are going to roll."

Rattle smiled to himself as he faded into a crumbling wall of people who had gathered near a side door of the Government re-employment office. He felt he had all the best advantages. He saw himself as not simply a petty criminal, but more a bit of a rebel. He was thinking that his work with JoË Dots had given him a cause as well as cash. He was moving light and lethal against a bunch of rental cops laden with heavy, state-of-the-fart technology, he thought. He was enjoying the chase.

Rattle pressed the dot behind his left ear and listened to the banter bouncing between the field feet and the captain parked in the middle of Times Square.

"Seal-ley-piggee," Rattle hissed as he calculated his next five moves. "Ah lil' piggee winTA marrKitt…, then dis lil' pig-gee wint kaa-boooom!"

Rattle hunched his shoulders and assumed the beaten-down silhouettes of the double file of men and women leaving the re-employment office as jobless as when they went in. It was Friday, so they would have to survive the weekend until they could try again on Monday morning.

Scores of these ghost jobbers staggered into the brisk streams of motor and pedestrian traffic of workers, shoppers, and African and Euro-Asian tourists flowing south past the T-shirt and trinket stalls lining Broadway and Seventh Avenue. Rattle fell into place among a half-dozen men who looked like even life was a job they were soon to lose. He had his own target in mind as he began to reach inside the sling strap of his shoulder bag for a hidden pocket.

Romaro couldn't believe what he was seeing. The target had somehow slipped past Gaghan and was heading north on Broadway, heading toward the command vehicle itself. Starr's squad was still six blocks to the north, but advancing fast on Times Square. Now the Viper was circling back.

"Gaggy," Romaro shouted, "the target is just behind you… no more than five or six yards."

"I'm not getting anything on my proximity scanner," Gaghan said, looking into his link's Opti-Dot suspended on a wire over his right eye. "I'm not picking up anything."

"Turn around," Romaro screamed. "Fuck the pad, use your eyes, man. He's a Viper with a striped knitted cap!"

Najima could see it all too plainly. A beefy man in a dark coat, scarf, and hat was moving along the crowded sidewalk, weaving aggressively, but expertly, among herds of heads and shoulders. He was closing on Gaghan, who looked lost—who looked, more by the second, like a victim.

Rattle could see the detective clearly now. His face was glistening with perspiration. His arms were up, bent at the elbows, forming a crude U that framed his stricken face. Pedestrians flowed around him as if he were little more than an inconveniently placed stone in a shallow stream. Rattle slowed his pace and took special note of the hand cannon the detective gripped in his left hand. The detective turned like a drunken dancer. Rattle eased forward, closer, so close that he could hear the detective's panic.

"I don't have the target in sight," Gaghan screamed. "Repeat-repeat. I don't have the—"

For Gaghan, time dribbled out like some tasteless syrup as he felt his stomach explode with a sickening, damp blow.

Najima squeezed her eyes shut; when she opened them, her tears refused to run.

Romaro cursed God, smacking his viewpanel so hard its face cracked and bled thick green fluids.

Rattle felt a spasm of satisfaction wiggle into his face just before a rush of deliciously satisfying sensations overwhelmed him. There was the surprising softness of the detective's belly and then the rush of warmth over Rattle's right hand, held tight against the detective's abdomen. There was sound: a bubbling belch as things tightly packed unpacked, as things internal burst to become external. And there were the detective's throaty grunt, and passersby singing shock at the top of their lungs.

Rattle gave the belly buster one last upward tug in the detective's gaping abdominal cavity, then dropped the device, withdrawing his left arm, which had supported the detective as if he were a pal too weary to stand. The detective's body crumpled to the sidewalk like an empty suit.

"Detective down!" Najima shouted. Romaro was barking orders to Starr to re-deploy her squad to box in the assailant. One of her men was to recover Gaghan's remains, and Reagan was ordered to leave his post on Eighth Avenue and replace Gaghan at 43rd and Broadway.

Reagan had been listening to the com traffic between Romaro and

Gaghan. When he got the order he didn't stop running until he reached Gaghan's corpse. He had seen many belly buster wounds before. In the right hands, it only took a few minutes to turn a cheap, laser flare into a belly buster's primitive laser blade. One had brutally eviscerated Gaghan, reducing him to little more than road kill that smelled like burnt bacon and green shit.

Starr's man was cordoning off the murder scene with laser wire, following body recovery procedures with mechanical efficiency. Rattle watched the recovery out of a corner of his eye as he stepped into a crowd huddled under the rotting marquee of the Paramount Building at 43rd and Broadway.

Reagan looked at his link's Opti-Dot and noticed that he was getting conflicting readings on the possible whereabouts of the assailant.

Rattle was watching the heavyset detective from across the street. He was wishing that he had another buster so he could watch the contents of the big man's stomach slosh onto the sidewalk, too. But all Rattle could do was to draw close to a wall and drop to one knee. He hiked up his pant leg and checked a twinkling device strapped just above his left boot line. He stood up, readjusted his pants, and moved slowly, but steadily, toward the command vehicle. "Seal-lee pig-gee," he said with a smirk.

"I need some help here," Reagan called over his link. "I'm getting nothing here. Nothing."

Rattle reached again into the hidden pocket and this time pulled out two six-inch lengths of Styx—one red and the other green. Still moving, he twisted the clay-like ropes together until they looked like an oversized piece of old-fashioned licorice. He carefully pinched twelve impressions along its length.

"Captain," Najima said, her voice low and heavy with disbelief, "The target is disappearing again."

"What?"

"He's gone. I'm reading no target." Najima said coolly as her seat swung her wildly around the bubble. "Just like Central Park."

Rattle began crossing Broadway on 45th Street, weaving through a swarm of cell-cycles to walk toward the outer edge of the traffic island, where the command vehicle sat behind a large triangle of laser wire. He could see the fat detective trotting back to 43rd Street, and Starr's recovery officer on his knees, collecting the last of the dead detective's entrails.

Without breaking stride Rattle pulled the Styx from his coat pocket and gave it a full twist. TWELVE... He was nearly at 44th Street when he lowered his head and ran like he was on fire. TEN... He was less than a yard from the command vehicle. He clutched his bag like a football, then hurled himself over the laser wire. EIGHT... He struck the gritty pavement and rolled beneath the command vehicle. SEVEN... He slapped the Styx to the command vehicle's underbelly—where it stuck. SIX... He rolled out and scrambled to his feet. A bullet whizzed by his face, ricocheting off of the vehicle's rear fender. FOUR... As Rattle jumped from the fender, clearing the laser wire, he caught a glimpse of the gunner aiming for another shot. THREE... He turned north, putting the vehicle's bulk between himself and Starr's officer as he sprinted. TWO... Rattle cut hard to the east, slipping behind a public VP booth, pushing confused pedestrians as he pushed himself to run, run, run.

Reagan heard a woman scream. When he turned toward the scream, he noticed a commotion in a crowd of passersby near the command vehicle. Reagan saw a man in a long, dark coat disappearing behind an office tower less than a block northeast of the command vehicle.

"Hey," Reagan said over his link. "I think I got the—"

ZERO.

Romaro felt it first. The rumble started deep in his stomach then radiated upward to his chest and then to his extremities, until his jaw picked up the vibrations in ever more insistent waves. His jaw rattled so violently that he couldn't stop himself from biting his tongue. His newly implanted wisdom teeth clacked like dice in a crapshoot.

The flooring of the command vehicle warped and buckled in ways he knew were impossible. His command pod folded and shattered, trapping him in his seat. Romaro realized he could not see his lower body, nor feel it. His head felt as light as a child's balloon while his arms and chest felt like dead weight. Romaro tried to speak, but only tasted bile and blood. Yet, inside his head he heard himself scream: *That fucking, head-snatching bastard got us!*

Romaro found that he could twist his shoulders and tilt up his chin just enough to peer through a break in the ruined equipment to see a small section of Najima's cracked surveillance bubble. In the low glow of the amber-colored emergency light, he thought he could make out the back of her head, a shoulder. Romaro noticed her arm backlit by a strangely restless illumination.

"Fire," Romaro mumbled softly. A nauseatingly dull ring in his ears muted his words. Najima's unmoving arm was on fire. Thickening smoke was making it painful to breathe. But Romaro puffed out his chest and forced out the simplest words he could out of his swollen mouth.

"Hel-lupp," he gasped, coughed. "Help. Help us."

Two blocks away, Rattle felt another wave of satisfaction over his handiwork. But there was much more to do, he reminded himself as he ran into the cover of a fleeing crowd confused and frightened by the exploding command vehicle. Rattle drifted from the crowd and began moving southeasterly to complete his mission.

"Seellee…" he said under his breath as he tugged his shoulder pack around until its bulge rested against his heaving chest. "SeelleeSeelleePIGGEE."

22

Hedz Up

REAGAN CLAMPED A BREATHER OVER HIS NOSE AND TROTTED TOWARD Lieutenant Starr, whose team had converged on Romaro's burning vehicle. Starr was an athletically built Light with sandy-colored hair tied back so severely that it drew up the corners of her emerald eyes, lending her hollow-cheeked face the confident bearing of a lioness after a kill. She stood in a cloud of dust and smoke with a squad of local police, ordering them to tighten their hold on Times Square.

Red-faced and panting from running full-out for a half block to reach 45th and Broadway, Reagan was bending over slightly, still trying to catch his breath, as he tentatively raised his voice over the din of disaster. "What— what can I do?"

Starr turned quickly toward the interruption. As she did, her elbow smacked Reagan on his jaw line, startling him by how much the bone-to-bone collision hurt. He absently rubbed his face as she shouted instructions over his head. Feelings of inadequacy rippled through Reagan when he noticed that Starr wasn't wearing a breather. He was certain that she noticed his breather.

"What a fucking mess," she said, almost looking through him to the bomb scene. "We're getting full communications back soon. Until then listen for updates on your links. The explosion fried the handheld hub. You good?"

"I'm o—"

Starr pressed her link at her ear, listening to other voices before she resumed speaking in full sentences. "Yeah. Yeah. I'm sure the assailant is still in the area."

Reagan wasn't certain whether Starr was talking to him or to voices on her link, or both. He decided that it didn't matter.

"You're going to have to eyeball him," Starr continued, after stopping to wordlessly shove a late-arriving detective toward the mayhem. "Tech is no match for good eyes and instincts. Ask Gaghan."

Reagan frowned, thinking, *Bitch.*

"Yeah, look for that ugly-ass cap, or Viper dreads," Starr instructed over her link. "He's probably not wearing the coat anymore. I doubt he ditched the fucking head, though.

"Yeah-yeah-yeah," Starr revved her verbal motor. "He's carried it this far. No, I *don't* know why this son-of-a-bitch keeps disappearing off our screens. Fuck that! If your sniffers are up and running, use them too. Understood?"

Reagan nodded like a cheap toy, but was certain it hadn't registered on the lieutenant. She was tapped in to dozens of Reagans. Better Reagans, he thought. Besides, he mused, Lieutenant Starr must be accustomed to people carrying out her orders as if they were natural law. Reagan was sure that his head-bobbing agreement was superfluous, a waste of time, as Times Square buzzed with detectives, police, emergency workers, fire suppressors, media drones, and rumors.

A new knot of detectives tightened around Starr, squeezing Reagan out of the loop. He could not see the lieutenant's face, but he could hear her raspy orders for an AirRush to jet Romaro to C3 Medical and ground transport to remove two bodies. Reagan was relieved to hear that his old partner had survived. But a sudden heavy sadness filled his ribcage when he realized Romaro's surveillance specialist obviously had not.

It didn't fully surprise him that he could feel anything for a Dark. He had respected Najima's mastery of surveillance systems. He envied her cool skill. Although Reagan never saw much of Najima outside of a cramped command vehicle, he remembered her features possessed an unusual sharpness for a Dark: thin lips, thin nose. She was striking—likely because of mixed Light ancestry, he reassured himself.

Suddenly, Reagan was wrestling with the question: Who would mourn him if he had been killed, like Najima and Gaghan? He could picture his sister sobbing in an obligatory display of grief while harboring a not-so-secret relief that she was finally rid of him. Romaro would miss him. Maybe. Reagan reminded himself that in the months after his dismissal from the Department, Romaro quickly lost touch.

A queer pleasure stirred deep in Reagan as he imagined his own death. Something quick, but not messy like Gaghan's. A smart-shell in the brain. A shock spear to the chest. He was death-dreaming. It was a rookie's lapse and he knew it. But he couldn't stop. It was like when he was five years old again and obsessed with tongue-toying his first loose tooth. It was a pleasure so entwined with pain that he wouldn't stop, couldn't stop, until the baby tooth lay dead and detached in his sweaty palm.

Reagan realized that dreaming about his demise was only a skeleton's skip away from inviting the real thing from crawling up his ass and chewing away everything that kept him alive. Yet...

Tug. Tug. Starr was tugging his arm, pulling him back to the moment, back to the crowds and commotion, smoke and sirens, good guys and bad. "Reagan," she shouted. She looked directly into his squinting eyes. "We've got a report of a suspicious figure in or around Times Square Tower." With uncharacteristic softness, her tone lightened until her voice was more air than sound. "Find the son-of-a-bitch who did this."

Without word or gesture, Reagan turned and ran toward the tower. He tried not to look at the charred wound of the bombsite as he trotted off. He ripped off his breather and took a deep breath of hell as he ran to meet the devil. A confusion of sighting reports blared from a handheld someone shoved into his grip as he waited for Starr's attention.

"Suspicious Viper-haired Dark with bag spotted on Times Square subway shuttle."

"Strange Dark entering public toilets in Bryant Park..."

"Dark in cap and coat driving city taxi on Tenth Avenue near 51st Street..."

Reagan glanced at the handheld and then into his Opti-Dot. He hoped all the reports were wrong; most of all he hoped that he himself was wrong.

He knew the assailant was Rattle. It had to be. And if Rattle was killing, he was killing for someone who was paying. And the only person who could pay Rattle enough had to be JoË Dots.

The night at Baghdaddy's came rushing back. The fear JoË Dots had worked so expertly to instill in Reagan was still there in his heart, like razor-edged shrapnel. Dots had made it clear that there were business interests at stake, big business. He made it clear that Rattle was part of that business, and that Reagan, even if he was back with the Department, had no business meddling with their business.

"You cost us," JoË Dots said, dropping his screech-slang for emphasis. "You pay. First with anybody your sorry old ass might care about. Then anybody we might think you care about. Then you. InI?"

Reagan didn't remembering saying anything except "Yes."

Underscoring the seriousness of the business in play, Reagan was convinced that JoË Dots had killed Taj, the informer, who had said next to nothing that night about rumors of a human head being kept in the club. The next day, the pleasurist's naked body was found bundled in a South Bronx trash receptacle, arms and legs broken and tied to make it resemble a Thanksgiving turkey for holiday cannibals. His head had been savagely hacked off, Reagan noted, convinced that it was a beheading meant as a message and not as a harvest.

The face of a new captain glaring from Reagan's Opti-Dot startled him. The dot displayed the captain's name. It was something Asian and, Reagan decided, too much trouble to try to pronounce. So, he decided simply that "Captain" would have to do.

As Reagan crossed 43rd Street, he told the captain that he was attempting to reengage the target on his handheld, that he had been dispatched to check out a report of the assailant near Times Square Tower."

"Proceed," the captain said brusquely. "My surveillance specialist— Kasuhiko Chongkittavorn—will patch you into anything pertinent."

"Damn good," Reagan replied, subconsciously mimicking the captain's subtly accented English and then added to his mental notes another name he couldn't be bothered to pronounce.

Rattle listened over his universal link and laughed. "Piggees plenTeeKONfusedNOWhuh?"

The tower's service entrance was open and unguarded, just as he had been promised that it would at the minute of his arrival. He was inside Times Square Tower, deep-breathing reconditioned air and readying himself for Phase Two. Pity, he thought, this was the deep stealth part of his mission. If all went as planned, no hand-to-hand, no blood play, would be required.

Rattle patted his bag before tapping in the security code for the high-speed service elevator. The keypad panel glowed green and he could feel the maxcrete floor tremble as the elevator began its ascent from the subbasement. Rattle kneeled to check the status of his c-jammer, still strapped tight to his calf. He caught a whiff of fetid odors. The stink of the bag and its decaying contents was getting stronger. The frezzpacs were giving out. He'd have to move faster, he reminded himself.

Rattle knew he had been pushing the c-jammer's underground technology beyond its design limits. When JoË Dots gave him the device, he'd cautioned him not to run it more than in fifteen-minute bursts before completing its recharging cycle.

But his disappearing act in Central Park had been costly. Now he was about to step into a freight elevator to ride nonstop to the building's rooftop. The c-jammer indicated that it had six minutes before shutdown and recharge. It would have to be enough time.

The doors snapped opened. Rattle smiled, and the maintenance man standing before him reflexively smiled back. The man was still smiling when he skidded into unconsciousness after Rattle slammed him, smile first, to the floor. The man's head cracked like a snack nut. He kicked the body out of his way as he stepped into the elevator.

As he rose, Rattle rummaged through a trash bin in the rear of the darkened elevator. *Perfect*, he thought, as he lifted out a bundle. The package was a spray-wrapped maintenance smock. Rattle ran his fingers along its collar to check if its security tape was intact. It was. Again as promised.

Less than halfway up the 47-story building, Rattle had a disturbing thought: What if the man he had just killed had been JoË Dots' inside guy? *Wrong place, wrong time*, he shrugged. He kept his head down as he rode nonstop to the roof.

Rattle chortled as he wondered what the building's security was seeing. The service entrance security cameras had been disabled. Now, there was someone in the service elevator who could only be seen as a dark blob—if that. The c-jammer was still working—four minutes to go. If the Insider had done his work, no one could stop the elevator from depositing Rattle on the rooftop. He rubbed the smelly bulge in the shoulder bag as the elevator doors opened.

Rattle walked into the late afternoon sun, alone on the windy rooftop. He yanked the bag from his left shoulder, letting it drop to the rooftop with a thud and a feeble bounce. He tore off his coat and slipped into the maintenance smock. As he hurried, he glanced at the shaft that rose two hundred feet into the sky.

He had seen this pole all his life on the Weave. Every year, Americans traditionally celebrated the official start of the new calendar when a ball of light slipped down its length at midnight. Rattle strode over to it and ran his hand slowly over its smooth thickness as his free hand pulled a metal hoop from his bag. He opened the hoop and snapped it around the base of the shaft.

Caterpillar-like rollers distended from the hoop and gripped the shaft. A police hoverplane startled Rattle as it noisily passed overhead on its way to the hive of police and Department action below in the square. He watched, dressed in the smock and looking very much like he belonged on the roof, as the craft stood in the sky and then descended swiftly through a swarm of aerial fire suppressers and media drones beaming the bombing scene to the Weave.

Rattle turned back to his bag and took a deep breath before opening it. The odor burned his eyes as Rattle reached deep into the bag's open mouth. He carefully removed a gray-skinned human head with a gaping square-cut wound, from which a thick nylon cord extended.

Quickly, Rattle hooked the head to the hoop that was hugging the shaft. He pressed a single button on the hoop and stepped away, watching the hoop crawl up the shaft, dragging with it the head. It steadily inched upward with the severed head dangling, swinging, and banging softly against the shaft and it rose higher and faster.

"MissionDoneDone," Rattle said, as he tapped his c-jammer. It glimmered in the sunlight before he dropped his pant leg and escaped to the elevator.

"How confident are you about this hunch?" Lieutenant Starr asked Reagan as he cautiously approached Times Square Tower.

Reagan looked into his Opti-Dot's shifting schematics of the tower, a fifty-year-old slab of steel and glass. All of the previous Viper sightings had proven false. But it was a miscellaneous report he picked up from the tower's automated security grid that struck him: A monitor had detected an odd blob in a service elevator. It was just like what happened in the mall with Romaro. *Same scum, same method*, Reagan told himself.

"I'm proceeding," Reagan told Starr over his link. "I've got a gut feeling about this one. If I'm wrong, you might be scraping my guts off the street."

"You mean if you're right," Starr said. "Don't be slow to call for backup if you run into trouble."

"You'll be the first to know," Reagan said, as he ditched his handheld and drew his service weapon. All the while he wondered what he would do if the man in the elevator was Rattle. Could he pull the trigger?

He banged his body weight against the first of the building's rear service-entrance doors. Locked. He leaned into the second door and nearly fell to his knees when it gave way and opened. A compact loading dock stood before him, dark and empty. He found a security port and waved his U.I.D. in front of it. The screen pulsed with the building's vital security networks.

A remote security guard's face filled the screen.

"Yes, how may I help you?" it said.

"Listen," Reagan said. "I'm a Department detective in your building's rear loading dock pursuing a T-4 suspect. A killer could be in here."

"We're not showing anything here," the piped-in guard replied.

"Where is here?" Reagan shouted.

The guard looked irritated. "I don't think that is pertinent."

"Where?" Reagan hollered, mumbling under his breath how he couldn't believe what was happening.

"Bangladesh," the guard replied, in better English than Reagan's. "I am physically in Dhaka, but for all purposes that matter, I am at Seven Times Square, in the Times Square Tower."

Reagan looked annoyed with the guard. "Read my U.I.D. scan and get me an elevator to the roof. Now, please."

Reagan saw his U.I.D. flash on the screen before the face returned.

"You may proceed, Detective," the guard surrendered.

Reagan trotted into the waiting elevator and nearly slipped as he entered it. He looked down. Blood. A drying smear of it. His eyes followed the chevron of blood that, just before the elevators doors closed, pointed to a pile of discarded shipping sacks and, among them, a lifeless face.

"Lieutenant Starr?"

"Yes, Reagan. You have something for me?"

Reagan cleared his throat. He held the man's dead stare in his head for a moment longer than he wanted as the elevator climbed like a rocket.

"Yeah," he said coolly, as his heart reflexively hardened. "He's been here and there's no reason to think he's not still here. You can send some sniffers to search for bodies. Just tripped over one in the loading dock."

"We've got you on an elevator…"

"Yeah, yeah," Reagan replied. "I think our man's on the roof. Why? I have no idea what the fuck he's up to."

Reagan checked his weapon and tried to shake off any apprehensions about killing Rattle. There'd be no contest if it was his life or the Viper's, he told himself. But worry kept washing back over his resolve. He envisioned himself found in some dumpster, bundled like the informant. He wondered if the head had been cut off first or last in the process. He had surely been conscious before all the cutting started.

"Detective. Detective," Starr called out over Reagan's link. "We have six officers surrounding your location. Tell me what you need."

"I," Reagan hesitated as he felt the elevator slowing to a stop. "I need for them to make sure nobody comes in, and definitely, make damn sure nobody comes out—except for me."

"Good," Starr said. "We'll lock the tower down. Keep your link open."

Reagan nodded, confident that Starr and the Department high-ups linked in would see him nod.

The elevator opened like the jaws of a toothless dragon. The sunlight nearly blinded Reagan for a moment. Stupid, he berated himself. Rattle could have torn his neck out in that flash of vulnerability.

Reagan dropped into a crouch, with his heavy penetrator leading the way. He saw nothing unusual on his Opti-Dot. The roof looked clear, nothing moving. He took another few steps and then spotted something on the maxcrete flooring of the rooftop. As he got closer to the clump of damp fabric, Reagan realized that it was some sort of bag. He kicked it with his foot and then had trouble shaking the bag loose from his shoe, now sticky with what looked like spoiled blood and thickening mucus.

High over his head, he heard something banging.

Reagan looked, straining his eyes against the sun to make out a shape. It was round and dark and apparently tethered to the pole, which he'd always assumed had been some sort of antenna when it was first erected. He looked harder at the object knocking against the steel tower, but couldn't make sense of it until he saw media drones swarming around it like flies.

"Can you see this?" Starr barked over Reagan's link. "We're putting it through to your Opti-Dot."

Reagan stepped back and craned his neck. The image of what he was trying to see with his unaided right eye revealed itself in high magnification in the dot positioned over his left eye.

It was a woman's head, wrinkled and rotten, buffeted by high sky winds. The head's hair hung limp, slimy, and gray, too thin to hide the yawning slot from which much of its brain had been stolen. The head's eyes offered nothing; their delicate tissues had congealed into cloudy mirrors of a long-lost soul.

Data flowed over images of the head in Reagan's dot. A preliminary identification indicated that the head had once sat on the shoulders of a young woman who recently disappeared with her husband in Harlem.

Starr and a group of security team leaders on the ground were gathered around a viewpanel that swung out from one of the command vehicles. Special Weave reports about the head's discovery were rapidly threading their way to VP knots everywhere.

"We are not sure what to make of this, viewers, but we are certain that we are looking at a human head. Some criminal element has inexplicably placed someone's head on top of the Happy New Year pole over New York's Times Square," a reporter said as media remotes and drones hovered around the butchered head.

"Stay with us, as we are attempting to make a positive ID on this head as we bring you further reports and informed speculation."

Another reporter broke in, inserting that the grisly face had been preliminarily identified but that government officials were withholding the information. "This, I venture to say, might well offer considerable validity to scattered reports and rumors that have been swirling around Upper Manhattan for weeks about gruesome beheadings for unknown purposes."

"That's true, Jill," the first reporter rejoined, his voice full of a practiced on-the-scene-up-to-the-minute enthusiasm. "Noting the large contingent of Department personnel here, it is a good bet that this afternoon's deadly Times Square attack—and now this recovery of a human head—indicates, or at least raises suspicions, that the origins of these recent attacks are terroristic in nature."

"Nelson, I'm not certain we can draw that conclusion just yet," Jill cautioned. "Department spokespeople have yet to respond to our questions."

Starr's link hummed in her ear. She took the call and was told to immediately recover the head.

A tap later, Starr was talking to Reagan.

"Still no indication that the assailant is on the roof?" she barked into Reagan's ear.

"Nothing," he said, now hoping more than ever he was correct. Seemingly overnight, Rattle had evolved into a cruelly cunning killer, Reagan realized. He was not sure he could take him out alone. Besides, he knew that he had to deal with much bigger game now. He was up against JoË Dots himself.

"Get the head," Starr instructed. "We need this circus to end right now."

"Understood," Reagan said, though he had no idea how he would manage to accomplish the task.

Seated on the metal floor of the descending elevator, Reagan embraced the head under his arm. Despite wrapping it in his suit jacket and tying the sleeves of his jacket around the head as tightly as he could, he could still smell its rot and see its eyes staring at him in his mind's eye.

The remote guard was back on a small screen in the elevator.

"I only wish I could have been more assistance to you, Detective," he said.

"Don't worry about it," Reagan said. "Hey, you did find a way to lower the pole so I could get this poor woman's head down. Right?"

"Listen," the guard said. "I am still sweeping the building and found nothing. But I have to report to you that I am confirming that the stairway sensors appear to be offline."

Reagan struggled to his feet, accidentally dropping the woman's head, which rolled to a corner of the elevator.

"How long did you know that little piece of news?" Reagan shouted.

"I'm just getting the hard info. A malfunctioning relay… difficult to say how long the monitors have been out."

Reagan kicked the elevator door hard and drew his penetrator. "You know what this means."

The service elevator's doors began to open onto the building's darkened loading dock.

"Be careful," the remote guard said, before the system went black.

Reagan tried to duck-walk off the elevator, abandoning the head. Sweat was pouring down his face, and his waistband was cutting into the tender flesh just beneath the overhang of his belly. He lost his balance twice, the second time falling with a crash into a nearby heap of discarded machine parts and more shipping sacks. He flipped back his Opti-Dot and waited for his eyes to adjust to the darkness. He'd kill for a pair of sunnyglasses, he thought.

"Starr. Starr," Reagan whispered over his link. Static.

"noUSEpiggeeeeeepiggeeee," a voice called out from one of two heavy haulers parked side by side. "Mr. Reagan. Mr. Reagan. WhyUchaseme?"

"Because you've become a soulless killer, Rattle," Reagan said, tucking himself closer to the wall and scanning the hauler dock for the Viper. "I remember when you were just a featherweight hustler."

"WebothThieves," Rattle replied from the darkness. "Ijustchose2steal-biggerthanU."

"So now you steal lives, huh?" Reagan said as he tried to unblock his link.

"MeONLYtakefromtheTAKERS," he replied. "NowGowan. Dotstold-UmegottaFREEpass. Free passage. Place2go."

Reagan heard the high-pitch whine and rumble of fuel-cell turbos spinning. He ran from his cover and into the loading dock spraying penetrator shells, as fast as a middle-aged fat man could run. Headlights lit up the dock just as one of the massive haulers roared by him and tore through the loading dock doors as if they were made of steel foil.

Reagan dropped to his knees and fired explosive penetrator shells into the receding hauler's exhaust grills. No effect. He could only watch as the hauler drove off, rumbling toward Broadway and plowing through a barricade of police and Starr's detectives.

Reagan's link went spastic in his ear. Starr's voice was back in his ear surrounded by a bevy of excited voices.

"Reagan? You okay, Reagan?"

"Yeah, but so is our assailant," he replied as he walked fast toward the nearest command vehicle, waving off the police running toward him. His right knee was stiffening up and his ass was aching. "It was Rattle. I am confirming. It was the Viper known as Rattle."

"Good work," Starr said. "We're in pursuit. Standby. And, oh… looks like your old partner is going to make it."

Reagan shook his head in relief. "Tough old gristle," he said under his breath.

The hauler roared toward Madison Square, catching Department ground and air units off guard. Reagan was reclining in the back of a mobile medical unit watching the scene on an overhead VP. He could not believe what he was seeing. The rampaging vehicle had apparently been retrofitted with offensive weapons, mostly automatic cannons that ripped up the streets behind it.

The hauler was bearing down on 38th Street before Department units began to catch up to it.

"Oh, shit," Reagan said, bolting up from his recovery cot. He watched a streak of light trace from the top rear of the hauler to the blunt nose of a low-flying Department hoverplane that was trailing one-hundred yards behind. The hoverplane rolled to its side and then split open in flames before it crashed—broadside—into two office towers along 37th Street. Fireballs crashed into the towers' midsections. Reagan could hear Starr in his ear, barking orders, coordinating local police and emergency crews: "Keep the target in view. Cut it off. Redouble barricades along Broadway from 34th to 23rd streets. We'll make our stand at the Flatiron."

Reagan could see the hauler slowing as it unleashed more precise fire on its pursuers. Three Department hoverplanes flew ahead to park in the air above the old Flatiron building, where Broadway and Fifth Avenue converge. Reagan could see thousands of people being herded away from the Flatiron's triangular block as flashing red and blue lights marked off the instant Department fortress.

It was too much for Reagan to simply witness on his back. He wheeled himself around and planted his bare feet on the floor, prompting a medic to rush to him.

"Get my shoes," Reagan ordered the medic. "I've got get back out there."

Hopping into the street with the medic trailing him, Reagan looked up and found himself engulfed in a cyclone of litter and dirt. The air whistled louder and louder. Reagan looked up and saw the flat, light-lined bottom of a Department hoverplane descending above him. Without a word, the medic ran back into the mobile medical vehicle.

Reagan began to hobble in the same direction while tapping his link to com-chat with the craft.

"Hold your position, Detective," a disembodied voice called. A green beam painted Reagan where he stood. Moments later, the craft opened its hop-hatch and snatched up Reagan with the ease of an owl fetching a field mouse.

"Welcome aboard," the hoverplane's co-captain shouted over the high-pitched motor wash. "Starr said you might want to join her at the fire line. We have instructions to hop you there ASAP."

Reagan felt the hoverplane tip forward and power itself south to the

Flatiron. Far below he glimpsed the hauler, which was taking heavy fire from aerial drones and rifle cannon positions along the barricaded corridor.

"We've got a full civilian panic down there," he heard Starr say to someone else. "Get 'em out of there. It's going to get a hell of lot hotter down here before it cools down."

"Reagan!" she snapped.

"On my way," he replied.

"Better hurry," she yelled over weapons fire. "The barbecue is about to start." She informed him that the hoverplane was going to deploy him at her command center.

But the barbeque looked like it was starting early, Reagan thought as he heard a tremendous explosion below him. As the hoverplane descended to land, he could see the hauler at a dead stop in the middle of 25th and Broadway. Black and silver smoke was curling from its cockpit. Flames were raging from its undercarriage.

Reagan could hear Starr confirming intelligence that the Viper had not escaped from the vehicle. A wave of relief swept over Reagan. Rattle was dead and he'd had nothing to do with it. He talked himself out of fear of any retribution. *JoË Dots can kiss my fat pink ass*, he thought to himself. *And that goes three times for his evil dwarf boss.*

Scores of police, fire and Department personnel surrounded the smoldering hauler. Starr was flanked by surveillance specialists who seemed to be delivering bad news to the lieutenant on the scene. More brass was landing in the shadow of the Flatiron building.

"You sure?" Reagan heard Starr scream at Chongkittavorn, whose eyes never left her palm-sized VP as they approached the burned out hauler.

"I am quite certain," Chongkittavorn said calmly.

"Sure of what?" Reagan asked as he walked up.

The surveillance specialist turned to face Reagan and Starr. "There is no body in the vehicle. No organic remains of any kind."

"Never was," Chongkittavorn's captain called from beneath the wrecked hauler. He was holding a fistful of ruined optical wiring and strands of Assisted Intelligence chippings.

"Remote control," Chongkittavorn said.

"Yeah," the captain replied. "Afraid so, Bobbie."

"Shit," Starr hissed. "I'll be goddamned."

Reagan felt his stomach and ass clench. Rattle was very much alive and on his way back into the hole he'd come from, waiting for his next assignment. Reagan said nothing but looked stricken.

"Don't worry," the captain said, slapping Reagan on his sweat-drenched back. "You came close, Detective, and still get the cigar. We'll get this bastard."

Reagan nodded and then looked away, letting his eyes fall on the path of destruction Rattle had leveled despite the assembled might of The Department. *But will he get me first?*

23

Passages

"**W**AKE... UP. WAKE UP... WAKE. UP!"

Army felt the shadows of the words fall over him, but their meaning was just out of reach. The drumming of tight little fists on his exposed shoulder was far easier to interpret: The time for sleep was over.

"Arm-mee." A whispery coo begged his eyes open. No fists this time. "You have to get up. They'll be here soon."

Army's eyes began to focus. There was the harsh glare of a table lamp and then the soft, dark oval of Oona's face. He could smell her breath. It was sweet and musky, like the scent of wildflowers blooming from rotting bark.

"Do you want some of this herb?" Oona asked. "It'll help clear your head."

"Nah, not this time. Trust me. It'll just put my black ass back to sleep."

"Your choice," Oona said as she quickly stood up, sucking hard on a joint she was trying to relight. He thought he noticed Oona's eyes pass quickly over his naked chest.

Army reached behind his head and grabbed his shirt, which he had rolled into a sadly inadequate pillow. He slept on the cot using his overcoat for warmth—but more importantly, to keep his cash close. He knew he was in a shack somewhere beyond the semi-urban fringes of Camden, New Jersey. Oona had slept on the other cot, the one she dragged each night across the shack's flimsy metal door.

He still didn't trust her. But he couldn't help feeling grateful that she had gotten him this far, out of Harlem and seemingly away from the omnipresent eyes of the Department. But he knew he was hardly far away enough to allow himself to relax.

"You sleep okay?" Army asked as he bent down to strap his boots.

Silence.

He followed Oona with his eyes as he fastened his shirt. Her back was to him. She was looking out of the shack's only window, an oily sheet of paper-glass that only confirmed that that it was still dark outside. In the hard light of the shack, he moved his eyes along the softness that he imagined just beneath her baggy slacks and shapeless sweater.

They had lived in the same one-room shack for about a week. Army gave free rein to his imaginings on how he would have preferred spending the time. His fantasies always began the same.

It was night and Oona was in her cot. She was naked. Army was incapable of imagining her in bed any other way. More specifically, she was naked and asleep on her stomach. *Yeah*, he thought, closing his eyes and letting himself fall more deeply into his fantasy. She was naked, asleep and the blanket was falling away to reveal the ripe-melon fullness of her ass rising and falling as she breathed, rising and falling as he slid slowly in and out of her. She'd moan and he'd sow tiny, moist kisses along her neck, along the chewy turns of her ears, along trails of goosebumps rising to meet his lips as he inhaled her, as he impaled her.

Army smiled as he felt his dick awaken and stretch a little at a sex fantasy that seemed unlikely to be realized anywhere else but in his head. Ever since the long car ride to Camden, their days were spent with equal parts preparations and boredom. Most of the time, Oona acted as if Army wasn't even there. There were times when she would disappear for hours.

Nonetheless, he gave thanks that he was here and not in some Harlem alley, scared, cornered, and alone. Oona stood at the window, staring out through a silvery haze of cannabis smoke. At first, Army hadn't noticed that Oona had turned the light off. There was something about her dark, upturned face catching the day's fragile first light, the thinness of her wrists, her delicate fingers pinching the joint to her lips. It had all combined in inexplicable ways to recast her as something soft. Not the warrior whore he first saw from Kattrel's hotel window.

"Oona?" Army ventured.

"Yeah," she replied, turning to find his face. "Change your mind about wanting to lung down some of this good smoke?"

"Umm… no," he replied and took a step closer to her. "What are you looking at?"

Oona smiled before turning her face back to the window, which was beginning to glow smudgily.

"Nothing."

"Really? Nothing?" Army took a half step then felt his nerve dissolve.

"I like the nothing, the stillness, out here. Really," Oona said slowly. "It's the spaces between things, the spaces between what's about to happen and then… it happening. Those spaces are bigger out here."

She paused. "It's like these nothings hold big secrets, important secrets, waiting to spring out, but only in their own time."

"Yeah. If we're patient enough," Army said, almost too softly for Oona to hear. "Then you know what I'm talking about."

Army smiled and somehow knew Oona sensed his answer without turning around to read it on his face. Oona waved her joint slowly under her face, air-doodling its smoke trail before bringing the last of it to her nose. She sniffed it like a connoisseur might a fine wine. She glanced at her wrist for the time.

They could hear the heavy rumble of long-distance haulers pulling in and out of the brightening morning. Army had grown accustomed to going to sleep and waking to the noise coming from the trucking terminal across a wild-onion field to the west.

Oona coughed up smoke as she turned to him. "You ready? We got a long trip in front of us—if you still want to come."

"I *have* to come," Army spat, as he ran his hands through his knotty hair.

"You ready?" she asked calmly.

"I think so," Army answered in kind as he slipped on his duster.

"Hungry? We've got about twenty minutes."

"I could eat something."

Oona opened her bag and pulled two mud-colored wafers and two shiny vials from a flip pocket.

"Apple or orange?" she asked, holding the hyper-condensed drinks in her open palms while Army weighed his choice.

Before he could decide, Oona tossed him the apple-flavored Swoosh.

Army watched Oona shake the thumb-sized container before carefully uncapping it. She tilted her head back and slid the vial's opening from her fingertip to her tongue. With the container held tightly between her lips, she yanked the pull-ring at the vial's base.

Oona's eyes bugged as her cheeks inflated into tight-skinned balloons. She held a finger to the wrinkled, brown circle of her straining lips. A couple of seconds later, she began to swallow.

"Well, are you going to drink yours?" Oona asked as she wiped a few drops of orange Swoosh from her chin. "Sorry we don't have any cups."

"Huh, I, uh..." stammered Army, who had never seen anyone ingest a Swoosh that way.

He knew that once the three-ounce sports drink was opened, it was chemically engineered to mix itself with the hydrogen and oxygen in the air and reconstitute into an eight-ounce beverage. He was certain he would gag on the concentrate blasting down his throat. *No way*, he thought. "I think I'll save mine for later," he said.

Oona laughed and explained that there was not going to be a later for a long, long time. She reached into another pocket in her bag and handed Army several tablets. She explained that one was an appetite suppressant, another a powerful laxative, and the last, a squared-shaped one, a long-acting muscle relaxant.

"Don't take the square one until I tell you to," Oona warned as she gulped down the laxative and hunger suppressant. "If I was you, I'd eat and drink something first. Take the laxative—that's the brown one—and go out back there and shit your brains out. Before you come back here, take the white one. Then we'll wait for our ride."

"What about the square one?" Army asked as he munched nervously on a meal bar and eyed his apple Swoosh.

"You just watch me, and do what I do," she said as she grabbed her bag and began to leave the shack to relieve herself. "And try not to embarrass me. Don't act like you've never done this before. Hear?"

Army heard Oona's voice trail off as she walked outside and around the shack. He could see glimpses of her through broken seams in the shack's plastic slat walls. She made her way to the edge of a littered field, stopped, and surveyed a patch of high grass and weeds before shoving her pants and underwear to her ankles and squatting like a Pygmy.

Army turned away and walked to the shack's window. With the sun up, he could see the transport terminal clearly. There were hundreds of haulers fueling, charging, and whatever else necessary, he surmised, for the vehicles and their drivers to traverse the Tri-Continent. He loved the idea of being able to travel like that, close to the ground, down where real people live real lives, passing in and out of different cultures as if you were no more than a warm breeze. Army was so lost in the idea of it that he didn't hear Oona return to the shack.

She rapped on the paper-glass to get his attention.

"Hey," she said brightly. "Take the brown tab and don't waste any time finding you a spot. It's really fast acting."

Army shook his head, took a breath, then popped the tasteless, chocolate-colored pill in his mouth. Oona handed him a napkin pack as they pressed past each other in the shack's narrow doorway. Army felt his stomach lurch so hard that he whimpered, "Shit-shit-shit."

"That's the idea. Go!" Oona shouted and smacked Army on his ass as he bounded into the morning. "Don't hold anything back," she screamed before laughing like a giddy girl. "Get all your shit out!"

Under her breath, she added, "God, please, get *all* your shit out."

Alone in the basement library, ZaNia could not get enough of the story. Who, she kept asking herself, would cut off a woman's head and then fly it like a flag over Times Square? *There was something intriguingly medieval about it all*, she thought. *A head on a pike. A message? A warning?*

There was surprisingly little about the incident on the Weave's official knots and threads. Most reports dwelled on property damage and the dead and injured. Nothing on the identity of the woman's head. ZaNia was most puzzled by the lack of a single mention of the retrieval of the head that practically fell in her family's lap. It had sent them scampering like roaches under foot. She had no idea where Army was, but sensed somehow that he was safe. There were no Weave reports—even after repeated deep searches—of his arrest, hospitalization or, she swallowed dryly, his death. The same was true for her father and husband. Not a word. She turned back to her work. She was calmer when she worked.

"You got to be kidding," Imani said, standing behind her mother. "Don't tell me that you're still on this chopped-off head stuff?"

"Good morning, daughter," ZaNia chirped as she spoke to Imani's reflection in her oversized viewpanel. "Your tea smells delicious."

"It does, doesn't it?" Imani replied. "I'm trying a new one this morning. The Mother Maternal said it's good for nerves. It's an Arabian blend with a touch of vanilla cream."

Imani took a long, loud sip.

"You found anything on Daddy and G-Daddy yet?" she asked her mother.

"Nothing concrete," ZaNia said as she patted Imani's hand, which rested warmly on her shoulder. "I also haven't found anything to make us worry, either. I know in my bones that they all are safe somewhere. Army too. Safe, just like us."

ZaNia played and replayed three separate news threads about the Times Square head, each ending in a government censor block.

"Why," ZaNia whispered, "would the government not want us to see this? Doesn't feel anything like international terrorism to me."

"I sweetened the tea with fish piss," Imani said with a guilty giggle.

"What?"

"What?" Imani said as much as asked. She shook her head like a disappointed tutor. "You haven't even been listening to me. You're lost in this head thing, playing data tag with the government. It's been almost a week and all you talk about is this head stuff."

ZaNia turned to look at her daughter, a teenager on the verge of womanhood. She reminded ZaNia of herself at about the time she was accepted into the Harlem Heights Order of Maternals Number 3. After a short apprenticeship, she'd climbed into a birthing chair and delivered the first of scores of transgenetic babies.

Imani pricked the bubble of bittersweet recall.

"There are murders everyday, all over Metro New York. Okay, this head on a pole is a little weirder than most of them, but—"

"I don't think so, honey," ZaNia said patiently. "Look at this."

Imani gasped when her mother brought up a life-sized, holographic model she'd made of the severed head. It revolved slowly, in full dimension, from her viewpanel. ZaNia explained that while much of the Order was asleep, she had been isolating and enhancing the head's attributes. A second head shared the viewpanel. This one had been significantly retouched. Lifelike color had been returned to its now taut, peach-colored skin. The wounds were gone, and its grotesque expression was rendered into a stiff-lipped smirk.

Imani took a closer look and pursed her lips. "Why'd ya make her look so stuck up?"

"I just followed her musculature," ZaNia offered.

"Be careful," Imani advised, putting down her teacup. "You know how carried away you get. But please get some rest, Mommy. Okay?"

ZaNia pushed back from the viewpanel and stood up to give her daughter a motherly embrace. She kissed the teenager on the cheek and whispered in her ear, "I promise."

Imani hugged her mother so hard it hurt.

"Imani?"

"Yeah…"

ZaNia returned to her seat in front of the viewpanel.

"We'll all get through this. All of us."

Rikki was eager for the private medical attendant to pack up his instruments and leave her home. She was eager to speak with Mac\Sheehan, and she needed absolute privacy before she could. She glanced at a hallway readout for the time. Another ten minutes to go.

The attendant had examined her mother, bathed her, fed her, and was now dictating a brief status report to Mac\Sheehan. Rikki looked in and noticed the attendant gathering his winking medical devices and carefully packing them away. *Ah, he's ahead of schedule*, she said to herself. Eight long minutes later, the attendant summoned Rikki to the doorway into her mother's room to issue the four words he always uttered just before he disappeared: "She is resting well."

Yes, Mother was resting well. She was seldom conscious, and when she was she stared, unblinking, at the ceiling directly above her. After the first few days, Rikki had an overhead viewpanel installed on which Mac\Sheehan displayed endless streams of family images and vidis. Despite the pictures, Rikki believed that during the increasingly brief moments in which her mother was awake, she saw nothing more than her life receding, like the party lights of a houseboat drifting off into the night.

Her condition remained unchanged, each day a breath away from being her last. Rikki despaired that death would claim all the wondrous things her mother had been—her wit, her spirit, her love—all she knew, all she'd experienced. It would be gone. Forever gone.

Rikki wished she were wrong. She wished there might be more. But

Rikki and her brother shared one inarguable thing. Neither had ever believed in Santa Claus, the Easter Bunny, Jesus Christ, Buddha, Mohammad or any other invisible investiture of good or evil. They disdained any promises of heavenly rewards, celestial paradises, reincarnation, or any other beliefs that promised second bites at the wormy apple of existence.

Rikki remembered Reagan telling her, after a Sunday-school teacher had made her cry with Biblical tales of devils and hell fires, "The only hell, little sister, is Sunday school."

It was precisely 9 A.M. when Rikki gave the attendant a matching faint-smile-and-wave, and her apartment's elevator doors closed.

"Miss Rikki?"

"Yes, Mac."

"I would like to confirm my noon shutdown today."

Rikki looked bothered as she leaned back into her overstuffed bamboo sofa. She swallowed hard.

"Yes, Mac. I need you to shut down for two hours—"

"If you need privacy…"

"No, Mac, that's not it at all," Rikki said, trying to smooth out the quiver that crept into her voice when she lied—even to machines. "I'm having someone over who gets nervous around, uh, home appliances like you. He's a Holistic."

"I know the discipline. Its members believe I'm an abomination because my higher functions are governed by Bio-Cybonetic Assisted Intelligence modules."

"Well," Rikki said, fascinated by the turn of the conversation, "some people think people are people and machines are machines, and they should stay that way—unmixed. Okay, Mac, I know most modern people have no trouble with accepting bio-cybonetics when they are implanted to, okay, keep diseased brains functioning properly. And, as far as I can tell, most people prefer having smarter cars, trains, viewpanels, games, and toaster ovens, even if it is B.C.A.I. that makes them all so smart."

"But," Rikki sighed, "super-smart machines like you make some people very uncomfortable, especially Holistics."

"Do I make you uncomfortable, Miss Rikki?"

"No, of course not. You know how I feel," Rikki said, sounding more defensive than she cared to. "I cannot imagine a day without you here."

"Thank you. I will, of course, operate and monitor all vital household systems, but will shut down my conscious capacities."

"Good," Rikki said as she walked into her mother's room and looked over the ashen little woman asleep beneath undisturbed blankets. "Put security on manual control as well. And place this conversation and all related conservations on this subject in deep mind-lock. The password will be... umm... vanaskhuru."

"Understood," Mac\Sheehan responded. "Vanaskhuru."

24

The Real Synthetic

THE BEAT WAS STEADY.

Bang. Bang. Bang. Bang. Sizzle-Sizzle. POP. Bang.

It was like a heartbeat, but its tempo was more reliable than a pulse. It never missed a beat for love, fear, or rage.

Bang. Bang. Bang. Bang. Sizzle-Sizzle. POP. Bang.

The drum drove the music, rich and complex. It was joy artfully finessed from the temporal to the para-permanent, Cutter thought, as he set his tiny teeth into a tight, toothy grin and let his shoulders loose to roll to the big band's swing. Ah, if only he could have lived in the Harlem of the thirties, he thought. The 1930s, that is.

Sunny Side of the Street…Ain't Misbehavin'…Don't Be That Way…Shine… One O'Clock Jump…Don't Mean A Thing If It Ain't Got That Swing…

"This is my music," he whispered. He just happened to have been born a hundred or so years too late to claim it. Billie and Ellington. Ella and Chick. Basie and Lester Young. Fletcher Henderson and Coleman Hawkins. Louis Armstrong.

Back then, in the 1930s, he would have known them all, when they were as alive as their eternal creations. He would have welcomed them to his club. He would have let their black brilliance shine from his polished dance floor to its twinkling chandeliers. And then again, he reminded himself, in the 1930s, the racial politics of the day, even way north in New York City, would not have tolerated a black man—even a milky-skinned black man like him—owning and operating a snazzy nightclub in Harlem. If he had wanted to toast every solo, applaud every fabulous flourish of sax, snare, and ivory, he would have had to do it from the kitchen, with a mop or dirty pot in his hand. Or from the stage—if he could have had a dab of the talent his great-great-grandfather possessed in those days.

Marvin "Sweet Feet" Hunter had been a Harlem hoofer, a dancer of such mesmerizing elegance that Cutter grew up listening to his grandmother's stories of white people stuffing money in his pockets just to get close enough to touch him. He remembered her stories of black people poking their heads out of their brownstones just to see the man carry groceries home to his family. Once a woman with breasts like satin pillows leaned out of her window and hollered, "You can carry my groceries anytime, Honey Feet ("Or did she say Meat?" his grandmother would laugh, when she didn't see any children around.)"

Cutter's grandmother used to arch her painted eyebrows and cackle with laughter when she got to that part of the story. It would be a decade before Cutter understood the currency of the sort of virility his great-great-grandfather had possessed. At about the same time, he realized that he would never—with his twisted spine and malformed legs—command such sexual power, at least not in any conventional sense.

In the end, what did it buy his great-great-grandfather? Sweet Feet's murder was never solved. He was found with his ankles crushed and his throat slit. Family lore says it was over a gambling debt. Cutter heard that some side woman had something to do with the killing. There were also tales that he talked tough to some white man who heckled a new singer he was working with. All Cutter knew is that Sweet Feet, even dead, helped raise him—whether in the stories he grew up with or in watching over him from the old posters that lined his grandmother's Harlem apartment.

Cutter grew into a man who cherished his ancestral connection to Harlem greatness. It was a bridge to a place and time he wished he could have known the way Sweet Feet had—and not as a cripple who had dragged a busted dream of being a jazz drummer for too long.

Bang. Bang. Bang. Bang. Sizzle-Sizzle. POP. Bang.

"Play those drums, Chick," Cutter murmured, as Webb's "Stompin' At The Savoy" filled his office, inadvertently providing a soundtrack to vidis of a woman's severed head swaying in the breeze high over Times Square.

"Hey-me-MONCee.Here-Ah-drink4U."

"Thanks, Dots," Cutter said, as he threw back a shot of cognac. "But please cut the screech-slang. I'm not in the mood. Straight English."

"Fine.Fine.The BitchQueen's-EngLASH," JoË Dots, said as he ran his huge, dark hand over his scalp, enlivening his kink-curled dreads in the process. He joined Cutter, who was seated behind his specially outfitted antique oak desk. A half-empty bottle of Louis XVI sat amid a clutter of read-outs, data pads, and broken handhelds.

Cutter said nothing, but kept his hooded eyes locked on the ceiling-to-floor display of the butchered head.

"My boy did a good job. Huh?" JoË Dots said, as Cutter never took his eyes from the screen. They both stared a few minutes at the slimy gray head set against a cloudless blue Manhattan sky.

"Nice, very nice job," Cutter said as he savored his drink. He felt a sugary satisfaction as scenes of the head played in multiple angles on his office walls high inside Baghdaddy's. "I've been monitoring the Weave. Try as they might, they cannot bury the truth. Everyone is talking about that goddamned head on a pole.

"Give your man my compliments, and then a little something special," Cutter said as he slowly shook his glass and watched the amber-colored liquor slosh about.

"I will," Dots answered.

"Where is he? Your man? Where is he now?"

JoË Dots took a long hard suck-and-gulp from his perspiring beer bottle before answering.

"Been laying low, like you told me to tell him," Dots said without emotion. "He's got some business way out of town. Thought the timing was good. Those Department bastards looked like dickless clowns on Times Square last week.

"They have no trace on him, except for our inside guy," Dots said.

"The hotel dick?" Cutter asked, as he shook his head in disappointment.

"No worries, no worries," Dots added. "We talked, again. I told him I know he got a baby sister. No more trouble."

Cutter shook his head and showed his teeth. "Pump him. We need to know what the Department knows. The sister is a nice touch. Exactly where is your boy heading?"

"He's driving a long-hauler south. Some light smuggling."

"We can use him when we start moving our product cross-continent," Cutter said from the side of his boyish mouth. "We're already seeing some spikes in demand in key locations. For some of our hottest prospective markets, the head-on-the-pole stunt was like a Weave-Wide commercial."

"Good for business," Dots added.

Cutter uncomfortably shifted his weight in his elevating office chair. He rubbed his forehead hard, so hard that his fingertips left tracks of red at the foot of his receding devil's peak. *Oh shit*, JoË Dots thought, bracing for the worst. If all his years working with Cutter taught him anything, it was the meaning of the laser eye. It could only mean one thing: The boss was pissed about something.

"Buz--ness?" Cutter closed his eyes when he spoke, his voice spitting the word in two, each as foul to him as the other. "With you, it is always biz-ness, biz...ness. Biz. Ness."

JoË Dots hastily poured Cutter another shot. But the hunchbacked little man sitting inches from him only glared at the cut-crystal glass.

"I'm just saying that your Times Square idea has been great for—us."

"Yes, right, of course," Cutter said sarcastically, as he brought his refreshed drink to his lips. "I only wish that you paid better attention to the bigger picture. Damn it, Dots, you're my right hand. I need you to use your head for more than something fuzzy for your whores to wrap their legs around at night.

"*Think*," Cutter said in a screaming whisper. "Think like a black man with a history and a future. That Times Square idea, as you call it, might drive some sales our way, but that is not why I ordered it.

"How many times do I have to repeat myself? I want the authorities— the government, the Department, the ruling elites, and the upper classes that hold this whole, sucking, sick society together—put on notice."

Cutter's face was blazing red as he spoke through clenched teeth. Dots listened and tried hard to calm a virulent mix of rage and fear. It spurred visions of reaching across the desk and ripping Cutter's heart out of his misshapen chest. Then other visions set in, of the consequences if he did. Without hesitation, Cutter loyalists would do the same to him, but not before they splayed open the chests of his children, his mother, and anyone else he cared about.

No one fucked with Cutter. Better than anyone else, JoË Dots should know that. He'd help liquefy dozens who hadn't known better, he reminded himself. So Dots smiled broadly and apologized for his lapse in judgment, for not keeping his eyes trained on "the big picture."

But Cutter was hardly finished with his lecture.

"You have to understand, Dots, that they must learn that even with all their wealth, power, privilege, and delusions of superiority, they are vulnerable," he said, as his thin lips curled back to reveal eyeteeth that looked inhumanly sharp.

"That was the world-class lesson of the Terrorist Wars. Of course, I'm glad that our side finally won. All that destruction, all that disruption of lives big and little, theirs and ours, had to stop. You know I lost my mother and father, exemplary people, in the nights of the Rain of Pain. But I have to admit, I enjoyed the early defeats we suffered. We were arrogant and we needed to learn some humility.

"I think the elites need some reminding, an elbow in the ribs from somebody like me, somebody not in the club, somebody they don't even fucking *see* when I'm standing right in their faces—unless I'm standing there, grinning, begging for a chance to make their day brighter, their way merrier, their sorrows my own. Well, I gave myself a new task, and it's a damn big one, Dots. We have to help them rediscover their humanity.

"Do you see what I'm showing you?" Cutter fumed as he turned in his office chair to face an extreme close-up of the lifeless head on his wall.

JoË Dots said he did. But whenever Cutter climbed onto his class-privilege soapbox, JoË Dots never fully understood the fullness of Cutter's outrage. By all accounts, Cutter was at least as wealthy as most of the elite patrons who pressed into Baghdaddy's every night. And, besides, Dots thought—considering his own dark brown skin—Cutter was, by every racial definition available, a Light.

"I want to keep these self-centered assholes up at night," Cutter continued, talking to the ceiling. "I want them to know that somebody is stealing what they hold most dear—their children's joys, their misbegotten joys. Now I can mind-suck it out, like sweet milk from a coconut.

"And," he began to laugh like it hurt, "I can sell that joy back to them, the fucking cannibals. I can peddle it for enough profit to make *much* more, and sell that, and make enough to steal big, like they do. It's not just business, Dots."

"I understand, Cutter, man. Really. I do, Cee," Dots reaffirmed, as he mindlessly played with the damp mouth of his beer bottle. "Look. It's my training. Remember, I was an economist before you saved me from myself."

"Dots," Cutter said, turning the room's music and his ire down a notch, "I get a little wound up over this Hedz shit. It's just so exhilarating thinking about what we can do with it. We have a chance to *change minds*, literally."

"Yeah," Dots followed. "Change minds."

JoË Dots took a deep breath and tried to gather his courage. He knew his timing was bad but it wasn't likely to get any better soon, he thought. He had to speak to Cutter about business—Hedz business.

He tried to speak, but nothing. He was having trouble concentrating. Cutter's old music was getting on his nerves, too. JoË Dots hated the stuff and couldn't understand how a man eight years his junior could enjoy all this jumpy noise no one except historians and eccentrics cared about. Then it happened.

"I need to talk to you about the Dups," Dots blurted.

Cutter chewed the corner of his mouth. "Biz-ness, again?"

"It's not so much business, really," JoË Dots rhetorically ducked and weaved. "It's like this. I think we need to clarify the Dups issue because it could help further the aims of, well, the big picture."

Cutter leaned back into his seat and closed his eyes. "I'm listening. Draw me a picture; draw me a fucking big, big picture."

Encouraged, Dots pressed.

"One of the white coats showed me a new kind of Dup he came up with," Dots said. "I know what you're thinking. But this one is stable, real stable. It ain't as good as the original memory print, but it's damn good."

"How good?" Cutter said, speaking to his office ceiling.

"Just a taste of a direct injection, but it's a hard high. Bangs the back of your skull and leaves an echo."

"A Hedz re-experience?" Cutter asked, lowering his face to look into Dots's eyes.

"Hell yeah," Dots replied enthusiastically. "But it's much shorter, and sweeter, sweet in a way that makes you want to re-experience again, then again, then again, then—"

"I get it," Cutter said. "You think these Dups are good enough to base a new secondary market?"

"Forgive me, but yeah," Dots said. "A very lucrative secondary market, because these Dups are very cheap to produce off a brain batch."

JoË Dots stopped to read Cutter's face before proceeding. He wanted to project diagrams and reports on the office wall, but didn't dare.

"Go on," Cutter said as he reclined in his office chair and crossed his tiny palms over his bird-like chest. "I'm still listening."

"Well," JoË Dots responded, "these new Dups could give us our first real chance to make Hedz a mass-market product. This could be bigger than Euro Fries and Swoosh drinks, Micro-Pizza and Chinese Eggy Rolls.

"We can get stepped-down synthetic Hedz to cost no more than a cup of Starbucks coffee," Dots said with a smile. "Now, who wouldn't dig in their pocket for a hot hit of borrowed joy?"

Cutter opened his eyes and drew small, imaginary circles on the ceiling as he turned the idea over in his oversized head. He turned to JoË Dots and raised his eyebrows. "Umm," he said. "Do you have samples of these new Dups?"

"We're doing some testing and can have some in a couple of days," JoË Dots replied, his confidence rising.

"Listen, bring 200 units and works here for the 'Scape next week, a week from yesterday."

"Sure," Dots said, and added that the new Dups did not require works. "You just squeeze them like grapes, but under your nose, and *Pow!* You're screwing some rich bastard's girlfriend in the French Alps—or at least you think you did, thirty seconds later."

"Jazzy," Cutter said coolly. "This is your initiative, Dots. I generously reward initiative and, as you know, I'm allergic to failure."

"MeNOworries," JoË Dots said, hardly able to believe that Cutter was willing to give the new Dups—sight unseen—a test run in Baghdaddy's.

Cutter hopped off his chair and leaned against his desk to help him stand as erect as he could. He turned to Dots and half smiled. "We plural on this?"

"Yeah. InI. We're together on this," Dots said, as left the office feeling his heart pounding like some ancient, jazz beat from Cutter's collection.

Bang. Bang. Bang. Bang. Sizzle-Sizzle. POP. Bang.

25

Welcome to the Darks' Side

THE SUBWAY DOORS BANGED OPEN ON THE WEST 125TH STREET station, but Rikki was too busy trying to hush her queasy disquiet to take full notice. She felt smothered, but it was not for lack of air. She wondered where were the touchstones that had given so many decades of her life the ease of reliability, the comfort of order?

Chaos. Rikki choked on it as bodies brushed roughly around her to be disgorged from the rear doors of the windowless car. One of those bodies—tall and stork-stumped—belonged to her hired guide, Mr. PIE.

"Are you certain this is where we are supposed to be?" Rikki shouted, as she stepped into a clamorous press of people.

"I'm sure," he shouted back, extending his bony hand to Rikki to help her navigate the crush. "We made good time. We should be able to make the 8:48 show. Hold tight and follow me."

Rikki reluctantly permitted the man's slender fingers to hook onto hers as he tugged her firmly behind him. *People. So many people and so little space*, Rikki thought, trying hard to keep up. Even the long, uncomfortable subway rides she had regularly taken to high school had not adequately acclimated her to this new world of extreme proximity.

In Philadelphia, or at least in *her* Philadelphia, space was a natural given, like air, water, and sunshine. She never thought of it as a luxury, even a privilege, until Mr. PIE insisted that they stand in the rear of that workers' subway car, packed with people so unnaturally absent of presence that she came to regard them as being in kind of suspended humanity.

Rikki and Mr. PIE were going nowhere. "It's a checkpoint," Mr. PIE yelled into Rikki's face. She was surprised that his breath smelled of mint and malt. "Since the trouble…" He looked around, then lowered his voice enough to urge Rikki to read his lips as much as listen for his words. "They've been stepping up random checks around here."

She nodded. What Rikki did not indicate was that she understood much too well. Since the beheadings, the Department was focusing its suspicions on the kinds of people who have always fallen under the spears, swords, rifles, and now electronic scanners of disdainful gatekeepers. She knew no limousines were being searched, that none of their well-dressed, well-connected passengers were being inconvenienced by hoggish sniffs for the scent of blood and savagery.

"How long?"

Mr. PIE hunched his skeletal shoulders.

"How long do you think this is going to take?" Rikki screamed over the drone of the milling crowd and departing trains and trams.

"Be patient," Mr. PIE replied. "And don't worry about your U.I.D. I got it covered."

Fear sliced though her like a cold scalpel. She had practically forgotten. She was traveling under a false identity. If the checkpointers detected that her U.I.D. was fraudulent, she would be arrested on the spot. Her mission would end in disgrace; she could face jail time, and certainly her brother's wrath. Worse, her mother would die. *Like any other mother*, she reminded herself.

Mr. PIE sensed his client's agitation. "Relax. It'll be okay."

Rikki was shaking her head in disbelief as the crowd squeezed into a single, snaking queue for the checks. She cupped her hands to still their trembling. *It could very well end like this*, she thought. She imagined a Weave thread: *Wealthy, middle-aged Philadelphia housewife nabbed in Harlem.*

"Listen," Mr. PIE whispered in Rikki's ear. "I told you I got this covered. This is what you pay me for."

Rikki discovered that she was holding tightly to Mr. PIE's outstretched hand. He was asking her to give him her U.I.D. card. She handed it over and then watched the private investigator expertly slip a folded $10,000 bill just beneath it.

"That's a bribe," Rikki whispered.

"No," Mr. PIE replied. "That's generosity."

The queue had stalled. Word filtered back that a whole family was being arrested for improper travel documentation. And she overheard two

Dark men saying that the checkpointers were asking about a Dark, a hired handsome who had been seen with a pleasurist. Rikki forced herself to relax. She let herself daydream.

She saw herself as she was when she entered the common rail train six hours ago, still cheery and optimistic about what she'd find in Harlem. Slowly, she'd wilted in the train's stifling air, in its heavy, moist heat, its movement without progress. Then, there were the faces, stoic passengers, surrounding her again with their sweat-stained clothing and unguarded bodily emissions that overwhelmed the train's ventilation system.

And there was that roasted meat.

For the first dozen miles of the ride to New York, Rikki had been convinced that she smelled roasted meat. Precisely what kind of meat, she couldn't quite determine. Surely, no one could have been eating cooked food in a train—not even a common rail train. Wasn't that strictly illegal? Health considerations and all, she considered. Besides, who among this pack of impoverished could afford to snack on roasted meat?

She had looked over to Mr. PIE for a clue. But he too rode in some sort of commuter's trance, his eyes closed and his hand holding fast to an overhead strap. Meat. Meat. Where was it coming from?

Rikki searched the shadowy rear of the train, snaking her sight over extended elbows, around raised forearms, past faces and open armpits, until she found a curious woman bent over in the single aisle with a heavy pack strapped to her back. She looked—especially around the deep set, worried sockets of her eyes—to be about fifty, Rikki's age. But this woman could also have been years younger, she reasoned, prematurely aged by the weight of too many hard days and harder nights. She noticed her smooth, unblemished brown skin, the same smooth skin of the small boy huddled a step behind the woman.

Was she his mother? Rikki wondered. *Grandmother? Great-grandmother?*

Rikki watched the child, who had unnaturally stubby limbs, a strangely flattened head and a vacant stare. A loop of nylon cord was tied crudely around his waist and knotted to the woman's pack. Just as Rikki was about to resume her search elsewhere, the train shuddered violently. Everyone involuntarily swayed as the train swerved into a hard, right turn.

The boy lost his footing, tumbling into a forest of passengers' legs. As the boy fell, the force of his weight on the cord tore open the woman's pack. A canvas compartment that held five, bulging pockets tumbled into view.

"Oh, God!" Rikki had not intended to scream and was embarrassed that she had.

A few faces turned in her direction. Mr. PIE opened his eyes and mouthed a question. She read his lips: *What's wrong?* She motioned with her head to the women in the aisle, who were checking to see if the boy was okay.

Rikki was sure that Mr. PIE could see as clearly as she did—five dead puppies wrapped in vendors' foil. Each has been carefully stuffed in the pack's pouches, leaving only their furry little heads poking out. The odor of cooked meat was overpowering until the woman secured a large plastic flap over the pouches.

Mr. PIE's smirk immediately angered Rikki. He shouldered his way closer to Rikki, standing directly in front of her and blocking her view of the dead dogs. She whispered, "Why is that woman carrying cooked puppies in her bag?"

Mr. PIE smirked again, enjoying the rich woman's ignorance. "She's a hot dogger," he said. "Hot. Dog-ger."

Rikki narrowed her eyes.

"She sells puppy meat on the street," Mr. PIE said matter-of-factly. "It's a delicacy. The meat is sweet and tender, especially when it is lightly roasted."

He smacked his lips.

"Why are their heads still on?" Rikki asked, trying hard to suppress her sense of superiority over the poor people on the train, over Mr. PIE.

"Two things," Mr. PIE answered quickly. "The eyes let you know how fresh the meat is. And some people like to see the head. It let's them know that they're buying real dog, not some oversized rat or park possum or something worse."

Rikki chewed her lip and tried not to imagine how a puppy might look roasting, with its hairy head hanging off the edge of a grill.

"I like toy poodle myself, but it's hard to find," Mr. PIE said, as he motioned to summon the woman for a sale.

Rikki violently shook the memory from her head. She opened her eyes as Mr. PIE began pulling her through the Harlem checkpoint. The checkpointers only glanced at Rikki but stared hard at Mr. PIE, who stared back with equal stoniness.

Managing a pace that nearly matched Mr. PIE's, Rikki plowed along the Central Harlem sidewalks. She could hear live music spilling from a café's open door. A guilty excitement filled her. How her husband would disapprove. But the bang of piano keys and the wail of a saxophone were irresistible.

Soon after Rikki and Ushala had met, he had told her that they were uncommon people. Much later she learned that her husband meant that they had no business with people who he deemed other than uncommon. Her husband hated crowds, especially crowds of "the unfortunates."

But who, she wondered, were the unfortunates here? She and Mr. PIE had just crossed Malcolm X Boulevard and everywhere she saw Darks and Lights together. All appeared full of a bubbling exuberance. There was energy, laughter, and smiles. Lots of smiles. Rikki felt herself smiling as she kept thinking, *I'm here. I am actually in Harlem. Harlem at night!*

She had heard and read so much about Harlem's history, its rebirth, and its celebrated debauchery. Carried by a touring sidewalk, Rikki swung around trying to get more than a glimpse of brightly lit storefronts, charming cafes, soaring grand hotels, and the huge nightclubs she knew Reagan had always happily frequented, even as he warned Rikki away from them.

Suddenly she was knocked to the moving pavement and flat on her face. She could feel the full weight of a man on her back, bucking and screaming as if he had lost his mind, before Mr. PIE tugged the man off her. Harlem security came running to assist.

"Sorry, sorry, mom," one seal-black officer said as he brushed off Rikki's grumbling assailant, while another officer, a hairless Asian Light, fastened a restraining band around the deranged man's arms and torso.

"Another Hedz case," the Dark officer said to his partner as they carted the sedated prisoner away.

Mr. PIE was helping Rikki steady herself and rubbing gritty dirt from her cheeks when she asked him what the officer meant by a "Hedz case."

"We starting to see a lot of them like that," he explained. "Too much Hedz up the nose."

Mr. PIE said the young man was probably from a leading Light family, most likely one with more wealth than he could waste in ten lifetimes. But when people became addicted to Hedz, he said, their minds eventually shattered like cheap glass. "They lose themselves," Mr. PIE said. "Too many memories not their own in their heads. Some kill themselves, usually with a shell to the brain just to shut it up."

In the distance, she could see a billboard with onion domes and minarets aglow with garish lighting, suggesting yet another nightclub. Despite Mr. PIE's apparent indifference to more bright lights, Rikki was grateful that he was her tour guide. Alone, she would have never ventured this far uptown. Never would have left the cozy SoHo hotel where she always stayed when she visited New York. Mr. PIE clearly knew his way around. Mac\Sheehan had done well to recommend him. She wanted to key up Mac and update it about her adventure.

But Mr. PIE forbade any communications. He had been emphatic: "No traces."

"Stand here," Mr. PIE shouted over the strained singing of a street performer. "I'll be right back with tickets for the 8:48."

Rikki nodded, thinking the idea of tickets was quaintly old-fashioned. No one seemed to pay much attention to her as she stood in a gaudy lobby, its walls covered in framed holographic posters and ads battling for attention in the misty, colored air. She was surprised by how easily she melted into the scene. At least a third of the crowd pressing into the lobby were Lights. Everyone looked to be less than half her age, but didn't seem to care.

Mr. PIE returned and handed her a red slip of coated paper. When she grabbed the ticket, it turned green and began showing previews of the show they were about to see inside.

"Okay, I know you've never had roasted poodle, so let me ask, have you ever been to a Screamer?" Mr. PIE asked as they walked slowing toward the auditorium's main entrance.

His question, like his smirk, annoyed Rikki. She did not like the way he seemed to enjoy rubbing her face in her ignorance about a world that, until a few weeks ago, never mattered much to her. She gave richly to charities for the shanty poor, and supported candidates who spoke out for sharing more of the nation's wealth with those who had none. There was something in Mr. PIE's manner that reminded her of the way her brother treated her whenever she asked him to take her to Harlem.

Mr. PIE did not wait for her to answer. He reached out to her as they entered the darkened theater, guiding her to a seat without asking her where she wanted to sit. "It's best to get a seat while most of these idiots party in the lobby. They're going to work themselves up for at least a few more minutes."

Rikki sat up straight as Mr. PIE slid low into his reclining seat.

"Listen," Rikki said to the investigator. "I'm paying you very good money to take me on this little field trip. So I don't appreciate your condescension."

Mr. PIE sat up and looked coolly into her face.

"Okay?"

"Okay," he said dryly before slipping back into his seat.

"And why," Rikki could feel her voice rising, "do I have to keep calling you by this ridiculous name 'Mr. PIE'?"

"Please lower your voice," he said, lowering his more as he spoke. "Remember what I told you in Philadelphia, when you hired my services? I must protect my identity as much as I must protect yours."

He whispered in Rikki's ear: Private Investigator Executive—P-I-E. Mr. PIE."

"Okay, Mr. PIE," Rikki said, pleased with speaking up for herself. "Now tell me what a Screamer is, and why we are here."

Mr. PIE spoke slowly. As he did, he noticed that in the darkened theater that his charge had an appealing profile. The fact that he noticed the delicate curve of her cheeks, and the soft upturn of her nose, surprised him. He usually didn't like women—especially women his own age.

Never taking his eyes from her, Mr. PIE explained that the octagonal theater exhibited movies specially made for it. They were shown in the round—but more importantly, unlike the movies she was probably accustomed to, these were nonlinear and highly interactive. Each movie was made with thousands of alternative scenes, soundtracks, and effects. He told her that special receptors built into the theater, including its seats, tracked audience members' moods and reactions.

"Depending on what the audience says or does or screams, the movie responds," Mr. PIE explained. "That's why they call these theaters, and the stuff they show in them, Screamers."

"Thank you," Rikki said, still annoyed. "And why, again, are we here?"

"A rendezvous," Mr. PIE said, rising in his seat to survey the rapidly filling theater. The suspended circular screen was dropping into place as clip-clop-hop music began to blare.

Mr. PIE and Rikki talked through the coming attractions and commercials for everything from DigiDots to vaginal tightening creams. She was impressed with his knowledge of Harlem life—especially after sunset. Maybe, she thought, he wasn't such a stiff. Their chatting stopped when the evening's first Screamer started, opening with what looked to Rikki like introductions of the cast. Each character was greeted with enormous blasts of cheers, catcalls, and foot stomps.

Rikki didn't know what to think. The Light couple next to her stomped feet and booed at the screen when it showed a pasty-faced actor Mr. PIE said was famous for playing villains in Screamers.

The movie started with an aerial scene of contemporary Los Angeles. A mid-tempo ballad played in the movie's background as the camera panned into the broad streets of downtown L.A. Rikki could hear hundreds of feet stomping, and hand-clapping coming at twice the tempo of the movie's soundtrack. In an instant, the music shifted up-tempo, matching the cadence of the claps. The audience broke into approving cheers. Some danced in the aisles.

The pasty-faced actor appeared, driving a gleaming sports speeder. The theater shook with boos. Everyone around Rikki was standing and booing—even Mr. PIE was making his displeasure felt.

Suddenly, the pasty-faced character's head exploded, and the audience screamed its approval. The scene panned and showed a handsome Dark man holding a penetrator rifle in the broken window of a nondescript office building. Rikki was frustrated that she could hardly hear what little there was of the movie's dialogue.

Mr. PIE reached over and pulled her ticket from her hand and peeled a circular tab from is back. He pressed it behind Rikki's ear, where it stuck. He told her it was DigiDot that would pipe the movie's audio directly to her head. Rikki smiled and returned to the Screamer.

Why, she wondered, *have I never heard anything about all of this? Why was there nothing about it on my Weave threads?* When a scene cut to some sort of morgue where the body of the pasty-faced character lay half-opened on a table, the crowd began shouting, "Rise! Rise! Rise! Rise!"

And the character did, sitting up with a yawning, brain-drooling hole in its forehead. Rikki realized that the audience, exercising the authority of its interests, had transformed the movie. It was no longer a detective tale but had jumped genres, now a horror movie with stiff-legged, stalking dead. Another scene featured the Screamer's heroine, a voluptuous Dark, climbing into an attic with a flashlight.

One viewer shouted, "Bitch, you better not go in there." Others yelled out other directives, chanting loudly, "Go in! Go in! Go in!" A few moments later, the heroine turned to face the audience, as if she needed help in making up her mind. Then, to Rikki's disappointment, she shut the attic door and backed down her ladder.

Rikki had gotten so caught up in the Screamer that she didn't notice that Mr. PIE had slipped away in the darkness. Frightened, she stared at the empty theater seat next to her as the theater erupted in chants of "KISS HER! KISS HER! KISS HER!"

She looked at the screen and saw the pasty-faced monster chasing the heroine back up her ladder and into the attic.

"GET HER! GET HER! GET HER! GET HER!"

The heroine fought him off, but he managed to corner her in the attic.

"FUCK HER(up) FUCK HER(up)FUCK HER(up)!" The audience convulsed as the monster wrestled the woman to the floor, ripping her clothing off between snarls. Rikki was trying to reassure herself that Mr. PIE had left only to relieve himself as she watched the audience try to push the story into a brutal sex scene.

Mr. PIE grabbed her arm hard and spoke loudly in her ear. "I found the man I told you about. We have to leave. He'll join us on our next rendezvous."

Rikki got up and took one last look at the screen, just as the monster ate the woman, limb by limb.

The room stank. Despite the earnest efforts of a frail, toothless man who stood in a corner of the room with a mop and bucket, the crowded waiting room's faux tile floor reeked with a sour stench that doubled Rikki over in her hard plastic seat. She was flanked by Mr. PIE and the man they had picked up in the Screamer.

"You'll get used to it," Mr. PIE said, as he let his hand linger on the small of her back a bit too long.

Rikki's thoughts swirled in a dizzying muddle: *What is this place? Why did they bring me here? When will I meet the dealer? Why does everything smell so terrible?*

"This is an InteliX Center," Mr. PIE said under his breath. "Well, it's more an off-brand, owned by InteliX. It's a donor station. It pays good cash and doesn't ask bad questions."

Rikki looked up just long enough to see a Dark woman behind him smear blood that was trickling down the side of her face. The woman made eye contact with Rikki, then promptly vomited on the floor. Rikki moaned as the woman's let her head fall into her lap. She could hear the mop bucket steering toward the latest spill.

"Don't worry," Mr. PIE said. "Everybody gets used to it."

Rikki was beginning to question the wisdom of her plan. From the start, she'd known it was audacious and would not succeed without undertaking major risks. Her plan was the only way. Mother was dying, dying completely. Harlem and its new drug held the only promise left available to her.

She had convinced herself that she could do this. She was a world traveler. And she could do this without Reagan's help. After all, he had helped enough by telling her about Hedz.

"I know we didn't talk about this," Mr. PIE said tentatively, "but my contact here says his people want you to perform a small act of, uh, good faith."

Rikki sat up and looked around the room. The knots in her belly had just begun to loosen. She was getting accustomed to the waiting room's stench. Even all the dazed faces there were beginning to disturb her less. Hell, she thought, this was their choice. No one was forcing them to sell their brains, a few milligrams at a time. They probably used the money to get high on some cheap junk. *What did she care?* she wondered, before pangs of guilt overtook her.

Rikki looked at the stranger, a hard-faced Dark wearing a brightly colored skullcap that was weirdly lumpy on one side. Somehow, she thought, he *looked* the role of a drug dealer. The man said nothing and stared across the room as if the wall wasn't there—as if the blown-particle benches crammed with wrecks of people weren't there either.

"If you want to do business, you have to make a donation," Mr. PIE said.

A white flash of anger snapped Rikki's head back.

"Isn't all the money enough?" Rikki screamed through clenched teeth just before she realized what Mr. PIE was actually suggesting. Confused, she began shaking her head in disbelief.

Donate? Me? How could he think I'd even consider that?

Of course, Rikki knew about InteliX.

Almost every device in her home operated on Bio-Cybonetic Assisted Intelligence modules. Mac\Sheehan would be little more than an expensive toy without B.C.A.I. And, of course, she realized that B.C.A.I. processors were developed from human brain cells. She didn't really understand the science, but she knew that it was common knowledge that InteliX operated donation centers all over the world. It was a huge corporation, a major provider of jobs and a source of pride to Greater America. But she had never considered visiting a donation center. On her Weave, they were always seen as bright, clean, and friendly places that help the poor make ends meet—not hellholes like this.

"DeseHowWePeepsLIVE24-365," the Dark said to Rikki without bothering to face her. "LETemSUCKyoBRAINSifUwantMYhelps."

Rikki stared unblinking at Mr. PIE.

"Looks like that's the deal," he said, not looking at her. "You can call it off now and I'll make sure you get back to Philly by dawn. Or you—"

"I know what I can do!" Rikki shouted, then began to sob.

"SHEain'tREDdee4us," the Dark grunted. "MeOUT."

"Wait," Rikki said as she wiped her eyes dry. *This had to work*, she told herself. "Just wait one fucking minute."

The Dark grinned.

Mr. PIE looked down at his plastic shoes.

"How long do I have to wait?" she asked.

Rikki let her eyes rest on a huddle of three teenaged girls, each wearing painted faces that inadequately covered their innocence. Their arms, legs, and bellies were covered with tat-toons—bouncing teddy bears and shooting stars auto-animated onto their brown skin. They looked frightened as they fidgeted on the bench. They looked, Rikki concluded, like desperate little girls.

"You don't have to do this," Mr. PIE spoke into Rikki's ear.

"ButUcomSOfar2do," the Dark said damply into her other ear.

"Okay. Okay," Rikki shouted, waving the men off.

Rikki took a shallow breath then spoke. "I'll do it, but no more surprises like this! You hear me? You know if anything happens to me, PIE, all you get is your deposit."

Looking at the Dark, she continued. "And your boss can't make a deal with me if I'm brain-dead—or dead-dead."

Mr. PIE nodded. "I hear it's not so bad," he offered. "It isn't supposed to hurt too much—the first time."

"ItJUSTaLiLPEN-na-TRA-tion," the Dark said.

The Dark dragged off his skullcap to reveal a spray of healed-over dots on a part of his head that was sheared to the skin. They looked to the untrained eye like insect bites. The other side sprang to life with snaking dreadlocks. The Dark began laughing loudly as if he were recalling punch lines from the asylum, rocking and clapping his hands to the music of his own amusement.

Rikki looked to Mr. PIE, who parked his equine nose an inch from hers before he spoke.

"Welcome," he said, "to the Darks' side."

26

Intercourses

"**I** CAN'T. I CAN'T, I CAN'T DO THIS."

Army's voice was faint, its sound so barely formed that Oona wondered if she had imagined the words. She said nothing, giving Army a chance to reclaim his confession—if he had actually made it. She preferred saying nothing. It was not only expedient, it was decent, she thought—given the circumstances. If he truly meant to cry out, he would do it again, she reasoned.

It had been ten hours since Oona and Army were packed and locked away into the smuggler's hold of Rattle's cross-continental hauler. Oona was an experienced hand at such travel arrangements. She knew no better way to move undetected through the many state, regional, and minor municipal security checkpoints. It was exponentially faster and easier than any other means she knew.

An aboveground, cross-county road trip was laughable. The interstate highways were among the most scrutinized strips of asphalt anywhere in the Tri-Continent. Off road was regularly patrolled by freelance toll takers and bands of robbers. Rattle's boys had pulled in a lot of due bills to get her and Army as far as Camden by car, she knew.

Without proper security ratings, air travel was out of the question. Oona sucked her teeth when she considered the steep cost of a flight ticket, even for a hop on a hoverplane. Only the rich or those who worked directly for the rich flew, and very few of them were Darks like her; even if she somehow possessed solid security status and an elite-class ticket, she would be too self-conscious to fly. She would draw suspicion, scrutiny, and then, without a doubt, trouble.

A deep sadness settled over Oona. She had no experience of the world of fancy skyliners and lazy sunsets off exotic shorelines. Worse, she knew she would probably never get that experience. But that didn't keep her from dreaming. She remembered a recent Weave thread that showed a delegation of Chinese businesswomen and global politicians waving happily from the open deck doors of super skyliners. "They are working so far from home for you at home," she remembered the Weave saying. Oona closed her eyes so tight she saw white. Why had she been born so Dark, and so broke? Why hadn't the double staircase of her DNA delivered her into a life less contentious? Less cruel?

She was twenty-four years old and had never been higher in the air than the top of a rickety Ferris wheel hastily erected for a Washington Heights street fair. What would it feel like to fly twenty times faster than the roar of your skyliner's engines? So high the stars didn't dare to twinkle?

A violent cascade of bumps shook Oona from her fantasies. The last crash threw her forehead hard into the rubberized aluminum ribs of the cramped smuggler's compartment.

Oona could hear Army struggling against his constraints. She could feel his head thrashing from side to side against her stocking feet. They were locked, flat on their backs, in a metal box tucked beneath tons of cargo. Strapped tight for their own safety, they laid beside each other, head to feet, in total darkness.

She wondered whether the crash had broken the skin. Her arms were still too numb with muscle relaxants to check for blood.

She heard Army stir again beside her.

"Can you hear me?" he asked, his voice hoarse and, if she didn't know better, creaky with sleep.

"Were you *asleep*?"

"Yeah, I guess so. But, yes-yeah, I think I was having a bad dream. Was I talking, talking in my sleep?"

"It's the dark. You sleep in it and wake up in it. Hard to know what's real and what's not. And, yeah, you were talking all right."

"Strange. It's disorienting. Like being a blind man walking in his sleep," Army said, his voice growing fuller. "It raises some metaphysical questions, doesn't it?"

"Yeah, like, does a born-deaf schizophrenic hear voices?"

"Now you're being silly," Army said, enjoying the way his laugh sounded in the closeness of the hold. "But that's all right. A long time ago, someone said: 'No sense makes sense.' "

"Manson. Charles Manson said it," Oona replied. "He's some kind of hero to my cousin."

"That maniac Rattle?"

"Be careful," Oona said with a chuckle. "He's the one driving this rig."

"Somehow that doesn't surprise me," Army replied.

The two permitted themselves some unguarded laughter.

"I never knew traveling in a double coffin could be so much fun," Army said.

"You surprise me," Oona said. "I was sure I was going to have to talk you out of a panic attack by now. A lot of people—even with the relaxants—go a little crazy their first time in a smuggler's hold."

"Did you?" Army asked reflexively

"No lie, my first time was a nightmare. I was traveling with this guy who basically just wanted to fuck me. He kept saying he didn't want my money, that he would do me this favor and sneak me cross-continent. Before we got in the hold, he seemed like a 'kay guy, you know? I paid him, and took my chances." Oona cleared her throat and half-laughed, half-whimpered. In the darkness, Army could not be certain which. He went with the whimper and wished he had never brought up the issue.

"About five minutes before the hauler picked us up, he hands me these muscle relaxants and tells me to take them. He says I'll need them to make the trip." Oona hissed.

"I was eighteen. I wanted to be an actress in the Screamers, but they don't make Screamers in Oaklyn, New Jersey."

"That's where you're from?"

"I lived there a while."

"Fine," Army said, trying to bury his annoyance with Oona's dodge. "Okay, so you are trying to get—where? Don't tell me Hollywood," he asked.

"Why?"

"Because it's such a cliché, that's why."

"It's only a cliché if you don't make it," she snapped.

"Granted," Army conceded. "So what happened?"

"Nothing. Nothing at first," Oona said softly. "I'd seen plenty of his type. Men started circling around me when I wasn't much more than pigtails and tit buds. I had no plans to be his little fuck-slave, trapped in the belly of a cross-country hauler."

"So, what did you do?"

"Nothing."

"What do you mean, nothing?" Army asked.

"Ah… that feels nice," Oona hissed in a voice faint, but clear.

"Go on," Army insisted. "What happened after you took the relaxants?"

"I didn't take them," Oona said blankly. "I let him think I did. When the hauler showed up, we were packed in side by side; there was just room enough to turn on your side. Whenever I did, he did. There we were, sealed away like spoons in some forgotten drawer."

"And let me guess," Army said. "He was behind you."

"You must have crystal balls," Oona giggled.

"No, just hairy ones. I know how men'll connive to get next to a pretty ripe peach like yours."

"Oh, that's what you call it?"

"Peach?"

"No," Oona grunted, "conniving. And Mr. Black, are you flirting with me?"

"What happened next?"

"I said nothing."

Army knew better than to believe that. He pictured the scene, the two of them all hugged up in the dark, bumping along the highway with nothing to do but each other. For a moment, he envied the scoundrel.

"Nothing?"

"Well, he starts talking all this nonsense in my ear about what he could do for me if I did for him. You know. Lame shit. I told him over and over again that I wasn't interested. But he started slobbering in my ear, trying to get me to turn on my side so he could rub against my ass. Oh—I mean peach. And I keep flipping onto my back."

"So what did you do?"

"Nothing. I mean, he thought the relaxants were going to make me all rag-doll and he would take me any way he wanted."

"Did he take relaxants too?"

"Hell no," Oona said with an edge to her voice. "He said he was a war veteran and could manage without the chemicals. He practiced some trans-med kind of shit."

"So…"

"So, he won't stop bugging me. I keep saying no, and now he's trying to get his hands under my clothes. Next thing I know he's got me on my side and he's trying to pull my pants down. He wasn't even bothering to unbuckle or unzip anything. Just yanking and tugging like he's skinning a fish.

"He's talking all kinds of shit now. He's all panting and moaning and saying I knew all along that he'd given me a pussy discount, that no one can hear me or help me, and a bunch more bullshit.

"But I'm resisting and he can't figure out how this Dark bitch can fight so hard with the relaxants in me," Oona said. "Then, just when he's just about got my pants and panties down, I finally get my pickle poker out of my sleeve sheath. And I start stabbing the shit out of him."

Army swallowed hard and fought the impulse to say something comforting. This was her liberation narrative, he realized—how she became the woman she was. It was clear to Army that she didn't need him or any other man to validate any part of it.

"I couldn't see a thing. But just like he was using the tight space against me, I was using it against him. Nah, I had no one to call for help. And now his ass didn't either. I think my first stab caught him in his stomach. I must have hit an artery, too, because he was a bleeder.

"By the time he realized what I had done, I'd poked him with three more deep ones. He started begging for me to stop and I could hear blood gurgling in his voice. But I couldn't. I wiggled myself around so I could face him. I kept stabbing and stabbing.

"Everything was slippery. I knew I was soaked in his blood. My hand and arm were getting tired. But I kept stabbing. Then he wasn't moving any more. I wasn't either—except I was alive and he wasn't."

Army murmured, "Damn. You killed a man."

"Damn straight I killed the fucker!" Oona replied. "But I didn't realize I'd have to lie next to that sack of shit for nineteen and half hours. It was horrible. He had all these muscle spasms. Like he didn't want to stay dead.

"It's enough to kill ya," Oona said, this time letting loose a wicked laugh.

"What happened when you got to your destination and they found the body?"

"Nothing," Oona said. "We'd paid in advance and the driver was no fool. He cussed about the mess, then yelled at me to get the hell out of his sight. He knew the deal. I didn't have to draw him a fucking diagram.

"I stumbled off into the woods. We weren't anywhere near California. It was some place in Louisiana. I heard the driver throw the dead man's body into some pond or something before he pulled back onto the highway."

"Damn," Army said, wishing he could muster up something more responsive, or more sympathetic.

"Scary story, huh?" Oona asked.

Army suppressed the urge to ask her more, or to offer his own scary story. But the companionship he felt with Oona—and the muscle relaxants—were freeing him from his inhibitions.

"Check this out," Army blurted. "I grew up in an apartment in a poor part of Harlem with a stepfather who wanted nothing to do with me unless he was drunk, and then it was to smack me around. My mother, who doesn't know who my father is, loves me so much she imprisons me in the apartment. She tells me that the neighborhood is too dangerous. There were still unearthed viral bombs going off. So, no playing outside. No school. My mother becomes my teacher.

"When I'm eighteen, I win a lottery scholarship to University, but it turns out that I'm the only Dark in my graduating class. I have only a couple of friends and find myself staying in my room or library most of the time. I graduate with a double degree in interpretative text. I'm twenty-four and as green as new grass. I work for my mother for a while in her home-based information-management business. I get a string of other jobs. All of them I hate.

"I finally get a job with one of the most successful corporate talent search companies in New York. The only hitch is that the agency's owner takes special interest in me—all of it while she's on her back. She pays me well, but she treats me like the whore I was.

"Then one day, after a few years of this, someone breaks into our hotel room on Chinese New Year. They knock me out, and they chop her head right off. I don't know how long I'm out, but after I get turned out on the street— by the *Department*, who've had me I don't know how long—somebody plants her rotting head on the roof of my family's apartment building.

"Now I'm running to God knows where, with a pleasurist with whom I've never had the pleasure and is somehow mixed up in the whole thing."

Army took a breath, but Oona was completely silent. Then he launched in again. "Here you are, talking openly about how you killed a man, but not a goddamned word about what you know about the night I became a murder suspect. Not a word about how I've been implicated, how my whole family has been implicated, IN! THIS! FUCKING! Bullshit!"

The distant whirl of heavy engine turbines filled the hold.

"You done?" Oona asked, her voice stern but oddly calm.

Army stared deeply into the darkness and tried to reimagine its pitch blackness as some infinite night. He wished he could cast all his confusion, regrets, and anger into that night. Then, quite to his shock, his eyes began to tear.

"Let it out," Oona urged him. "Let all your shit out, Army."

"What?"

"I said let go. You're holding too much inside," Oona said in a voice Army could only describe as feathery. "It's obvious. Just let go of it."

For an instant, Army wanted to lash out at Oona. Who was she to tell him what he needed to do? But before he could sharpen words to hurl at her, something in his throat caught him unawares. His eyes moistened and his nose ran.

Army was crying, trembling with tears, sorrow and regret.

"That's right, Army," Oona said softly. "Let it all go."

Army cried, embarrassed and relieved. He cried for his mother, his sister, grandfather, stepfather. He even cried a little for Kattrel, for the way she died and for the instances of genuine kindness she had shown him from time to time.

Then he felt Oona's feet leave his shoulders. She was turning in the tiny space, awkwardly—he felt what must have been her knee bump into his side—and then, with a soft exhalations, she was slowly tumbling down over him. Her hands were at his shoulders and unbuckling his safety constraints.

"Don't. Don't say a thing," she whispered as she laid her body on his.

"Turn under me." She urged him with a gentle push.

He obeyed and soon felt Oona's supple body scoot back behind his. He could feel her hot breath on the back of his neck. Her warm, soft hands roamed his body. Army instinctively closed his eyes—even in the dark. His heart was pounding a satisfying counterpoint to his deep, steady respiration of the hold's recycled air.

"Turn. Turn," she insisted in a whisper.

Army felt Oona's hips pull in close to his as her hands pushed back his coat and opened his shirt. She buried her head on his breastbone and kissed his heart. He smelled her hair, fragrant with sweet oils and the richer scent of her. He reached out and found her waist. Her clothing had rode up her back as she'd wiggled over him. Her bare skin was hot and impossibly smooth.

He moaned when she opened his trousers. She kissed him from head to head. Army mustered only short, approving grunts. Army reached into the near darkness and found Oona's breasts. Her nipples were erect for his touch, for his tongue.

Oona's kisses lingered on Army's tear-salted cheek before returning to his lips.

"Oona…"

"Shhh. Hush…" she said before gliding her tongue back into his mouth to find his tongue—wet, heavy, and responsive.

Oona enjoyed the taste of him, the solid, proud feel of him. She was enjoying the seduction, too. He was a man who had grown accustomed to being taken by a woman. Oona understood how that felt, so she purposely prolonged each erotic act of her passion play.

She wanted Army, as much as she wanted Army to want *her*, and not some fabrication she crafted night after night for the Harlem alleyways. She knew Army had been attracted to Oooh—most men with a working dick and balls were. But she wanted to give him so much more. Oona, not Oooh. It pleased her to hear her name—"Ooon-naaaa…"—on Army's breath as she turned her ass to him.

"Hmmm," Oona purred, as she parted her thighs.

27

The Weight of Waiting

I T WAS 2:20 IN THE MORNING AND REAGAN WOULD NOT ACCEPT THE WIDE-eyed fact that he could not sleep.

Why? He'd never felt so secure, never the recipient of so much peer courtesy, respect—or perhaps it was fear. At the Department, he had acquired authentic authority after being named a captain following a lightning series of successful raids on Hedz operations. He was a major case manager, and with the position came newfound power. At last, Reagan thought in a shimmering bubble of satisfaction, he'd acquired a quotient of redemption.

Secretly, he wished his mother could wake from her deathbed just long enough to see how wrong she had been about him. Then die.

He kept his old Bronx apartment. Reagan enjoyed being "a big ass bass in a little muddy pond." Since being named to management class, he could now be a big bass in much vaster ponds. Nevertheless, he chose to live where he had spent the last twenty-five years—if not among friends, at least among a few friendly faces.

Reagan savored the idea that his sister was jealous of his class-status-skipping. He knew his net worth didn't approach anything like her accumulated booty. But he knew that she knew that hers came by way of matrimonial proximity—from an absentee husband, his connections, his resourcefulness. Reagan, on the other hand, had polished his own penny. And he knew that she knew that, too.

His apartment was spotless. He had a cleaning woman coming in four days a week. Rumors spread at the tavern that she was polishing more than his doorknobs. To spite his sister, Reagan bought a SmartSlumber just like hers—except with all the latest features, even if he'd never bothered to use them.

But in the first official hours of this particular weekend, the fancy bed might as well be made of rusty nails.

By 2:45 A.M., he was wandering the listless street just outside his old building. "*Spent all those fucking credits and still can't sleep in the fucking thing,*" Reagan thought. He paused, bent his knees, and leaned into the distressed brick facade of a libations shop, looking like a man half asleep in an invisible chair.

A gaggle of crackleheads spinning like wobbly tops in the gray shadows across the street caught his attention. He never understood a drug that forces its consumers to whirl like children's toys to heighten its high. But the stuff was popular, so much so that the Federal Drug Council was thinking of legalizing it to better monitor its use and, Reagan concluded, collect yet another new stream of rec-narc taxes.

A dark sedan pulled up fast to the curb and loudly stopped just inches ahead of Reagan.

"Nee-da-ride, Captain?"

Reagan peered into the car with his big shiny penetrator in his hand.

"Jesus H. Shiva," the taxi driver shrieked. "Don't shoot! Don't shoot me! Just wanted to know if I might carry you somewheres. Free of charge. For the Department. FREE!"

"You know me?"

"No, sir," the red-faced driver nervously sputtered. "My grill scanner IDed you Department/Captain and just thought you might need a ride— no charge. My part to keep the city safe and all."

Reagan looked at his wrist scanner and confirmed that the man was a Class II gypsy driver, decent security status. And it did not strike him too unusual for a gypsy driver to invest in a grill scanner in these especially dangerous days. Poor fare jockeys like him can never be too trusting who they stop for.

"Take me to Harlem, the Apollo," Reagan said as he got into the car's sickly-sweet-scented backseat.

"Harlem. Yep, of course. Since those rich kids got butchered I don't get calls to take many there—at least not civilians. Hedzhunters bad for business."

The driver guided the car confidently into high-speed traffic and headed for the colored lights of Harlem's jagged skyline, rising in the black morning. Reagan worried. Despite all of the Department's media restrictions on the case, too much information was leaking. The gypsy driver spoke as if he knew almost as much about the case as Reagan knew.

"I hope you guys get 'em real soon," the driver said as Reagan stared off at Harlem's ghastly glow. "I hear these fuckers are spreading out. Hitting the road."

"Yeah," Reagan asked catching the driver's eyes in his rearview screen. "What else you hearing?"

"Nothing," the driver said with a grin.

"Hey you shifty shit," Reagan growled at the back of the driver's head. "Your meter's been runnin'."

"Oh," the driver said with a start, "habit."

Rattle readjusted his OptiTechs for distant night vision. The stretch of highway slicing through central Ohio was as uninteresting to him as the rurals he imagined working the commercial farms of the region. His grandfather used to call it flyover country, and he understood why. But Rattle enjoyed driving his hauler through the hearts of states like Ohio, Indiana, Arkansas, the Dakotas. *A man can think when he's alone behind the wheel*, he reminded himself.

Rattle unfastened his pants.

High above the roadside, harnessed into his Kustom-contoured driver's seat, Rattle kept one hand on the hauler's steering wheel and one hand adjusting his OptiTech vision to scan the road for smoochers. The night was warm and clear. He knew it would only be a matter of time before he'd spot an open-bed truck blanketed with hay, sacks of feed—and smoochers. They'd be desperate to get away from their steamy, crowded hostels, away from parents and grandparents, and lay under the cool open sky. And fuck.

He commanded his hauler's entertainment deck to mute. Rattle welcomed the relative quiet of his hauler's cabin. He needed to concentrate. The left-eye lens of his OptiTechs went into thermal-telescopic mode. The right lens searched for fine telltale movement.

And then Rattle found reason to congratulate his patience. His OptiTechs spotted a low-bed truck less than three miles ahead traveling at moderate speed. He tapped his glasses for more data. *Promising*, he said to himself as he pressed the hauler's accelerator and closed on the truck ahead. Its driver paid little mind to Rattle's gradually approaching headlamps. To Rattle's delight, neither did its joy riders.

Rattle glanced at his dash data. His navigations indicated another twenty-five miles of relatively flat, vacant highway ahead. Rattle slowed his hauler to eighty-five miles per hour, nearly matching the truck's speed as he pulled in behind it.

Rattle carefully fingered his OptiTech's to give him the best view into the truck's flatbed low-bed.

The smoochers never suspected that they had an audience of one.

"Yessss," Rattle oozed as surveyed the scene. There were five young couples, and a few threesomes, twisting, withering, pumping, licking, sucking, and sweating in the hay.

"Damn," Rattle whispered as he flicked on his hauler's anti-collision system.

He loved to watch, especially those who didn't know he was watching. Rattle locked on a pair of liberally fleshy women orally satisfying each other, before becoming worried that he might be missing more elsewhere. He bifurcated his vision so he could keep at least three groups of fornicating farmers' daughters and sons in view. He could hardly contain the seedy thrill of it.

The hauler's viewpanel startled Rattle.

"Goddamn it to fuck," Rattle screamed as he watched the truck pull around a length of cornering highway.

He tore the OptiTechs from his face and tossed them into the hauler's passenger seat.

"Speak!"

"Dat-daWAY-U!-Speaky2yaBALDY-headedMutha?"

Rattle glared at the dash-mounted screen and saw JoË Dots staring back.

"Fucka," he said with a grin. "WhatchaNEEDnfrom-ME!-now?"

"U-fooool!"

"Me? SahWha?"

"ThaThangUdoN4me. LATER."

Rattle glared at JoË Dots' emotionless face, waiting for what had to be a punch line.

"UwantNme2cumBock? MePackN-P-duct?"

"UdoTHAThang4MeLATER."

Rattle couldn't believe what he was hearing. Come back? Back with a full load of Dups? What about the deal in St. Louis? And what was he going to do with the full tank of flight fuel he hid the Duppys in? And why did JoЁ Dots want to meet him back in Camden?

Damn, he thought, wondering if he could find another truckload of smoochers as promising as the one he had to let go. He thought about catching up to the one he had just found, bursting a nut, running the truck off the road, and then killing everyone on it. But he was getting tired, he thought, and where would the profit be in killing a bunch of oversexed farmhands?

Complications. Rattle despised complications.

Oona stiffened in Army's arms just before muscle tremors rocked her naked body. The shock startled Army from the sweetest sleep he had experienced in months. His eyes opened wide as Oona's arms tightened around his neck with more affliction than affection.

"Hey. Hey," he firmly called out.

Oona's grip loosened, then fell away.

"Are you all right?"

"Yeah. I'm okay," Oona replied unconvincingly. "Your goddamned nightmares must be contagious."

"You're sure that's all it is?" he asked as pulled the coarse fabric of his duster tighter around the two of them.

Army could feel Oona slip back into a familiar pose, the confident calm he was learning was only a guise.

"I don't know how to say this..." The sounds of the hauler, the road, even the fluid tons of fuel sloshing just outside their compartment punctuated the painfully long passage of her pause.

"What?" Army snapped. "What?"

"Can't you feel that?" she shouted. "We're slowing down. And if we are slowing down now, that means something is wrong."

Army could feel the hauler decelerating to a stop.

"Get your pants on—fast," Oona commanded, as she felt around for her clothing.

"What do you think it means?" Army said, as he struggled to get his long legs into his pants.

"Could be anything," Oona said, "from engine trouble to a hijack."

Army cursed under his breath. He was nervous and scared. What a shitty way to wake up, he groused.

"You think it's the Department?" he asked, as he refastened his safety constraints.

Oona didn't answer. She was tapping a tiny panel glued to the ceiling of her compartment.

"Find my shoes, Army," she called down to him.

The panel flashed red, then green.

"Rattle-Rattle... Rattle," Oona spoke into the panic panel, trying hard to keep the fear from finding her cousin's ear.

Silence.

"Rattle... Rattle," she repeated just short of screaming his name.

"CuzGal.IearUgood."

"What's going on out there? It feels like we just turned around."

"UgoodGAL.Changzplanz.GoNboch."

Going back? Oona thought. *No way.* She was done with New York, done with its hustles and bad cops and Jellies and johns. She was looking forward to Kentucky and introducing Army to her getaway in the hills. Waking up in his arms got her thinking about all the mornings they could wake together beside a fire to those cold Kentucky sunrises. She needed a break and she was determined to get one.

"Shit," she whispered. "What are we going to do now?"

"Oona, here. I found your shoes," Army said.

"Forget it," Oona replied. "We're not stopping, at least no time soon."

"Huh?"

"Yeah, we got to go back. Change of plans. We're going back."

But Army had done the math of mayhem if they returned to Harlem. The Department would surely be waiting, as would whoever wanted to blame him for Kattrel's death. He also knew Oona was running from something herself. *We can't go back*, Army thought. *Not now.*

Reagan wasn't certain how he ended up at the locked door of Oooh's sweet-suite at 3:30 in the morning. He knew she had disappeared almost a week ago. For a second or two he felt badly about that, thinking he had run the young pleasurist off. He hadn't meant to. Then again, he knew how hard it could be to truly know his own intentions. He was always drunk when he pounded on her door in the middle of the night. He was always drunk when he smacked her around.

The last time—the last night he saw her before she vanished—had been the worst. He remembered the surges of satisfaction he felt with each heavy-footed kick he gave her sex-techs that night. He had promised to do the same to her and meant it. Every punch was practically orgasmic as the Jelli bruised and bled synthetics. But when he struck Oona, Reagan could only recall a suffocating shame.

Reagan stood in the humid, late winter morning, staring at Oona's door, retching with remembrance of that last night they were together. He had wanted Oona, not Oooh, nor any of her dead-eyed twitchers. He wanted to talk to Oona: make her laugh at his bad jokes, make her understand that he had once been a decent man, and might someday be one again. But everything he said and did just deepened her disgust for him. And the more he sensed that disgust, the more it fed his rage.

"I know why you do this to me, why you torture me," Reagan recalled Oona screaming at him through snot-smeared lips. "I had nothing to do with that killing."

Reagan stood over Oona, recoiling to smack her again when he realized that she was talking about the Avanti killing. Had *she* somehow been involved in these Harlem murders?

Reagan glared at Oona as she lay crumpled on the floor, sobbing and trying to cover herself with her badly ripped robe.

"I was paid to watch that man—JUST WATCH!—watch him in that hotel room," Oona cried. "That's all. That's all. I didn't know anybody was going to get killed."

"But somebody did get killed, bitch," Reagan bluffed, lowering his face to scream in hers. "And I'll snap your pretty neck right here if you don't tell me who paid you, and why."

"I don't know who he was. I barely saw him. He gave me some cash and the night glasses," Oona said, as she pleaded with Reagan to stop twisting her arm. "I didn't know that Light woman was going to get her head chopped off. I didn't. I was just working my spot across from the Robeson." Then she cried like a dying kitten and hoped her lie had taken hold.

"And the woman in the Robeson, Kattrel Avanti? You didn't know her either?" Reagan boomed as he tried to get a tighter grip on the truth, and Oona's hair.

"No! No! No! I didn't know her. Just saw her face on the Weave when she came up missing," Oona whimpered. "But the next day I knew, everybody on the street knew, that she was killed, that someone ran off with her head."

Reagan didn't say a word. The sweet-suite was quiet except for the low, choppy moans and sobs rising from Oona at Reagan's feet. The detective didn't say a word. He slowly unfastened his pants.

Oona peered at Reagan from the corner of her swollen right eye. Staring at the floor, she slowly reached for the gathering bulge in his silken undershorts. She shuddered and sickened at the feel of her own surrender.

She had played the scenario in her mind over and over. What would she do if the detective ever tried to rape her? What could she do? She knew it happened to other pleasurists all the time. But never to her.

Before she could find her answer, Oona felt the cold, hard tile of her apartment floor as she was being forced to her knees. She could smell the foul scent of his genitals as he shook them free in her dead face. Now the sound of the detective's hard breathing overwhelmed her.

Reagan narrowed his eyes as he watched Oona mechanically part her lips. He could feel her breath as she extended her dry tongue and he gently rose to the balls of his feet. He held his breath and closed his eyes.

In an eruption of self-loathing, Reagan seized Oona and threw her from her knees. She flew like something inconsequential, banging her head hard against a fake brick wall. She felt something give in her upper back as she tumbled in to a heap. Oona felt submerged in the watery weight of momentary paralysis. Her eyelids involuntarily fluttered. Everything seemed like something in an antique movie: gray and jerky and silent.

But she could see Reagan clearly enough. He stalked to her bed nook. She saw him yank her best Jelli from its storage compartment and roughly throw it on the bed. He threw it face-down and penetrated it from behind as he locked eye contact with Oona. As he spread the Jelli's legs ever wider he tugged its braided hair. He rode the warm-skinned machine with crushing abandon. He tugged and tore at its hair until it started coming out in chunks in his hand.

Oona heard the Jelli's neck snap, then shatter. But the detective kept pulling and twisting its head.

Moments before Oona passed out, she realized that one night soon, Reagan would come for her. It would be *her* on the bed, being invaded with no more semblance of humanity than a sex-tech's programmed panting. And in the end, the detective would snap her neck too, with as much regard as he gave the Jelli's finely tooled vertebrae.

When Oona regained consciousness, she was alone. But Reagan had left the Jelli's detached head next to hers.

"I," she said, as her temples throbbed and her muscles ached, "got to get away from here. Gottarun. Gottarun."

28

DuppyMan

JOË DOTS OPENED HIS COLLAR, THE BETTER TO FEEL THE STRESS SOAKING through the imported fabrics of his tailored shirt. Any pretense of cool was being drowned, along with his sinking nerve. He was a capitalist.

What had seemed like his most brilliant move now appeared to JoË Dots as nothing more than a suicidal impulse, more proof that he was powerless over his addiction to cutting deals. And perhaps a new addiction.

Why hadn't he waited for Cutter's approval before moving the Duppy westward for distribution? He wondered aloud whether his growing appetite for his own product was wounding his judgment. He swatted away the notion.

Dots was still convinced that the Duppy deal made solid business sense. The drug was stable, cheap to make, and exquisitely addictive. And St. Louis was the perfect test market. Dots preyed at the altar of human frailty; he knew that once the Duppys reached the river city's two million-plus poor and desperate, they would be transformed practically overnight into herds of cash cows for the milking.

But after just suffering through the "big picture" speech, JoË Dots was convinced that even mountains of money would not be enough to dissuade Cutter from insisting that he pay for his "biz-ness" misstep with his life. *Cutter would never trust me again. And without trust...*

"MuthaFUCK," JoË Dots whispered, as he punched the code for a secure link to a trusted fixer. *I must be going out of my head,* he thought, but knew, in fact, that too much had been going into his head lately. Just as the truth crackled in his brain pan, he found himself wanting to reach for a quick squeeze of Hedz. *Just to smooth out the fuzzy edges.* Dots fumbled with a Duppy, its rubbery teardrop inhaler as red and shiny as a child's balloon. It slipped from his fingers and struck the polished wooden floor with a soft thud and a few feeble bounces, only to wobble to a stop between Dots' size thirteen-and-a-half square-toe oxfords.

Dots stared for a syrupy long moment at the Duppy that was within easy enough reach. He only realized that he had been holding his breath until he involuntarily exhaled, long and hot and loud. He stomped the Duppy, kicking the smashed inhaler under a heavy oak cabinet before he straightened his back and turned his attention to his link.

"Audio only," JoË Dots said, as he fought the urge to drop to his hands and knees and snatch up any remnants of the ruined Duppy—wet with spilled memories—from the floor.

"Speak," a familiar voice answered flatly.

"Yeah. Need a delivery." Dots spoke slowly, carefully as his confidence gathered its legs.

"What and where?"

"Doom. Location to follow."

"DoomDone," the voice said, with a kind of finality that chilled Dots for a second or two. "The meter's runnin'."

JoË Dots yanked his link from his ear and shoved it into his inside jacket pocket. He took a deep breath and a drink before readjusting his sweat-dampened collar around his tree stump of a neck.

Cutter was coming. Second guesses. Dots hastily fell to the floor to retrieve the smashed Duppy. He folded his pocket square around it and stuffed them both into the pocket of his sports coat. He could hear a melancholy cascade of trumpet and strings spill into Baghdaddy's upstairs hallway. The music swelled when Cutter opened the door of his front office. JoË Dots crossed his legs, torturing the crease in his pants, and tried to assume a posture of calm. Out of habit, he yanked his pocket square from his jacket to dab the sheen from his neck and forehead. His heart seized when he realized what he had done. *Did Cutter notice?* Dots quickly tucked the ivory-colored handkerchief square back into place. His face was quickly shined with a new coating of nervous perspiration.

As Cutter stepped toward the front inner office room, he gave Dots a quick glance. "Warm?" he asked, offhandedly.

"Ita-lil'CLOSEnHere," JoË Dots replied, as he did his best to seem nonchalant, meeting Cutter's slightly amused stare. He stood up, then instinctively took a couple of steps back to de-emphasize the enormous difference in the men's heights. Cutter turned with all the ease of a two-legged tortoise and headed out of his office. JoË Dots was forced to take uncomfortably small steps to follow.

"I hear you got a new batch of Dups," Cutter said over his shoulder, as he headed toward the club's most opulent private party space, the Dome.

"Calls`emDUPPYSnow.YEAH."

"Dup-pees?" Cutter mouthed the name. "Excellent," he said as he proceeded down a wide hallway. "I don't want any fucking foul-ups tonight, Dots. I am expecting some of my better clientele, the Cloud Class. You understand? I want them to thoroughly enjoy my famous hospitality."

Dots nodded, as his mind ached for a way to change the subject.

"Say—what was that music playing in your office? It sounded familiar."

Cutter looked back to stare at his lieutenant in surprise.

"You've never expressed much interest in my music, Dots," Cutter said, as the two men stepped into the Dome's dedicated elevator. "I always had the sense that you didn't share my taste."

Dots blinked, then smiled, but even in the confined space of the elevator, he was careful not to look down at Cutter. He knew how much Cutter hated people looking down at him.

The elevator doors parted on the padded entryway of the Dome, a space at the top of Baghdaddy's opulent sprawl along 116th Street. Dots thought he saw a smile playing on the corners of Cutter's thin lips. "Have you been checking the Weave today?" Cutter asked, changing the subject and his mood. "Hedz killings have been on every Weave knot. Almost wish we could have done more. Something more grand. More smoke and broken mirrors."

"No, naw, naw," Dots sputtered. "C2nite."

Cutter shot Dots a sharp glance.

JoË Dots fell deep into the cushions of a sofa chair. Cutter beckoned a waiter to bring them flutes of his favorite old-century champagne as he hopped into an adjacent matching chair.

"Yeah," Dots feigned interest. "I've got to catch up on the news."

Cutter sipped his champagne and flashed a grin that unnerved Dots more than he thought possible.

"You *are* the news, you big fucking teddy bear," Cutter practically sang, and then laughed like a demented child. "'Got to 'catch up'?" He laughed some more and stopped with a hiss to sip his champagne.

Dots shuddered—worse yet, he was convinced that Cutter noticed that he had. He could not determine whether Cutter was genuinely pleased or pissed. Dots felt like a mouse under a paw. He wanted to scream, or run away. But he knew he couldn't, not if he wanted to keep his head on his shoulders.

"You know, I've been hearing more about your inside boy," Cutter said, as he savored his champagne and watched the progressing decorations for the Dome party. "Seems like he's become quite the hero around the Department."

Dots said nothing, but nodded.

"He's taking a lot more than he's giving us, I think. Right?" Cutter asked no one. "I think it's time for him to be reminded of exactly what bit part he plays in our little production. Get a decent haircut, Dots. I want you to take care of this personally."

"What," Dots asked weakly, "do you want me to do?"

Cutter shook his head like he'd lost his hearing.

"Make him hurt, and let him know I did the hurting."

Cutter hopped out of his chair and continued, alone, to inspect his pleasure dome. Just as abruptly, the diminutive Big Man's mood had darkened to pure black.

"I do not fully understand, Miss Rikki."

"Damn it! I know, I know, Mac. Listen, my logic might sound a little confusing. But you have to trust me. I know precisely what I want, and right now, Mac, I simply want you to follow my instructions without fail—or hesitation. You understand me?"

"Of course," Mac\Sheehan responded.

Rikki was tired, and the puffy circles beneath her eyes betrayed any illusions she might have had of fooling her Personal Home Appliance that everything was fine. She tried not to think about it, but she knew the appliance could hear her respiration, analyze her heart rate, and detect the most minute fluctuations in her skin temperature and color. She knew it sensed when she was lying to it, but it also knew better than to challenge her. So, they both worked hard to maintain her deception that all was as it should be.

Final preparations had to be completed. She hadn't slept well in days, and now she could see early evening approaching, being drawn like a sheer dark curtain before the heavy drapes of night fell. There was little time left.

She instructed Mac to reset all its primary security protocols to specifications that Mr. PIE had supplied. She had informed her building's security desk that a new medical staff would arrive tomorrow morning at 8 to perform tests before transporting Mother to a special op-center for an emergency procedure. Now, Rikki thought, if she could only quiet the quiver in her hands—and stop Mac from asking so many goddamned questions.

"Miss Rikki?"

"Yes," Rikki said, with barely masked exasperation.

"The new protocols call for a self-induced meltdown at 8:03:05 tomorrow morning. Such a radical termination may do serious harm to several of my key B.C.A.I. sectors. Are you certain this is what you want?"

"Mac, I understand the risks. Okay? Believe me, I do. All right? But there is simply no other way."

Rikki stood in the middle of her living room and, out of a habit she could not explain, pitched her voice upward as she addressed her P.H.A. She tried to remind herself of everything that was at stake. She had set in motion events that were quickly building their own momentum. The painful truth was that Mac might have to be sacrificed.

"Mac," she lowered her voice as if she was about to share a dark secret, "I need you to do this for me, and for Mother. If there is any damage to any of your sectors, I promise to get your parent techs to restore you to full health. You have to—"

"I know… 'trust' you," Mac whispered. "Then I have to hurry. I have an appointment tomorrow at 8:03:05 A.M. And, as you know, I am never late."

"No," Rikki replied, pausing to swallow a lump in her throat. "You're never late.

"MISS RIKKI!"

The sound of Mac\Sheehan's sudden scream unnerved her so much that she hardly noticed the tightening sensation around her wrist. But the second one was so intense that the MediSentry almost sent her right hand into spasms.

"Mother!" Mac\Sheehan shouted. "She is going into cardiac arrest!"

Rikki ran into her mother's room to find her skeletal figure convulsing

against a backdrop of clamorous medical monitors. Her mother's arms were
thrown stiffly back as her spine arched, throwing her chest upward as if it
were trying to break free from the netting of wires, contacts and umbilical
tubing.

"Mac, call her medical emergency team, now!" Rikki hollered, as she
struggled to push her mother's thrashing figure down on to the bed.

"Miss Rikki, Miss Rikki. Wait. Mother is beginning to stabilize."

The cacophony of the room's monitors rapidly subsided to its usual
drone of metronomic pops and airless hisses. Rikki could feel her mother's
implanted respirators restoring the rhythm of the old woman's unnatural
deep breathing. Rikki could even detect traces of pink returning to the thin,
wrinkled skin of her mother's sunken cheeks.

Rikki's stomach lurched as her wrist tightened again.

This time the feeling was not accompanied with the tingle of electrical
charges. She looked down and was shocked to see her mother's hand gripping
her right wrist. Her grip was surprisingly strong.

Rikki involuntarily bared her teeth with pain and then strained her face
into an unconvincing smile. She stared down at her mother's pale, bony
claw of a hand as she rubbed its faint warmth.

"You hear… you hear it?" her mother rasped.

Rikki gasped.

"Mac, do you hear her? Did you hear her speak?"

"Yes," it answered. "It is a miracle."

"Mother?" Rikki asked softly. "Momma? I'm here. It's me, your
daughter. Do you hear me?"

Rikki's mother spoke through dry, thinly parted lips. "Oh, my God,"
she whispered. "The music. The music is so sweet. Da-da-daaaa. Dee. Dee.
Oh… the music."

Rikki lowered her face close enough to smell her mother's breath, which
suddenly reminded her of cave water. All around her clung the odors of
medications, and of an old woman's waste cycling through the machines
that maintained her.

"Her eyes…" Mac\Sheehan spoke up.

Rikki pulled back just enough to behold the most radiant smile she had
ever seen on her mother's face. Her eyes glistened as they focused on Rikki,
who tried to look brave through her tears.

Confusion drew up Rikki's eyebrows. "Momma?"

"Not so bad. Not so…," Rikki's mother continued, but her lips moved in silence. Rikki violently shook her head—*no*—as her mother nodded, then closed her eyes.

"Let go," Rikki's mother whispered. "Let me go… to the… music."

Rikki's mother smiled, and then let the smile slip gradually off her narrow, craggy face.

"No, Momma… don't," Rikki begged, as her tears dampened her mother's face. "Just a little longer."

"Rikki. Rikki. Mother's asleep," Mac\Sheehan consoled. "She needs her rest."

JoË Dots rolled the rubbery purplish bulb between his thumb and his forefinger over and over again. It reminded him of a large grape, the kind he remembered from his youth, but was difficult to find anymore. Robotic pickers performed better harvesting square-shaped grapes, so in the name of progress, grapes had been genetically coaxed into growing rectangular edges. He'd always loved the old grapes, not just for their roundness but for the delight they'd promised when he popped them into his mouth and bit down on their ripeness. There was an explosion, sometimes so intense he could hardly contain all the sweet flesh and juice in his little-boy mouth.

The Duppy pinch dispenser, he knew, contained its own promise of explosions and delights. All he had to do was place it under his nose and squeeze. Its stem membrane would rupture, and the Duppy's hyper-psychotropic agents would speed into his nostrils and smash into his brain, then excite his memory centers with duplications of stolen experiences.

"I'll need another couple of minutes to recalibrate my monitors," a dour-looking man said to Cutter in a hushed monotone. Cutter nodded his approval as he ran his eyes over JoË Dots, who sat stripped to the waist in a wire-webbed chair. His dark skin glistened with the medical transducer gel that was streaming the minutia of his physical and psychological states to the MedTech's portable sensor displays.

"He seems a bit agitated," the MedTech half-whispered to Cutter. "Tell him to relax, to take deep breaths."

"You heard him," Cutter shouted over thunderous dance music that was hemorrhaging through the pleasure dome's radiating acoustic walls. "And what do you have to be so agitated about, anyway?"

"NutN, Cee-mon. Nothing," Dots shouted between deep breaths.

Cutter glanced at the MedTech, who was tightening the harness that held JoË Dots snugly in the netted chair.

"You ready, Dots?" Cutter said. "You ready to show me that your Duppies are as good as you say they are?"

The MedTech jerked his trigger finger as if he was shooting a pistol.

"It-B-BETTER," Dots said, as he held his head back and squeezed the Duppy under his nose.

The sound started low, a hum that Cutter mistook at first for some malfunctioning ventilator. But the hum quickly grew louder and more ragged until it became clear to Cutter and the MedTech that the sound was coming from Dots, whose mouth had flown inhumanly wide open. His eyes were closed and the veins in his neck and temples bulged large and ropy just under his skin.

"He's all right," the MedTech told Cutter, who had no idea what the data screens were reporting.

Dots was tumbling inside, seized by a deliciously warm and exhilarating sensation of ghostly G-forces that suggested he was flying, landing, and bouncing back into thin air—all at the same time. The sense of wonderfully reckless speed stirred in his gut, while his brain happily simmered in a gumbo of adrenaline, dopamine, and endorphins.

He gnashed his teeth and moaned with pleasures both familiar and foreign. He forgot all about Cutter, whether he suspected anything, whether there would be another day.

White. White and blue. Flashes of white and blue, blue and white. Cold. His face was cold. His body hot. The earth beneath, slick and crunchy.

JoË Dots realized he was on a slope, in a state that bordered on what's dreamt and what's done. He knew not to overthink. He smiled as he tasted high-priced winter in a spray of snow that stung his cheeks and dampened his lips. Dots was hurling forward on what he guessed were composite-fiber booted blades fitted to his feet. He didn't care; he didn't even think to look down to check. He was overwhelmed with the fullness of his mastery of sugary slopes. He reveled in the feelings—mostly his, and yet imported. Again, he didn't care. He embraced the feelings, squeezed them hard under a cloudless, fluorescent blue sky that he knew only existed in his head. He didn't care.

Suddenly, all Dots cared about was lost. Emptiness swallowed him, and then strangled him as he was swept with an insatiable need to do it all over again. Dots felt himself fall back into his body, back into a webbed chair, back into a life he wanted more than ever to escape. He felt heavy, tired, and nauseous.

"Wake up," Cutter shouted into Dots' face.

JoË Dots opened his eyes to see only Cutter and the MedTech staring at him. Dots sputtered to speak, but only managed to cough up phlegm and a little blood that darkened his large, overwhite teeth.

"Amazing," Dots rasped, as he started to cough again. "I... I told you."

Cutter took a step closer to JoË Dots and smiled like Louis Armstrong in a New Orleans cathouse. "I just wanted to be sure before I added your little treats to tonight's menu. I'll take all you can give me. And I trust that that will be considerable."

"IcanLITEmUPaulNITE," Dots replied. "All fuckin' night." He started babbling about the experience he'd had.

The MedTech told Cutter that the re-experience had lasted 33.72 seconds. Cutter was impressed that JoË Dots was blathering on about the smell of pine he'd never smelled, the sound of wind flapping a ski jacket he'd never worn, and the enormous skill he'd displayed to narrowly miss a tree, when all he had really done was squirm and moan in a lab chair for half a minute. Dots was talking like a man who had actually accomplished something, when in fact he'd only popped an illicit substance under his nose.

Cutter began to wonder who the bastard was who had actually skied those slopes. No doubt his head was long ago whacked off, his brain scooped out and mined for nuggets of experience like the one JoË Dots had just re-experienced.

"U-likee?" Dots asked as the MedTech began to pack up his gear.

"I-likee, DuppyMan," Cutter replied. "Now I'd like to get you to finish up some business you promised me a couple of days ago."

"InI," Dots said holding up a finger on each hand. "InI," he repeated as he brought the fingers together.

"Yeah, motherfucker," Cutter oozed. "I and I."

29

Final Rest Stop

REAGAN SAT IN AN ARMORED TACTICAL COMMAND VEHICLE AS HIS surveillance specialist monitored several dozen feeds directed at Baghdaddy's. His driver guided the A.T.C.V. in slow, four-block-square radius of the crowded Harlem nightclub. It was early evening.

"So far no surprises, Captain. None," the surveillance specialist reported.

"Good. Real good. Anything from our operative inside?"

"Pee-Diddy-Squat," she replied, as she gently spun inside the vehicle's surveillance bubble. "Still early."

Reagan scanned the readouts of the command pod that enclosed him. He was struck by how different Harlem appeared when it was stripped to its bare ass through 4-D scans, waveform analysis, and thermal-sonic prints. The surveillance specialist was drawing attention to recent arrivals that had slipped into the club's underground VIP entrance.

"I'll have metadata on the last dozen big bangers in a couple of minutes," she said. "Ultrasonics indicate that they're heading for the dome. I'm capturing their in-house vid feeds. Your operative was right. There's going to be a big party in that space tonight."

"Yeah," Reagan said flatly. "Keep an eye and an ear glued to the shit and get me that guest list the nano instant you've got it."

"I'm on it."

Reagan was bored. And it didn't help that now he was the boss. One thing he had come to realize, once he scampered to the top of his modest pyramid of power, was that there were always much larger—inverted—pyramids of bosses to which he'd have to answer. Reagan stewed on that realization until it began to bore him, too.

Waiting. Reagan hated waiting, especially on machines. Even more infuriating to him was how dependent his profession was on machines. *Too many damned gizmos,* he lamented. Monitors monitoring monitors. He prided himself on being an eyes-and-ears man. Real police work, he was convinced, depended on what a detective could see, hear, and feel on his own.

"Bullshit," Reagan mumbled to himself, glancing up to see the young Dark surveillance specialist he'd personally selected for the mission. "Bullshit."

"Captain, I'm getting a high-priority communication from C3 that I think you want to take," the specialist yelled down to him.

"Patch it over."

Reagan tapped his secure link and an Opti-Dot wire displayed a familiar face in its glow tip. It was the kid who had been Reagan's personal driver during his first weeks back with the Department. He had lost touch with the cadet and forgotten his name. But he'd remembered his Beaver Cleaver face.

"Captain," he said. "I'm sorry to interrupt, but—"

"Go ahead, dispatcher."

The young dispatcher's face flushed before he spoke again.

"The surveillance team here has intercepted unauthorized fragments of communications that have been traced to your target location. It places transmission between 5:48:03:21 P.M. and 5:48:07:49 P.M yesterday."

"And?" Reagan barked.

"And... the team leader here believes it is relevant to your investigation, and wants me to—"

"I determine what's relevant," Reagan snapped, just for the hell of it. "Give me the intercept. And thank your leader." The dispatcher could not decide whether the grouchy captain had just smiled or grimaced.

"Yes, sir," the dispatcher said. "Stand by..."

Yeah. Need a delivery.
What and where?
Doom. Location to follow.
DoomDone. The Meter's runnin'.

Reagan played the audio snatch over and over and nearly shit in his pants. He knew the first voice right away. It was JoË Dots, Dots trying not to talk screech, but straight English. But the second voice? He knew he'd heard it before, and not too long ago. Reagan closed his eyes and searched his memory. He paused the audio loop for a moment, and repeated the words ringing in his ears: *The meter's runnin.'*

"Damn it to hell's gate," he screamed and then called out to his surveillance specialist. "Search all the male voice prints of gypsy taxi drivers who were operating in or around Harlem in the last two weeks. Do a search and compare to the second voice on this clip. Track what you find!"

"Got it," she said, snapping into action.

Reagan already knew what his surveillance officer would find. He called in a jumper and prepared to fly to wherever the mysterious voice might lead him. "DoomDone," for fucking sure, Reagan said under his breath as he struggled out of his seat harness.

"DoomDone."

"Where the hell are we?" Army asked Oona.

They were huddled behind a wreck of a structure half hidden beside encroaching woods in the early night. Its windows were long gone, replaced by fiberboards that looked hastily sealed into place, overlapping the modest building's flanks like the scales of a giant, ancient fish. A gated door stood bent and rusting at the entrance, which reeked of something recently dead.

"I dunno," Oona said while she gathered herself and sat on her haunches near the entrance. "Rattle said for us to stay put until he got back."

"You trust him? I mean, really trust him?" Army asked as he worked the circulation back into his legs.

"He's all the family I got," Oona said, looking up at Army, who nervously wrapped himself tighter in his duster. "Yeah. Of course I trust him."

"Bandits'Blind," Rattle hummed as he walked toward them out of the darkness. He stopped in a shaft of moonlight that gave him a pearly, otherworldly aura. "WeSTayhereTilmornN."

Rattle shouldered past Army and aimed something small and silvery at the sagging building's door. The moan of a magnetic lock releasing made Army turn to Oona in stunned bewilderment.

They all walked inside. Army and Oona were surprised to find the structure was warm and smelled of reconditioned air. Army sensed lights glowing from the walls, which appeared to be made of some sort of thick canvas stretched tightly over a ribbed frame. He also made out several cots, immaculately made and stacked with neatly folded extra bedding.

Rattle was directing Oona to a far corner. Army could barely make out cabinets and a folding table with chairs that completed what struck him as a cozy, patchwork palace—compared to the smugglers' hold he and Oona had crawled around in much of the last eighteen hours.

"Look, Army," Oona whispered excitedly. "Rattle says there's food here, and a bathroom with a sonic shower behind that curtain. He says it's sound- and light-proof, too. Secure."

Army folded his arms. "Where are we?"

"Western Pennsylvania, somewhere," Oona spoke under her breath as Rattle disappeared behind the bathroom curtain.

"And what about the hauler?" Army asked, his patience for his own ignorance running on low.

"He said he hid it in some ditch nearby."

"And," Rattle piped up from behind the curtain, "gotMY-GiulianisSET-all`ROUND. Lax. 'Kay? LaxEZBOY."

"We appreciate this, cuz," Oona spoke up. "We're fine. Get yourself some sleep. I know you have a long drive back in the morning."

"WezDashN@Dawn," Rattle said, as if the statement was a single word. He pushed through the curtain, obviously relieved. He waved Army and Oona goodnight and threw himself on the nearest bed, kicking off one of his filthy boots as he landed. "DawnUP."

Rattle turned roughly to his side and tugged a bright blue blanket over his face.

The sound of Rattle's other boot falling startled Army.

"Well," Oona laughed.

"Well," Army mocked as he reached for Oona and guided her into his arms.

She playfully bit his cheek and wiggled away. "I'm starving. But first, I've got to clean up."

Oona grabbed a folded blanket from one of the beds and wrapped it around her shoulders. Army watched, turning from Oona to a snoring Rattle and back to Oona, who walked to the middle of the room. Army understood when he noticed Oona leaving a trail of her discarded clothing.

He stripped in the middle of the darkened hideout. Oona smiled and then dropped her blanket, baring her naked bottom.

Rattle inched down his blanket and shook his head. "Kidz," he said, grinning before replanting his weary head in the bed.

30

Hillside Hop

W HEN ARMY AWOKE HOURS LATER, HE FOUND HIMSELF IN ALMOST total darkness. He realized that the hideaway's illumination was tied to motion detectors. Oona told him that Rattle had set up Giulianis all around his hauler, too— sophisticated security devices, in screech.

He recalled when his mother had taught him his first screech phrases. It was their private joke.

She'd say, "Jeet (*Did you eat?*)?"

And he would answer, "JU (*Did you?*)?"

One morning, Army decided to let his stepfather in on the screech joke when he unexpectedly sat down for breakfast after working all night.

"Jeet?" Army had asked.

"What?!"

"Jeet?" an eight-year-old Army repeated. He shook his head disapprovingly and told his stepfather that he was supposed to say, "JU?"

"Jew? I say fuck you," Jae-J. thundered, then smacked the back of Army's head. "You're not going to get anywhere in life talking like a goddamned tongue-tied hoodlum."

Now Army's stomach was fluttering. He had eaten too much of the hideaway's canned tuna and flash-radiated cheese and crackers. He took a deep breath and stepped carefully toward the bathroom. Army could see an outline of Rattle asleep in his bed as he inched toward the dry toilet that sat behind the curtain.

Army hit the floor chin-first in a rude crash.

As he was going down, he reached for something to help break his fall and instead pulled the table and two chairs onto him. It all happened so fast, but not so fast that Army couldn't wonder why the crash made no sound. None at all.

He saw Rattle scrambling to his feet and screamed something in his direction. But he heard nothing. He reached for his ears and felt something warm and oily between his fingers. He pulled them to his face as the hideout's lights suddenly turned harshly bright. His fingers glistened with blood, and he felt his right knee blossom with pain.

A blast of cold air struck Army's naked back. He whipped in its direction to see the hideout's metal door tumble toward him, trailing smoke, flame, and debris. It silently tumbled past him, striking Rattle's legs as he tried to roll away and leaving the Viper bloody and dazed.

Oona? Army looked toward the bed where hours earlier they had made love. It was ablaze, as was the paper money spilling from his duster, sprawled out on the blind's floor. He spun around to see that the structure's canvas walls were burning away.

"Oona!" he called through the choking air, horrified that he did not hear her call back and terrified that he couldn't hear his own voice. Army scrambled behind the overturned table and broke off one of its legs for a weapon. When he peeked out, he saw Oona crouching in the shower's stall wearing only a pair of under strings. He motioned to her to stay down.

Rattle was crawling toward her. She extended her right arm to try to drag him into the shower stall with her. Something winged and spear-like embedded itself in his back. Its wings fell away as the thing's shaft drilled deeper into Rattle's bloody back. He turned his head to look back at Army, hiding behind the table.

In the flames, Army could see the predatory gleam fading from Rattle's eyes. For a moment, Army felt sorry for the Viper, for the only family Oona had. He could just begin to hear her screams as a broad-shouldered figure dressed in all black ducked through a burning hole into the blind. The figure fired a long-barreled weapon, shooting another winged harpoon at Rattle, this time into his chest; the Viper curled into a fetal position.

"Nooo. Oh, nooo." Army could hear Oona scream as she cowered in the shower stall.

The figure was picking his way through the ruined hideaway toward Rattle when Army saw something he knew he would never forget. The

Viper's whole body shook as his fingers and feet twitched frantically. A moment later Army sensed a great rippling thwack as Rattle's ribcage sprang open, exposing shards of snapped ribs, torn tissues, and traumatized organs. Army thought the opening looked like the gaping mouth of some grotesque creature. Then everything—bone, hair, skin, muscle—became gelatinous, then liquified.

Oona looked as if she was going into shock as the black-clad figure moved to stand over Rattle's vanishing remains. Army tightened his grip on the broken table leg but knew he had no chance against the assassin with only a leg of furniture to serve as a weapon. He crouched lower behind the table and searched for anything he could use to protect himself and Oona.

The figure kicked a bubbling hunk of meat that had been Rattle's upper thigh.

"Niggerboy," the man called out as he waved his harpoon launcher in the air. "You can hide behind that table all night for all I care. I'll come for you after I come for her."

Army cowered, frozen with terror, as he watched the man walk over to Oona and scoop her up in his arms as if she had no weight at all. *Oona. He had Oona,* Army said to himself over and over until the words spilled out of his anguished lips. The man draped her limp body over his shoulder as if she was a trophy kill. Her hair covered her face. Army dry-heaved with helplessness.

Without thinking Army was on his feet, charging the black-clad man until he felt contact. Army's lowered shoulder struck the man at his hip, bone-on-bone, sending him stumbling. Oona fell hard to the floor and took a full roll until her body stopped, face down. Army careened off the man, landing in a heap six feet away.

"Should have stayed under the table," the attacker said as he pulled himself to his knees and then his feet. "Should have let me have my fun. Huh?"

Army stood, flat-footed and cornered.

The man raised his launcher and aimed it at the center of Army's heaving chest.

Army defiantly stared into the man's laughing eyes. He tried to fix this image of himself: upright, clear-eyed, ready to fight, to defend himself and his woman. He tried hard not to think about what the next moment might bring. The harpoon launched with a ferocious suddenness, ripping through the blind's heavy canvas ceiling and shattering when it struck the building's old wooden roof. Army looked up as he fell back, just in time to see the man's upper chest and back explode in a geyser of blood.

Army crawled on his hands and knees to reach Oona.

"Back here!"

Army started dragging Oona by her arms as he tried to guide himself through the smoke and haze to reach the voice.

"Over here."

Army strained his burning eyes to make out a heavyset man holding open the hideaway's metal door. "Yeah, this way, keep coming this way!" the man hollered as he reached out to grab Army's hand. The man's other hand gripped a black and nickel-plated penetrator. *Police*, Army thought as he tried to resist the urge to run. He was hurt and knew he couldn't get far. And he knew he could never leave Oona.

"You okay?" the heavyset man asked Army, as he stood and lifted up Oona with what remained of his strength.

"I'm more worried about her," Army told the man who was dressed in a heavy suit and fedora. "But I think she just fainted."

Army carried Oona as the man led the way down a trail, past the smoldering carcass of Rattle's hauler, to a clearing in the night woods.

Army saw a four-wheel All-Utility Vehicle sparkling in the moonlight.

"Yours?" Army asked as the man helped him lay Oona across the A.U.V.'s rear seat compartment.

"The Department's."

Army sat back in the front seat as it strapped him in. His head and heart warred in a confusion of conflicting thoughts and feelings. Who had come for them—who was that man in black? Who was this other man who had saved their lives? Were they under arrest?

He could feel the vehicle's engines whirl and then watched the man drive, as the teardrop-shaped A.U.V.'s independently-powered wheels tore into the underbrush. They reached a wildly twisting dirt road that led away from the burning blind toward the highway. Army glanced at the A.U.V.'s in-dash display, which showed the burning heap of the hideaway receding into a haze of white smoke and approaching off-white dawn light. The man silently redirected one of his ancillary sightlines to scan skyward. Next, he tapped up a secondary control panel on his forward dash and gunned the

A.U.V. to roar near the edges of its top land speed. The woods blurred then disappeared as the vehicle's shuttered windows closed and flickered into navigational viewpanels.

A red dot raced across the vehicle's dash, stopping on a slender display that alerted the man that automated fire suppressors were en route to the smuggler's site. He rubbed his heavy jowls while checking the navigational data that wiggled across his blackened windshield.

"Where we going?" Army asked.

"You don't remember me, do you?"

"Should I?"

"I dunno. I was part of a group that questioned you last month at Department headquarters. In the morgue."

Army squeezed his eyes shut.

"If it helps," Reagan said calmly. "I wasn't the one who was yelling at you. My name's Reagan Reynolds."

"I'm not going back there."

"That's fine," Reagan said turning to offer Army a crooked smile. "I ain't, either. Here, put this over her," Reagan said, handing Army a blanket pack from beneath his seat.

Army popped the seal and watched the blanket spread over Oona, pulling itself up to her chin.

"My medicals read that she's okay. Just mild shock."

"Mild shock," Army repeated with disbelief.

The A.U.V. trembled before slipping swiftly over what Army could see from the air was an early-spring cornfield. Its wheels folded into its belly with a satisfying seal. The craft's engines growled and the A.U.V lifted higher to streak over the treetops of the Pennsylvania hillside.

They were headed north by northeast.

31

Born Again

RIKKI WANTED TO CRY OUT TO MAC, BUT CHOKED BACK THE IMPULSE. It was 12:43:04 P.M., and her Personal Home Appliance had not uttered a word or responded in any way to her wants, needs, or mere existence since its meltdown four hours and forty minutes ago. With programmed efficiency, Mac\Sheehan had not hesitated to carry out her orders. Its many eyes and ears were dead, along with its wit, wisdom, and voice.

Rikki felt enormously alone.

She paced along the lower lip of her sunken living room. The doors to Mother's room were closed. But occasionally, Rikki was certain, she heard an errant bleep of unfamiliar technology, the jangle of metal tools in unfamiliar hands. And there were the muffled voices of men she had only just met. She had followed Mr. PIE's instructions and let them in with their gurney and equipment cases and hollow, hungry looks.

She had personally taken the big man into Mother's room and then watched him close the doors behind him. More than three hours had passed since their arrival. Rikki sat on her sofa, wracked with trepidation and, underneath, excitement. Perspiration beaded on her forehead. Rikki could hardly believe that she had done it.

There were actual Harlem Hedzhunters in her mother's bedroom.

A great sadness swept over her as the realization settled in her head that her mother was probably already dead. Despite the promise she'd made to herself, Rikki had not been at her mother's side when her final moment on earth had come and gone.

She tried hard not to think about the actual procedure, the necessary desecration of her mother's body and her mind. She tried not to think about Reagan—what he would say if he ever learned of what she had done. She was breaking the law, both God's and humankind's. Her hands trembled.

No, she told herself. *This is right.*

Rikki dropped her head into the latticework of her opened palms. She stared at the floor until a pair of shoes covered in pea-green hospital booties stepped into view. She looked up. He looked down.

"Our work, Madame, is done."

The man, dark and thickly constructed with a large, close-shaven head, reminded her more of an African porter than a back-alley brain surgeon. His English was good, but she detected a hint of an accent she could not place. She was, however, certain that the Queen's English was neither his first nor his preferred language.

When they had first met at her apartment's elevator, he'd introduced himself as Dr. Joseph. Rikki thought his manner was amusingly courtly. *Weren't they a bunch of headhunters?* she'd thought at the time.

Dr. Joseph moved—glided, she thought—to sit on the loveseat positioned just outside her mother's bedroom door.

"Your mother is gone," Dr. Joseph said in his best bedside manner, stepping soundlessly toward Rikki as she sat in her living room. She looked up without surprise, as if the scene had been rehearsed in a dream. "She passed without pain or struggle," he continued, speaking to the top of Rikki's head. "Our procedure was successful."

Speaking from a daze, Rikki looked past the Dark doctor and stared at the bedroom door, set slightly ajar. She asked a single question: "May I see her?"

Dr. Joseph rose and guided Rikki to sit down next to him on a loveseat positioned at an equal distance between the entrance to the living room and bedroom. Rikki complied, and then noticed that he was holding an exquisite little case just above his lap. She let her eyes drift down to it, and then up to the man's broad, impassive features.

He opened the case as if it were a prize.

"Now she is yours, forever," he said sounding more like a shaman than a doctor as he placed the case in Rikki's waiting hands.

The case felt shockingly light in Rikki's trembling hands. The very fact of it frightened her. As she opened it, she noticed that the man was avoiding her eyes again.

"We isolated, of course, for optimum hot memories," he said as he let his gaze settle on an elephant-eared houseplant seated in an elaborate pot a few feet beyond the loveseat. Rikki said nothing. She opened the box and gasped when she noticed that less than a third of it held a stand of slender, glass vials containing fluids of varying tints of red and pink.

"You must understand something about memories; they come in different temperatures," Dr. Joseph explained. "Hot memories are the most intense memories, the ones people will do anything not to forget. They are usually among the happiest, the most satisfying. The most gratifying.

"People re-remember them all their lives, recalling them for their own satisfaction, talking about them, preserving them in diaries, memoirs, vidis, in retracing their contours, refreshing their colors and textures until they die with their keeper.

"That was before Hedz," Dr. Joseph said, pride reverberating in his breathy voice. "We color-code them," he continued as sat a little closer to Rikki.

"The red memories are the most intense. The pinker ones are less so, but still hold quite a bit of happiness."

"These are all you could find?" Rikki asked, eyeing the practically empty case of vials standing upright in illuminated racks of cushioned brackets. "You are certain that there are not more? Many more?"

"She was old, your mother, and very sick," Dr. Joseph said. "Her mind was affected. There could once have been more, but these are the ones we could secure and remove. Then again, this could very well be the extent of it."

"The extent of what?"

"Her happiness," Dr. Joseph told Rikki. "There are easily one hundred hours of happiness here. If you keep them mildly refrigerated, and you are careful with your injections—no more than a few minutes at a time—there is enough here to re-experience your mother's happiness for the rest of your life."

Rikki shook her head. This was not what she had imagined. She began to worry if the men were telling her the truth. It would not be beyond them, she thought, to hoard some of her mother's memories to sell on the open market. How would she know? What could she do?

"Hold on," said Dr. Joseph, who, in Rikki's eyes, began to look as if he had something to hide. "I have to make a call. About your payment."

Rikki got up to leave the room when her mother's bedroom door opened and she caught a glimpse of Dr. Joseph's assistants splattered in blood. She felt panic banging in her head. The man had told her that the procedure would be bloodless. She had to get to her bedroom, its locked door, its viewpanel. Just then, she felt a strong hand grip her hard around her right wrist.

"NoNeedaRush," Dr. Joseph said. "Let's drop the formalities. Call me JoË. I have a question for you: Have you ever shot Hedz?"

Rikki felt the room draw in on her. She felt dizzy with fear. She suddenly realized that she was alone in her home with four criminals, demonstrated murderers. Her scheme had worked too well. Reagan had no idea what she was doing. And she'd timed the procedure while her husband was away on another extended business trip abroad. Even building security believed a legitimate medical team was in her home attending to her dying mother.

And Mac. Rikki had ordered him into a hard shutdown.

"Excuse me," JoË sqeezed her arm harder. "Did you hear me?"

Rikki nodded absently.

"You should sample da goods before you pay4daGoodees," he said, motioning to his associates to prepare an injector.

A shiver shook her shoulders when she looked at the injector's long, silvery needle. "Here," JoË Dots said, "let me showyUhow."

Rikki glanced at the time. It was almost 2:00. Two of the men steadied her by holding her shoulders as JoË Dots eased the long, red-tipped injector needle up her right nostril. Her right eye began to tear. His hand was there to dab it with a surgical swab.

She felt pressure building high in her nasal cavity. Rikki felt the needle's dull penetration, then its warm release. Rikki smiled, or believed she did, thinking for a moment how much the sensation conveyed an odd sense of intimacy.

PAIN!

So much pain crashing about in her lower body—not her head. Rikki instantly thought something had gone wrong. This was not how it was supposed to be. Then the pain subsided, but never disappeared. Then, again, she was slammed with a clenching, searing pressure. It was in her back, her hips, her lower abdomen. Her head throbbed as her heart pounded and her breathing raced to keep up.

"Breathe. Breathe. Chain breathing."

Rikki sensed a reassuring presence looming somewhere between her outstretched thighs as she instinctively prepared to push. The pressure of hands was tight on her ankles as she sucked air and took long, deep breaths. And there was music, folksy, twanging guitar cords, a reedy girl's voice... "Oooh Oooh child, things are gonna get better..."

It was a woman's voice, a doctor's, which had spoken with understated authority and calm.

Blood. There was the smell of blood.

"Now push!"

The doctor again, and more voices, familiar and not.

"Push. Push!"

Pain, but pleasure, too. Deep, sweet pleasure—and satisfaction, too— poking through. Rikki knew. She was experiencing uterine contractions. She reveled in their primal power, their gaining strength. Rikki was heaving and laughing and crying—and pushing.

Her gaze was affixed on a large, overhead mirror. She could see latex-gloved hands slick with amniotic juices, mottled with blood, reaching and pulling, too.

"Push. Push!"

"I can't see," she screamed, as hands scattered like startled starlings.

"Here she comes, Mrs. Reynolds. Here she comes."

If there was pain, she could not sense it beneath the waves of determination and joy that flowed through and over her. She could see the tiniest of a human ear, as perfect and pink as a morning rose. Gloved hands. The doctor's head. Then a face, so small, so wonderfully wrinkled.

There was no pushing now, as the rest of the baby slipped from her as if it was a stick of butter. A last push and the placenta spilled out.

Rikki, childless Rikki, felt a profound happiness that she'd long ago believed would never be possible for her. Her eyes darted toward the sleeping baby on her chest. The delivery room filled with cheers and applause and a new life's high-pitched cry.

"Listen to those lungs," the doctor said as she cut the umbilical cord. "You have a happy, healthy new daughter, Mrs. Reynolds."

The baby whimpered in her ear as she cradled the soft, warm creation to her chest. "Now, now, my little angel girl," she cooed, silently counting ten fingers, ten toes. "Now, now."

PAIN!

This time, all the pain was in Rikki's chest. Rikki opened her eyes, briefly, but long enough to see Dr. Joseph plunge one of her kitchen knives into her chest.

"Why?" she asked, choking on her own blood and the realization that the child was not hers, but *her*, a memory of childbirth stolen from her mother. "You'll never get paid."

Dots laughed. "We've already been paid. How much do you think your mother's Hedz—and yours—will be worth? Lot more than what you were going to pay.

"Oh, almost forgot to tell you: I got something for your fucking two-faced brother, too," Dots said, as he unleashed another savage knife thrust to Rikki's heart.

32

Ashes to Answers

FROM THE AIR THE NEXT DAY, THE SCENE WAS PRECISELY WHAT REAGAN had expected: a quarter-acre of scorched earth and overcooked steel, plastic, and glass that looked like the footprint of a one-legged giant in a hurry. But on the ground, the destruction threatened to overwhelm him. The fumes of things organic and inorganic fused in a rage of flames.

Reagan looked around, then up. The day was young and hazy, and smoke was still snaking off wreckage strewn all around him. A sheriff's deputy offered him a breather, but Reagan gruffly refused. His left eye was running and that was bad enough, he thought. He didn't want strangers thinking the big-city Department captain was crying over an investigation. Yet he could not escape the sense of dread weighing harshly on his shoulders.

He toed around what looked to him like a great mound of manure, in the midst of a small clearing of charred concrete blocks encircled with old-fashioned police tape. Dropping into a wobbly crouch, Reagan used a stick to poke the mound, which was drawing flies.

"What am I looking at here?" the sheriff's deputy asked Reagan

Without looking up, Reagan spoke in a dry, seen-it-all tone: "It was a man, a Viper called Rattle. I saw him killed here last night with some kind of dissolving agent."

"Excuse me," the clean-shaven deputy said under his breath, as a dozen other local investigators gathered around the smelly mound. "This is a body?"

"Yeah," Reagan said as he stood and began to walk away. "Scan its DNA. I knew 'em when he was a man, even though he was still a shit.

There should be a second body in this mess somewhere. I dropped him somewhere over there." Reagan pointed over his shoulder, then slowly stood to further survey the wreckage.

Reagan heard a boyish voice calling from inside the burned-out hauler.

"A lot of real funny readings here," the voice told Reagan as he ducked under a metal rib and stepped into what was left of the hauler's tanker. "The fuel it was carrying is what went up in a fireball…"

A slender man with blazing red hair stepped out from behind a charred compartment that looked to Reagan like some kind of shower stall or double coffin.

"—But… I'm picking up that another substance, and a helluva lot of it, burned too.

"Oh," the young man said, extending his hand to Reagan. "My name is McKee Gavock. I'm the forensics investigator here in Allegany County."

"Good for you," Reagan replied. "Now what do you think was being transported in here?"

McKee looked at his flip-up mobile VPs and kicked around the ash.

"Hard to say, exactly, but I'll guess some illegal narcotic. The chemical composition I'm getting is not like anything I've seen—"

Reagan scoffed: "We could build a whole new world out of all the things you ain't seen, sonny boy."

McKee ignored the jab and kept reading his flip-ups. "It's the packaging, see," he continued. "Common synthetics, and lots and lots of it."

McKee began walking into the woods, looking up in the trees as he walked with an exhausting puppy's energy. Reagan trudged for about fifty yards until he saw no point to going any further.

"There," McKee said, pointing at something stuck in the crook of the upper trunk of an old oak. "Can you reach that?"

Reagan rolled his eyes and began walking closer to the tree.

"A boost?" McKee asked.

Reagan bent down and held out his cupped hands, an impatient taunt on his face. The young investigator stepped in and up and began climbing into the tree's lower, leafless branches. Less than a minute later, McKee jumped down.

"This is what was being transported," McKee said as he handed Reagan what looked like a bunch of artificial grapes. "The force of the explosion musta blown 'em way over here."

"Eat something," Oona coaxed Army.

He nervously looked around the modestly appointed room high in the Hotel Theresa. Army had been grateful for a couple of comfortable nights' sleep, but after getting up early, he had grown restless as he looked down on a hurrying Harlem. There was no link, and the room's VP was locked from sending outgoing data. There was only a single message from Reagan that crawled across the screen's edge on the quarter hour: *Will you help us help you?*

"How can you look at another one of those silly old movies?" Army asked Oona, who was stretched across the room's centerpiece, a triple-wide bed. "I keep thinking about Rattle, the way he died. Your cousin was an asshole, but nobody should have to die like that."

Oona looked up from her nest of fluffy smart pillows and hand-sewn comforters. She rolled over onto her back and reached for a buttery croissant. Her oversized robe gaped at her neck as she turned, helping Army steal a glimpse of her unrestrained breasts before the robe closed on its own.

"Did you know that these things ain't even French?" Oona asked, trying to decide which would be the yummiest end to bite first.

"Yeah, I heard," Army deadpanned, dispatching her question. "And what's that got to do with anything? Huh? Huh? Rattle's dead, and we almost got killed. We're locked in this goddamned room by this Department guy who you've told me is a monster. And you're talking about some bread's nationality?" Army pounded his fist into his thigh in frustration and then turned back to the hotel window.

Oona carefully tore open the flaky layers of her croissant and inhaled its aroma. Her eyes scanned the serving table of breads, cold cuts, and lukewarm tea that uniformed cops had rolled into the room earlier that morning.

"Rattle was a soldier," Oona said. "He died like a soldier. That's all I want to say about it."

Army nodded without turning to look at Oona.

"Tell me," Oona asked, munching on her croissant and wondering why in the movie Deckard would dream of unicorns, of all things, "Did you hear that detective say anything about us being under arrest?"

"I told you—I know that fucker, too," Army replied, annoyed that Oona seemed more interested in the movie on the viewpanel than their captivity. "He's got us trapped in here and he keeps asking us to help him. HIM?"

"He did save our lives," Oona said, half-watching the movie.

Army shoved his hands into the pockets of his hotel robe and stewed.

"Yeah, I guess he did," he replied. "But saved them for what?"

"C'mon," Oona pleaded as he swung around and sat up in bed.

"I've been thinking about this," she said, walking over to stand next to Army. Slipping her hand inside his matching white robe, she began massaging his bare chest. "Listen. Old Reagan wants the bad guys. And you and I know that you ain't one of 'em."

"Yeah," Army said, as he warmed to Oona's touch.

"What if we help him for a while? What if we help him get the real bad guys? Wouldn't that let you off his hook?"

"Might," Army said, "if he doesn't get me killed first."

"I'll have your back," Oona said impishly, as she reached down and gave Army's ass a squeeze. "Now, eat something. I know I'm about to."

Reagan was breathing hard as he ran, then lumbered, toward the sound of the hoverplane's whining engines. When he broke through the weedy field, he could see the craft hovering several feet off the ground. The pilot skillfully inched toward Reagan, then tipped the vehicle, bringing its side entrance steps within Reagan's reach.

When he grabbed the short stair's handrail, Reagan lost his grip on his coat and watched it get sucked into one of the craft's engines.

"Fuck," Reagan said, as he flopped into his seat beside the pilot. "That was my favorite fucking coat. Couldn't you have gotten closer to the ground?"

"Sorry about your coat, Captain," the pilot hollered, as he pointed to a forward viewpanel. "It's the Department, and it's for you."

"Yeah?" Reagan yelled back, as he watched the crime scene recede to a shrinking rectangle, then a smudge, then nothing but Pennsylvania hillside. The engines calmed as the craft flattened out of its climb.

"Ray," a comforting voice sprang in his head. A second later, the viewpanel filled with an image that comforted as much as confounded Reagan. "It's Romaro. How-ya-doin', buddy?"

"Rome?" Reagan asked incredulously, as his eyes drank in a background that looked starkly familiar.

"What are you doing back? And what are you doing in my sister's apartment?"

"Ray, listen to me. We need you—all of you—on this one."

The hoverplane banked hard, and Reagan felt his seat close tighter around his flanks and shoulders, but not as tightly as the fear that had him by his throat.

"Ray, look at me," Romaro said tenderly. "Look me in my eyes and remember that the Department, that I, need you on this one."

Reagan narrowed his eyes and shook his head. *Why all the jacking off?* he thought.

"What's happened?" he demanded. His jaw clenched. "Just tell me what the fuck happened, Rome."

Romaro looked away, then quickly turned back, composed. He stared into Reagan's eyes through the screen.

"They're gone, Reagan," he said flatly. "Your mother and your sister. They've been murdered. I'm very sorry."

The pilot tried hard not to appear as if he had been listening over the craft's com system. He said nothing, as the hum of the hoverplane's engines filled the cabin. Then he heard it—something akin to the sound of metal giving way under great pressure, like the wail of a bridge falling away into deep waters. The sound was getting more insistent as it wormed through the pilot's head.

The pilot turned to Reagan, then quickly turned back to his cockpit readouts. Reagan's mouth was wide open, and his eyes were bulging like marbles. The wail grew louder and louder, until it morphed into a kind of inverted scream. For a moment, the pilot wondered if the detective was having a stroke.

Reagan's grief blinded him to everything except what played in his head. He had seen thousands of murder scenes. He pictured the mangled corpses, the abundant evidence of the killer's utter disregard for the humanity that was so violently stolen. Blood. He knew there had to be great amounts of blood. Everywhere, blood.

He wondered if they had suffered. Probably not his mother, but surely Rikki. She would not have surrendered to the Reaper easily. Suddenly he was cold with terror. Romaro was there. The Department. He forgot about all his plans for his captives in the Hotel Theresa.

"Dots," Reagan whispered. "JoË motherfucking Dots."

A light rain began to pelt the hoverplane as Reagan wiped his eyes and glared into the darkened sky. Philadelphia's Fairmount Park materialized just ahead. And high over a line of ash, red oak and sugar maple trees, Rikki's penthouse came into focus, glowing with the ghostly white light of expert inquiry.

33

Bucked Up

DESPITE HIS PRONOUNCED LIMP, ROMARO STILL WALKED LIKE A MAN accustomed to the mantle of leadership. At times, he privately worried whether he would regain full use of his biobuilt right leg. Yet he found some accommodation with the affliction. It was an aging warrior's wound, a wordless reminder of the Times Square Incident he had survived, while some had not. On days like these, he found it irresistible not to milk the leg, just a little.

Romaro peg-legged around a trauma detect-deck that blocked his access to the apartment's living room which, only ninety minutes after the bodies were discovered, looked like anything but a room for living. Most of the large, sunken room's furniture and fixtures were being foamed and removed for thorough analysis downtown. In the room's center stood twin Medical Emergency Surgical Shelters, ready for on-site autopsies. Where once a sickle-shaped sofa the color of damp sand had bathed in the penthouse's morning light, a mobile crime laboratory had taken its place.

"What a shit bomb," Romaro said as he made his way to the apartment's ample country kitchen, which had been wiped and turned into his case conference center.

"How the fuck could this happen?"

No investigator within eyeshot dared to answer. Three were carefully removing the primary memory nodes from the partially dismantled Personal Home Appliance. Another two were reviewing Towers Majestic entry desk vidi logs of the suspects entering and leaving the north tower's lobby. A swarm of White Coats wordlessly fluttered in and out of the MESS tents.

"I've got a question for you, Captain," a tight, dry voice croaked, as its possessor poked his head out of a PopUpPottie pitched near the kitchen's arched entrance. "Just one. Do you honestly think your old partner is going to hold up in the face of all of this?"

Romaro turned to pour a cup of coffee, considering the question posed by the Federal agent who had been trailing Romaro all day.

"I'm not going to bush-shit you, Rome. I know my capacity here is strictly oversight—you are the crime-scene coordinator. But making a detective—one just recently reinstated—the lead investigator in the murders of his own mother and sister?" The agent shook his head in disbelief.

"He's the best investigator the Department has on this goddamned headhunting shit," Romaro replied, pouring coffee. "Check the record. Why do you think C3 called me out of my rehab to lead this little detail? It's 'cause the Department wants to, let's say, more fully invest in Detective Reynolds. They were looking for a sensitive touch to keep him in the fold on this one."

The agent reached for his cup of black coffee and blew the steam that rose over it before he spoke. "The Department is banking that you can keep your boy from having some kind of massive breakdown, from walking."

Romaro took a mouthful of coffee and swished it around his mouth.

"He's become too valuable to lose now," Romaro said. "He's up for another field promotion, probably a full captain, like me."

"You're shitting me!" the agent said, sitting his coffee cup down. "It wasn't that long ago when your old partner was, as you so aptly like to say, a fucking mess."

Romaro shook his head. "He was always a good detective. He just had trouble keeping his hands in his pockets."

"The records *I've* seen have him cold for accepting favors—mostly cash and sex—from the people he was investigating, or should have been investigating. I'm sorry—in Washington, he'd have been lucky not to go to prison."

Romaro shook his head again.

"That was more than twelve years ago, and you weren't there," Romaro said. "I was. Most of that stuff was petty crap, and the shit that wasn't was—well... I told our supervisors, but nobody wanted to hear it. Can't say Ray was ever very likable.

"He definitely had a problem with Darks, and two of our key supervisors at the time were Darks." Romaro said and then chewed his lower lip. "I'd say he was set up."

"By his Dark superiors?" the agent asked.

"Hell no," Romaro said, with a chuckle. "The bad men did all the setting up. I just think our supervisors, Light or Dark, just weren't that motivated to look into the thing."

Romaro felt his link pulse in his ear.

"What?" the agent asked.

"Reagan's on his way up."

Both men looked over the bustling crime scene.

"Don't worry about Reagan," Romaro said, then drained his coffee cup.

"He's a tough son-of-a-bitch," Romaro said, as he unwrapped a square of mint vapor gum. "Even on his worst days, he was better than most I know on their best days."

The agent shrugged.

"Wait 'til he gets a look at those bodies over there—his mother and sister are missing persons from the neck up," the agent replied.

Romaro smiled as he blew streams of mint green vapor from his nose.

"He'll buck up," he said. "He'll be fine."

34

Storm's Buildin'

"**I** HATE JERSEY," JOË DOTS GRUMBLED, AS HE AND HIS DRIVER BURST from the shallow light of Lincoln Tunnel. They saw a sudden morning of billboards enlivened with unvarnished come-ons for cheap motels, cheap narcotics, cheap pleasure, and cheap training for work certificates in general hygiene, general food services, general elder care, and general work-certificate training.

He turned from his backseat window in disgust.

"It really makes you fucking wonder what the Old Jersey must have been like if this is the New Jersey," Dots said, speaking to the familiar back of his driver's head. "Much longer?"

"Twenty minutes, tip-tops," the driver said, keeping his eyes on the highway and his heavy foot on the accelerator. "Want some music?"

"NawMeNo," Dots snapped. "I just wanna get there, do the business, then flip the hell back to Oz."

The dark sedan sped in silence onto a sparsely traveled stretch of Port Imperial Boulevard. Alone in the car's backseat, Dots slammed a clip of explosive shells into a vintage 9 millimeter Glock automatic he used only on special occasions.

He could not believe his good fortune. He didn't have to bother with hunting his down his old inside guy; Reagan had arranged the meeting, and had even made it clear that he would be alone, operating far off the Department reservation. This was between the two of them, the detective had emphasized over a secured link. He said he just wanted the heads, and in return had offered to do one last favor.

But did he want much more? Did he want revenge? A shoot-out, one swinging dick swinging at the other? Dots couldn't be certain. He'd never have believed it if someone had told him. But right before his eyes, the fossilized has-been had grown a pair. He patted his Lucky 9 on his lap and rested his stocking feet on the cooler on the floor. If there was to be a contest between them—new stones or not—Dots knew he could make quick work of the fat man.

A double thunderclap over the Hudson River derailed Reagan's train of thought. He had been sitting for most of the morning in a rickety, high-backed wooden chair up against a wood-paneled wall. Thunder rumbled again, closer this time, he thought, as he allowed his eyes to wander over Romaro's tumbledown boathouse, which smelled of mildew and dead fish.

He had suggested that Reagan go there to get away from the Department for a while, take a couple of days to be alone with the better memories of his mother and sister before coming back to the case. Reagan smiled, recalling his old partner's look of surprise when he actually took him up on the offer. Reagan reassured himself that Romaro need not know of his ulterior motive for accepting the keys to the Jersey boathouse.

Reagan let his heavy head fall back against the chair's uncushioned back. He mindlessly rubbed his service penetrator in his lap and thought of how yesterday still refused to accept its place with the rest of days past. He couldn't stop thinking about how Rikki's home was no longer her home, but a crime scene, a place of work for his kind.

Anger flared again. *How could Rikki have been so stupid to be a part of this?* Reagan asked himself, as he replayed Romaro's words in his head.

"I know how this sounds, Ray, but let me tell you what we know so far. Three Darks, posing as Medical Emergency Techs, were scheduled and cleared by Ms. —uh, by your sister. They entered her penthouse at 8:16.08 AM—that's confirmed by building security vidis—to assist Ms. Reynolds, your mother, who was suffering from acute V-HIC-related collapse.

"It looks like Ms. Reynolds expired between 12:15 and 12:30 that afternoon. Cause of death was decapitation. There was no sign of a struggle, but we are still trying to figure out what else was done. The cut through the throat—like with all Hedz cases—was surgically clean. But there was also a lot of blood and brain tissue on the bed and dressing table.

"Now this is the part that really has us all confused. Your sister apparently disabled her Personal Home Appliance just before the fake techs got here. And her post-mortem scans show that she took a heavy injection of Hedz shortly before she was killed. Probably forced. But we can't be sure until we do a post on her head.

"Now all of that was only minutes after your mother's death. We estimate that your sister expired shortly after 2 p.m., also by decapitation, but not before she was stabbed in the heart—twice.

"We have to assume their deaths represent another set of Hedz killings, but you know as well as I do that we've never had any involving someone of your mother's age and poor health and with the violence that was inflicted on your sister.

"It doesn't make sense," Reagan recalled Romaro telling him. But Reagan had already figured it out. He knew the truth would be irrefutable once the Hedz residue in his sister's head was tested. He had to retrieve her head, he told himself, not only to make her whole again, but also to bury with her a secret that was apparent to him, as it would be soon to the rest of the Department if he didn't act.

Reagan's Giuliani flared. Someone was coming. Seconds later he heard the crunch of tires on the crushed-rock driveway leading to the boathouse. By that time he was on his feet, his penetrator leading the way. He peered out of the only window in the little house, alone in a field of weeds and crickets.

"That's close enough," Reagan hollered out of the cracked window. "Get out of the car—ass first—and keep your hands where I can see 'em."

He watched JoË Dots back out of the car and cooperate with exaggerated compliance. He was immediately struck by the change in his appearance. Dots had shaved his head, revealing a huge tat-toon of a snake coiling and uncoiling around his scalp.

"I am REACHING for the CoolIT. Okay?" Dots said, as he moved with caution and care to remove the cooler from the car's backseat.

"Keep your hands on the CoolIT," Reagan barked, as he kept an eye on the driver who had parked in a patch of weeds and river trash.

Dots nodded as he walked toward the boathouse's door, which Reagan was holding open with his foot.

"Stand over there, facing the wall," Reagan ordered Dots, who stood in the middle of the boathouse's dingy, warped floor. "Tell your driver to disappear until you call him back."

Again, Dots complied.

"Sit it down," Reagan snapped. He watched the big man bend deeply from his waist and gently place the cooler on the floor by his feet.

"So you're going to shoot me in the ass while I'm bringing you what I promised?" Dots asked as he, still facing the wall, straightened up slowly.

"No," Reagan said, with an eye on Dots' hands, which hung at his sides. "You deserve much worse, but that's between you and your fate."

"Fate? Uh-oh. I thought you didn't believe in that kind of shit, Reagan," Dots said.

"Startin' to."

Reagan felt a stab of fear in his gut. Dots suddenly seemed so much larger and more lethal now that they stood face-to-face, no more than four feet from one another. Standing so close, Reagan could see that Dots' cobra tat-toon bore a fanged head on both ends of its steel-blue body.

Reagan ordered Dots to remove his pistol and place it on the floor in the middle of the room. Next, he motioned for Dots to take a seat on a crate of fishing gear on the far side of the room.

Dots hesitated to relinquish his pistol: "Only if you do the same."

"Fair enough," Reagan said, "but first I gotta see if you really kept your word."

Reagan kept his penetrator trained on Dots as the Viper lumbered to the middle of the room and placed his Glock on boathouse's floorboards. A moment later, Reagan sidestepped his way to the cooler. He unlocked its pressure seal with a tap of his toe and watched the cooler's lid slide back.

"AsPROMised," Dots hissed as Reagan looked inside.

The boathouse's atmosphere was seized with the smell of disinfectant and frezzpacs.

Reagan glanced in. He only wanted to have to look into the cooler once. Lying face up on a bed of frezzpacs were the heads of his sister and mother. Each of their faces was gray and puffy and partially obscured by their wet, tangled hair.

"As promised," Dots called out again, as he sat with his hands on his knees and his eyes on his pistol in the middle of the floor.

Reagan quickly blinked back tears and turned to Dots, his face more stern than before.

"Thank you," Reagan said, as he placed his weapon on the floor next to

Dots's Glock. "Remember those two words, because you'll never hear them from me again."

"Okay," Dots said. "I did everything you asked me. I brought your people back. I cleaned them up and my driver's probably somewhere joyriding around Weehawken with his dick in his hand. Now it's your turn to deliver so I can get the hell out of here."

"You know, you're right, you murdering piece of dog shit," Reagan said, glancing back to the opened cooler. "As promised."

Both men said nothing as the sounds of river life intruded on the silence.

Reagan took a breath and returned to the rickety wooden chair, which was directly across from where Dots sat in a muscular heap.

"We're going to hit you," Reagan whispered.

"Excuse me?"

"I said we—the Department, Spook-Ops— are going to hit Baghdaddy's in forty-eight hours. We know what we need to know about your operation. We know all about Cutter and your merry band of headhunters."

Reagan spat on the floor.

"We're going to shut the shit down for good," he continued. "Believe me. No more Hedz. No more Duppies. No more you."

Dots began to clap his hands. "I think you and your fancy-ass cops deserve a standing ovation for your inflated sense of importance. You might stop Cutter, you might stop me, but no one in all of this fucking Greater America can stop what's coming. What's happening is so much bigger than you and people like you can ever understand."

Reagan listened with a raised eyebrow. He'd never heard JoË Dots spout more than mongrel gibberish. It was easy to forget that this tat-tooned Viper had once been an academy-educated suit.

"I'm just satisfying a hunger, Detective," Dots said with unswerving conviction. "That's the easy part. The hard part is creating the hunger. And I, and devils like me, had nothing to do with that. You ask yourself, Reagan Reynolds—now Captain Reynolds, I'm told—what would make people so desperately hungry that they would feed on somebody's memories? Not a shoebox of vidis or old photos, but direct source. Somebody's—almost always a stranger's—goddamned brains? I didn't create that kind of hunger; neither did Cutter. But people like you, all the suits and the protectors of the suits, just got too accustomed to winning. After a while, you people didn't care about what happened to the losers.

"They're looking for a key to escape their awful little lives," Dots said, his voice rising in anger. "They're looking to break out of the cages where they've been imprisoned, places where there is no hope, no optimism, no happiness. My job is to simply provide them a key for a modest price. A skull cage key, Captain. It's not terrorism. It's not even revolution. It's pacification. And you should thank me."

Reagan leaned forward in his chair, which popped and crackled under this weight, and stared at Dots. "You sound like you think I should give you a medal or some shit. You're a murderer making money by turning ordinary people, good people, into savages."

"Was your sister a savage?" Dots said, visibly pleased with his retort. "Yeah, your sister was *desperate* for that key, and she was rich. She realized, all alone up in that big, shiny apartment, that she was trapped in her own cage, too."

Reagan bellowed. "You don't know anything about my sister."

"I know she suffered before she died," he replied. "I made sure of that. Cutter would have killed me if she didn't. He says you betrayed us, got caught up in all your Department bullshit, forgot your friends. Forgot who used to help you pay your bills. That's why she suffered. That's why she's dead."

Reagan jumped to his feet and stomped to the center of the room before Dots could stand up. Reagan smiled as he snatched up his penetrator and then kicked the Glock to Dots.

"We may have history, but we have no future," Reagan said, as his rage simmered. "Call your driver. Get the fuck out of here."

Dots blew the dust off his silvery pistol.

"We're hitting Baghdaddy's in forty-eight hours. I'll leave instructions to arrest your murdering ass. That's all I can do for you for returning them to me. But your boss..." Reagan shook his sweat-drenched head. "Cutter... he'll never make it to trial. Remember, forty-eight hours."

Dots nodded and chewed the corner of his lips.

"What if I go to the Department, tell your people how you used to help us?" Dots asked, tucking his weapon back into his waistband.

"If I don't go to prison, I guess I'll be back at the Theresa working security," Reagan said without remorse for his prospects. "But you won't live long enough to know which one. And believe me. I'll make sure you suffer first. Suffer!"

Dots took a couple of steps toward the boathouse door. "You've really grown you a set, Captain. Congratulations."

Reagan watched Dots walk into the Jersey sun and signal for his car to return.

"Nice new balls, Captain," Dots yelled out as he was driven away. "Shame if they get you killed."

Reagan locked the boathouse door, knelt next to the reeking cooler, and cried like a frightened child.

35

Pre-Doom

G-DADDY QUIETLY WEPT AS HE BLINDLY FINGERED RIVER GRASS FOR bits of trash.

"I know, Gee," Jae-J. told him, as he combed the grass for trash too. "I hate thinking about it. But Cosi said it was the only way to get 'em out."

Jae-J. spoke haltingly as he stooped to lift a decaying water fowl with his gloved hand. He held his breath as a swarm of flies followed the stinking mound of dissembling features and slime into a long canvas shoulder bag.

"He told me that he was personally taking care of their transport."

Jae-J. moved a step closer to his father-in-law as the two worked the Hudson bank with a crew of about a dozen others in the RiverNorth Church's Next To God cleanup crew. "I know it's dangerous. But Rev says they can't stay where they are. It's the only way."

G-Daddy let out a long, loud breath before he spoke.

"You still thinkin' 'bout Army?" he asked. "You wonder if he made it, if he's still alive and gettin' over?"

Jae-J. nodded that he did, as the men worked under the oppressive sun.

"You think he made it out of the city?" Jae-J. asked. "Think he's still alive?"

"Yeah," G-Daddy said. "Shit yeah I do."

He watched Jae-J. walk off alone toward the river and knew his son-in-law was trying his best to hide his misery. G-Daddy regretted that he could not give Jae-J. more comfort. He was thankful to Jae-J. for getting them to safe harbor at RiverNorth. He was surprised that his son-in-law not only knew Rev. Cosi, but that the grand old minister actually owed Jae-J. a few favors.

The RiverNorth Work Project had been an excellent cover for them both, G-Daddy thought. Even the weeks of hard physical work had been good for both of them. But the necessity of keeping their communications with ZaNia and Imani to a minimum was killing them a little each day. The exposure, Rev. Cosi's people frequently reminded them, was too risky for everyone involved. The explanation offered little comfort to G-Daddy and Jae-J.

It'll be so good to have 'em back in the house," G-Daddy said to himself, dragging his trash sack along the river bank. *Damn skippy, Skippy.*

Imani lay on her back and peered at the sky through an opportune rip in the packing materials that enshrouded her and her mother. The sky spoke to her, and she wanted to answer the sun and clouds by breaking free and swimming up into its milky depths.

"Lay still," ZaNia hissed, as they began to inch out onto the street.

Imani wanted to correct her mother, tell her that she was lying as still as anyone could, and it was only her breathing and heartbeat that her mother felt beneath the layers of their wrappings. Imani was excited. After weeks of living in the Maternals' compound, they were finally leaving. They were being wheeled out in some sort of automated cart, Imani figured. ZaNia had warned her that they were at their most vulnerable when they were being taken to and from the vehicle. Their sensor masking would only white-noise their bodily functions, not their outward movement.

Imani felt the mechanics of something lifting her, then shoving her firmly into darkness, then soft afternoon air. ZaNia had prepared her for this. She told her that they would be smuggled to Washington Heights in a laundry truck, taken to where her mother told her Rev. Cosi had promised them safe shelter while his church's legal team sorted out their situation.

"The Department has no right to make you refugees," Rev. Cosi told Jae-J., who'd told ZaNia. She permitted herself a bolt of giddy energy over the prospect that the family was on its way to be reunited. *Only Army*, she mused. *He'll find us*, she told herself.

A heavy door slammed hard, causing Imani to tumble onto her side. She felt a bony pressure in the small of her back. She pushed against it, hoping that her mother would read her signal and move her foot. But nothing.

"Mom, mom," Imani whispered.

"Shhh."

"Your foot. It's in my back."

"That's not my foot, honey. Quiet. You have to stay quiet."

ZaNia shuddered with guilt. She had not told her daughter the full truth regarding their escape—or about her former Order of Maternals, either. It was more, she had thought, than Imani could handle knowing.

Besides carrying and delivering perfectly healthy, V-HIC-free babies into the world for anyone wealthy enough to pay for the service, the Harlem Maternals also operated a lucrative gray-market business: collecting, preparing, processing, and delivering human organs and body parts for medical and industrial applications. From the beginning, ZaNia understood its perfect logic. Maternals were in the birth business; why not take on the human recycling business, to help give life or extend the life of ailing humans? There were so many discarded embryos and other genetic materials that were a natural byproduct of Maternal work. Why not sell it?

But ZaNia did not think Imani would understand. Worse, ZaNia worried, Imani would think less of her if she knew that her mother was not only a birth cow, but a gut reaper, too. Even Army did not know that part of her.

"Try to shift your body," ZaNia instructed her daughter as she imagined a cadaver's foot jabbed in the small of Imani's back. "Get as comfortable as you can. We still have quite a ride before Cosi's people intercept us."

"Yes, Momma," Imani replied, her voice sounding muffled and faraway to ZaNia's ear. "These dirty clothes sure smell funny. Like vinegar and underarms."

"Try to sleep," ZaNia urged her. "Try to dream you're somewhere nice."

Imani tried to find that rip in the packing materials. But all she could find was darkness as she felt the creaky machinery of a small hauler taking them away, taking them to, Imani prayed, Rev. Cosi, family, and a new start.

JoË Dots stood transfixed and dry-mouthed in the center of Cutter's office. A Department bust of a small-time Hedz dealer was being shown live, in full spectrum, on every wall of the spacious room.

"Those bastards have some balls on them," Dots said, chortling nervously.

I hope they can hold on to them long enough to be buried with them," Cutter added, pushing his light voice to sound heavier.

Dots ignored Cutter. He tried to hear the media chatter playing over the hypernatural sounds of penetrating rifle fire punching through a four-story brownstone in Washington Heights. He could make out antitank cannons blasting returning fire. A command vehicle was fully covered in flames. Bodies were burning in the pockmarked streets. "That's A.V.'s spot," Cutter said, amused. "We've done business with his outfit from time to time. Remember? One-sixty and Saint Nicholas?"

Dots nodded blankly. His attention was drawn to a series of extreme close-ups highlighting the menacing approach of more Department ground and air firepower. Dots could feel the muscles in his belly twitching. It was not difficult for him to imagine a similar onslaught ripping into Baghdaddy's. How could Reagan guarantee his life tomorrow? Could he somehow find a way to hustle him out of the club before the attack went full blast?

Cutter set his viewpanel to randomize, prompting the visual perspectives to rapidly melt one into another and another. He cut the commentary and amped up the immersion sound.

Department hoverplanes let loose a volley that collapsed the building's top floor, silencing the antitank cannons.

"Ouch!" Cutter chuckled. "Never liked them much any way. Vaporize their arrogant asses!"

Aghhhhh, Dots thought as he watched the three hoverplanes open and sustain fire on the brownstone, which was staggering on its crumbling foundation. Surrounding buildings were burning like a garbage fire.

Army and Oona could see the smoke from the Theresa on 125th Street, but neither knew exactly what was happening. The night before, the hotel had disabled the room's viewpanel when it discovered that Army was attempting to use it to jack into an outgoing Weave thread.

"Whatever it is," Army told Oona, "it's ugly. People are dying tonight."

The office had a sunset quality about it, G-Daddy thought, as he sat with Jae-J. in age-swollen leather chairs that had seen much better days. The room was dimly lit. He could not decide whether this was a consequence of design or neglect. Every window was shuttered. Some also wore drawn curtains, but the smell of noxious smoke from the street was everywhere in the room.

With the exception of two overdressed young men standing silently at the door to the main office, G-Daddy and Jae-J. appeared to be alone in the dusty old room. No one seemed concerned that Armageddon was unfolding close enough to choke on it. On this early evening, as on all others, highlights of Rev. Cosi's speeches played softly in the background, barely audible over the antipersonnel fire.

"Why do you think he had us brought here?" G-Daddy asked Jae-J., who only shook his head and stared at the threadbare paisley-patterned carpet under his dirty shoes. It reminded him of his grandfather's funeral home back in Cleveland, too long ago to remember much more.

Then, as if he had materialized from a luncheon in heaven, Rev. Cosi appeared before them, standing between the sliding doors that led into his adjoining private office.

"Good of you to join us, gentlemen," Cosi began, as he motioned to G-Daddy and Jae-J. to sit in matching African-print chairs that looked like thrones. Before they could get settled, Cosi glided into his generous seat behind an even more generous walnut desk.

As if on cue, the two young men in their dark suits planted themselves on each side of Cosi's desk. He acted as if he hadn't noticed.

"What I wish to discuss with you is of grave concern," Cosi said as his cinnamon-colored central wall became the largest viewpanel Jae-J. and G-Daddy had ever seen. "The matter at hand pertains to your loved ones en route to us."

Jae-J.'s heart trembled. All he could see on the wall were bombs and bullets, the dead and dying.

"Are they okay?" G-Daddy asked feebly, trying to force down his fear of the worst.

"For now," Cosi said in quiet, honey-roasted tones, "your women are safe. But their progress has been halted by this big police action on Saint Nicholas. The transport they were traveling in has been held up near Columbia-Presbyterian Hospital.

"My understanding is that they are in a sealed transport, so it could be dangerous for us to permit the ladies to stay there for the night," he explained as clasped his hands in gesture for miraculous mercy. "I know the Lord is with us in our many mortal ministrations, but He also implores us to act as He might—boldly and resolutely."

"What can we do?" Jae-J. asked firmly.

Multi-dimensional maps of Washington Heights filled an upper quadrant of Rev. Cosi's viewpanel. "My sources tell me that the hauler is under light guard. We plan to use a small, highly resourceful group of followers to reach the hauler, free your women, and bring them here. I was hoping you would go with them, Brother Jae."

Jae-J.'s chest swelled as he thanked Rev. Cosi for making him a part of the rescue.

"And me?" G-Daddy asked. "What do I do?"

Jae-J. and Cosi looked at G-Daddy.

"I'm going too," G-Daddy insisted, as he almost rocked out of his chair to stand. "If I'm strong enough to work like a cotton-pickin' slave—no ingratitude intended, Rev.—I'm strong enough to help rescue my daughter and grandbaby."

"Yo, I'm going!" G-Daddy shouted to an emptying room. His insistence grew louder as his realization deepened that he was going to be left behind. "I'm going," he whispered as Rev. Cosi's guards left the office, locking its door behind them.

Romaro followed Reagan's instructions to the letter. He had gone to the Hotel Theresa and released the couple Reagan had stashed there. When he saw Oona, he thought, *Damn, what a sugary little chocolate,* and wondered, for a moment, if Reagan was back up to his old tricks. He recognized Army right away and was stunned by how hard and focused the young man looked, compared to the dazed wreck he'd interviewed in the morgue.

"As far as I'm concerned, you two are free," Romaro told Army and Oona as they rode the hotel's elevator down to the lobby. "It's not completely my call, but I have been authorized to offer you the Department's apology for—"

"Apology?" Army hollered as the elevator began to slow. "You people have destroyed my life and have my family hiding no telling where." Looking down on Oona's stoic expression, he added, "People have *died.* Maybe *my* people."

The doors opened onto the lobby. "Like I said," Romaro pressed, "this is not my call, and I obviously don't know everything that has gone on between you and Reagan. But he asked me to personally get an answer from you two."

Oona stopped Romaro as he walked into the opulent, high-ceilinged lobby filled with Asian tourists and hotel staff rushing to their tasks to please. There were uniformed cops posted at the exits. "I know. He wants us to *help* his psycho ass! Why the hell should we? Tell me that!"

"He said you," Romaro said, directing his words at Oona, "know your way around Baghdaddy's, especially the upper floors where the owner lives and has offices. And that big dome on top of the building, where they have parties for their top-class members..."

"So?" she responded defensively. "I've worked in there a few times."

"Reagan says we need all the help we can get in terms of finding our way around up there," he said, explaining that the nightclub was heavily shielded and that it was difficult for surveillance techs to see through its walls.

"You've got to be kidding," Army snapped. "Maybe you didn't get the memo, Sherlock, but we don't have anything to do with this shit. Hell, we've been *locked* in that room up there for the past three days. Plus, we ain't soldiers, or agents, or whoever you're sending in there."

"My apologies," Romaro said, stopping just outside the hotel's opulent main bar. "Reagan says that he can give your woman the best protection if she helps. Or—on the other hand—he can build a damn good case against her if she refuses."

"You're crazy," Army screamed, as tourists moved away from them.

"Listen, Black," Romaro said, his frustration sharpening the edges of his tone. "We know that pile of shit, Rattle, was her cousin. We've got enough just on the illegal interstate travel in his hauler alone to put you both in upstate work camps until you drop dead of exhaustion.

"Be smart," Romaro said, turning to Oona. "You play ball, and Reynolds will give you a way out."

Army slammed his open hand hard and flat on the bartop, rattling glasses and drawing a look from the bartender. "You can't make—"

"I'll do it," Oona said softly.

Army snapped his head to look at Oona, who was staring at Romaro.

"I'll do it," she repeated, raising her voice. "I'll go."

"Then I'm going with you," Army volunteered. "No way in hell I'm letting you go off with them unless I'm there too."

Romaro shook his head and reached inside his suit jacket and slipped out a handheld VP. As soon as the room's light fell across its polished, micro-onyx surface, it glowed to life and he began to speak. "Yeah. I'm standing right here with both of them," Romaro said into the viewpanel. "She's in.

But they insist the guy come too. Yeah. I don't know—to keep tabs on her. Yeah. Okay."

Romaro handed the VP to Army.

"I'm not going to bullshit you," Reagan said, his face spilling off the VP in all directions. "I know your girlfriend has extensive knowledge of our target site. The Department needs her. But you? You'll be in the way."

Army looked to Oona and Oona looked to Army. Romaro stared at both of them.

"You want her, you take me, too," Army said. "I go where she goes. That's our deal."

Reagan stared back from the VP before he spoke. "Suit yourself. But you've picked the wrong time to play the hero. *Boy.*"

"When do we get started?" Oona asked.

Romaro lowered his face to within inches of Oona's.

"You already have," he whispered.

"UknowzTHEYcoming4us," JoË Dots said, turning away from Cutter's vidi of yesterday's recaps of the raid on A.V.'s, which he had looping on all four walls of the office.

"They're already here, Dots. And how many times do I have to tell you? Fucking English. Please!"

"Then what the hell we going to do, Cee? I can't see us going down like A.V."

JoË Dots looked as if he was on the edge of panic. He hastily poured himself another drink from the first bottle within his reach. He had to be careful not to overplay his concern, nor underplay it. Either would tip his hand that he knew something, something that could get him killed.

Cutter leaned back in his office chair. "Relax. I've got security at triple strength, and I instructed access management to spread the word that tonight's a special event: free entry for non-members and no class-codes in the sweet-suites. That should clog the place up really good. Human shields and all that."

Two wall screens flipped to multiple views of the club's main level. The dance floors were teeming with gyrating partygoers. The bars and dining islands were overflowing. Another screen showed crowds stretching for blocks along 116th Street, all clamoring for a chance to get into Baghdaddy's.

"Judging by the attire, I'd say we have some first-timers in that queue," Cutter said while never dimming the brilliance of his smile. "And I got a dinner going in the dome—some regional administrators and very special guests getting a head-full up there.

"Who would hit us tonight?" Cutter practically sang the words. "The mayor's boy is up there hogging the Hedz. He loves the stuff, especially female Hedz."

JoË Dots nerves got the better of him. "What the fuck?" he yelled, spilling his fresh drink. "Maybe I didn't speak clearly or plainly enough in the *Queen's English* for you, Cee. The Department is coming. For us! I *know* this. For me. For you. Check the Weave. Streets all over Harlem are being shut down and cleared. The heavy shit is heading our way."

"And maybe you didn't hear me, Dots!" Cutter shouted back, incredulous that an underling, even JoË Dots, would raise his voice to him. "My inside guys tell me that the Department is *already here*, but that it's looking for a little fish. There'll be a routine search-and-seizure so the assholes can say they've done something. Someone utterly replaceable will be arrested. We'll make the Weave, and then it will be back to business as usual.

"You know the routine," Cutter said, eyeing Dots from sweat to twitch. "What's your problem tonight?"

JoË Dots shook his head and sulked, and began thinking again about how he should find a way to put some distance between Cutter and himself. He didn't want to be in the same room when the Department came gunning for his boss. *Routine search-and-seizure my ass*, Dots thought. He was working out his exit plan as Cutter rambled on about the preparations for the evening's festivities.

Dots was on his feet. He paced a while before he charged Cutter's desk.

"Because you're already dead doesn't mean I want to be," JoË Dots blurted, his face inches from Cutter's startled expression.

"You better sit your big ass down," Cutter growled at Dots, "before I sit it down permanently."

"You're crazy," Dots hollered, as he thought about running for his life.

Cutter glared, reached into his desk drawer and slammed an Atlas automatic hand cannon onto his desktop.

"We're all dying, Dots; that's the beauty of life, the certainty of it all. I

find that our knowing we will die gives life its essential urgency," he said as
he slowly spun his pistol on his desk as if were about to play a deadly game
of spin the bottle.

"And, Dots," Cutter said, "if you keep getting on my nerves this way, I'm
going to pump some urgency, point-blank, into your fat fucking head."

"You and your jokes..." Dots walked in ever-smaller circles in front of
Cutter and eyed the door.

"Who says I'm joking? I should blow your goddamned head off right
now for that side deal you tried to pull in Missouri. You think I didn't
know?"

Dots spun around.

"Don't bother," Cutter cut him off. "I know you've been trading with
that Department shit, Reynolds. Very disappointing. I bet you cut a deal for
tonight with him too? He gives you a get-out-of-jail-free card if you deliver
my head to him on a paper plate."

Dots tried to appear unfazed.

"Jokes, again," Dots said, realizing that Cutter could end their
partnership by splattering his brains on the office walls.

"Could be joking—then again..." Cutter said, smirking as he fingered
his glistening hand cannon. "Maybe I don't blame you for being addicted
to profits, or then again, maybe I do."

JoË Dots hated that smirk, and he hated the man wearing it even more.
Before he fully realized what he was doing, he had his big hands wrapped
around Cutter's stout, short neck. The office automated security system
fired, but Dots realized that leaping with Cutter in his arms had mostly
shielded him from its fire before he fell behind the desk.

As he laid beneath the desk, Dots felt a burning in his lower left calf.
A glance confirmed that it had been hit. At the moment, Dots thought,
the terrible throbbing in his leg was worth the pleasure he'd gotten in
pinning Cutter to the floor by the throat. He was surprised by how little the
diminutive man resisted the mounting pressure of Dots's hands.

"Die, you evil little fuck!" Dots screamed. "My English clear enough
for you now?"

Cutter smiled faintly as his dollish lips passed from pink to violet.

JoË Dots could hear pounding outside the sealed office door. He gave
Cutter a final, neck-snapping choke, then propped himself up to peer over
Cutter's desk. He frantically looked over the desktop controls and began

hitting buttons, first to double-seal the outside door to the office and then to pull up images of the club's security personnel pounding at it to get inside.

"Fuck!" Dots screamed, as he scanned the security controls for anything that might help barricade him in Cutter's office. He stuffed Cutter's cannon in his waistband and rummaged through the desk until he found the steel box of first-run Duppies he had given Cutter after his demonstration.

Then he heard more pounding, now from the sweet-suites a floor below. Weapons fire. His whole leg was aching.

Fuck. They're here, Dots said to himself, just before pinching a Duppy under his flaring nostrils and cozying up to surrender.

36

Ying's Yang

ROMARO SAT TO THE LEFT OF REAGAN, AND WAS AMAZED AGAIN BY HOW quickly his old partner had made himself invaluable to such a high-priority case. The Federal agent's assessment still rang in his head: It wasn't long ago that Reagan was swatting Vipers in a Harlem tourist trap. Romaro felt a jolt of jealousy over Reagan's battlefield promotions to operation commander. Here Reagan was, leading the Department's mission to eradicate the Hedzhunters and anyone who aided them, harbored them, or profited with them.

Reagan was oblivious to his former partner's musings. He hardly looked up as the shadowy mobile command center filled with more than two dozen detectives and forensic and surveillance specialists. The low-ceilinged MCC, bolted between the upper floors of a Harlem parking garage, had become Reagan's war room. The center's concave walls danced with data.

"My condolences for your tragic loss, Captain."

Reagan looked up from an interrogation transcript to see Lieutenant Starr. She firmly patted his back before power-strutting to her seat near the end of a triangular bank of reconnaissance specialists.

From the corner of his eye, Romaro checked Reagan for any indication he might be loosening his grip from grief or guilt at not being able to save his mother and sister. But what he saw was a man who had somehow found himself in the midst of great loss. He looked, Romaro thought, like a man who had finally found redemption. Suddenly, Romaro felt useless, and with his busted leg, literally out of step with the Department.

For a few minutes, Reagan studied his screens in silence. He was still trying to figure out what Cutter had gotten out of his bid at misdirection, with his people's half-hearted attempt to cast Armstrong Black as a Hedz killer. For his part, Reagan had long ago concluded that Armstrong had nothing to do with any of the killings. It made no sense. But then again, Reagan was convinced that an animator of fates and fools like Cutter had to be insane; making sense was not a requirement for a madman.

Reagan took in the scene around him. Practically everyone in the MCC was watching him. The moment seemed to require something. He cleared his throat before he spoke.

"We are about to take our operation right to these head-snatching bastards. We are about to launch, by far, our biggest operation yet. And with it, we will crush this hideous trade before it spreads. We stop it here. We stop it tonight."

The room crackled with applause just as Army and Oona were escorted into the command center, where attention seemed to them to be on everything but them.

"Captain Romaro has worked up an attack and capture plan with three Spook-Ops assault units—Alpha, Beta, Gamma," Reagan said, as he settled back into his seat. "Those of you involved will find your orders uploading."

Reagan turned to check a four-dimensional grid map of the target site when he noticed an information officer guiding Army and Oona in his direction.

"So you're ready to join our little raiding party tonight?" Reagan asked Army and Oona, who were looking up to him in his platform command center.

Army glared at Reagan. Oona spoke before Army could say something they might both regret later in an upstate labor camp.

"Yeah, we're in," she said, coldly, "like we had any choice."

"Put her with Beta team," Reagan ordered. "They'll feed her intel to Alpha and Beta as we go in.

"You just do whatcha have to do for me in there," he growled at Oona. "I don't give a damn why. And as for your 'boyfriend,'" he continued, turning around to sneer at Armstrong. "I hear you're insisting on going along to 'keep an eye on things'. Okay, fine—we'll let you tag along with Gamma, the back-up team. But how's about you stay out of the way and not fuck up our operation, and try not to get yourself hurt in the process. Okay, loverboy?"

"Ex-cel-lent," Lieutenant Starr said, stepping up and addressing the group. She cast a cool glance at Oona before eyeing Army from his head to his feet and smiling broadly.

"Remember me, loverboy?" she teased. "Wish upon a…"

Oona's head jerked toward Starr, and Army grimaced reflexively. Starr switched off her grin and moved smartly back to her battle position.

Romaro watched it all silently. He knew Reagan wouldn't lose any sleep if Armstrong got his head blown off in the raid. But he couldn't say Reagan would feel the same thing about the girl. He suspected that however Reagan felt, he probably wasn't finished with her.

An hour later, Reagan was scanning the status of the Baghdaddy's raid as it spilled before him on multiple viewpanels inside the MCC. The whole command bunker was assembled from ten command vehicles parked in a great rectangle in the center of West 119th Street, each conjoined and mechanically reconfigured—in minutes—into a fully-enclosed, hardened command structure.

The assault was proceeding like clockwork—though not without heavy action and heavy Department losses. Reagan whirled in his command seat, fielding requests, interpreting data, and shouting orders. His piggish eyes brightened as each new progress report rolled in. A dozen field captains, their surveillance officers, and staff were hunkered over their own MCC control decks' translucent viewpanels. Romaro, sitting side-by-side with his old partner, found himself increasingly impressed by Reagan's total absorption in leading the assault effort.

"Goddammit," Romaro heard Reagan murmur in a voice much lower than the one he used to direct the Department team. He glanced at Romaro quickly. "We just lost all signal on Oona Woods."

Romaro leaned forward meaningfully, and replied in a voice just as low, "What about Black? He still in there?"

"Wish I could say," Reagan said, feeling his voice empty. "Turns out Gamma is taking a lot of fire on that damn dorm floor, where we thought things would be quiet. Got two dead, but not him." *Not yet, at least*, he thought to himself.

"Small wonder you lost her," Romaro hissed, before yelling in a louder voice, "Okay, people—looks like Beta's been ambushed on five. They're taking serious heat."

Starr called from her post. "I've got Gamma Team making its way to five to assist."

Romaro nodded as he tapped his link and watched his viewpanel. "My people tell me that floors one through four and the sixth floor are secure. We have Alpha team assembling weapons in the bathrooms on six for deployment on the offices on seven, Cutter's loft on eight, and then that fucking dome on the roof."

"This is it," Reagan said. "Get Gamma to five quick—we need the girl to help us find the way in to that dome."

Army was had been repulsed and excited as he'd followed close behind the Gamma Spook-Ops team. He'd watched closely as the agents—whose resentful disregard for him was palpable—loaded and charged their hand-cannon weapons. Since they'd gone into the building, he'd been completely focused on Oona and seeing her out of this nightmare safely. But it dawned on him that maybe he hadn't ended up in the middle of a fire fight between Department agents and the security forces of Harlem's top crime lord— pretty much defenseless without the helmet and body armor the Gamma team members wore, and armed with nothing more than a link they'd given him to hear orders in the midst of the firing—without that sick fuck Reagan wanting him here.

Gamma team had entered the original rear wall of the eight-story building through an air-compressor port. As back-ups, they were making their way along the already-cleared fourth floor, high above the club's cavernous dance and dining level and yet just as many floors from the seventy-foot tall party dome where Alpha team was ultimately heading.

Army heard Starr's voice come over his link: "Gamma team—get to floor five to support Beta—Beta under heavy fire on five, repeat, heavy fire. Access through the northern stairwell, left of your present position."

"Copy. We're moving," Army heard the team leader reply. "Saddle up, Gamma! Time for a piece of this action."

Beta team. Oona.

Army's worst fears ignited, animating unspeakable scenarios in his head from which he could neither turn away nor shut out. He wished he could kill like the Department's best. He wished he could kill his way to Oona. But he found himself only capable of keeping his head down. Scampering voyeuristics reported nothing on the northern staircase as the team prepared to climb it. He tagged along as the team rushed up the stairwell, prepping their cannons.

Army thought he could feel his heart pounding, but he knew what he was feeling through the stairwell walls was the sound of heavy fire coming from five, with a backbeat of distant music emanating from massive air speakers music far below and above him. His mind flashed for a moment all the Freds and Gingers grinding and humping to the music without a hint that war was spreading over them.

"Stay close and don't be afraid to let your trigger bounce," the leader said as the team prepared to burst through the door to the fifth floor.

As he burst through the door behind the team members, Army saw the fifth floor light up with a blinding blue-white light, as Cutter's security met the reinforcements. A hot spray of debris pelted Army's face and chest as he felt himself being thrown backward.

Like counter beats to the beat-bop that saturated the building, Army could now hear gunfire playing all around him. Army could make out the team leader and several Spooks emptying fire into bodies that seemed to be pouring from every open door.

Then, another blast, and Army felt himself hurled through a sliding door that closed behind him. He landed on his ass in total darkness. His whole body hurt.

He tried to lie back but felt something hard against his back. Army rolled to his side and was surprised to find himself staring at a Department hand cannon. He grabbed it and pushed himself upright, grunting. The sharp pain in his back was from the helmet of the Gamma team leader. Army looked down the leader's torn body, the torso blown wide open. When he took the fire that killed him, his body had pushed Army into this room.

Army stripped the team leader's OptiTechs off his helmet and put them on. Instantly, he could get a better sense of where he was—what looked like a dorm room, filled with bunk beds. Some kind of staff quarters, he realized.

Army turned up the OptiTech's brightness. He could hear the pop and thunder of hand cannons in the hallway outside as Gamma and what remained of Beta (he hoped) engaged with the bad guys. He knew he would have to make his way back into hallway to avoid being left behind. He was certain no one would dispatch a rescue mission for him the way Reagan's people had for Oona.

Army looked at the cannon, his mind racing over what he'd seen the Gamma team members do to prep their weapons. It was loaded for bear. He flipped on the safety and jammed the blunt-nosed weapon in his pants pocket so he could move fast once he got into the hallway. Just as he prepared to step out of the dark room, the door was thrown open by a barrel-chested Viper. The Viper stumbled into him, as if he had been born out of darkness itself. Army yelled, and the Viper yelled back, firing wildly as they both fell. The muzzle flash illuminated movement in the room's far corner as plaster flakes fell like snow. Army's concentration went into soft focus as fear cemented him to the floor. He reached for his weapon. It was not there. He reached for his OptiTechs. Nothing.

"Where you at?" the Viper called out as he fingered the blackness in search of his own weapon. Suddenly the Viper kicked blindly into the darkness, and his booted foot found Army's ribcage. The pain drove Army to attack.

Before he realized it, Army was wrestling the heavy-limbed man, who tried to drive him into one of the room's walls. Army was determined to hold on—until the Viper butted Army skull to skull.

Army fell back with loosened front teeth and a bloody face. He was too disoriented to defend himself, and the Viper seemed to sense that.

Get up! Get up! Army screamed in his own head. *Find the cannon!*

The next sound chilled Army into total stillness. The Viper flash-charged his penetrator. Time seemed to slow, as Army felt his racing heart drum in his ears. Death, he thought, was wrapped and ready for delivery.

The room lit up in a sudden strobe of rapid weapon fire. Army felt his shirt grow heavy, hot, and wet. He felt a great suffocating weight fall across his chest, and blood gushed into his face, running across his lips and down his neck like a thick, salty sauce.

"Get up... get up, Army!"

Army felt the weight roll off of his body.

"Get up. It's me, Oona. Get up! Hurry—and take this!"

He could feel her pressing the cannon into his numb hand. He could feel the OptiTechs being slipped over his head and down over his bleary eyes. His first sight was Oona. She kissed him swiftly, through the battle blood, and told him that she was all right. He looked back at the dead

Viper—like the Gamma team leader's, the body looked as if it had been turned inside out by the penetrator fire. From the penetrator Oona was hefting in her right hand.

"Ms. Woods—where did you get that weapon?" the Beta team leader said as he slipped into the dorm room. He took in the scene of carnage around them. "Let's go—we're heading out," he finished, and held open its sliding door for Army and Oona's escape.

37

Last Call

"RAY," ROMARO HOLLERED, "MY GUYS HAVE YOUR CIVILIANS HEADING back to four. The girl is getting ready for EVAC. Alpha is set for the assault on seven, but still no sign of Cutter."

"Confirmed," Reagan replied, and then turned to Romaro. "How are we doing with isolating all the Very Important Assholes on the ground floor?"

Romaro's chief surveillance officer swung around from her perch to report that all of the remaining guards on the lower floors had been neutralized. "Most of the VIAs ready for evacuation," she smirked. "No injuries worth mentioning."

"Good. Very good," Reagan replied. "Let's get them home in time for a midnight snack."

"Hey, Ray," Romaro interrupted, "we're getting some new chatter—our chief target might be fuckin' dead."

"Goddammit," Reagan screamed and punched his control panel. "Was it one of ours who bagged the little shit?"

Romaro shook his head as he pressed his link deeper into his ear. "No. No physical evidence—no body. No hard confirmation, yet."

"Then we have to assume he is still with us and sitting pretty up on seven or eight, or in that stupid dome of his," Reagan barked. "We press on till we learn different."

"My surveillance leader says to expect voyeuristics getting to the rooftop and dome any minute now," Romaro replied. "Two minutes to the offices."

Reagan nodded and turned back to Romaro. "I want all power cut on everything but the dome. I want everything sealed except for our access points. Where are the civilians now?"

Romaro hurriedly tapped up his mission screen. "They're at the EVAC point on four and ready to start descending. They're looking good. Here," he pointed to a viewpanel shot of Army and Oona, dressed in oversized battle gear, following what remained of the Beta and Gamma teams as they released a new batch of voyeuristics skittering for the staircases.

"Captain," Reagan's chief communications officer interrupted. "I have a Harlem police unit officer who says it is urgent that he speak with you."

"How urgent?"

"He says really urgent," the com officer replied.

"Then patch him in," Reagan said as he dragged the feed window to the center of his viewscreen. "Officer, we are a bit busy. What do you have for me?"

"At first we thought it was simple vandalism up here," the officer spoke, stumbling to retain his official tone. "But we observed that the suspects were specifically trying to break into a hospital meat wagon a couple of blocks from Columbia-Presbyterian."

"Gang stuff?" Reagan asked. "Hot body parts can buy a lot of crackle and MethPops."

"Yeah, but I wouldn't consider a bunch of Baptist youth leaders a gang," the officer replied.

"Like I said, we're really busy here," Reagan said. "Why are you bothering me with this?"

"Well, one of the vandals is the guy your people have been searching for in that Hedz case. The one that had that rich woman's head on the roof over on—"

"I know the case," Reagan snapped.

Romaro turned to look at Reagan before he spoke.

"You mind?" he asked. Reagan gave him a be-my-guest look.

"Who is this vandal?" Romaro asked.

"He says his name is JJ Justus," the officer replied. "Here's an image."

Reagan and Romaro exchanged looks over the screen.

"Hold him, and we'll send someone to take him off your hands," Reagan told the officer.

"We found his wife and daughter in the meat wagon. Want them, too?"

"Yeah," Reagan barked. "Pick up the whole lot. And hold 'em, ready for transfer."

* * * * *

For five blocks in every direction around Baghdaddy's, nothing moved unless the Department ordered it. Even the wind seemed reluctant to dare more than a humid breeze without proper authorization. Every shop, restaurant, apartment building, church, mosque, temple, theater and shoeshine stand in the lock-down zone had been quickly and quietly evacuated.

From 10,000 feet above, media drones beamed back to the Weave a neighborhood under siege. Streets that were usually bright, bustling, and festive as a carnival were jammed with Department vehicles and personnel. Several hoverplanes held their station high above Baghdaddy's huge dome while others loudly flew in and out from designated parking lots and plazas.

Rev. Cosi watched from his office as several close associates fed him the latest reports from the streets. His subordinates guarded a fuming G-daddy in another part of his office. His fears were confirmed. The operatives he'd dispatched to rescue the Justus women were being held by authorities.

"The Department has them in custody," Cosi's security chief told him.

"And the mother and young girl?" he asked.

"Them too. The Department is holding them at a transport post. Destination unknown as yet. But everyone is safe—no aggression, no violence."

"Then they are in greater hands until He can perform some earthly miracles," Rev. Cosi said, as he studied his central viewpanel.

Reagan looked at the same Weave feed on his viewpanel, but saw something Rev. Cosi and his inner circle did not.

Salvation. Justification. Redemption. Salvation. His own.

It was not a Harlem nightclub that was at the center of the Department operation, but him, Reagan Reynolds. He was convinced. And through the operation's execution—*his* operation—he realized that he had finally achieved the life he had long ago convinced himself he would never have.

"Captain," a field captain reported. "We are preparing to fully sweep the office suites on seven. We're reading that loft on eight as abandoned."

"Good," Reagan said over his link. "But go easy. Our scans indicate about fifty partiers in the dome above you, and another dozen heavily armed security along with them. They're probably keeping anyone from leaving, figuring we won't storm the place with them in there.

"Go in smart," Reagan instructed. "I want that twisted little bastard's head in a bucket. I think he's in the dome."

Starr walked over to stand behind Reagan. She looked on, concerned.

"I've been looking at this thing for a while now," she began. "I just got a patch from the EVAC point—the pleasurist is saying there's another way into the dome, but it's risky."

"And?" Reagan asked, laughing for the first time all night.

"JoË. You bitch."

The voice was pinched and pained, rising from a pile of overturned office furniture, trash, and a broken vase of fresh-cut azaleas.

Dots heard the voice, but was preoccupied with his own gnawing pain. It felt like his leg was coming apart like a cheap shoe. Whenever he tried to move it, his agony stilled him. And now he had to listen to this voice needle him.

"You big dumb bastard."

Cutter. As soon as he'd thrown the little man's body aside, Dots had regretted it. He wanted to rip his heart out, or gut him like a fish, or smash his head under his heel. But he hadn't, and now he had to listen to his boss man die in one corner of the office while he struggled in another.

"You know, you're turning to shit," Cutter said, as one of his stubby hands pushed aside a small end table that had fallen on him. "Just like your Viper pal you had killed. I have the same compound loaded into my office's Ballistic Defense System."

"I just got nicked, you stupid fuck," Dots screamed. "Just nicked."

"That's all it takes, you vastly more stupid fuck," Cutter replied. He chuckled weakly. "I think you broke my legs, but they weren't any damn good anyway. But you? You're shit."

Both men could hear small-arms fire over the office viewpanel that neither could see.

"They're coming," Cutter shouted over the stabbing pain of his broken ribs. "There're up on seven. Shame that all they're going to find under your desk is a big pile of shit."

Army and Oona were waiting their turn to leave through the EVAC point. From the combined Gamma and Beta teams, only a few Department agents remained. The Beta communications officer's shoulder wound was bleeding heavily, so he was being removed from the building first.

"It was hotter than we anticipated, Captain," the Beta team leader reported to Reagan. "Once Alpha got up to six, I think the bad guys' plan was to try to take the rest of us out underneath them, then get Alpha from above and below. But we locked our floors, and we're secure now on up to Alpha on six. We're bringing in our casualties—should be back to the bunker in a few minutes."

"Get the wounded out—but we've got a change in objectives for you, and whichever of your people can still go," Reagan said. "We need the girl civilian on six to show Alpha another way into the dome."

The team leader turned to the rest of the group. "Okay. We're going back in to support Alpha on seven," the team leader. His eyes locked on Oona. "Our orders are to get you up there to show Alpha your way in.

Army pulled back his OptiTech goggles to look into Oona's eyes, which gleamed in the EVAC's dim light.

She stared back at him for a moment before she spoke. "Get your ass out of this mess," she said flatly. "I saved it once, Army. I don't know if I'll feel like doing it again."

Oona tried to smile. He noticed the blast abrasions burning along the edges of her ill-fitting battle vest. Army shook his head and kissed her quickly on her dirty forehead. "No fucking way," he said.

"Let's move!" the team leader screamed. "Cavalry's coming!"

Reagan and Starr looked at a cross-section of Baghdaddy's party dome. It stood seventy feet and was topped with an ornamental minaret crammed with security sensors. The dome was covered with bullet-resistant glass tiles and reinforced at the base with self-correcting pylons. Two of the four also served as shafts for two inclinators that ran from the club's ground level.

Reagan could not help but wonder what such a structure must have cost. Everything from the lighting to the contoured seating and lounges had to be custom-made. Starr said that some pleasurists she'd busted had told her that only the most-valued members of the club saw the inside of the dome. Each member granted entry had to deposit millions of dollars in nondisclosure agreements before entering.

"What happens in the dome…" Reagan said.

"Yeah," Starr replied. "You got the idea."

She pointed out that the dome principally had four tiers, each smaller and more exclusive than the one below. Cutter's private lift opened onto each public level and also onto a hidden fifth, high above all the others, that few patrons even knew existed. But, Starr told Reagan, Oona knew about it.

"You think Cutter is hiding up there, on that highest level?" Reagan asked Starr.

"Hard to say. His loft and offices are sensor-shielded, and cracking that dome is like trying to look through a walnut with a candle."

The mobile command center bristled with activity.

Before Reagan could open communications with the Alpha team leader, Romaro reported that Cutter's office shielding was being shut down. He said he still had no idea if anyone was holed up in there.

"We've got to warn the teams," Romaro added.

Reagan looked worried. "We have to take that office to get to the loft and dome," he told Starr. "Tell 'em what you got to. No. I'll talk to 'em."

"Assault teams," Reagan's voice vibrated on their links. "We've just gotten some critical intelligence. Cutter's office might be hot. You can't trust your readings. It might be hot."

The remains of Beta and Gamma found the Alpha team with surprising speed. Oona noticed that Army had picked up a long-nosed sniper pistol that he'd strapped to his thigh alongside the hand cannon. She had never backed away from a fight when her survival depended upon it. But she was sensing something more budding in Army. He seemed, she thought, to genuinely want to kill someone.

"We understand, Captain," the assault leader said. "We'll take it as we find it."

Romaro nodded at Reagan, acknowledging the team's bravery. He and Reagan looked at their viewpanels, watching the teams set up robotic sentry guns in front of the reinforced office door. The teams' explosives specialists moved in to set charges at the door's hardened hinges and locking mechanisms. Reagan's lips pursed as he watched Army and Oona advance with weapons drawn.

"The music. Feel it?" Cutter said, speaking between bursts of violent coughing. "Missing my own... fucking party."

Cutter heard a slow thrashing. There was the sound of uneven breathing.

"Not doing... Not doing so well, huh?"

"I'll live long enough to get over there and… and stomp the last sour breath out of you… " Dots panted.

"Where. Where you hit?" Cutter grasped. "Arm? Leg? Ass?"

Cutter coughed more than he laughed as he clung to consciousness. "Meat must be. Falling off… your bones."

Cutter was right. JoË Dots didn't have to look down to know that there was nothing below his right knee. Fifteen minutes ago, he'd seen his shoe fall from his leg with his foot still in it.

Dots knew he was dying. For a moment he thought about Reagan and their chat about fate in the boathouse. He wondered if he would outlive Cutter. He began to wonder why he cared.

"I'm still here, bitch," JoË Dots said, finding the strength to sound unscathed as his legs slowly dissolved into shit.

"Talk. Talk," Cutter hissed. "Won't be. For long. Time you die. Dots."

JoË Dots shrugged and squeezed another Duppy under his nose.

"Ray, the assault team says it is ready for a green light—they've talked to Woods and gotten her intel," Romaro said. "Charges are set and immobilizers are ready."

"Let's do this," Reagan ordered. "Link and sync the teams."

The command center screens went white as the sound of several explosions ripped open the wall of Cutter's office. Voyeuristics ran forward sending back new scent, tactile, and image feeds.

"We've got a life sign," Starr reported. "It's very weak. Also something else that is barely registering as human. There is no indication of weaponry. There's a BDS, but it has been manually disengaged."

"Captain, our readings concur," the assault leader reported as his teams readied to storm the empty loft above and have Oona show them how to access the dome.

"We're picking up a horrible smell on voyeuristics," Starr injected. "Same stuff, it looks like, that you picked up on that Viper's remains in Pennsylvania."

Army kept his head down as he pushed in behind the three team members who cautiously led the way into the dark office. The odor almost took his breath, and he heard other team members coughing on the scent. Then he felt a hand on his ass as he crouched behind an overturned desk.

"It's still there, big boy," Oona said as she gave Army a playful pat before moving off to a far corner of the office, away from the source of the smell. The team leader signaled all clear.

Army's eyes followed Oona until she stood over a small mound of trash and broken furniture. Oona heard a single word over her link: "There."

Army poked the pile of trash with the nose of his sniper's rifle. It moaned. Three team members quickly uncovered Cutter laying face down on the floor, his limbs frozen in mid-crawl.

"Get him down to EVAC," Reagan shouted to the team leader. "Medical, stand by."

"We're getting the other—I think," a voice broke in the assault leader's ear.

Army trotted toward the office's large desk, slipping on what looked like excrement from a very large animal.

"Where's the second...?" Army asked.

"I think you just stepped in him," the surveillance officer replied. "Follow the trail."

Army did. It led him to a huddle of officers, including the team leader, staring at what looked like a human head attached to a large upper torso and beefy arms. Nothing else, except ropy piles of the same reeking mush that Army had stepped in, remained.

Its hands were clutching a small, decorative box.

Romaro pressed his link hard to his ear. He shook his head and bent down to speak into Reagan's ear.

"The teams have the dome. Total surprise attack. It fell without a shot. Baghdaddy's—all of it—is ours.

"And oh, Cutter didn't make it," Romaro added as if it were an afterthought. "Seemed he had a bullet hole in his head our people missed when they transported him to medical."

Reagan nodded approvingly.

"Let's foam the whole place for evidence and shut it all down," Reagan said, as the command center began to fill with applause.

"Tell medical that I want an autopsy," Reagan said. "I want the head sent to Kobec at C3 and the rest of the remains to the boys in DC. Let them know we play a mean end game. And have the civilians from the dome put up in the Theresa. Feed 'em and have them tucked in bed for debriefing in the morning. You got that?"

Romaro looked around the command center for someone he could order to carry out Reagan's orders. He soon realized that he was the only one who could be spared.

Reagan stood up and walked past Romaro, who was shaking hands with the command center staff. He reached the door and opened it onto the approach of a new day. It was Sunday. Soon, Harlem's church bells would begin to ring. Life would lurch forward, Reagan thought, as he made his way to Baghdaddy's shell-riddled face.

Two security officers trotted out of the command center to trail him. When Reagan ducked his head and stepped inside the club's charred entrance, Department guards posted there stiffened to attention.

Reagan stepped past them, stopping deep inside the dead club to inhale the closest thing he hoped he would know of hell. He screwed his hat down tight over his balding head and tried his best to remember everything he knew he would want to forget.

Epilogue

THE BEACH'S RHYTHMS WERE AS PRIMAL AS THE PALETTE THAT colored it. Layers of blues, greens, and browns splashed with whites. The Bronx coastline was all Army and Oona could see from their All-Utility Vehicle. The insistent sweeps of the tide and syncopated caws of seagulls gliding on late-summer breezes were all they could hear.

"Mmm," Army sighed, breaking the spell.

"Do you think he'll come?" Oona whispered. "Are you really going to do it?

Army gently nodded yes, rousing the scalp-ful of dreadlocks Oona had Spun-woven the way she used to Spun-weave her cousin Rattle's hair, back when she was just a kid.

"He'll be here," Army said softly, so as to not further disturb the harmony of the beach song with an intrusive chop of spoken words.

He closed his eyes and fully reclined in the open cockpit of their flaming red A.U.V. He rested his seemingly untroubled head on his folded palms. His tropical shirt lay open, exposing his taut brown chest and stomach to the already warm, late-morning sun. Oona nestled at his side, her troubled face beginning to find peace again next to his. She turned slowly to her side. Her pearl-colored wraparound skirt freed the supple fullness of her right leg, which came to rest between Army's slightly parted thighs.

"Mmm," she murmured. "You know you're a devil, don't you?"

Army smiled, his eyes closed. He heard a distant whine growing closer.

Oona tried to ignore it, but Army startled her to alertness. He quickly turned his head in the direction of the approaching sound.

It was a Department sedan, black, and overpowered for the sandy road leading down to the beach. Army and Oona hopped from the A.U.V., their bare feet landing on the beach's loose, cool sand. They stood together, each with an arm encircling the other's waist, and waited.

The vehicle stopped. Its forward hatch slid open, and Reagan stepped tentatively down to the sand. He was wearing a dark suit with no tie, and his shirt was open at the collar. He'd pushed his porkpie hat back on to the crown of his head to appear more casual.

He waved, more as a signal that he saw them than as a greeting. They watched Reagan walk awkwardly toward them as his vehicle closed and shut down.

Oona could hardly believe that this was the same man who had terrorized her in Harlem, the beast that had brutalized her, who had run her out of town. It was not so long ago that the very sight of this man would make her nauseous, Oona thought. She remembered her promise to her ancestors to never forget what she and Army had endured because of this fat man, who was huffing and puffing toward them.

"Orchard Beach," he said, taking off his hat and wiping his brow. "They've really cleaned it up. My mother used to come here when she was a kid. It was a public beach back then."

"This is my first time," Oona said, letting her eyes wander from Reagan to the splendor of the surroundings. "It's just like paradise."

"Yes, paradise," Reagan said softly, then cocked his head and began staring at Army's head.

"What's with the hair?" he asked. "You a Viper now?"

"No," Army said, as he shook out his dreads to full effect. "But tell me, why does a white man always have something to say about how a black man wears his hair?"

"I… I…"

"Forget it," Army said wearily. "We heard about your friend, Romaro," he continued. "A suicide?"

"Yeah. I can't completely believe he's gone, not even after the funeral," Reagan said, his voice sounding dull. "None of us could have known what was in his mind, especially after he got hurt in that Times Square attack. He was never the same…"

Army and Oona stared at Reagan, who cleared his throat before continuing.

"Well, it looks like the Department is closing the whole investigation. There were leaks, but no hard proof linking Romaro to Cutter and his crew," Reagan said as he looked off into the sky. "Looks like some Department agents had unauthorized contacts with Cutter's people, though. Was it part of a case outside of our chain of command? I don't know."

"With Romaro dead, along with Rattle, JoË Dots, and Cutter, we'll probably never know the whole story," Army said, as he held his eyes on Reagan's. "Doesn't look like any of it hurt you none."

Reagan stared back, but kept silent.

"Look—sorry to get into all that," Army said. "We know you've pushed the Department to be fair with us, and with my family. The settlement was generous. Our records have been cleared. Our U.I.D. security ratings are fully upgraded. The Department research contract you landed for my mother has been a big help. We appreciate it. That's why we asked you here."

Oona looked at Army and wondered if he would actually have the nerve to bait the trap.

"So," Army said. "Did you come alone like we asked?"

Shit, Oona whispered, as her heart raced.

"Of course," Reagan said. "I was going to ask you about that."

Army walked to the rear of the A.U.V. and unlocked a compartment tucked beneath its rear seat. He returned with a small wooden box in his hands.

"Listen, you can play this anyway you want," Army said, standing next to Oona.

"You can turn it in to the Department," Oona said brightly.

"Or keep it for yourself," Army added as if he didn't care one way or the other.

Reagan furrowed his brow. "What is it?" he asked, stepping close enough to be darkened by Oona's shadow.

Army slowly pulled back its lid to reveal ten rows of red-capped Hedz vials.

"These are your sister—her memories," Army said, his voice low.

"... How?" Reagan asked hoarsely.

"We're the only ones who know that these exist," Army said. "They're untraceable. We found them, labeled but untouched, during the raid. It was like someone knew we were coming and made sure we'd see it. Investigators, if they assume anything, will think that they were lost in the Baghdaddy's raid.

"At first, we were going to turn them in with the others found that night. But then we thought, no, the Department has enough evidence. She belongs to you," Army continued.

"Call this our way of paying you back for being straight with us," Oona added. "Even though she's gone, she's alive here in these memories, memories that can live in your brain they way they lived in hers." She looked into Army's approving face, then quietly said, "There's an injector."

"In the drawer," Army added.

"In the bottom of the box," Oona clarified.

Army gently closed the box and placed it in Reagan's open hands.

Reagan swallowed hard as he drew the box to his chest and lightly rested his cheek against it. Could he resist its contents, he asked himself. Should he?

Army and Oona climbed into their A.U.V. without words or waves goodbye. Its engines hummed. Its knobby tires dug into the beach. Reagan watched as Army and Oona pulled away in a spray of sand.

Oona turned in her seat to catch a last glimpse before they disappeared behind a distant swell of earth and stand of swaying trees. The last thing she saw was Reagan standing there on the beach, staring at the little box in his hands.

THE END

Acknowledgments

While it is my name that appears on the cover of this book, it would not have been possible without the enormous support, patience and encouragement of the following: Rose Moss, Henry Louis Gates, Jr., Brett Renwick and members of the Dark Body Writers Collective, Jill Nelson, Glenda Marriott-Foster, Jennifer Lyons, Doug Seibold and Agate Publishing, Jon and Louis Marriott, Don Terry, Howard French, Gerry Migliore, Jeff Weber, Sherry Turkle, Ralph Keyes, and my offices away from the office, Starbucks Coffee shops from Bangkok to Harlem.